THE BOY OF DUST AND ASH

To Sam

Enjoy your adventures!

THE AETHER STONES SAGA
BOOK ONE

THE BOY OF DUST & ASH

JOSHUA NEAL

978-1-7393523-1-8

First published by Joshua Neal Fiction in 2023.

Cover design by Ebook Launch.

PART ONE

1

Devi and his father worked in silence. They each raised their scythes above their heads, their silver blades cutting the sky in two, glistening for a moment in what little was left of the setting sun. Then, they brought them down once more, and one hundred tiny, golden heads tumbled into the dirt, severed from the bodies that continued to stand defiantly upright. At Devi's father's feet, only the very tips of the wheat plants laid scattered across the soil, whereas Devi's blade had taken half the stalks along with it. One more elegant sweep of his blade laid the next row of plants to waste, and Devi's father was moving effortlessly on towards the edge of the field.

Though Devi did his best to follow close behind, he was never quite able to keep up with his father. Devi was quick with his scythe, but his father moved through the fields like a wildfire, clearing in a single morning fields it would have taken Devi a week to clear himself. Of all the farmers in the fields of Rakhas and beyond, Devi had never seen a man more efficient with a scythe than his father. Trailing only a few steps behind, Devi knew that his father was working slower than he was able, and if he so wished, at any moment he could be out of sight.

As he continued to hack away at the wheat plants that reached almost to his chest, Devi watched his father closely. He studied his body – the way his shoulders twisted as he raised his scythe above his head; the way his torso seemed to squeeze and pull as he brought it back down towards the earth; and the way his arms reached out in front of his body as his blade cut through the air. No matter how closely he watched, however, and no matter how hard he tried, Devi couldn't seem to force his own body to do the same. It seemed as if his father had been made for the fields. It seemed as if he had been crafted from the earth itself, as if he wasn't tending to the fields at all, but instead as if the fields were tending to themselves.

"We should head back to the village," Devi's father said as he waited for Devi at the edge of the field, finally breaking the silence that had followed them diligently as they worked. "We won't have the light for much longer."

The sun hung low in the sky. It wouldn't be long until it disappeared below the horizon for the night, and the field still needed to be cleared. As Devi reached the edge of the field and stood alongside his father, he turned and looked back towards the village.

Between Devi's position and the small, unassuming shack that he called his home, the fields had been completely razed. It had taken them all day, but Devi and his father had left a golden trail in their wake. There was not a single wheat plant left standing that hadn't been cut down for harvest. Beyond the village and far out towards the orchards on Devi's left, however, the fields still shone gold in the half-light, and Devi could still see his neighbours hard at work, setting their own scythes to the crops in a race against the sun. Though they were often shorthanded when compared with their neighbours, most fields being filled by five or six farmers, Devi and his father always seemed to be the first to finish.

Devi watched as his father tossed his scythe to the ground, took the empty burlap sack he had slung over his shoulder, and dropped to one knee. He scooped up a handful of soil and wheat, spreading his fingers a little to allow the soil to sift through and fall to the ground, whilst the heads of wheat remained. Rather than toss the wheat into the burlap sack, however, he inspected it closely, running his fingers across the tips of the plants in his palm, the expression on his face far more grave than Devi could provide explanation for.

"I thought we had a little more time."

Devi's father held out his hand, and Devi allowed him to pour the fallen wheat heads into his own palm. They were pale and pallid, somewhat withered – not the same fresh, golden brown the plants at the centre of the field had been. As Devi ran his own fingers across them, the heads of wheat crumbled to dust, falling apart and drifting away on the gentle wind that drifted in from the Tharakun Sea just beyond the edge of the field. Devi crouched beside his father and scooped up his own handful of wheat. Hidden amongst the soil, almost imperceptible to the naked eye, were several tiny grains of sand. They were difficult to spot amongst the dust and the dirt, but they were there, nonetheless.

"Kalier warned of this," Devi's father said. "But I thought we might have another harvest. Perhaps two if we were lucky."

The Sands had been drifting west for as long as anyone could remember. They had been steadily nibbling away at the hills and the grasslands and the forests that stood before them, and they had already begun to eat away at the farmlands further south, just beyond the mountains where Katai faded into Darmeen. Now, it seemed they had reached Rakhas too.

Devi tossed his scythe to the dirt as his father had, unslung the burlap sack from his own shoulder, and began to fill it with wheat. When the sack was bulging, he pulled at a short string of rope tied loosely around the leather belt at his waist. The knot in the rope immediately gave way, and the length of rope was suddenly dangling by Devi's side. Devi wrapped the rope around the top of the sack, pulled it tight, and tied it in an uncompromising knot.

"To plant the seed within the ground," Devi's father began, tying his own burlap sack tight.

"To turn the dirt and plough the field," Devi continued.

Devi lifted his sack from the ground. It was heavy – it likely weighed as much as Devi himself – but years of lifting sacks filled with wheat, corn, and maize had strengthened his slender body, and he hoisted it up onto his shoulder without a struggle.

"Is but to search for what is found."

"Within the good Son's sacred yield."

It was traditional to end the working day with the second of the Psalms. Devi and his father had been doing so for as long as he could remember, particularly during harvest season. Devi had known all ten Psalms by heart since he was able to speak. They had been carried by his ancestors from the Hinterlands to Darmeen, and then after Vagan's war, from Darmeen to Katai. Devi's father lived by them, as did most of the other farmers, and he spoke their lines with fervour and zeal. They provided the motivation to continue working through the heat of the sun, the compassion to share when there was so little to give, and the strength to face the terrors that might come with the night.

Whenever Devi spoke the lines aloud, however, they sounded empty and hollow. He and his father had planted their seeds within the ground, they had turned the dirt, and they had ploughed the soil. It was he and his father that would pull the crops from the ground and carry them to the market in Narkasee too. As far as Devi could tell, the yield was his own, and he struggled to see what contribution the good Son had made. He struggled to understand what it was he was supposed to have found in their yield too. He had spent his whole life searching, and he had found nothing but heat and hunger.

"Are you able to finish up alone?" Devi's father asked.

"Of course," Devi said.

"Very good. I'll meet you back at home."

Devi's father lifted his scythe from the dirt, propped it against his shoulder, and began to stride across the field in the direction of the setting sun and Devi's neighbours, who were still hard at work. Without his father's help, they may not finish before sunset. With his help, they would likely be finished with time to spare.

A short distance behind Devi, a small, wooden cart stood, its wheels sunk deep into the ploughed dirt of the field. Approaching the back of the cart, Devi bent at the knees before hoisting the burlap sack from his shoulder and adding it to the pile that he and his father had already begun to stack there. Harnessed to the front of the cart was an enormous white ox, and its head drooped so low that its horns almost touched the ground.

"I know, boy," Devi said, patting the hulking creature on its side.

The ox's great, black tongue hung from the side of its mouth, and even in the twilight of the setting sun, its eyes were narrow and squinting.

"We'll get you some water back at home."

Devi collected the burlap sack that his father had filled and tossed it onto the cart with the others. Then, he patted the ox once more, this time at the top of its hind leg, and laboriously it began to move away in the direction of the shack on the other side of the field. The cart itself ground slowly into motion too, the weight of the wheat sacks driving its wheels even deeper into the loose soil.

Rather than follow the ox and cart that trundled steadily back towards the village, Devi cast his gaze around the empty field. That morning, he had been greeted by row upon row of golden wheat plants that brushed against his midriff as he forced his way through them. Now, all he saw was dirt and the mangled stubs of the plants that had been hacked in two, some flat and level where his father's blade had been, others awkward and uneven where he had swung his own scythe. He had stood in the same spot the year before and looked out across the same scene, and he had done the same the year before that, and the year before that.

There was a time when Devi had enjoyed harvest season. He would anticipate the sun pouring in through his window earlier and earlier with each passing morning, and he would relish standing shoulder to shoulder in the fields with his father from sunrise to sunset. Whilst he grew taller and stronger, however, the fields never changed. Year upon year, harvest upon harvest, they remained the same, each as neat and precise as the next, turned, ploughed, and sown in perfect, even rows. The fertile soil would bear its harvest, the ground giving rise to an endless sea of wheat, but the seasons would turn, the fields would be cleared, and the cycle would begin again.

Devi made his way to the edge of the field and walked a short distance beyond, where the ground sloped away towards a narrow beach that gave way to the Tharakun Sea. Unlike the fields, the water seemed to have no end, rolling out towards the horizon for as far as Devi could see, and even further beyond that. A gentle breeze drifted up the beach and across the fields, but the water itself was quiet and still, catching the light from the sun as it continued to set at Devi's back.

Devi had never set foot in the water, but he had always found himself drawn by its allure. When he looked out across the sea, he saw freedom, and he saw possibility. He saw the endless sprawling of the world, and he saw the opportunity that was left in its wake. Every time he saw a tiny set of Katai sails carrying a ship through the water, cutting the stillness of the Tharakun like a knife, he couldn't help but wonder who was on board and what corner of the world they were heading to.

Were they pirates venturing north to pillage Darmeenian traders? Were they traders themselves, heading up into the Hinterlands in search of their fortune? Or were they Stone Seekers sailing out towards The Sands in search of the Fire Stone, likely never to return but knowing that, if they did, they would bring glory home with them?

Rakhas was Devi's home, and though at times its fields seemed as endless as the sea, he couldn't help but feel there was no glory to be found amongst them.

Devi turned his back to the water. He found his scythe in the dirt, and he carried it back towards the village, its handle at his side and its blade leading the way out in front. By the time he reached the other side of the field, Devi saw his father making his own way back towards the village, but he was no longer alone.

"It is a bountiful harvest once more!"

The man that walked alongside Devi's father was tall and sleek, and his narrow face always seemed to be wearing a smile. The boy at his side did not smile, however. Instead, his face was as surly and sullen as Devi had always known it to be.

"The Son shines on us again!"

"Indeed he does, Elya," Devi's father said. "Indeed he does."

Though his father was likely unaware, Devi's ears caught the subtle hint of agitation he had allowed to creep into his voice. Elya's unshakeable optimism was too much for Devi to bear, and though his father would never admit it, Devi knew he found him somewhat sickly too.

Elya was nothing if not a good neighbour, however, and he immediately began to lift the sacks of wheat from the back of Devi's cart along with his father. At the front of the cart, the great, white ox stood with its head plunged into a trough that was half-filled with water, snorting loudly as it drank.

"I think you've earned a rest," Devi said, patting the ox on its thick, muscular neck and unlatching its halter chains.

The ox lifted its head briefly as Devi pulled the chains free, and then it fell to drinking once more.

"Have you heard the news?" Elya asked, hoisting the last sack from the cart.

Devi wasn't sure whether the question had been directed towards him or his father, and as he lifted one of the sacks on the ground onto his own shoulder once more, he was grateful that his father answered before he felt the need to.

"The news?"

"Jerod will leave for Narkasee after this harvest. He has come of age, and he wishes to seek the Aether Stones."

Devi looked over Jerod, who was struggling to lift one of the sacks of wheat from the ground. His bony knees trembled as his thin, fragile fingers gripped the burlap tight, and his whole body seemed to shake as he lifted the sack up onto his shoulder.

"Is this true, Jerod?" Devi's father asked.

"It's true," Jerod forced out through gritted teeth.

"But you are a farmer, not a Seeker."

Devi had heard the same words on his father's lips when he had come of age two harvests ago. His father had gleaned his wish before he had even managed to speak it aloud, insisting that his place was in the fields.

"Narkasee is no place for a farmer," Devi's father pressed. "I'd urge you to reconsider, Elya."

"Nonsense," Elya said, refusing to allow his eternal optimism to be stirred. "Jerod is a strong boy, and he has Katai in his heart. He'll make a fine Seeker."

By the time they approached the centre of the village, Jerod's strides seemed to have shortened significantly, and Devi wasn't sure whether Elya was aware that he had slowed himself to a snail's pace so as not to put too much distance between himself and his son.

Overhead, strings of colourful bunting stretched between the wooden shacks that surrounded a large clearing, cutting the sky into countless uneven shards. At the centre of the clearing, sack upon sack of precious wheat had already been stacked high, the preparations for the harvest festival already well underway.

Devi's father was the first to haul his sack of wheat onto the pile, and Elya and Devi soon followed. When Jerod stepped forward to throw his sack towards the top, it took a helping hand from his father to prevent him from toppling over.

"A bountiful harvest," Elya said again, looking over the pile from top to bottom. "Katai will eat well this winter."

As Devi looked over the pile for himself, he couldn't help but wonder whether he was looking upon the same harvest. The pile seemed to be smaller than it had been the previous year, and even smaller than it had been the year before that. It seemed The Sands had been creeping into the fields of Rakhas for longer than either he or his father had realised.

"Thank you, Elya," Devi's father said.

"I can help you with the rest if you –"

"No, no," Devi's father said quickly. "You've done quite enough. I wouldn't like to keep you from your family any longer."

"Very well," Elya said, bowing his head a little in a gesture of farewell. "The Son belongs to one and all."

"The Son belongs to one and all," Devi repeated along with his father.

By the time Devi and his father had carried the remaining sacks of wheat to the pile in the centre of the village, their ox no longer stood with its head buried deep in the water trough. The sun barely managed to peek over the horizon, and the fields were almost empty, most of the village having made their way back to their shacks, the windows of which glowed with the gentle amber of the small fires in their pits. At the centre of the field they had cleared, however, Devi spotted the white coat of the beast, grazing on the remnants of the wheat stalks they had cut down, and he started in its direction.

"Let him eat," Devi's father said. "We'll manage ourselves."

Devi followed his father to the side of their shack, where they kept a small stack of barrels. The barrels were heavy, each filled to the brim with oil, and Devi and his father each stumbled across the sandy road with one end of a barrel in their arms until they reached their cart. They hoisted it up onto the back, turned it over onto its side, and tied it in place, running a length of rope through the wooden slats of the cart and around the barrel itself. At the front of the cart, where the ox had once stood, Devi and his father each crouched beneath one of the wooden beams where the halter chains hung, and they lifted the front of the cart from the ground.

As they dragged the large, wooden wheels across the turned dirt towards the field they had spent the afternoon clearing, they seemed to haul a thick fog of tension along with them. Devi hadn't been able to resist casting sideward glances at this father as Elya had made his announcement, and he knew he must have felt his eyes upon him.

Devi could tell his father was waiting for him to broach the subject again. Instead, he set the cart down, made his way around to the barrel at its back, and pulled the cork stopper from its top. Oil immediately began to spill out, dampening the soil at Devi's feet. Then, he returned to his place at the front of the cart, and he and his father dragged it forward once more, its wheels churning laboriously through the dirt and discarded wheat stalks they had left behind that afternoon, the oil in the barrel forming a thick, damp line in the soil behind them.

Devi and his father walked in silence up one edge of the field, lacing the dirt with oil as they went. As they approached the corner of the field, they were shrouded in the looming shadow of the great signal tower that stood there like a lonely sentinel, its rotting wood creaking almost inaudibly and the metal bowl at its top long since having succumbed to rust. Then, they lined the top of the field and made their way back down the other side, the gentle waves of the Tharakun whispering softly as they made their way up the shore to Devi's right.

By the time they had lined the final edge of the field with oil and dragged the cart back towards the village, the barrel was light enough for Devi to haul it from the back without his father's help, and he carried it back to the side of his shack, placing it at the front of the stack, where it could be collected the following evening. Devi's father pulled the empty cart to the edge of the field himself and began up the wooden steps at the front of the shack.

"I'll be right in," Devi said as his father disappeared inside.

Devi heard the door at the top of their wooden steps creak open and closed, but he did not follow his father. Instead, he stepped back to the edge of the empty field at the front of their home, which they had already lined with oil days earlier. He gazed out across the soil to the fields far off, which were still thick with crops of tall, golden wheat. Their gentle silhouettes swayed softly in the breeze, the setting sun behind them trying its best to cling to the fragile lip of the horizon. Beyond the fields, Devi could just about make out the orchards, the thick, dense trees there rising and falling like the rolling hills between Rakhas and Narkasee.

Soon, all of it would be gone. Devi and his father would lay waste to those fields as they had the others, and the fruit pickers would soon be picking the trees and vines clean, leaving behind nothing but their empty carcasses. Then, the fire would come. Devi would watch as his father would glean the blade of his scythe with oil, light it in the flames of a small fire, and touch it to the already dampened soil. In a second, the flames would burst into life, clawing and grasping at the air around them, clambering over the soil and the stubble of the stalks – something sparking from nothing. Before long, the entire field would be alight, and Devi and his father would stand on the steps of their wooden shack, watching as the fire washed away all memory of the days they had spent raising their harvest from a single tiny seed into a golden field that would feed a kingdom.

Standing at the edge of the field, Devi wished the fire would wash away all memory of who he was and who he had been. He was a tiny seed, and he was certain that, if allowed to grow, he could shine brighter than a thousand fields of wheat. But the sun had all but set, and the darkness had all but crept in.

Devi turned his back to the fields, crossed the sandy road towards his shack, and climbed the creaking wooden steps to join his father inside.

11

Devi's knuckles whitened as he gripped the handle of the sword and lifted it up towards his shoulder. It felt awkward and heavy, the tip of its blade wavering a little as he struggled to find its centre of balance. He raised a second hand to the base of the handle to steady it, and he held it there for a moment, one elbow hugging tight to his body, the other protruding at a sharp angle as if poised to strike out.

Then, Devi brought the heavy blade flat against his palm. It was so clean that his own dark, innocent eyes stared back at him, their almond shape warped a little by the shallow groove that ran all the way up the centre of the blade. Devi ran his finger along its sharpened edge. He couldn't imagine the time and precision required to create a margin so fine. He also couldn't imagine how effortlessly it would cut through the flesh of a Sand Dweller.

"It's a fine blade isn't it, boy?"

The keeper of the market stall was a tall, broad-shouldered man, his arms thick and greasy, his large face hidden behind a mask of soot.

"The perfect weapon for a young Seeker."

Devi glanced up at the man, and when his gaze fell upon the blade once more, a second pair of eyes were suddenly staring back at him in its reflection.

"Copper and brass, silver and gold, rubies red and diamonds bright."

Devi knew the proceeding lines of Psalm Three – he'd wager he had heard them every time he and his father had visited the market in Narkasee – but he refused to speak them aloud. He knew his father would be more than happy to do so on his behalf.

"Are merely trinkets, bought and sold. The Son's true worth lies in his light."

Devi felt his father's hand fall upon his shoulder, but he couldn't bring himself to place the sword back on the blacksmith's counter just yet. He wanted to hold it a little longer.

"I'll thank you, friend, to choose your words more carefully when speaking of my work."

The blacksmith's voice was deep yet kind, but the almost imperceptible moment of hesitation before and after he spoke the word 'friend' told Devi that it could cut as keenly as his blades if necessary.

"You'll find no trinkets here," he said. "I make only weapons – amongst the finest in all of Katai."

Devi's father glanced up at the man before he too returned his gaze to the sword in Devi's hands.

"In hands meant for fighting, it would make a fine weapon indeed," he said. "In hands meant for the fields, it is merely a trinket. Nothing more."

The blacksmith glared at Devi's father for a moment. Then, he reached over the counter of his stall, wrenched the sword from Devi's grip, and turned to walk away. Before he was able to do so, however, Devi's father called out to him once more.

"Hold on, friend."

The man paused. Devi could not see his face for his mountainous shoulders, but he felt sure it no longer bore the same smile he had flashed Devi when he had first approached the stall.

"I mean no offence," Devi's father said. "You do fine work – masterful, even. But we have no need for such a weapon, as finely crafted as it might be."

The blacksmith turned back to face Devi and his father.

"Our scythes need fresh blades," Devi's father continued. "We'll take four if you have them.

With his gaze fixed firmly on Devi's father, the blacksmith thrust the tip of his sword into the ground, and the weapon stood perfectly upright, its handle teetering back and forth just a little. He made his way to the back of his stall towards a small, wooden bucket from which several curved, steel blades protruded at all angles like the needles of a thistle. Devi watched as the man leaned down, took up the bucket, and dropped it heavily on the counter in front of him. Then, he carefully lifted four blades from inside, inspecting each one closely before he placed it on the counter in front of Devi's father.

When the stall keeper was done, Devi's father reached into his pocket and pulled out a small, velvet pouch, placing four copper coins on the counter next to the blades. With one enormous palm, the stall keeper scooped the coins into his other, and he turned away from Devi and his father once more.

As Devi turned back towards the road that ran through the centre of the marketplace, he was consumed by the crowd. The dusty streets around the stalls were always busy during harvest season, but they seemed even more tightly packed than Devi had been expecting. The stalls themselves stood at regular intervals along the road, stretching away from the central thoroughfare in neat, little rows. Their light fabric roofs did little to protect against the relentless heat of the sun, but they did at least cast shadows between the rows, shrouding the people beneath them in a slightly more tolerable shade.

"What use is a sword?" Devi's father asked, though Devi himself had remained silent. "Swords are heavy, clumsy. They're no good in the fields."

Devi knew the sword would be no use to him back in Rakhas. If he was to spend the rest of his life in the fields, he would want for nothing more than his scythe. Its long handle and curved blade made sweeping through row upon row of golden wheat plants an effortless task. But the sword hadn't been crafted for the fields. It had been crafted for combat. It had been crafted, as the blacksmith had put it, for a young Seeker.

"Swordfish! Yellowfin! Oysters by the shell!"

The gravel voices of the fishermen filled the air. It was early, but the sun was already high in an otherwise vacant sky, and they would have hauled their nets in long before Devi and his father had even drawn close to Narkasee.

"We have Trout, we have Skipjack, we have Barramundi! All caught in the waters of Katai! You'll find none more fresh!"

Devi's stomach rumbled as the aroma of fresh fish wafted across his path. His hand drifted towards the pockets of his britches, and his fingers began to turn the single coin they found there over and over.

As they reached the cart that stood motionless in the centre of the road, Devi's father placed his four fresh blades in the back, whilst Devi approached the ox that stood up front. He took hold of the halter chains that hung from its thick, muscular neck, gave them a gentle tug, and the cart ground slowly into motion once more.

Devi and his father walked in silence, but all around them, the marketplace was a hive of activity.

On his left, Devi watched as a small band of pirates laid out a handful of treasures. The faces of the men were framed by thick, greasy hair that hung over their eyes from their foreheads and that hung down to their chests from their chins. It looked to Devi as if they had been sailing for weeks but, in spite of their wide, toothless smiles, they seemed to have little to show for their time at sea. Peering a little closer, however, Devi caught flashes of gold across their fingers and beneath their half-open shirts. They had little left to sell on the market, but it seemed the sea had been good to them after all.

On Devi's right, the stalls were fewer and further between. It was in this area of the market that Devi and his father, along with every other farmer in Katai, would eventually be hauling their harvests, but for now they mostly stood empty. Only a single stall had been packed with sacks of grain, and the man behind its counter stepped forward towards the road, holding his arm out towards Devi and his father as they approached.

"Ah, Kalier," Devi's father said, greeting the man by gripping his forearm tightly, whilst Kalier returned the gesture.

Kalier nodded at Devi's father, and he gave Devi a gentle nod of his own.

"I thought it likely I would be alone," Kalier said, glancing towards the near-empty cart at Devi's back. "Where is your harvest?"

"Our harvest is not yet complete," Devi's father said. "But we draw near. We have come for fresh blades and oil, some other essentials for the festival."

Devi's father looked beyond Kalier to the stall behind him. There were several sacks of grain stacked amongst the shade, but in years past, the stall would have been overflowing.

"You have sold much already," Devi's father said, but Kalier's face was blank and stoic.

"I have sold nothing," he said. "This is all I have."

"This is your harvest?"

"The Sands came quickly" Kalier said. "Last year, they merely ate away at the farm's edge. This year, they took half our harvest."

Devi watched as his father looked over the pile of sacks, which now seemed even more meagre than it had moments earlier.

"The Sands haven't come for you yet?"

"This harvest," Devi's father said. "It seems we have even less time than I thought."

A short distance beyond Kalier, tucked away amongst a cluster of other empty stalls, Devi's rumbling stomach dragged his gaze towards a stall that he had not seen before. It seemed to sell dried meat, and strings of cutlets hung from the rafters of the stall like macabre curtains. Behind the counter stood a tall, thin man, dressed from head to toe in maroon robes, and in front of the man was a glorious loaf of bread that sat front and centre on his counter.

Devi wasn't sure that his stomach had ever been full, but it began to roar like he had never known it to roar before when his eyes fell upon the loaf. Sliced open at its centre, and with half already missing, it seemed to be packed with so many nuts and dried fruits that Devi was unsure how the stall keeper had managed to find room to add the grain. As Devi slipped away from his father and Kalier and approached the stall, he saw that the crust of the bread was hard and cracked like the cooked sand beneath his feet, but the centre of the loaf looked as light and fluffy as cotton.

"How much?" Devi asked, slipping his hand into the pocket of his britches in search of the single copper coin he knew he'd find there.

"Too much for you, boy," the stall keeper said.

The man behind the counter possessed a flamboyant air, and he seemed to speak as much with his hands as he did with his tongue. Devi's stomach rumbled again. It was clear he would not be able to settle it in the way he had hoped, but he felt obliged to offer it some form of appeasement.

Devi gestured towards a thick cut of cooked steak, which laid next to a stack of uncooked cuts that still seemed to be bleeding. The edges of the steak were heavily greyed, and the little fat that ran through the grains of the meat seemed to have all but melted away.

"How long has that been out?" he asked.

The stall keeper shook his head and shot Devi a grave look.

"Perhaps you would prefer something dried," he said, reaching behind his head towards the several strings lined with meat that hung towards the back of the stall.

The man took down one of the strings with one hand, took up a knife with his other, and hacked the string in half in one fluid motion. The bottom half of the string fell onto the counter, one of its ends landing in the pool of blood that had collected at the base of his chopping board.

"Very cheap," he said. "Only two pieces."

Devi longed for the taste of fresh meat. He couldn't remember the last time he had placed a fresh, succulent cube of beef, or horse, or yak into his mouth. He couldn't even remember the taste of wild dog. He knew the stall keeper was right, however. There was nothing fresh about the slab of beef on the counter, and the string of dried yak would be more than he could hope to get for two pieces anywhere else on the market. Devi reached into his pocket, took out his coin, and placed it on the counter.

"I only have one," he said.

The string of meat was already generous in length, worth the single coin on the counter and more. He expected the stall keeper to snatch the cutlets away again, but instead he slid the coin from the counter into his open palm and dropped it into a leather pouch that hung from his waist.

"Thank you," Devi said, speaking as much on behalf of his stomach as on behalf of himself.

"Take not more and give not less," the stall keeper said, his hands articulating the words along with his mouth. "Lest you should your fate forestall."

"But share yourself at his behest," Devi replied, reaching for the cutlets of meat. "The Son belongs to one and all."

Devi turned back towards the road in search of his father once more, gnawing away at the first of the meat cutlets on his string. At the very edge of the marketplace, however, away from the bustle of the streets, Devi saw six men reclining in the shade of the low wall that ran around the perimeter of the stalls. Cloaked in long capes of deep beige, each of the men's chests were covered by light armour, and their biceps spilled out from under their half-sleeves. They wore swords sheathed at their hips, and they wore hide boots that covered both their feet and their ankles completely.

Devi could still remember the first time he had seen the Stone Seekers. Like every boy in Katai, he had long dreamed of joining their ranks. To give your life for Katai was the highest honour. To give your life seeking the Aether Stones was something even greater. It was the kind of honour and glory that Devi could only dream about back home in Rakhas, and it was the kind of honour and glory that called to him whenever he cast his gaze out across the endless waters of the Tharakun, or whenever he visited the buzzing marketplace in Narkasee.

Two of the Stone Seekers sat with their backs against the wall, each with a woman, only half-clothed, perched upon his lap, their arms draped around the shoulders of the men, their hands lost somewhere beneath their capes and armour. The other men stood filling their stomachs, hugging tight to the wall so that even the very tops of their heads were protected from the sun. When Devi looked a little closer, he realised they were eating the bread that he had seen on the stall a short distance back

– thick slabs of the loaf, packed to the crust with dried fruits and nuts. Devi looked down at his cutlets of dried meat. They would assuage his hunger for a short time, but he wouldn't be eating again until he and his father arrived home, and even then, it would likely be only thick soup, perhaps with some bread and cider.

Tucked away in the shade of the low wall, the Seekers seemed, for the most part, to have gone largely unnoticed, their raucous laughter lost amongst the din of the crowd that continued to filter around the stalls from the main road a short distance off. They clearly were not noticed by the man that clambered over the low wall beside them, his foot almost coming to rest on the head of one Seeker rather than on the ground.

Devi watched as the thin, frail man, all bones and knocking knees, took a crate from a nearby market stall, turned it on its head, and threw it to the ground. Then, he clambered unsteadily on top of the crate, and spoke as loudly as his sunken chest could manage.

"The Sands are coming west," the man shouted.

He held one arm outstretched and pressed the other firmly against his stomach, as if his voice would travel further if he squeezed every bit of air from his lungs.

"The Sands are coming west," the man repeated. "And King Vagan continues to hide away in his Keep!"

Devi glanced towards the distance, where the King's Keep loomed high above the marketplace. For a building as large and imposing as the Keep, it looked strangely vulnerable, teetering perilously atop the Salt Cliffs. The Keep had been built into the cliffs themselves, but like The Sands that had begun to nibble away at the fields of Rakhas, the Tharakun Sea had worn away their face until the Keep almost hung over the rocks and water below.

Most in the marketplace paid the man little attention. They merely continued to walk to and fro around him, as if he was a statue erected on a low plinth, rather than a flesh and blood man addressing them from the pedestal of his overturned crate. One or two did stop to listen to him, however. Perhaps, with more courage, they would have stood in his place.

"Recall the last time you saw Vagan walking the streets. You cannot! He is old, and he is paranoid. How can he lead a nation if he cannot even leave his Keep?"

What the man said was true. Devi had never seen King Vagan walking the streets of Narkasee. In fact, he had never seen King Vagan at all. He knew from his father's words what King Vagan looked like, but he had never been able to verify his father's testimony for himself.

The mention of King Vagan's name sparked a murmuring to spread amongst the crowd, like the gentle striking of stone on stone giving rise to fire, but Devi was unsure whether the disapproving murmurs were directed towards the man speaking against King Vagan or towards King Vagan himself.

"Time is of the essence," the man said. "We cannot stand idly by and allow King Vagan to lead us into oblivion any longer."

The man paused for a moment, eager to allow his words to settle over the marketplace that continued to pay him less attention than he clearly felt he deserved. Then, he spoke again.

"I have word from Darmeen," he said, his voice as loud as it had yet been. "They have the location of the Fire Stone. When they reach it, Katai will –"

The man was on the ground before he was able to finish his thought. He quickly found himself beneath the hulking bodies of two Stone Seekers, their hands grasping at his flailing arms and their knees driving into his stomach and his ribs.

"We cannot allow them to –"

The man continued to attempt to speak as he was lifted from the ground and carried away from the marketplace, but a swift blow to the liver was enough to silence him for good.

Two of the remaining Seekers immediately moved out into the clearing. One of the men kicked the upturned crate aside, its wood cracking under the force of his boot. The rest moved out amongst the crowd that had finally begun to form and began to move people along. The few that had surrounded the man were initially reluctant, unsure what to make of the revelation they had heard. The state of the man that had delivered the revelation, as well as his treatment at the hands of the Stone Seekers, seemed to be enough to dissuade them from lingering for too long, however.

"You, boy!"

Devi turned to see one of the men returning to the clearing and bearing down on him.

"Do you have trouble hearing? Move on."

Devi began to walk away, but before he had the chance, his father was already striding towards him. He glared at Devi intently, yelling his name as he marched away from the main road in his direction.

"And what's your business, old man?"

Devi's father wheeled on the Scroll Seeker that had addressed him.

"My son is my business," he said. "And he is no business of yours."

The Stone Seeker seemed to step towards Devi's father almost without moving. His teeth clamped together so that his thick jaw grew tense and unmoveable. At the same time, the other Stone Seekers a short distance off each took several steps towards Devi's father until they flanked the first man on either side.

"And who, in Vagan's name, are you to be telling us about our business?"

The man spoke slowly and with conviction. The deep and penetrating timbre of his voice would have been enough to shake any man, but Devi's father did not seem even to flinch.

"After all," the Seeker said. "Perhaps he *is* our business. The trials draw near. Has he come to enlist?"

The Seeker turned to Devi and beckoned him over. Devi looked back at the Seeker, glanced at his father, and returned his gaze to the man that had addressed him. Then, he stepped forward.

The Seeker looked Devi up and down.

"Is that it, boy? Have you come to Narkasee to enlist?"

The mischievous grin plastered across his face made it clear to Devi that the question had been asked merely for the purpose of irritating his father.

"With arms like those," he said. "I hope not."

. The Seeker grabbed Devi's arm by the elbow and pulled it away from his body. His hands were enormous, and Devi felt for a moment as if his arm might get lost inside them. Devi's bicep began to tense a little as he felt the urge to resist, but the Seeker's grip was far too strong.

Devi looked to his father again. His face had remained stoic, his expression one of impatience rather than intimidation, as the Seeker seemed to have hoped. Devi could almost hear his father's voice speaking the words of Psalm Eight aloud in his mind:

Deep within the truest heart
There lies a darkness all but rare.
Every soul must do its part
To bring the good Son's light to bear.

The man twisted Devi's arm so his palm faced the sky. There, on Devi's wrist, was a scar made up of two rudimentary heads of wheat intersecting to form a figure of eight. Like every other farmer in Katai, the mark had been burned into Devi's skin when he was a child, branding him and forever marking him as belonging to the fields.

"You're just a farmer, boy," the Seeker said. "Why don't you stick to the fields?"

Devi allowed the muscles in his arm to flex, feeling the tension from his shoulder all the way down to his clenched fist. He knew he was small, but he also knew that years of working the fields had made his body strong. He caught a flash of surprise in the Seeker's face before he tightened his grip a little more. With this, Devi wrenched his arm free from the Seeker's grip. His fists remained clenched at his sides, and he stared back at the Seeker before him.

"The boy is stronger than he looks," the man said, smiling as he turned to face the other Seekers at his back.

"Or maybe you're just weaker than you look," one returned.

The Seeker laughed for a moment, but his smile fell from his face as he turned back to Devi's father.

"You're a peasant," he said. "And we're Stone Seekers, sanctioned and ordained by King Vagan himself. Speak to me with such insolence again, and you'll lose your tongue. Understood?"

Devi watched as his father took several deep breaths and swallowed them down like water.

"Of course," his father said finally. "Please accept my apologies."

Devi felt his father's hand come to rest on his shoulder once more, and he ushered him back towards the dusty road, where their ox and cart were stood waiting.

III

Though the dirt at his feet was littered with the stubble and debris of crops that had already been cut down, Devi raised his scythe high above his head as he had done countless times before. The fresh blade his father had collected from the market cut through the air with unparalleled ease and precision and, though it was likely slightly heavier than it had been the previous day, the blade being slightly larger and more weighty, Devi's scythe felt lighter than ever.

Devi spun away to his left, leaving his right arm to trail behind. When his right hand came swinging around to meet his left, it brought the blade of his scythe with it, sweeping effortlessly through the dusk, slicing it cleanly in two. Then, Devi slid each of his hands outwards so that one came to rest just beneath the blade of the scythe, and the other came to a halt close to the base of its handle. He thrust it out in front of him, as if to block the oncoming blow of a weapon – a sword or an axe, perhaps. He spun once more, pirouetting on the very tips of his toes, blocking the imaginary attacks as they came, finally dropping to a low squat and sweeping his blade across the shins of the enemy he had created in his mind. Devi rose to standing once more, bringing his scythe to his chest and holding it there with both hands, and he looked around to survey the damage he had caused.

As he turned to his left, he saw a figure lurking in the periphery of his vision, and he didn't need to face the man to know it was his father that was now watching him.

"You know," Devi's father called. "We'd be finished much quicker if you did that in the fields I hadn't already harvested."

It was his attempt at humour, but Devi didn't smile.

Though he had worked as quickly as he had ever worked that morning, Devi had still been unable to match his father's relentless pace, and he was beginning to doubt that he ever would. When his father was old and grey, when time had caught up with him and his days in the fields were numbered, though Devi would still be in the prime of his life, he couldn't imagine his father wouldn't remain one step ahead of him at every moment. By the time the sun had begun to set, Devi's mind was elsewhere, and his father was already at the edge of the field, scooping the fallen heads of wheat from the dirt.

"To plant the seed within the ground," Devi's father said as he pulled his burlap sack tight and tied it in a knot.

"To turn the dirt and plough the field," Devi said reluctantly, finally lowering his scythe and slinking towards his father.

"Is but to search for what is found."

"Within the good Son's sacred yield."

Devi's father lifted his burlap sack onto the back of the wooden cart which, as always, lingered a short distance behind them. He found his scythe where he had dropped it in the dirt and turned to look out across the fields to his right. Like usual, Devi could hear the muffled shouts of his neighbours and, when he looked over his shoulder in their direction, he saw them still hard at their own tasks, whether packing their carts, still hacking away at their last remaining rows of crops, or even carrying baskets of freshly picked fruit back towards the village from the orchards by the hills.

"Finish up here," Devi's father said. "And I'll meet you back at home."

Devi nodded, and he watched as his father strode across their own field into that of their neighbours, content to continue to toil, even though his work was done.

Devi tossed his own scythe into the dirt. He took up a burlap sack from the pile his father had carried with him and dropped to his knees. With both hands, Devi scooped up the fallen heads of wheat from the ground and stuffed them inside the bag, widening his fingers ever so slightly to allow the soil he had taken up with them to filter through. He worked his way back towards the spot where he had last stopped to fill his sack. There, he pulled his newly filled sack tight, tugged at one of the short lengths of rope at his waist, and tied the bag. Devi hoisted the sack of wheat onto his shoulder as his father had done and lifted it up onto the pile on the back of the cart.

The great, white ox at the front of the cart snorted loudly as the sack shook its halter chains.

"I know, boy," Devi said, making his way to the front of the cart. "Harvest is almost over. It'll be winter soon. Then, your only job will be to get fat."

The ox snorted again, as if in recognition of Devi's promise. Devi slapped the ox hard on its hind leg, and it forced itself back in the direction of the line of shacks beyond the fields once more, dragging the heavy cart awkwardly through the dirt along with it.

During the winter months, Devi found himself growing somewhat envious of the village oxen. It was true the animals bore a brutal load from seed sowing until harvest, but Devi's load was almost as difficult to bear. Whilst the oxen spent the winter growing fat and strong for the following harvest, however, Devi's work never stopped. He spent the winter months repairing tools, building outhouses, and preparing the fields to receive their seeds once more. Not to mention hauling their countless sacks of wheat up to Narkasee to be sold on the market and beyond. As Devi picked his scythe out of the dirt and began to make his way back to the village, his stomach rumbled, and he wondered whether he would ever get to enjoy a winter dining on the fruits of his labour like the oxen, and like the rest of Katai.

As Devi arrived at the edge of the field, he found his loaded cart still behind his ox, its head plunged deep into the water trough once more. Devi lifted the halter chains over its neck and began to unload the sacks of wheat from the back of the cart, carrying each to the centre of the village, where the coloured bunting cut the sky overhead.

As he hoisted the final sack up onto the pile and turned to head back towards his shack, Devi found himself face to face with Jerod, struggling to keep his own heavy sack from falling to the ground. Their shoulders met, and Devi sent Jerod sprawling across the floor, his sack bursting at the seams, the wheat inside spilling out across the ground.

"I'm so sorry," Devi said. "I didn't hear you coming."

Jerod looked down at the sack, which was now half-empty.

"It's ok," he said, his face glum and defeated. "It's my fault. I shouldn't have snuck up on you."

Jerod dropped to his knees, and Devi thought for a moment about leaving him to refill his sack alone. It wouldn't take him long, and Jerod's despondency was almost as tiresome as his father's good cheer. Though it was true Jerod had snuck up on him, it was ultimately Devi that had caused the accident, however, and he dropped to his knees alongside Jerod, scooping the heads of wheat back into the open sack.

"When do you leave for Narkasee?" Devi asked, the silence that had briefly lingered between them quickly becoming too uncomfortable to bear.

"I'm sorry?"

"To enlist in the Seeker trials," Devi said. "When do you leave?"

"Oh, yes," Jerod said, his voice low, his mind seemingly elsewhere. "I leave immediately after harvest – when the sun rises after the festival."

"You are not eager to begin?"

"Of course," Jerod replied, but the tone of his voice betrayed the words he had spoken. "It is every boy's dream to seek the Aether Stones."

Devi looked Jerod over as he continued to pick the fallen wheat heads from the dusty ground. His arms were thin and wiry, and his fingers appeared so fragile that it seemed as if they would snap if they were to somehow wrap themselves around the handle of a sword.

"It is the dream of most boys," Devi said. "Are you sure it is yours?"

Jerod squirmed a little under Devi's questioning. His lips withdrew, his nose scrunched up, and his narrow eyes belied his discomfort.

"In truth," he said. "It is not. But my father insisted."

Devi did not speak, and the brief moment of silence that fell between them was encouragement enough for Jerod to continue.

"It's just… I don't think I'd manage well in The Sands. I don't much enjoy the heat."

Devi glared back at Jerod for a moment, and it took every ounce of strength he could muster not to grab him by the shoulders and shake him until he wasn't sure who he was any more. Devi longed for a chance to prove himself in the Seeker trials, and to earn glory for Katai, but his father would never allow him. Yet here was Jerod, reluctant to leave the confines of his own shack but being sent away to Narkasee on his father's instruction.

Devi scooped the last few heads of wheat into the sack and pulled a string of rope from his waistband. He re-tied the sack as best as he could, trying to hold together the opening at the top as well as the seam that had split when it had hit the ground. Then, he threw the sack on the pile with the rest, and he and Jerod turned back towards their shacks.

"Well good luck," Devi said. "To seek the Stones is the highest honour. I hope you bring glory to Katai."

"Thank you," Jerod said, still immeasurably unsure of himself.

As Devi climbed the wooden steps up into his shack, he could already hear his father busy in their kitchen in the back. Devi slipped off his thick hide boots and placed them by the door. The evening was still warm, but his father had already lit a fire in the pit, and the air was heavy with the heat. Devi knew the cold would soon draw in once the sun finally set, however, and he was content to be a little too hot now so he wouldn't be a little too cold later.

From the kitchen in the back, a rich and earthy aroma drifted through to the front room, and Devi knew immediately that his father was preparing the hearty soup they ate most evenings. It was usually thick with vegetables discarded from the previous harvest, and it was occasionally accompanied by slices of dense grain-bread. A couple of winters back, when their last ox had grown too old and weak to tend the fields any longer, it had even been laden with meat.

Devi took two bowls and two spoons from the dilapidated cabinet on the other side of the room and set them down on his father's heavy, wooden table.

When Devi's father finally came through from the kitchen, carrying a large metal pan by its handles, he opened his mouth to speak, but Devi never gave him the chance.

"I want to train to become a Stone Seeker," he said.

Devi spoke with more conviction than he had anticipated, and the firm tone of his voice surprised him as much as it seemed to surprise his father. Devi's father placed the heavy metal pan at the centre of the table, leaving a trail of steam behind it.

"Devi," he began, but Devi barely allowed him to begin, much less finish.

"I know I can do it," Devi said.

Already, the conviction with which he had managed to steel his voice had been lost, and he was almost pleading with his father.

"I am strong. The Seekers in the market yesterday said so themselves."

Devi's father huffed derisively, seemingly recalling the incident with the Seekers. He took up a bowl, fished the wooden spoon from inside the pan, and began to serve.

"I am fit, and I am good with my scythe."

"Seekers do not carry scythes, Devi," Devi's father said, his voice flat and low.

He placed a bowl in front of Devi and pulled the chair out as an invitation for him to sit.

"Seekers carry swords, and you have barely held such a weapon, much less swung it in the direction of another man."

"I can train," Devi insisted. "I *will* train. I can become as good with a sword as I am with a scythe. Better!"

As he poured himself a bowl of the thick soup and took his seat, Devi's father glanced out towards the fields he and his son had spent all day tending, the remnants of the crops on one side flat and even, the stalks on the other all hacked and jagged like torn fabric.

"Perhaps you are not as good with your scythe as you like to think."

Devi stood in silence for a moment, taking a few deep breaths to steady himself. His father was as good with a scythe as any living man, and it seemed unfair to compare Devi's work with his own.

"I came of age two harvests ago," Devi said finally. "Every boy of age should have the chance to win glory for Katai. If I am not successful, I will return to Rakhas and dedicate my life to the fields as you have dedicated yours. And if I *am* successful, I will bring glory to Katai. Is this not what you want for me? For you? For Katai?"

Devi's father breathed deeply. He seemed perturbed but ultimately unmoved. He took up a spoonful of soup and blew away the steam. Rather than place the spoon in his mouth, however, he returned it to the bowl.

"The life of a Stone Seeker is not a life to envy, Devi. It is not a life to strive for. Perhaps there was a time when the Seekers were the best of Katai, but you've seen them in Narkasee. They spend more time lounging in the shade of the market than they do in The Sands. They have become lazy and arrogant. They do not bring glory to Katai; they bring shame. There is too much of Darmeen in them."

Devi opened his mouth to speak, but his father simply raised a finger, and Devi remained quiet.

"Katai does not stand on the shoulders of its Seekers. It stands on the shoulders of its miners, who venture deeper into the darkness of the Salt Cliffs with every passing day. It stands on the shoulders of its pirates, whose ships are dwarfed by those of the Darmeenian traders they board and pillage. And it stands on the shoulders of its farmers. Men and women like you and me, Devi, who toil in the fields day after day, year after year, raising and razing the good Son's sacred yield."

Devi's father held his arm aloft, gesturing towards the door that Devi had left open.

"You have brought more glory to Katai in those fields than you could bring in a lifetime seeking the

Aether Stones. Our hard work feeds a nation, Devi. Without us, Katai would wither and die."

Devi had heard the ramblings of the man on the crate in the marketplace the day before, and he knew his father had heard them too. The man may have been wild in the eyes, but his words could not be faulted. It was true that The Sands were moving west. They had already begun to eat away at the very edges of the fields in Rakhas, and it was even worse further south. It was also true that King Vagan barely left his Keep any more. If it was true that the Darmeenians were closing in on the Fire Stone, then it seemed to Devi that Katai would soon wither and die whether he remained in the fields or not.

"From kindred embers burning low."

Before Devi was able to speak his thoughts aloud, as if he had read his mind, his father gave his response.

"From dust and ash in darkened skies. From tainted soil never sown, the vision of the Son shall rise."

Psalm One was the foundation upon which each of the following Psalms was built. It was a promise of deliverance – a promise that to live according to the teachings of the Psalms is to be redeemed.

"And where is the Son?" Devi asked.

"Excuse me?"

"When can we expect the vision of the Son to rise? These words have been repeated for generations, and yet we continue to work the fields day after day, year after year like our ancestors. We're little more than the slaves Vagan fought to free. The Son of the Psalms never came for them. How long are we to wait for him to come for us?"

Devi looked deep into his father's eyes as the steam from his bowl rose in faint wisps around his face.

"We are to wait for as long as our faith will allow," his father said simply. "Now sit and eat. Your soup is getting cold."

IV

A cool breeze drifted in from the Tharakun Sea, meandering down the dusty streets of Rakhas like some lonesome vagrant, and though the air was alive with the sounds of the harvest festival, Devi was sure he could hear its waves whispering their way up the shore. The strings of coloured bunting that hung from the rafters of the wooden shacks swayed with the rhythm of the drums, and the bouquets of wheat plants that adorned the wooden platforms at the front of the shacks relinquished their kernels to the wind, which carried them across the fields and off into the night. At the centre of the clearing in the village, the huge pile of burlap sacks was stacked high, though not quite as high as Devi had seen it during harvests gone by.

All around the clearing, the night pulsed with the endless beating of the drums. They had burst into life as suddenly as a flame from a spark, and they would perish just as quickly, though not until the sun rose to quiet them. The dancing would continue until sunrise too, men and women throwing their bodies to and fro in the half-light, doing their best not to topple the boys and girls that flowed around their legs and feet. Devi knew his father would be somewhere amongst the crowd, not dancing but otherwise basking in the energy of the evening.

The smell of freshly cooked meat hung on the air, bitter yet enticing, the charcoal and smoke emanating out from the firepit to reach every corner of the clearing. Ordinarily, the harvest festival was the only time of the year when Devi's stomach was anything close to full, but he barely felt like eating. He had almost picked his leg of meat clean, but doing so had taken him all evening. Across the clearing, Devi saw Jerod sat on the stoop of a shack, nibbling away at his own enormous leg of meat, which seemed almost too heavy for him to hold to his mouth.

Devi threw his meatless bone to the ground, and he slipped through the shadows between two shacks and out of the clearing. With the relentless beat of the drums at his back, he made his way through the village out towards the edge of the fields, where his own shack sat on the dry, cracked sand like the discarded shell of a crab. The sun had all but slipped below the horizon far off in the distance, leaving behind only the moon and an endless blanket of stars, but it seemed to be dissolving as it set.

The sun itself was an orange disc, only a small portion of which was still visible, but way out amongst the orchard trees were several tiny orbs of orange light. They bounced and flickered on the horizon by the hills, shifting slightly from left to right as they moved, and they appeared slowly to be growing larger. As Devi squinted through the half-light, he realised it was not only the orbs of light that seemed to glow in the distance but the horizon itself was also a menacing, fiery orange. A thin, pulsing line ran from left to right, cutting the fields from the sky.

It looked to Devi as if the setting sun was melting across the farmlands, spilling its light over the fields and all that came before it. The light seemed to glow and waver in a way that Devi had never seen in a sunset, and as he continued to gaze out towards the sun, it looked almost as if the orchards, and the fields just before them, were on fire.

Devi held one hand to his eyes, sheltering them from the little light that remained and squinting in the direction of the horizon. Harvest season was at its end, and the fields had each been lined with the flammable oil that would wash away all memory of the crops they had held. The fields weren't supposed to be lit until morning, but it was possible some of his neighbours had begun to burn their fields early, Devi thought.

Devi climbed the wooden steps at the front of his shack and looked out towards the horizon again. He was barely higher than he had been on the ground, but he saw that the tiny balls of orange light had grown even larger, and they continued to bounce from left to right as they seemed to make their way towards him. As Devi squinted his eyes, trying his best to narrow his gaze, he also saw that the darkness of the evening hid a wall of thick, black smoke that rose up from the orchards beyond the fields, which was now so high that it had begun to mask the stars.

Devi wasn't sure what could have caused the fire. When he had slipped out of the clearing, he had left the entire village behind, and the sun had not been hot enough to have caused a wildfire at any point throughout the day. It certainly wasn't hot enough now that the day was all but over.

Devi stepped down from the wooden platform at the front of his shack and stepped onto the field. He walked slowly towards the horizon, still unsure whether it truly was fire he was looking upon. As he reached the middle of the field, however, he heard his father's voice calling out to him, and he turned to see half the village spilling across the field behind him.

"Get back to the house, Devi," Devi's father said, pushing him by his shoulder back in the direction of the shack he had left.

He had only run a short distance, but Devi's father's breath had already left his lungs, and he panted furiously as he spoke.

"What's going on?"

Devi's eyes leapt from his father's own to the glowing, orange horizon then back again.

"Just get back to the house. Don't stop, don't think, don't even turn your head. Just get back to the house and block the door. Do you understand?"

A sudden panic gripped Devi. He had never seen fear in his father before. He barely even thought it possible. But his father wasn't just afraid; he was terrified. Devi could see it in his eyes. His father grabbed him tightly by the shoulders, and it was then that Devi noticed that he carried his scythe. Its handle pressed painfully against Devi's bicep as his father brought his face close to his own.

"Listen to me, Devi. Do you know my knife? The one I use to cut meat?"

Devi nodded.

"Do you know where I keep it?"

Devi nodded again.

"Go and find it. Then, get inside the house and block the door. Find somewhere to hide if you can, but don't come back out until you hear my voice. Do you understand?"

The look in his father's eyes entranced Devi. He had never seen anything like it before, not in his father nor in anyone else. He had seen fear before, but this was something different, something more.

"Do you understand?" Devi's father said again, louder this time, his eyes fixed on Devi's, their noses almost touching.

Devi nodded one final time. Then, he turned in the direction of his shack. At first, he walked, intermittently turning his head over his shoulder in the direction of the glowing horizon. The orbs of orange light he had initially seen there were large now, and they bounced violently as they continued to grow. Their edges too were now warped and hazy, and they seemed to dance in the twilight like wavering flames. Devi picked up his pace, walking briskly, before jogging and then breaking out into a run.

By the time Devi reached the house, he was panting as much as his father had been. He made his way around to the back of the shack and found his father's knife where he always left it – embedded in the stump of a tree that he used to chop wood and carve meat. Devi gripped the knife by the handle and pulled, but it didn't move an inch. He knew his father was strong, but it seemed even he had underestimated his true strength.

Devi placed one foot on top of the tree stump and gripped the handle of the knife with both hands. He pulled with every fibre and sinew in his body and gradually managed to work the knife loose. Then, a final tug brought it free.

Devi glanced down at the blade, still stained deep red with blood. It was sharp enough to carve through ox meat, and it was sharp enough to cut a man's head from his body. Devi had never used the knife before. He didn't know what was going on in the fields, but he hoped he wouldn't be forced to use it before the night was over.

Devi made his way back around to the front of the house and froze where he stood. All along the horizon, the faint orange glow he had seen had risen to a blazing wall of flames. Even from such a distance, Devi could tell that the hills were alive with fire and that the orchards would already be all but smouldering ash. The field immediately before him was beginning to catch fire too.

All around, women and children hurried through the village, abandoning the clearing at its centre for the refuge of their shacks, the cries of the young filling the once jubilant evening air. The men did not follow, however. Instead, they stepped from the solid ground onto the ploughed dirt of the field.

It shocked Devi how quickly the scene had descended into chaos. Only moments earlier, the field had been empty, quiet, peaceful. Now, the sound of horse's hooves rumbled across the dirt like thunder, and the torches in the hands of the men on their backs flashed against the darkening sky like lightning.

The men were covered from head to toe in black so that their bodies were camouflaged by the rapidly darkening sky, and their half-lit faces danced about the fields like macabre spectres. Their heads were covered by sweeping black hoods that trailed behind them as they rode, and Devi caught a flash of a trident on one rider's chest – the insignia of Darmeen.

In the near distance, the Darmeenian horses spilled across the open terrain, bearing down on the village with relentless force. At their backs, the fields were now filled with fire, the stubs of the harvested crops there suddenly aflame, just like the trees in the orchards beyond. And ahead of them, a mass of farmers stood ready to face them down.

Away to Devi's left, one of the signal towers burst into life, lighting the corner of the field below, but the flames atop the others were weak and meagre, and they seemed to peter out before the villagers at the base of the towers could get them going. One by one, the men abandoned their efforts to join the crowd at the centre of the field. Then, before Devi could even blink, the two forces met.

The evening erupted with the sound of battle cries and iron meeting iron. The men on horseback swung their swords as they ducked and weaved amongst the throng, darting in and out of the crowd with brutal elegance. The men at the feet of the horses, Devi's neighbours and countrymen, also swung their weapons. They did not hold swords, however. They held axes and knives, they held rakes and sickles, and they held scythes.

Devi searched amongst the chaos for his father, and finally he spotted the curved blade of a scythe held high in the air. The blade cut through the darkness and found its home in the chest of a horse as it galloped by. The horse whinnied a frightful cry and fell to the ground, its front legs collapsing beneath it, snapping the handle of the scythe embedded in its chest in two.

The Darmeenian rider tumbled to the ground too, rolling twice over before his body came to a stop. He did not remain on the ground for long, however. He rose quickly, still gripping his sword in his hand, and he strode towards the man that had cut down his horse. As another horse passed behind, Devi caught a glimpse of the man's face in the fleeting light of the rider's torch for long enough to determine that it was not his father. Then, the man bent over double as his midsection was sliced open, and the contents of his stomach spilled onto the ground.

Devi's entire body shook violently. Everywhere he looked, there was fire and slaughter, and somewhere amongst it was his father. Devi knew his father. He knew he would be fighting, and he knew he would be fighting well. He wanted desperately to be at his side again, to defend his village from the violence and destruction that was unfolding before him, but he could not move. He simply stood at the edge of the field, his father's knife in his trembling hand, his feet deeply rooted to the dirt. When Devi finally moved, it was not in the direction of his father and the field. Instead, he turned towards the shack at his back.

Slamming the door frantically shut behind him, Devi searched in the darkness for something to grab on to. The setting sun bled through the window at the front of the house, but its dying light did little to illuminate the room. Devi's hand landed on the table where he and his father ate every evening, and he found his bearings. The table was thick and heavy, and it took all of Devi's strength to pull it towards him, kicking one of its legs out from underneath so that it came crashing to its side.

Devi bent at the knees and dragged the table across the wooden floor, heaving it into place against the front door, the only point of entry into the house. Then, he dropped to his knees and crawled into the corner of the room beneath the front window.

As the light from the setting sun seeped over the window ledge, Devi pulled his knees tight to his chest and gazed down at his hands. They trembled uncontrollably.

Devi had never seen real violence before. He had seen other villagers fighting, but Rakhas was generally peaceful. Days spent in the fields were typically long and tiring, and energy spent fighting was energy wasted. He had listened to his father's stories of the raids he had seen in his own childhood too, but it had been so long since any Darmeenian had stepped foot on Katai soil that they seemed almost like fairy tales, the signal towers at the corners of the fields the only lasting remnants of what Katai had once overcome.

Devi wondered if his father had fought when he was his age, or whether he had also sat in the darkness, cowering like the women and children in the neighbouring houses. He had never fought before, but he wanted to fight now. He wanted to fight more than anything, but he could not bring himself to his feet.

Devi looked down at his father's knife, which he continued to clutch in his trembling hand. Its blade was large, but in that moment it felt tiny. The Darmeenians would be much taller and much stronger than Devi, and he knew that, if he was going to stand up, step out, and fight, he would stand little chance of survival if he stepped close enough to put the knife to use. He thought of his scythe laying in the dirt where he had dropped it, and he yearned to feel its long, wooden handle in his grip. He had never used his scythe in actual combat before, but he had spent countless days cutting down shadows. This, and his years of using it in the fields would at least give him a fighting chance of defending himself.

Devi imagined himself bursting out of the house and ducking beneath the sweeping blades of the Darmeenians, darting between the rolling hooves of their horses. He imagined scooping his scythe up from the dirt and turning it on his attackers. He imagined holding the blade of his scythe high into the air as one of the Darmeenians approached and swinging it ferociously in his direction. Then, from just beyond the window, Devi heard his father's voice calling his name.

His voice sounded close – so close that Devi wasn't sure whether he had actually heard it, or whether it had simply echoed in his mind. Then, the voice sounded again.

"Devi, you need to run," Devi's father called this time.

From beyond the window, a woman's cry punctuated the sounds of battle.

"No!" the woman screamed. "Leave me! You can't!"

When Devi rose to his knees and turned to peer over the window ledge, he saw the woman from the neighbouring house on her hands and knees, struggling to keep her face out of the dirt as she was dragged by her hair towards the field.

Then, he saw his father. He was as close to the house as his voice had sounded, but his back was now turned, and he strode away from the house in the direction of the woman. Devi's father held his scythe in both hands, and Devi could see blood dripping from the blade down his father's back as he walked.

Devi watched as his father neared the helpless woman and brought the blade of his scythe down into the neck of the Darmeenian man that dragged her. The man's legs immediately gave way, and he collapsed to the ground, the scythe still embedded deep in his flesh. Devi looked on as his father helped the woman to her feet, and then as the woman ran back in the direction of her house and her children. When Devi's father turned to face his shack once more, his eyes instantly met Devi's own.

Devi's lip quivered as he stared back at his father. He couldn't move. He couldn't speak. He couldn't even think. He simply knelt by the window, staring at the blood-soaked figure before him, whose face was cut and bruised, and whose tunic was half-torn from his torso.

"You need to run, Devi."

Devi's father did not shout this time. Instead, he spoke as if the field was empty and silent. Yet, Devi heard him clearly. He wanted to disobey his father. He wanted to walk through the door with his knife in his hand, return his father's scythe, and lay waste to the Darmeenians as they had laid waste to the harvest crops that afternoon. But he could not. As Devi continued to stare, trembling, out of the window, his father spoke again.

"In darkness lie all terrors true."

Devi was silent.

"Say it with me, Devi. Be they many, few, or one."

Devi spoke now too, echoing the final two lines of the Psalm along with his father.

"Yet, through the darkness, he pursues, to lie in wait, the rising Son."

From behind Devi's father, a horse suddenly appeared, and a menacing glint flashed in the eyes of the Darmeenian rider on its back. The man reached the blade of his sword towards the sky, and when he brought it down again, Devi's father's head fell from his neck, and it came to rest on the ground at his feet.

V

A thin shard of pale, yellow light hovered by the leg of the overturned table just inside the door to Devi's shack. He had watched as it had crept out of the blackness of the night and over the sill of the window, slowly growing larger and larger as it ventured steadily deeper into his home. Amidst the trail of light the shard had left behind, countless specks of dust hovered in the air, floating to and fro, visible one second, only to be seemingly snuffed from existence the next.

Devi shifted his foot, and the floorboards beneath his body groaned in protest. His muscles were stiff, and his bones felt as if they were locked in the contorted position in which they had spent the entire night. Devi's shoulder still rested in the corner of the room where two of the wooden walls of his shack met. One side of his head was numb, having been pressed against one of the walls for what felt like an eternity.

Devi wanted desperately to move. Not a minute had passed since he had curled himself up in a ball when he had not felt a deep and burning desire to force himself upright and step out of his front door, but his body simply wouldn't allow it.

Inside the room, all was silent. Devi had fallen still once more, and the floorboards had acquiesced by falling quiet themselves. Not a creak nor a murmur punctuated the dry, dusty air. Devi could barely even hear himself breathe.

When the screaming had started, Devi had been almost unaware. He had still been in the fields, his father's frantic eyes searching through the darkness to find his own, his mind struggling to piece together the fragments of thought that had fallen from his head and shattered at his feet. Once he began to hear the voices, however, it was as if he had never heard another sound. He had begged, over and over, for them to stop, but it wasn't until his wish was finally granted that he realised the silence they left behind was even worse.

Outside the window, the faint crackling of fires still burning sifted in through the cracks in its panes. The fires snapped and hissed so low that Devi felt almost as if they were whispering to him, breathing softly into his ear and calling him to step forth and feel their warmth. When he had turned his back on the fields, the fires had loomed only in the distance, the orchards and the fields around them clearly ablaze but not yet beyond hope of salvation. By the time he lifted his head to peer out of the window in search of his father, the fires were all around him, already waist-high and seeking to climb ever higher.

Devi covered his ears, and his entire body shook as the image flashed across his mind – the blade of the Darmeenian rider glistening in the silver light of the moon, the sound of death as the blade sliced through his father's flesh, and the moment of sheer confusion when his head fell from his body and hit the ground at his feet.

Devi had never seen a dead body before, but he had always imagined that death would be immediate, that when life left the body, the body would simply collapse into a heap where it had stood like a half-empty burlap sack. His father had remained standing for what felt like an age, however, and when he finally fell, he fell forwards, his body stiff and tense rather than lax and flaccid. Every time Devi closed his eyes, he saw his father fall again. Every time he saw his father fall, blood pounded in his ears, his entire body shook, and he couldn't tell whether or not he was screaming.

On the opposite side of the room, a sliver of light began to eek its way in through the door that led to the back of the shack. By now, Devi should have been in the fields with his father for some time, the blades of their scythes basking in the gentle heat of the rising sun. For a moment, Devi felt as though, if he were to stand up and step outside, he would see his father hard at work along with the rest of his village, tending to the fields and preparing them to receive their next harvest. But he knew his mind was running away from him. He also knew that, sooner or later, he would have to stand up and face what truly laid beyond his door.

Devi's legs trembled violently as he forced himself up from the floor. He stumbled as he stood upright, laying his palm flat against the wall beside the window but refusing for the moment to look outside.

Devi took a few tentative, uneasy steps towards the door. He bent at the waist and leaned against the table he had overturned the night before. It had felt heavy when he had thrown it to the ground, but now he struggled to simply pull it aside. The wood cracked and splintered as he dragged it across the wooden floorboards of his shack until it was far enough away from the door to allow him passage outside. Devi stepped over the table, one foot catching on its side but not enough for him to topple over, and he took hold of the door handle.

As he stepped outside, the smell struck Devi even more strongly than the heat. He had grown used to the sweltering days spent under the gaze of the sun, and he had even grown used to standing at the edges of the fields, watching on as they burned with the oil that had been soaked through the soil and the stubble that had been left behind by their harvest.

There was nothing that could have prepared him for the smell, however. Like rotten flesh and scorched sewage, it hung in the air like the thick fogs that would roll in from the Tharakun every winter. It choked Devi as he stepped forward onto the wooden steps that led down onto the sandy road, smothering his eyes and seeping into his throat, placing its wiry fingers around his neck and squeezing the air from his lungs. An acrid smoke lingered over the field too, and it clawed at Devi's eyes the moment he stepped outside.

Stepping from his shack down onto the sand and shuffling slowly towards the edge of the field, Devi's feet kicked up a cloud of dust. He kept his head pointed squarely towards the ground, unwilling to allow his gaze to drift to one side or the other. Already, however, he could see the blackened stubs of wheat plants at his feet, carried by the gentle morning breeze from the fields and onto the road. He could hear the fires crackling more loudly now, and though he knew the only fires still left burning would likely be far off, he was sure he could feel their flames licking and spitting at his feet.

When Devi finally saw the sand of the road meet the dirt of the field, he continued to stare down at the ground, unable to force his eyes to fall upon the one thing in the world he never thought he would see. For a moment, he considered turning away. There was no reason he had to look, no reason he couldn't simply turn and run.

He had fled the night before, however. He had spent the night cowering away whilst his neighbours had each stood their ground. He had turned and fled, and it was his father that had paid the price. If he was ever going to be able to live with himself, if he was ever going to piece together the shattered remains of his life, he had to look. He knew he had to look.

As Devi raised his head and gazed out into the field where his father's body laid, he felt as if his stomach had been sliced open, and he bent over double, his entire body shaking violently, his throat closing so tight that he felt as if he would never breathe again.

Devi heaved once, and then he heaved again. There was nothing in his stomach to dispel, but he placed his hands on his knees and spat a thick mouthful of bile down into the dirt at his feet. Devi's stomach twisted in a knot, and he heaved again. He tried taking deep breaths to calm himself, but the smell was so intoxicating that his head began to swim, and he felt his eyes beginning to haze.

Instinctively, Devi raised one hand to his face and brushed away the tears that had begun to form in his eyes. He hadn't even known he was crying, but his hand was immediately slick. He took a final deep breath and stepped forward onto the dirt of the field.

Beneath Devi's feet, the soil was thick and black with soot. The darkened stubble of the wheat plants instantly crumbled to dust when he stepped upon them, and after only a few steps in his father's direction, his boots were already black. The leather soles on the base of his boots quickly succumbed to the heat of the soil too, the smouldering fires beneath the dust and debris still glowing with menacing, orange embers.

When he finally reached his father's body, Devi felt as if his world had been split in two. There, at his feet, laid his father's lifeless corpse. A short distance away, laid his father's head, his eyes wide open but black and empty, staring vacantly up at the clear, blue sky. Devi turned one way and then the other. His father had been cut in two, and a searing pain pulsed through his temples as he struggled to make sense of the mess of blood and flesh in the dirt before him.

Devi wanted to drop to his knees beside his father's body, to throw his arms around his shoulders as he did when he was just a small boy, clinging to his neck so tightly that it felt as if he would never let go. Then, he felt the desire to look into his father's eyes, to see the limitless strength and devotion that swirled like a thousand stars within them.

That he could not do each of these things at the same time was so puzzling, so wildly incomprehensible, that Devi merely fell to the ground and threw his face to the dirt. His face was immediately thick with soot, which clung to his hair and eyebrows, and his skin began to singe amidst the smouldering ash the fires had left behind. Devi's tears dampened the scorched earth somewhat but only enough that the embers hissed and spat at his eyes as they fell.

"I'm sorry, father," Devi begged.

His sobbing was loud and uncontrollable. He did not speak the words but rather allowed them to fall from his mouth, over his quivering lip and into the dirt along with his tears.

"I'm sorry," he repeated.

Devi's hand searched the dirt for his father's body, and he took hold of his soot-covered tunic. Devi pulled his face from the dirt, his skin red and hot, and he buried it in his father's chest. The world around him seemed to tilt and spin, and he clung tight to his father so he might not fall from its edge. Devi's entire body felt numb, and time seemed to evaporate until he was unsure how long he had spent kneeling in the dirt. When he finally stood, his britches were blackened and burnt, and they seared into the flesh of his legs.

Devi stumbled away from his father's body, the horizon in the distance lurching wildly in the opposite direction. He took a moment to steady himself, and then he took a few steps in the direction of his father's head. He stared down into his father's eyes, and he wanted so much to feel as if his father was looking back at him. But he didn't. It felt as if his father was already a world away, distant and unreachable, lost. Devi's stomach began to heave once more as the grim realisation of what had happened finally began to settle over him.

"I'm sorry," Devi said again.

Then, he took several stumbling steps forward once more until his father was at his back.

Stumbling his way heavily through the ash and dirt, Devi gazed across the rest of the field. The thick smoke that lingered in the air made it difficult to see too far ahead, and the ground at his feet was hazy and blurred. Each morning, he would make his way out into the fields, venturing closer and closer to the orchards on the horizon the closer they drew to the end of harvest season. Looking out to the distance now, Devi couldn't even see the orchards. Where he had seen the faint glow of orange light the night before, now he saw nothing but fog and smoke.

Devi almost tripped as he continued to walk, and looking down, he saw his foot had trodden across the ankle of one of his neighbours. Devi knew everyone in his village and, though he recognised the man's face, the distant, vacant look in his lifeless eyes made him seem eerily unfamiliar.

As Devi raised his head again, it felt as if he was truly taking in the scene for the first time. Scattered across the fields were not just dead bodies but the dead bodies of his neighbours and countrymen. Some were covered in blood, some still had blades stuck in their bodies like pins, and some were slumped over in a position so contorted that it seemed as if they were all flesh and no bone. There were horses in the fields too, their broken legs pointing to the sky like angry mountains. And there were Darmeenians in the fields, their light armour broken or split by the axes and sickles of the farmers that had been brave enough to defend the village.

As Devi neared the top of the field, he caught a flash of something shining in the dirt. Blades had been dropped and scattered all over, but Devi knew his scythe the moment he saw it. He bent and brushed the blackened wheat stalks from its handle. It too was burnt, portions of the wood crumbling like charcoal as Devi's fingers closed around it. It felt rough and foreign now, no longer smooth and supple as Devi had known. The blade of the scythe was also blackened at its edges, the fire having grown so hot that it had begun to eat away at the metal, and the centre of the blade was no longer clean and fresh but was instead stained with deep blues and reds.

Devi held the scythe in his hand for a moment. He imagined the fires were still burning around him. He imagined he could still hear the roars of the Darmeenians in his ears and the cries of his neighbours as they ran, some towards their attacks and some away from them. He imagined swinging his scythe through the air as he had done on so many occasions before, but this time swinging it in the direction of those that would turn their swords on him. He imagined cutting the Darmeenians down from their horses, slicing their stomachs open with his blade, or cutting their own heads from their bodies as if they were merely golden stalks of wheat.

As Devi turned back to the field, however, he saw another dead body laying in the dirt. It was not the body of a Darmeenian man, nor was it the body of one of the neighbouring farmers. Instead, laying in the dirt before Devi, his body as lifeless as if his heart had never beaten, was Jerod.

For a moment, Devi wasn't sure whether his eyes were betraying him. The lingering smoke continued to claw at his face, and tears continued to well in his eyes, but there was no mistaking it. Before Devi laid a boy, smaller and younger than himself, his fragile fingers still grasping the handle of the sickle that had not yet been stained with blood, and any strength that had somehow continued to linger in his body immediately drained into the earth. Whilst Devi had turned and ran, Jerod had remained in the fields. Whilst Devi had been cowering in his home, trembling and shivering beneath his window, Jerod had taken up a sickle. And, whilst Devi had watched his father's head being cut from his body, Jerod had watched whilst the blade of a Darmeenian came to slice him in two.

Devi turned back in the direction of the row of shacks at the opposite end of the field and began to walk. From the clearing at the centre of the village beyond, a single plume of thick, black smoke rose towards the sky like ash from a volcano, and Devi didn't need to wander in its direction to know that its source was the pile of burlap sacks that he, his father, and the rest of the village had spent tireless months building. Rakhas was nothing more than a fire pit, a pile of smouldering ash and ruin. Even if there had been anything left to salvage, even if his neighbours were not all dead, and even if the harvest had not been lost to the smoke and fire, Devi knew he couldn't stay in Rakhas another second. All that was left for him there was shame and chagrin.

Devi dropped his scythe in the dirt once more, and he continued to walk. He walked until he drew near to his father's body, but he could not bring himself even to glance down in its direction. He wiped the tears from his eyes, forced his chin from his chest, and walked past his father as if he had already been consumed by the earth. He continued to walk as he drew close to his shack beyond the edge of the field, but again he did not stop. He walked past his home into the fields beyond, and he continued to walk until Rakhas was nothing more than a smoking pile of dust and ash at his back.

PART TWO

VI

From a distance, the King's Keep appeared large and formidable, etched into the very rock of the Salt Cliffs themselves. Until now, Devi had only ever seen the Keep from the sprawling marketplace that found refuge in its shadow, but as he drew near, it seemed immeasurable, hanging over the Tharakun Sea by a thread yet looking as if it may never fall.

The crowd outside the Keep seemed almost immeasurable too. A sea of faces flooded the clearing in front of the great building, where a set of stone steps led up to a walkway and eventually to two impenetrable wooden doors. Each of the faces belonged to a boy, most of whom appeared to be slightly older than Devi. Devi was unsure whether this was truly the case, or whether their height and the width of their shoulders merely gave them the appearance of maturity, most standing a full head taller than himself, and some even taller still.

Devi took his place at the edge of the crowd. The air was abuzz with the low chatter of voices, some suffused with a distinct air of anxiety, others impatient and irrepressible, but none willing to raise his volume so high that he might draw particular attention to himself or disturb the peace of those that might be lurking inside the Keep itself.

As Devi looked around, he saw that most boys, like him, stood alone. They each glanced cautiously from left to right, surveying the other faces in the crowd, just as he did. Some of the boys seemed to stand in small groups, however, loitering together, whispering and murmuring as discreetly as they could manage, occasionally daring to point a finger out in the direction of one boy or another that they happened to deem of particular interest.

"Citizens of Narkasee only."

Before Devi could even turn around to match the face of the person behind with the voice that had greeted him, he already felt their chest pressing against his shoulder.

"Excuse me?" Devi said, stepping forward to create some space to turn, his voice tentative and unsure.

"Citizens of Narkasee only," the voice repeated.

Devi found himself staring up into the face of a boy who was a little more than a head taller than him, and whose blond hair and youthful complexion suggested he was roughly Devi's age. His piercing eyes and the tone of authority that ran through his voice, however, gave the impression of a boy much older.

"Only citizens of Narkasee can enlist in the Seeker trials," the boy said. "You're not from Narkasee, are you?"

Devi declined to answer for a moment. Instead, he looked to the left and right of the boy that stood before him.

At each of his shoulders, the boy was flanked by two others, each much closer to Devi's height but each with the same smug, superior countenance as the boy that had confronted him. All five of the boys, including the one that continued to stand too close for Devi's comfort, wore uniforms of rich, black velvet that were laced at the edges with ornate threads coloured in gold. Their collars were turned up at their necks, and their chests were uncovered beneath their tunics. Their uniforms did not match exactly, but it was clear they had been chosen intentionally.

"Who are you?" Devi asked, returning the question he had been asked not with an answer but instead with a question of his own.

"Never mind who I am," the first boy said. "You can answer my question first. You're not from Narkasee, are you?"

For a moment, Devi began to panic. The boys barely looked older than him, but between their attitude and their attire, they were conspicuous amongst the crowd. They looked almost official.

"Answer me, peasant boy."

The boy at the front of the group poked a finger into Devi's collarbone, and he immediately stepped forward to close the tiny gap that had been created as Devi had stumbled back.

"You're a farmer, aren't you?"

Devi still wore the same clothes he had worn on the last day of harvest. His loose, ragged tunic was torn up from working the fields, and his worn and withered boots were still covered in black soot from walking through the smouldering ash he had left behind. Even if he had managed to clean himself up before he arrived, his dark skin and the branded mark on his naked wrist would have given him away. He'd had no intention of hiding his identity, however. It was the right of every citizen of Katai to enlist in the trials, Narkasee-born or otherwise.

"Away with you, peasant boy," the boy in front of Devi said, grabbing him by the shoulder in an attempt to force him back in the direction of the sandy road that led up the hill to Vagan's Keep.

Just then, however, another boy stepped forward into the group, and he joined Devi at his side.

"What's wrong, Orlain?" he asked, the question seemingly directed towards the boy that had initially confronted Devi. "Trying to scare off the competition?"

Orlain scoffed, apparently unable, for the time being, to find the words to adequately convey his scorn.

"I have no competition," he said finally.

"Then why are you lying to the other trainees?" the boy that had just arrived pressed.

"He's not a trainee yet."

"But he will be. As will I."

The boy raised his hand to indicate the crowd that, whilst already large, still seemed to be growing.

"As will every other boy here. Because we are all citizens of Katai. And every boy in Katai has the right to seek the Stones and to protect his nation. Isn't that right?"

Once more, Orlain struggled to provide his answer, This time, however, it seemed he was less eager to allow himself the time to find one to provide. He simply glared at Devi for a moment, huffed derisively, and pushed past him, thrusting his elbow out to catch Devi's own, whilst the four boys that had flanked him followed obediently behind.

"Pay him no notice," the boy that remained said. "He thinks because his grandfather was a Seeker it will come naturally to him. He'll soon find out it's not so simple."

The boy held his hand out towards Devi, and Devi returned the gesture, gripping the boy's forearm and allowing him to do the same.

"I'm Vikas," the boy said.

Before Devi could thank Vikas for his intervention, the great, wooden doors at the front of the Keep burst open, and a hulking giant of a man stepped forward onto the stone walkway at the top of the steps.

"Cease your noise and gather before me!"

The man's voice boomed around the clearing like thunder. Immediately, the gaggle of boys that were loitering outside the Keep began to converge on the steps, none daring to place so much as a foot on the steps themselves.

"My name is Farruk," the man bellowed.

His voice seemed to rise up from below the earth and force its way out of his great barrel chest like a geyser.

"If you are lucky, this will be the last time you hear my voice. If *I* am lucky, I will never hear your own."

Devi forced himself up onto the tips of his toes so he could see Farruk in his entirety. He stood almost as tall as the doors at his back, his shoulders appeared wide enough that the entire world could rest upon them, and his arms were as thick as tree trunks.

"It is the right of every citizen of Katai to defend his nation, and to bring her honour and glory. Today, you will be afforded the opportunity to exercise that right."

Since the day he had first seen their sails flapping fitfully in the wind off the coast of Rakhas, and since the first day he had ever stepped foot in Narkasee, Devi had dreamed of enrolling in the Seeker trials. Standing outside the King's Keep, about to make his way inside, he only wished it hadn't been a nightmare that had brought him there.

"If you will follow me," Farruk said, gesturing with one arm towards the great, wooden doors that still stood open behind him. "King Vagan awaits you."

Devi followed the mass of boys up the stone steps, along the walkway, and through the doors into the Keep. Just beyond the entrance was a vast, open hall, and the boys filtered slowly in, flooding the space until they were pressed up against all four of its walls. Devi shuffled his feet, careful not to allow his soles to lift from the floor for fear he might stumble and be buried beneath a mess of bodies. The floor beneath his feet was polished stone and seemed, like the rest of the building, to have been carved out of the cliff directly.

Devi looked around the great room, its walls lined by doors of various sizes, as well as archways that seemed to snake away in all manner of directions. The Keep looked enormous from the outside, but it seemed as if the corridors and walkways inside were endless. All around the hall, great banners and pennants hung in green and brown, each bearing two intersecting scythes – the sigil of Katai.

Devi saw no sign of King Vagan, but he did see a balcony on the opposite side of the room, flanked on either side by sets of stone steps that curved up and away from the Great Hall before disappearing out of sight. As he had on the stone steps outside, Farruk emerged and addressed the trainees in a voice that shook the very walls of the Keep.

"Stand in silence for the King of Katai. King Vagan!"

Not a soul in the room dared speak as Farruk stepped aside, nor as he was replaced at the edge of the balcony.

The man that emerged from behind Farruk was almost as tall, and it seemed as if, in years gone by, he would have been almost as wide. Though Vagan's shoulders were still broad, his chest had grown sunken, and the muscles beneath his heavy robes had long since succumbed to the passage of time. Devi had never seen Vagan in person before, and he struggled for a moment to pair the stories his father had told him with the man he saw before him.

Devi had been told of Vagan's fire-red hair that glowed like burning embers, but instead his hair was withered and grey. He had heard that Vagan could crush a man's skull with his bare hands, but the fingers that gripped the stone bannister at his waist were bony and wrinkled. And he had heard that Vagan's voice could cut through stone like a diamond blade, but compared to the efforts of Farruk's thunderous lungs, Vagan's voice seemed to peter out, falling flat onto the stone floor at the feet of the boys beneath him.

"Young men of Katai," King Vagan said. "It is an honour to welcome you all today. To seek the Aether Stones is to serve Katai in the most noble of ways, and it is for this purpose that you have found your way to my Keep."

King Vagan paused for a moment, casting his eyes over the boys that gazed up towards him. Then, from the shadows behind the king, Devi watched as a girl stepped forward and took her place beside him.

The girl stood a little taller than half the height of Vagan himself, and her hair did burn orange like fire. It hung in thick locks around her pale face and ran down her back, sweeping over her shoulders and across her chest like a molten waterfall. Even from his position across the hall, Devi could see that the girl's eyes shone a brilliant blue like elegant daggers, and she moved with a poise and grace befitting only royalty.

"It is no secret that Darmeen wishes to regain what they believe to be rightfully theirs, and by now many of you will have heard that The Sands continue to draw ever closer. To seek the Aether Stones is to defend Katai from such perils, and Katai thanks you for your sacrifice."

Devi did his best to return his gaze to King Vagan himself, but he couldn't draw his eyes from the girl that stood beside him. Her red hair lit her pale skin, and there was something about the playful half-grin on her face that was irresistibly enticing, almost alluring. Devi watched as the girl's eyes began to scan the crowd below her as Vagan's had. When he saw them fall upon him, Devi's heart began to beat out of his chest and it seemed for a moment as if he had forgotten how to breathe.

"To seek the Stones is a privilege afforded only to a chosen few, however," Vagan continued. "Most of you will fail. Many of you will return to your families to continue whatever tradition those that have come before you have established. Some of you may not be fortunate enough even to do this. For the chosen few that prove themselves worthy of joining the ranks of the Stone Seekers…"

King Vagan paused again. Not to survey the audience this time, but instead to allow a gnawing tension to creep into their guts.

"Glory," King Vagan said finally. "Awaits you.

Vagan raised his arms almost in jubilation, and the crowd of trainees below saw this as an invitation to release some of their pent up anticipation, a measured and somewhat subdued cheer echoing around the hall.

Amidst the cheers, Devi turned to Vikas.

"Who's that?" he asked, gesturing towards the balcony where the mysterious girl stood behind King Vagan's outstretched arms.

When the boy beside Devi turned to face him, however, he saw it was not Vikas that was by his side. A blank face stared back at Devi, but it gave no response, and the boy turned away once more. As Devi turned back to the balcony, he thought perhaps he saw the girl's mouth twist into an almost imperceptible smile, but suddenly her eyes were elsewhere, and she was following Vagan back towards the shadows from which they had emerged.

~

The corridors that ran through the King's Keep were long and narrow. They cut through the Salt Cliffs in all directions, and they harnessed Farruk's booming voice like a trumpet.

"There will be six trainees to each room," Farruk had bellowed as he led the trainees through the corridors in the barracks, those at the very back of the procession more than able to hear him, though they could not see him. "The bunk you are assigned will remain your bunk for the duration of your stay. That may not be long, so don't make yourselves too comfortable. You are to change into the clothes in the chest by your bunk and be out in the training yard on the hour."

Devi peered in through the open doors as he passed. In spite of the passing audience, some of the boys wasted no time in dispensing with their clothes and replacing them with the beige tunic and britches it seemed would be their uniform. Inside each room, Devi caught a glimpse of several cloth hammocks hanging from metal hooks on the stone walls, each with a wooden chest at its head.

As another group of six boys were assigned their room, and the mass in the corridor was beginning to dwindle, Devi scanned the heads in front of him in search of Vikas. He had only spoken to three other trainees so far. One of them had told him to leave, and another he had addressed only by mistake. Devi didn't much care who he would be bunking with, but Vikas seemed as if he would make as fine a roommate as any. Just as Devi reached the front of the procession, Farruk's enormous face glaring down at him, he felt a warm breath against his neck and he heard a menacing voice in his ear.

"Looks like we're going to be bunkmates," Orlain hissed.

Before Devi had a chance to respond, Farruk's great mitt of a hand was on his shoulder and his thunderous voice was booming down the corridor once more.

"Six more!" he yelled.

Farruk ushered Devi into the room as effortlessly as if he was brushing a fleck of dust from his shoulder. Orlain followed closely behind, and Devi turned to see the four faces that had flanked Orlain earlier filing in after them.

"Well, aren't we fortunate," Orlain asked, turning to survey his four companions. "To be bunking with a friend?"

A menacing grin fell across his face.

"And to think," he said. "We could have ended up with anyone."

The gormless chuckles from Devi's four other bunkmates seemed to be a sufficient response, as Orlain turned his attention to Devi.

"I believe you know my name," he said. "But you never gave me yours."

Devi considered ignoring Orlain. He also considered spitting in his face. He knew making it through training would be the greatest challenge he had ever met, however, and it would be even more difficult with someone like Orlain breathing down his neck every step of the way. Perhaps, if he kept his head down and did nothing to anger him, Orlain would grow weary and leave him be.

"It's Devi," Devi mumbled, his voice low.

Orlain stepped quickly towards him.

"Speak up," he said, glaring down into his eyes.

"My name is Devi," Devi said again, louder this time.

"Well, Devi. I plan on staying here for some time. You, on the other hand, will never see this room again."

Orlain pushed past Devi to the hammock that, since each of the others had already been spoken for, would be Devi's. He bent down, lifted Devi's small, wooden chest from the floor, and turned it upside down. Two pairs of britches and two beige tunics fell to the ground.

"So I'm sure you won't mind if I take this."

Orlain pushed past Devi once more and dropped the wooden chest by his own hammock. Devi stood in silence, watching as he did so. Then, he simply took his clothes from the floor and, one by one, slipped his feet out of the withered, blackened hide boots that had carried him from Rakhas to Narkasee.

VII

Devi made sure he was not the last boy to emerge from the back of the Keep out into the training yard, but the space was already crawling with trainees when he did so. Just as they had out front earlier that morning, some boys formed into small groups, more so now than before. Devi found a space where he could stand alone, and he took a moment to survey his surroundings.

The training yard itself was large, spanning the entire width of the Keep and extending even further beyond on each side. It stretched all the way back to the edge of the Salt Cliffs, but the perimeter wall lined only the edges of the yard on two sides. The back of the yard was completely open, and Devi could see the Tharakun Sea stretching away from him towards the horizon, where it met the clear blue sky so perfectly it was impossible for Devi to tell where the water ended and the sky began.

Far off to Devi's left was a small barn and stables, which appeared at first glance to be empty. To his right stood several large, wooden structures, each seemingly fashioned into some wall, platform, tunnel, or other obstacle. Some of the walls had ropes hanging from their tops, and others had wooden planks that protruded at awkward angles. The space at the centre of the yard between the structures and the stables was vast but empty, and towards the back of the yard, beyond the wooden structures and nearing the edge of the Salt Cliffs, was a large wooden board with a tall ladder leaning against one side.

"Right, you worthless lot."

Farruk's voice was no more quiet in the open air than it had been in the narrow, stone corridors of the Keep. He emerged as the trainees had, lowering his head as he passed through the door to avoid taking a chunk of the stone archway along with it.

"Gather around and listen closely."

Devi joined the throng that was already beginning to form around Farruk as he made his way to the centre of the yard.

"Though all of you have made it here today, only half will remain tomorrow. The life of a Stone Seeker is a gruelling existence, and it is not for the faint of heart, nor the weak of mind, nor the feeble bodied. Beginning immediately, you will run laps of the obstacle course."

Farruk raised his arm towards the wooden structures away to his right.

"If you refuse, you will be ejected," he said, his voice flat and devoid of emotion. "If you fall behind, you will be ejected. If you stop before my say so, you will be ejected. Do I make myself clear?"

A handful of the trainees that had gathered around Farruk mumbled their assent.

"Do I make myself clear?" the giant of a man bellowed.

This time, every trainee in the yard yelled at the top of his voice, Devi included.

"Then what are you waiting for?" Farruk shouted. "Get moving!"

Devi took off towards the obstacle course with the rest of the crowd. Roughly half of the boys were already in front of him, the other half behind.

The pack was thick and dense as they approached the first wall, those at the front clambering over the top and down the other side, but those behind being forced to wait their turn. Several of the trainees around Devi began attempting to push their way to the front, but Devi stayed put. Farruk had said nothing to indicate this was a race and had made no mention of finishing first. Rather, his words had suggested a test of endurance. Devi knew he merely needed to hold his place in the middle of the pack and keep moving until enough of the other boys had given up.

As more and more of the trainees clambered up and over the wall, the pack began to stretch. Devi finally reached the base of the wooden structure and took his turn grabbing hold of the rope. He leaned back, placed his feet flat against the wall, and pulled himself towards the top. There, he released his grip of the rope, clambered over the wall, and dropped to the other side. The ground at the bottom was hard and dry, and he stumbled awkwardly as he landed, taking several lunging steps forward to prevent himself from falling over.

As Devi approached the next obstacle – a tunnel that seemed to slope down under the ground slightly – he dropped to his knees, and dust from the trainees ahead kicked up into his face. The tunnel was barely wide enough for two trainees to slither through side by side, and Devi was forced to hold his ground for a moment to prevent the boys immediately behind him from clambering over and ahead of him.

The vibrant sun almost blinded Devi as he rose to his feet again, bursting out of the other side of the tunnel with a string of trainees following behind. Up ahead, a handful of boys had already managed to separate themselves from the pack, opening up a lead on the crowd that followed behind them. Devi was unsure whether or not it was Vikas that he could see way out in front, but he was certain that he caught a flash of Orlain's luminous blond hair following close behind.

As Devi clambered up the heavy netting that hung from a thick, wooden beam high above his head, he managed to advance his position in the crowd, the boy to his left holding up those behind. In his haste to climb the obstacle, the boy thrust his ankle through the netting, falling back on himself until his leg was twisted painfully at the knee. The boy screamed out, but just as Devi had clambered past him towards the top, the trainees behind merely navigated over or around the boy, leaving him to work himself free. It wasn't until Farruk came and lifted the boy from the netting, his gargantuan hands grabbing him firmly by the shoulders and tossing him back towards the Keep, that the crowd of trainees began to flow more freely again.

To Devi's surprise, it wasn't long before boys began to drop out, and after just two laps of the obstacle course, Devi had managed to advance his position, gaining ground on the front of the pack. Some of the boys were simply too large and too heavy, their bodies strong but too cumbersome to carry them over walls and through tunnels. They quickly fell behind, and after three laps, Farruk began to grab them one by one as they passed him, tossing them aside back in the direction of the door at the back of the Keep. Others of the boys streamed with sweat, their heads dripping and the backs of their tunics sticking to their bodies, and after four laps, seeing the looming figure of Farruk bearing down upon them, they opted to slink away back to the Keep of their own volition.

Though Devi was hot and tired, the sweltering midday heat proving as fearsome an adversary as any boy in the yard, he had spent years toiling away in the fields. He was used to the heat, and he was used to the relentless strain that farming had placed on his body. He was light, he was nimble, and he was smaller in stature than most of the other trainees, but he was likely almost as strong. His muscles ached and his skin burned, but Devi knew he could keep going all afternoon if necessary.

As the boys up ahead continued to slow, and those behind continued to be plucked from the ranks by Farruk, Devi made steady progress towards the front of the pack until he was only a stone's throw from Orlain, who continued to trail the tall and slender body of Vikas. The next time he turned to look back over his shoulder, Devi saw that the crowd had thinned far more than he had realised. It looked as if the yard was only roughly half as full as it had been when they had begun, and Devi estimated far more than the half that remained were behind him.

Sweat dripped from Devi's forehead, dampening his tunic, and his head spun wildly. He would continue until his muscles gave way and he dropped to the floor unable to move, but it seemed to be growing ever more likely with each passing minute that he may not be able to prevent himself from doing so for much longer.

When Farruk's voice finally thundered across the yard once more, Devi immediately dropped his hands to his knees and sucked in several deep, gasping breaths. The entire world seemed to lurch one way and then the other, and though his stomach was empty, Devi felt his body begin to retch, and he forced down the tide of bile he could feel rising within him.

"Congratulations," Farruk said, his voice once more entirely emotionless. "You have proven you are not utter failures, and there is the slimmest of chances you have what it takes to bring glory to Katai."

Farruk stepped towards the front of the pack where Vikas and Orlain were each doubled over as Devi had been. He took Vikas by the wrist and raised his hand in the air.

"This boy has set your standard," Farruk said. "If you wish to seek the Aether Stones, you will match him, and you will beat him."

Vikas had led the pack, but he did not stand with a smile on his face as Farruk raised his hand. Instead, Devi thought perhaps he had seen him wince, and he was sure he had seen Orlain glare at him with wry derision.

~

A wave of rich aromas washed over Devi as he passed through the Great Hall and through the pair of large wooden doors that led to the mess. The muscles in his legs were on fire, and his head was still moist with sweat. He followed the line of trainees all the way along one wall in the direction of a set of hatches that had been carved into the stone along another. Down the line, the trainees each took a tray, which they slid down to the serving hatches to receive their food. Devi's stomach was roaring with hunger, and he certainly felt as if he had earned a good meal.

When he finally took a tray of his own and approached the first of the serving hatches, Devi was greeted by a large troll of a woman, who stood over a vast cauldron with a blackened ladle in her hand. She took up a wooden bowl, sloshed a ladleful of some concoction inside, and tossed it onto Devi's tray, spilling half of the liquid across his hands and his tunic.

Devi slid down to the next hatch, where another trollish woman threw a slab of crusty bread in his direction, and he was met at the final hatch by a tiny man, whose hands were dwarfed by the thick leg of meat that he struggled to lift onto Devi's tray. Whenever Devi had been fortunate enough to eat meat back in Rakhas, it had almost always been blackened by the firepit at the centre of the village, and even the meat on the marketplace appeared to have been barbecued. The leg on his tray was pale and slimy, however, and it seemed to have been boiled rather than roasted or grilled.

Devi turned to face the bustling mess of tables and trainees that confronted him. He cast his gaze across the sea of heads, and he realised it was not only trainee Seekers that were sat around the tables. Way off in the corner, he saw a small band of real Stone Seekers, and the golden helmets of the King's Vanguard were also scattered across a handful of tables, their green cloaks draped over their thick, shining armour. One of the men seemed to hold his chunk of bread up to the light of the flickering torches, and whilst at first Devi thought he might be admiring the flecks of mould that were scattered across its crust, the look of disappointment on his face suggested he was more concerned by its scant and unimpressive size.

Scanning the tables for a familiar face, Devi's eyes finally lighted on Vikas, who raised his hand in Devi's direction, gesturing to the empty seat opposite him. Vikas seemed to be joined by two other trainees, but just as Devi began to make his way towards them, he found himself flat on the stone floor, his tray clattering to the ground and his food scattering away from him in all directions. Roars of raucous laughter filled the room for a moment, but they died away almost as quickly, the trainees in Devi's immediate vicinity managing to find something else to occupy their attention.

"That was clumsy."

Devi heard a voice call out to him from the table to his left, and he glanced over his shoulder to see Orlain glaring down at him, a smug, sanctimonious grin plastered across his face.

"I'd be quick, or you won't have anything at all to eat."

Orlain nodded ahead of Devi where his tray had clattered to the floor. Just as Devi turned to look, two other trainees swooped down and scooped up his slab of bread and his leg of meat, peeling away the filth and hairs as they scampered back towards their tables.

"Would you like me to help you up?" Orlain asked, his voice all mock sincerity.

Devi placed his palms flat against the floor.

"I'm fine," he said, forcing himself upright.

When Devi finally made it to Vikas's table, he was greeted not by a handshake but instead by a leg of meat. Vikas tossed it on the table in front of him without a word as he sat down, and he introduced the two boys to his left, one on his own side of the table, the other on Devi's.

"Warwick, this is Devi," Vikas said. "Devi, Warwick."

Warwick nodded, scooped up his slab of bread, and placed it in front of Devi.

"Pleasure," Warwick said, sinking his teeth into his own leg of meat.

"And this is Tsurzan," Vikas said, indicating the boy beside him. "Tsurzan, Devi."

Tsurzan held his bowl to his mouth and was slurping the liquid from inside.

"Pleasure," he gurgled as he swallowed it down.

Tsurzan drained his bowl and slammed it back down before him, and if it wasn't for the boy's frantic exuberance, Devi would have been convinced that Warwick had merely stood up and taken a new seat across the table. Each looked identical to the other, and Devi knew it was only by virtue of their contrasting mannerisms that he would be able to tell them apart. As Tsurzan took up his slab of bread and crammed it into his mouth, Vikas looked down at his empty tray, then back up at Tsurzan expectantly.

"What?" Tsurzan asked, breadcrumbs flying from his mouth and striking Vikas in the face. "I'm hungry."

"You'll have to excuse my friend," Vikas said. "Apparently, he's hungry."

Vikas gestured towards the food in front of Devi.

"Go ahead," he said. "Eat."

Devi lifted the leg of meat from the table and held it up to the light that flickered from the flame torches around the mess. A chunk of meat fell from the bone and landed in Devi's lap, leaving a thick, gelatinous string of grease behind it.

"Thanks," Devi said, and he bit into the meat.

"You're a farmer, aren't you?" Vikas asked as Devi tried his best to force down the cold, moist meat that had already turned almost to a paste in his mouth.

"I am," Devi said.

"You don't see many farmers in Narkasee after harvest. And you almost never see them enlisting for the trials. Where are you from?"

Devi thought for a moment. Rakhas was the name that immediately sprang to his lips, but for some reason, he decided to hold his tongue.

"Doku," he said finally.

Doku was a small city, home to the library that Devi's father had taken him to on occasion.

"Not many farms out that way," Vikas said.

"It's small."

"Well, I don't know what they've been feeding you out on the farms, but you did well today. It wiped the smile off Orlain's face when he saw you were still standing."

Devi continued to eat, but he took a moment to smile.

"Did I see that you're stuck bunking with him?"

The smile fell from Devi's face, which was enough of an answer for Vikas.

"You need to stand up to boys like that," Vikas said. "I know Orlain. Even if I didn't, I know his type. He's tough, especially when he's got those other idiots behind him. But get him on his own, and he isn't much of anything. He's all fluff."

Devi nodded his head.

"I mean it, Devi," Vikas said, his voice firm and sincere. "If you really want to make it as a Seeker, you can't let people like him push you around. He'll have you turned out the first chance he gets, so you better get ahead of it now."

Devi stopped chewing for a moment. He wasn't sure why, out of hundreds of boys in the crowd that morning, Orlain had chosen to single him out. It was clear he was a farmer, descended from the those that Darmeen had first ripped from the Hinterlands all those years ago, whilst Orlain's pale skin indicated that his veins ran with the ancient blood of the Lagunian Kingdom. They were both citizens of Katai, however, both ready to sacrifice themselves to ensure her longevity. They should be kin, rather than foes.

"I will," Devi said, tossing his meatless bone onto the table and handing his slab of bread back to Warwick. "Thank you, but I'm not hungry."

Then, Devi rose from the table, and made his way back towards the two great, wooden doors that led out into the Great Hall.

VIII

"All rise!"

Devi felt as if he had only just closed his eyes, but already he found himself forcing them open again. The door to his right thundered, sending three dull shockwaves pulsing through his entire body.

"All rise!" Farruk's unmistakable voice called from beyond the door again. "We're up with the sun!"

The room was still cloaked in darkness, but Devi heard the tired groans of his five bunkmates as they too forced themselves awake. When Farruk's voice boomed around the corridor for a third time, it sounded further off, but the room still seemed to shake a little as his fist pounded against the door just down from Devi's own.

Devi swung his feet over the edge of his hammock, and they came to rest on the cool, stone floor. Being in the heart of the Keep, and with no windows to open, Devi imagined the barracks must become swelteringly hot when the sun was at its highest. The almost imperceptible shiver that ran up the backs of his legs told him it must be early.

"You better get dressed quick," Devi heard another voice mutter in the darkness from across the room. "Sounds like Farruk rolled out of the wrong side of his hammock this morning."

Devi was under no illusion the words had been spoken for him and for him alone. He listened as a pair of feet shuffled across the room towards the door that had been at the mercy of Farruk's fist just moments earlier, and Orlain slowly came into view as light from the corridor beyond flooded in around him.

Devi looked around the small room, all five of his bunkmates already up and out of their hammocks and dressing themselves. Orlain returned to his own hammock, his lower half covered by a pair of beige britches, but his upper body exposed. His chest was thick and bulging, and the skin of his stomach was pulled tight against the ridges of muscle beneath. Devi couldn't help but wonder what his own body would look like if food had been a little easier to come by. He watched as Orlain lifted his tunic over his head and pulled it across his body.

"See you out there."

Orlain leaned close into Devi's ear as he passed by, leading the procession of trainees out into the corridor until Devi was alone. Devi took up his britches from the floor, folded where his wooden chest had once sat. He slid one leg in, then the other, and they seemed to fit as well as any clothes he had worn before. Then, he took up his tunic and pulled it over his head. It hung loose over his slender body, but no more so than the ragged tunic he had worn since the day he had fled Rakhas.

When Devi finally sat down at an empty table in the mess, his tray firmly in hand, he didn't look too closely at the food he had been served. The leg of meat Vikas had given him had been enough to sustain him through the night, but his body had worked hard the previous day, and his stomach turned over as if it was rolling down a hill. The food appeared to be exactly the same as the previous evening, but Devi immediately took up his slab of hard, stale bread and crammed it into his mouth.

Devi looked around the room as he ate. A few tables down from his own, he found Orlain and his other bunkmates. They talked and laughed as they ate, their voices distinctly audible above the general commotion of the other tables. Devi saw Vikas across the room too, sat at a table alongside Warwick, Tsurzan, and a handful of other trainees, who Devi assumed were the rest of his bunkmates.

Devi ate quickly and, though he had arrived in the mess later than many of the other trainees, he was one of the first to be ready to leave. He stacked his empty tray with the others at the end of the row of serving hatches, and he hung back a little until another group of boys rose from their table to leave. Then, as they made their way out of the mess towards the training yard, he followed close behind.

Outside, the sun was low in the sky, casting dense black shadows across the half-lit ground, but already Devi could feel its warmth. Far off in the distance, just beyond the edge of the Salt Cliffs, Devi saw the glint of Katai sails way out amidst the endless Tharakun Sea.

As he made his way out towards the centre of the training yard, he turned and gazed up at the towering wall of the King's Keep. The entire face of the wall was smooth, lined at the top by rows of crenels, and it was so tall that it seemed to lean over Devi. A handful of windows were scattered at various intervals across the wall, only the floor at the very top of the building possessing a row that ran from one side of the Keep all the way across to the other. Devi imagined that to stand at one of those windows and look out across the Tharakun was to peer over the edge of the world.

By the time Devi levelled his gaze again, the yard was filled with trainees. There seemed to be roughly half as many as had gathered outside the Keep the previous morning, but there still looked to be at least one hundred faces milling about around him. One or two of those faces winced as the yard erupted with the same booming voice that had yanked Devi from his sleep that morning, and Farruk strode out into the yard amongst them.

"Gather around," Farruk yelled. "And make it quick! Seekers can't afford to be idle."

If there was any lethargy lingering in the yard before Farruk's arrival, it dissipated immediately. The trainees were suddenly alive, hustling over from all corners, and it was all Devi could do to hold his position at the front of the circle that quickly formed around Farruk.

"Today," Farruk began. "You will learn how to defend yourselves."

At Farruk's feet, a mess of wooden swords had been piled in the centre of the yard, and he bent to pick one up. It looked nothing more than a toothpick between his enormous fingers, and it looked as if the handle might shatter as he gripped it in one hand.

"The Sand Dwellers are vicious, fearsome warriors," Farruk continued. "If you cannot defend yourself against the boy across from you, you will have no hope of survival in The Sands."

Devi had heard countless tales of the Sand Dwellers. The last remnants of the ancient Kingdom of Emirya, and protectors of the Fire Stone, they lived amongst The Sands, basking in it as it overwhelmed their towns and cities, rather than cowering away or running from it. But The Sands had worn away their faces as well as their homes, the harsh winds and storms gradually eating away their features until only the vacant, anonymous flesh of half-men remained. Masters of stealth, they could disappear into the dunes at a moment's notice, and with no more effort than the blinking of an eye.

"You will fight with swords only. No shields," Farruk said, holding his sword aloft. "The only thing a shield is good for in The Sands is digging a grave. And if you're dead... Well, you probably won't much care whether you get buried or not, will you?"

Farruk tossed his wooden sword high into the air, and it lingered above the crowd for a moment before a hand flew up to snatch it. One by one, Farruk scooped up the swords at his feet and tossed them into the crowd, some falling to the floor before they were sheepishly seized by the red-faced trainees for whom they had been intended.

Devi caught a sword as it was tossed his way, and he held it in his grasp for a moment. He thought back to the elegant, ornate blade he had held in the marketplace, its handle encrusted with jewels and its blade an ethereal silver. The wooden sword he clutched was nothing more than a toy in comparison, but though it was much lighter than the blacksmith's sword, the blade still felt awkward and unwieldy in his hand. Devi's instinct was to raise a second hand and clutch the weapon as he would his scythe, but there was only space on the handle for one.

"The Sand Dwellers do not carry shields. In The Sands, a shield will only slow you down – there's nothing out there but desert and dunes. Instead, they will use their bodies to defend themselves, and they will use your body against you."

Farruk raised his sword and began to rotate in the centre of the circle, his arm outstretched like the hand of a clock. The tip of the sword slowly made its way around the circle, creeping closer and closer towards Devi with each half-step of Farruk's feet. Devi's breath caught in his throat as the sword landed upon him, lingering there motionless for a moment. Then, it continued on past him before lighting on another trainee a few places further down.

"You," Farruk yelled. "Step forward!"

Devi leaned his head towards the centre of the circle. He looked in the direction of the unfortunate boy Farruk had chosen, and he saw Vikas stepping forward.

"Now," Farruk began, as Vikas joined him at the centre of the crowd. "Our ready position will remain the same. Our shield arm will be held forward, and our sword arm will remain back."

Farruk positioned his body accordingly.

"But instead of holding a shield, our arm will act as a counterbalance, allowing us to shift and move with ease. We have nothing to block oncoming attacks, so instead we must avoid them."

Farruk thrust the tip of his sword in Vikas's direction. "Attack me," he said.

Vikas tossed a weak and lazy blow towards Farruk, and Farruk retaliated by knocking his blade to the dirt. Then, Farruk brought his own blade painfully against Vikas's knee, sending a bone-splitting crack around the yard. Vikas's teeth sank into his lip as he struggled to suppress the pain, but he barely allowed himself to wince.

"Fetch your blade, boy," Farruk barked.

Vikas darted down to his left where his blade had fallen and scooped it up from the dirt.

"Stand tall," Farruk barked again, delivering a second blow to Vikas's elbow. "And never allow your blade to touch the ground!"

Vikas sheepishly straightened his body, lifting his sword until its blade pointed rigidly towards the sky. Devi was relieved the tip of Farruk's blade had lingered on him only for a second, and it wasn't him at the centre of the circle.

"Now swing at me," Farruk yelled. "Like you mean it."

Vikas picked up his sword and swung it viciously at Farruk.

"Better," Farruk said, smiling as he effortlessly avoided the blow.

Vikas continued to swing, and Farruk continued to evade, his huge upper body moving in tandem with his feet, his arms always remaining outstretched.

"Your feet remain apart," he said. "Never side by side. If I step back, my body turns. If I step forward, my body turns again."

Farruk allowed Vikas to swing his sword twice more before he brought the demonstration to an end.

"Pair up," he said. "And let me get a look at you."

All around Devi, the other trainees scattered themselves around the yard in pairs, positioning themselves across from each other ready to attack and defend. Devi looked around in search of another trainee who stood alone in need of a partner, but he could see none. Then, he saw Orlain across the yard, one arm around the shoulder of one of his other bunkmates and the other outstretched in his direction. The smile on Orlain's face was menacing, and his eyes flashed with excitement. Then, the boy next to Orlain began to stride across the yard towards Devi.

The boy was the tallest of Devi's bunkmates, and he cut an imposing figure. His body was wide, and his hands, though not close to the size of Farruk's, also seemed to consume the handle of his sword.

"Looking for a partner?" the boy grunted as he approached, a gormless smile plastered across his face.

Devi swallowed hard. If he was ever going to venture into The Sands to seek the Fire Stone, he would face enemies far more fearsome than the boy that stood before him. Only, the boy that stood before him barely seemed to be a boy at all. Compared to Devi, he was already a man.

"I suppose I am," Devi sighed.

"After you."

The boy opened up his body and bent slightly at the knees to mimic Farruk's demonstration. Devi raised his sword gingerly and began to circle the boy. The blade felt cumbersome, and his empty hand felt limp and useless hanging loosely at his side. It ached, almost as if it longed to feel the thick handle of a scythe in its grip.

The boy turned as Devi turned, shifting his body so his feet always remained apart, one hand outstretched towards Devi, the other holding his sword aloft at his shoulder. Devi swung his wooden blade awkwardly towards the midriff of the boy, but it failed to find its home. The boy quickly weaved away from the blow, shifting his stance so his empty hand was now behind him, and his sword was pointed towards Devi.

Devi lunged in again, swinging towards the boy's thigh this time. Again, however, the boy was able to dodge the blow, sending a counterstrike in Devi's direction, almost knocking his sword from his grip.

Devi was surprised by the boy's dexterity. His body was large and heavy, but he moved with relative ease, carrying his substantial weight forwards and backwards seemingly without effort. By the time the boy was ready to take his turn to attack, Devi had failed to land a single blow with his sword.

"Now me," the boy said, rising from his defensive posture and allowing Devi to find the position for himself.

The boy turned away from Devi and, when Devi followed his eyes across the yard, he saw Orlain staring back in their direction.

"Let's go," Devi said.

The boy's head snapped back around. He swung a ferocious blow at Devi's shoulder, and Devi was almost caught off-guard. He pivoted on his back foot, leaning his upper body away from the oncoming blade, which narrowly avoided contact. He was barely able to regain his balance before the second blow was on its way, this time coming straight down towards his head. Devi shifted to his left and then ducked away to his right, out of range of a third strike. The gormless grin had returned to the boy's face, and he pressed forward to narrow the gap between himself and Devi.

The boy swung his sword one way and then the other, and Devi did his best to avoid each blow. Though he had moved well against Devi's attacks, the boy's heavy upper body made his own attacks slow and easy to predict. He was relentless, however, and he seemed to have the advantage of prior training. He swung a vicious blow towards Devi's head, and Devi stumbled backwards, his feet crossing in their attempt to shift his body out of harm's way. Devi came crashing to the ground, and immediately the boy was upon him. Devi rolled to his left to avoid the first blow, and then rolled to his right to avoid the next. When the boy raised his sword to deliver a third strike, Devi scrambled to his feet, and the boy's wooden blade found the dirt.

As Devi rose, he circled away from the boy so that he faced the Keep and his back was to the sea. There, in the window that hung just above the training yard, Devi saw a girl seated on the ledge inside, one leg pulled up to her chest under her chin, her crimson hair flowing over her shoulders. It was the same girl he had seen on the balcony beside King Vagan the previous day, her brilliant blue eyes utterly unmistakable. The girl seemed to see Devi too, and she smiled down at him from the window ledge. Before Devi was able to smile back, however, he felt his head crack and his ears explode, and the whole world seemed to turn sideways.

When Devi opened his eyes again, he saw a handful of other trainees circled around him, their faces all blurred and hazy but each seeming to wear a smile.

Then, the sun disappeared behind a great shadow, and Farruk's shapeless face veered into view.

~

The rest of the afternoon passed in a blur. It wasn't until he walked into the mess again in the evening that Devi felt as if he had his wits about him. Even so, his head throbbed, and his cheek was already tender where the wooden blade had struck him. As Devi lined up for his tray, he ran his finger down his nose, grateful it was still straight and in one piece.

Devi took his tray. The rich aroma of meat filled his nostrils, and he immediately felt a little more alive. He crossed the mess and thrust his leg of meat into his mouth before his tray had even come to rest on the empty table, scanning the sea of faces around him as he ate.

Across the hall, he saw Vikas sat at the same table where he had seen him sitting that morning, surrounded by the same group of trainees. This time, Vikas noticed Devi too. He did not rise from the table to join Devi, however. Instead, he simply nodded his head. Devi nodded back, and he tossed the bone that he had already picked clean down onto his tray. Then, as he took up his slab of stale bread and stuffed it into his mouth, he heard the unmistakable grating of Orlain's voice.

"I wonder if you left a mark," he said. "Why don't we see for ourselves."

When Devi looked up, he saw Orlain approaching his table, his four other bunkmates following close behind like hungry house cats.

"Ouch," Orlain said, wincing as if the bruised knot ran across his own brow rather than Devi's. "Looks sore."

"I'm fine," Devi muttered, tearing at his bread.

"For now," Orlain snarled. "But not for long. You don't belong here, farmer. I know it, you know it, and Farruk knows it. In Vagan's name, the whole Keep knows it."

Devi continued to chew as Orlain inched even closer to his table, the flame torch on the wall behind him casting a shadow across his body.

"You won't last long here. Trust me. Your days are numbered."

Orlain stepped away from Devi's table, but Devi could feel his eyes still fixed upon his face until he finally snapped his head around to search for a table of his own, each of Devi's other bunkmates also glaring at him as they filed past.

When he was alone once more, Devi cast his mind back over the portion of the day that was still clear to him. Standing in the circle around Farruk, he had been dwarfed by the other trainees. They were all larger and stronger than him, and they could all likely best him in hand to hand combat. Devi was sure he was quicker than the others, but even his bunkmate had moved with surprising agility given his size, and he had not hesitated to punish Devi when he had let his guard down for a second. If he was going to survive his training, Devi couldn't afford to make mistakes. He needed to be sharp, and he needed to be ready.

By the time Devi's meat and bread were gone, and his soup bowl was half-empty, the mess had already begun to clear. He did not eat more quickly, however. Instead, he slowed down. He laboured over his soup until he was the only one left at the tables. Even the serving hatches were empty. As he slurped the last remnants of the thin, tasteless concoction down, Devi rose from his table, returned his tray, and made his way through the heavy double doors and into the Great Hall. Rather than turning towards his barracks, however, he turned towards the training yard.

The sun had already set by the time Devi emerged out of the back of the Keep once more. Beyond the edge of the cliffs, he could hear the Tharakun Sea lashing at the rocks, but the night was otherwise silent. He made his way to the pile of swords that had been scattered at the centre of the yard, and he took one up.

Devi held the weapon in his hand, trying to accommodate its additional weight as he held his arm aloft. He swung the sword forwards and then backwards, turning to his left and to his right as he lashed out with its blade. Then, he dropped into the ready position that Farruk had demonstrated earlier that morning.

He bent slightly at the knees, held his sword arm aloft at his shoulder, and stretched his empty hand out in front of him to balance the weight. He imagined Sand Dwellers coming at him, one at a time, from all angles, and he spun away from the shadows, twisting his hips one way and then the other under the light of the full moon, swinging his sword out in retaliatory blows.

But then, just as quickly as he had begun, he stopped. There, across the yard, beyond the wooden structures of the obstacle course, stood the vast wooden board that had been empty that morning. It was no longer empty, however. Instead, it was filled with names organised into rows and columns, each with a large, painted number next to it. In the top left corner of the board, Devi saw Vikas's name hanging from two small, metal hooks next to the number one. Just below it hung Orlain's name next to the number two.

Devi searched the board for his own name, scanning the remainder of the first column and working his way across to the next, and then the next. For a moment, Devi thought his name had been excluded from the list. But, as he reached the final number at the very bottom right corner of the wooden board, he saw it scrawled there in thick, white letters.

IX

The sun beat down on the dry, cracked dustbowl of the marketplace, and though Devi was loitering in the shade of the low wall that ran around its perimeter, he could still feel the heat. He stood some distance from the main road that ran through the centre of the market, but the stalls at the periphery were bustling nonetheless, a dense crowd filtering through the shade afforded by the thin cloth strung over and between their roofs. Little eddies of wind carried a light dusting of sand across the ground so that it whirled around the feet of the passers-by as they moved from one stall to the next, some carrying burlap sacks slung over their shoulders, others carrying heavy wicker baskets in their trembling arms.

Farruk had woken Devi, along with the other trainees, in the same way he had woken them the previous day – by pounding his heavy fist against their wooden doors and bellowing in his thunderous voice for them to rise. Once Devi had forced down his meal in the mess and headed out to the training yard, however, Farruk's instructions had been far different than they had been the morning before.

"Not only are the Sand Dwellers fearsome in combat," he had said, the trainees gathering around him at the centre of the yard once more. "They are also masters of stealth. Their bodies are like vapour, and they are able to vanish into the sand of the dunes in an instant, leaving behind no trace of their former presence. If you are to survive in The Sands, you must be able to match them."

Devi was quick and agile. He was light on his feet, and he was small enough that his presence was often unobtrusive. He was all flesh and bone, however, and he knew that he and the other trainees had no hope of training their bodies to evaporate on command.

"You are to head down into Narkasee's market," Farruk had continued. "The vigilant eyes of the stall keepers will be everywhere, but you must evade them. Return to the Keep by sundown with one item stolen from the market, and your training will continue. Fail to return by sundown, and you may never return. Return before sundown *without* a stolen item, and you will wish you had never returned at all."

A hum of murmurs began to rise amongst the crowd of trainees, but Farruk's booming voice snuffed it out almost immediately.

"One more thing," he had bellowed. "If you are caught, you will no longer be of any use to me. There is no room in the ranks for a one-handed Stone Seeker."

Farruk's departing comments had sent a shiver up Devi's spine, and he heard the words echoing around his mind once more as he continued to survey the stalls that were sprawled out before him.

To Devi's left, one stall keeper seemed particularly reluctant to keep a watchful eye over his wares, but this was primarily because they were being snapped up so quickly, and coins were being thrust into his hands at such a rate, that he was unable to devote too much of his attention to anything other than cramming the coins into the leather pouch at his waist.

To his right, the stalls were quieter, but this only meant their keepers were perched on the very edges of their counters, reaching out hungrily towards the men and women in the streets as they passed. Devi had been in the market for some time already, but as yet, he had failed to find a stall he felt comfortable targeting.

Amongst the crowd directly ahead of him, Devi caught a flash of Orlain's thick, blonde hair, but for once, his other bunkmates were nowhere to be seen. Instead, Orlain moved alone amidst the throng, clinging tightly to one group of people before seamlessly letting them go and latching onto another. He scanned the stalls, twisting his head from left to right as he walked, apparently still as empty-handed as Devi.

Devi stepped out of the shade beneath the wall he was leaning against. He began to move in the direction of the market stalls, each of which seemed to be stalked by the somewhat familiar face of a fellow trainee. Across the street, standing at the counter of a near-empty stall, Devi saw Vikas. Before him, laid out across the counter, were several silver trinkets formed in various shapes and sizes. From a distance, they seemed to serve no purpose, having been crafted merely for decorative purposes. They looked as if they might hang from a cape or a tunic and, upon closer inspection, each seemed to be modelled in the shape of an animal.

Devi watched as Vikas reached a hand towards the trinkets, the woman to his left dropping a few coins into the palm of the momentarily distracted stall keeper. Vikas did not lift just one trinket from the counter, however. Instead, he gripped one in the palm of his hand, whilst lifting another up more delicately between his thumb and his forefinger. Then, he tucked his remaining fingers around the second object and lifted the first up to inspect it in the light of the sun. Almost invisibly, Vikas dropped the second trinket into the palm of his other hand, concealed as it was by his torso.

Then, he returned the first object to the counter in front of the stall keeper, shaking his head and muttering a few words as he turned away to become lost amongst the crowd once more.

Vikas had carried out Farruk's instructions precisely.

"Choose your item wisely. Then, get in and get out. You are to remain concealed, undetected. The successful trainee is the humble trainee."

The item Vikas had stolen was small and inconspicuous. So much so that he had been able to conceal it within the palm of one hand. By the time the stall keeper noticed it was missing, Vikas would be laying in his hammock, safe within the impenetrable walls of the Keep.

Vikas's name was at the top of the rankings on the board in the training yard, however. His impressive start had given him the luxury of being conservative. But Devi had no such privilege – his name was at the very bottom of the list. Though he had survived the obstacle course without too much difficulty, he had been the only trainee to have been downed during combat, and he could still remember the look of pity on Farruk's face as he had hauled him up from the dirt. To make it back to the Keep in one piece would be a victory in itself, but it would barely lift him from his place at the bottom of the rankings. Whereas, to make it back to the Keep with something impressive to show for it could give him the breathing space he needed to survive another day.

Devi cast his eyes around the marketplace once more. The farmers were busy unloading their harvests from the back of their wooden carts, but Devi knew the toil it took to do so. The pirates were also busy hauling their treasures from their chests, plucking only the finest of the loot for their own collections, but Devi knew it wouldn't simply be his hand they would take if he was caught. And the jewellers stood with their eyes fixed to their rings and necklaces, some of which Devi was certain were cursed, but he was far from certain which.

For a moment, Devi's mind flashed back to the stall his father had dragged him away from the last time they were together in Narkasee. He remembered the sheer weight of the jewel-encrusted sword he had hauled from its counter and the way its blade caught the light, as if it was reluctant to return it to the sun.

Devi's pulse raced with excitement as he imagined walking out to the training yard the following morning, sword in hand, its blade resting against his shoulder as he strode towards the centre and pointed it in the direction of Orlain. But he could barely lift the thing. There was no way he could carry it out of the marketplace without being seen. Then, his stomach rumbled, unsatisfied as it was by his morning meal, and he knew exactly where to go.

Devi was sure he could smell the bread from streets away, and when he turned the final corner and saw it laying on the countertop in all its glory, he would have sworn he could taste it. When he had last visited the stall, the loaf had already been cut in two, several thick slices having been handed out to the Stone Seekers. As he gazed towards the market stall now, the loaf was still full and untouched. Though its thick crust hid the bounty inside, Devi knew it would be packed with nuts and dried fruits that would send his mouth watering.

Moments ago, he was imagining walking out into the training yard with the ornate sword resting against his shoulder. Now, he could only picture dropping the heavy loaf of bread onto the table in front of Vikas, Warwick, and Tsurzan, tearing off a handful for himself before allowing the other trainees to each take their fill.

Devi approached the stall and the same tall, narrow man that had greeted him the last time he had visited, still shrouded as he had been then in light, flowing robes of maroon. The man's eagle eyes danced over Devi as he stepped forward, his inquisitive gaze seeming vaguely to recognise Devi's face amongst the countless it would have encountered. As he explored Devi's beige tunic and britches, however, his half-smile fell from his face.

"A Stone Seeker?" the man asked, one arm outstretched towards Devi, his fingers long and wiry, beckoning Devi closer to his counter.

"A trainee," Devi corrected.

"Ah, of course."

The man's hand retreated into the waterfall of his robes.

"The Seekers come to me often," he said.

Devi thought for a moment that he could detect a thin layer of resentment beneath his warm, inviting tone.

"My name is Varash. Perhaps we will get to know each other well."

"Perhaps," Devi said.

"And what can I do for you today?"

Devi was unsure how to proceed. Vikas had made it look so easy, slipping the silver trinket into his palm right under the nose of the stall keeper. Yet, he hadn't even decided how he would conceal the loaf, which Varash would undoubtedly immediately notice was missing, much less how he would make it out of the marketplace.

Devi looked back towards the wall that he had left. It was just low enough to clamber over, and his path away from the stall and back in its direction was, for the moment, completely clear.

"I'll take a cutlet of yak," he said, nodding in the direction of the grisly curtains of meat that hung at the back of the stall.

"Very good," Varash said.

As Varash turned to the back of the stall, Devi froze. Time was already against him, but he could barely bring himself to take the loaf in his hands and turn away without leaving at least a coin or two behind, though the loaf would be worth much more. Just as Devi managed to force himself to lean towards the counter, his hands almost clasping the thick, dense loaf, he heard a voice call out above the throng of the crowd a short distance off.

"Stop! Thief!"

Devi turned to see Orlain across the aisle of stalls, a finger pointed in his direction. The bread remained on the counter, but already there were a number of people staring in Devi's direction and, acting on instinct alone, he took off running.

Devi burst towards the wall that ran around the edge of the market, but one of the stall keepers close by stepped out across his path. Devi darted away to his left, and he heard the pounding of footsteps close at his back.

"Stop him!" a second voice yelled, distinct from Orlain's, and Devi was sure Varash had abandoned his stall in pursuit of him.

Devi cut between two stalls as their confused keepers stepped back to avoid him. He bounced between the shoulders of men and women making their way down the next street over, but he managed to remain on his feet as he darted to his right, doing his best to vary his direction in the hope of losing whoever was still on his trail.

"Someone stop him," Varash yelled again, and the keeper of another stall stepped out from behind his counter and snatched at Devi's tunic as he passed.

Devi felt the tunic tear, his shoulder now exposed. He continued on, but the collision had slowed him enough that one of the men who followed him, now amongst a small crowd, was able to reach out a foot and catch Devi's own. Devi took several long, stumbling steps forward, and finally he felt a great force against his chest. He slumped into a heap on the ground and, when he rolled over and looked up, he saw several angry faces scowling back at him.

"Make way! The boy is mine."

Devi scurried back on his elbows as Varash stepped into the centre of the circle that had surrounded Devi, but Varash reached down and grabbed a handful of his tunic.

"In Vagan's name," he said. "When will the King realise his Seekers are nothing but a band of roving troublemakers?"

Varash shook Devi fiercely.

"What do you have, boy?" he snarled. "Give it up."

"I don't have anything," Devi said.

Just then, at Varash's shoulder, Devi saw Orlain step forward into the circle.

"He was about to steal the bread," Orlain said, his face the picture of innocence. "I saw him looking at it with my own eyes."

"But I didn't steal it," Devi insisted. "You can search me. I have nothing."

Varash lifted Devi from the ground with one hand, still clutching a fistful of his tunic. Then, he wheeled around to glare at Orlain.

"You mean to say we chased this boy down merely for the crime of *looking* at my bread?"

Varash turned his attention back to Devi, and he lifted Devi's tunic up around his head, revealing the waistband of his britches. He dropped the tunic, and patted at Devi's legs, searching for some item that had been concealed within them.

"The boy has nothing," Varash said, looking Devi intently in the eyes. "He has stolen nothing, but I do wonder how he was planning to pay for his cutlet."

Devi shrank sheepishly into his shoulders, but the cutlet, just like the loaf of bread, was still back on Varash's stall.

"The boy is no thief," Varash said, and the crowd around him immediately began to dissipate, some murmuring their disappointment that Devi still possessed both his hands.

Just as Devi's knees had begun to cease trembling, however, he heard another voice.

"This boy is no thief," the voice called, and Devi turned to see Vikas stepping into the circle beside him. "But can we say the same of this boy?"

Vikas gestured towards Orlain, who scoffed derisively back at him.

"I am no thief," Orlain said.

"You lie. I saw you with my own eyes."

Orlain sneered as Vikas repeated his own words back to him.

"If you are no thief, then consent to a search."

Orlain cast his gaze around the circle. He was surrounded by expectant faces, some keepers of their own stalls, others merely excitable citizens. Then, he scoffed again.

"Fine," Orlain said, thrusting his hands into the pockets of his britches and turning them out. "I have nothing to hide."

As Orlain removed his hands from his pockets, a shiny, silver trinket in the shape of a bird fell to the ground, and a hush fell over the small crowd.

"That's…" Orlain began. "I don't know how…"

Orlain tried his very best to protest his innocence, but his confusion dumbfounded him and twisted his tongue in a knot.

"I knew I put that piece out this morning," a man in the crowd said. "You little –"

As the man stepped towards Orlain, Devi recognised him as the owner of the stall Vikas had stolen from earlier that morning. Devi felt Vikas's hands on his shoulders pulling him from the crowd as it closed in around Orlain, and he heard Orlain's stuttering protests continuing to falter as he and Vikas turned to flee.

~

Devi's lips were dripping with moist, succulent meat as he sat across from Vikas and Warwick, whilst Tsurzan was at his side, chewing noisily away on his chunk of stale bread. All around them, the mess was abuzz with the chatter of the trainees that had made it back to the Keep safely, some of whom were boisterous enough that they drew irritated glares from the Vanguard close by and were on the verge of drawing something more sinister like the back of their hands.

At the centre of Devi's table sat the string of pearls that Tsurzan had dared to take from under the noses of the pirates, and Warwick swapped his boneless leg of meat for the catapult he had managed to wile away from some unsuspecting weaponsmith.

"What do you think?" Warwick said, swallowing his last mouthful of meat and pulling back the empty rubber of the catapult. "How many Sand Dwellers could I put down with this?"

He released his grip of the rubber, letting it fly in Vikas's direction.

"Not many," Vikas laughed. "What are you going to fill it with? Sand?"

Just then, the great, wooden doors on the other side of the mess burst open, and Devi turned to see Orlain bearing down on his table. He strode across the room with fury in his face and ire in his bloodshot eyes.

"You set me up," Orlain spat, glaring at Vikas, his face glowing red and his brow unimaginably furrowed.

"I don't know what you're talking about," Vikas replied calmy.

"You stole that trinket, and you planted it on me."

Vikas smiled.

"I did no such thing."

Vikas lifted his bowl to his mouth and slurped down some of the thin, soupy gruel from inside. Orlain lashed out, the palm of one hand meeting the side of Vikas's bowl, sending it clattering to the stone floor. The chatter that buzzed around the hall had quietened the second Orlain entered, but the room was close to silent now.

"I almost lost my hand," Orlain snarled. "You have no idea how much you owe my father."

When Orlain had struck Vikas's bowl, Devi had seen Vikas's hands fall to the table and curl up into fists.

Now, however, they began to relax once more, and Vikas's face began to twist into a satisfied smirk.

"What does your father have to do with this?" he asked.

Orlain bit his tongue, but he knew he had already said too much.

"Did you..."

Vikas paused for a moment, ensuring the attention of the trainees in his vicinity was fixed upon him.

"Did you have your father pay off the stall keepers?"

Vikas's grin was irrepressible now, and Orlain was almost steaming. Orlain breathed heavily, his eyes narrow and his forehead dripping with sweat.

"Are you planning to take him with you to The Sands?" Vikas asked. "To have him drop a coin in a Sand Dweller's hand every time your life needs sparing."

The trainees on the adjacent tables began to laugh.

"I'm warning you," Orlain seethed.

Vikas lowered his voice.

"And I'm warning you," he said. "Stone Seekers don't take handouts from anyone. Leave the boy alone, or Farruk might just hear what happened today."

Vikas made no move to gesture towards Devi, but Orlain knew exactly who he was referring to. Devi shifted awkwardly in his seat, relieved that he might finally be granted some reprieve, mildly anxious that this might only deepen Orlain's dislike of him, and unspeakably frustrated that it had been Vikas that might finally have forced Orlain to back off, rather than himself.

"You better watch yourself," Orlain said. "You might be Farruk's golden boy for now, but you'll slip up soon. And when you do, it'll be my face you see staring down at you."

Vikas held Orlain's gaze unblinkingly. Then, Orlain turned to face Devi.

"And I'm not finished with you either," he spat.

Orlain turned on his heels and strode out of the mess. The quiet lingered for a moment longer, but the buzz of conversation quickly started up once more.

"Come back," Vikas called in the direction of the wooden doors that Orlain had just passed through, his voice muted so that it barely travelled beyond the table. "We have something for you."

Vikas and Devi reached under the table, and they each pulled out one half of Varash's dense, heavy fruit and nut bread. They dropped their halves on the table, the tough crust thudding against the wood and shaking their trays. Devi couldn't help but laugh as he grabbed a handful of the bread and stuffed it into his mouth, passing it to his left, where Warwick's eager hands were waiting to receive it. Soon, half the trainees in the mess were gathered around the table, their clawing hands clutching at the hearty loaf, their tongues raining sweet utterances of gratitude down upon Devi and Vikas, who could barely stop smiling for long enough to chew.

X

The next morning, Devi's stomach purred rather than roared. He had gorged on Varash's fruit and nut loaf with Vikas, Warwick, and Tsurzan the previous evening, and his morning meal had been easier than usual to force down. As he stepped out of the back of King Vagan's Keep and into the training yard, Devi felt full for what he thought might have been the first time in his life.

As it had the previous morning, the sun hung low in the sky, sending its light sprawling across the vastness of the Tharakun Sea. Back home in Rakhas, Devi had always been overawed by the immensity of the water. From high up on the Salt Cliffs, it looked as if the Tharakun was endless. The tiny ships that skated across the water, perfectly still and smooth, looked nothing more than grains of sand carried across the desert on the wind. They looked as if, at any moment, they might be whisked up into the air and thrown across the other side of the world, where the water would be just as still and just as sprawling.

Devi looked towards the back of the cliffs, where the great wooden board stood, painted names hanging from its small metal hooks. The great crowd outside the Keep had been whittled down almost immediately, and now it seemed only half of the surviving group of trainees remained, several of the metal hooks now empty. Devi wondered how many of those missing had failed to make it back to the Keep in time and how many had simply bowed out. He shuddered as he thought how many had been caught and had one of their hands taken from them.

For a brief moment, Devi was relieved – fewer trainees meant less competition. Whilst he had made it back to the Keep with Varash's stolen bread, however, it had been Vikas that had used the distraction to obtain it, and though Farruk would never know he hadn't stolen it himself, Devi's name still lurked precariously close to the bottom of the board. Fewer trainees did mean less competition, but it also meant that weak links would be easier to find.

Between Devi and the rankings board, the wooden swords the trainees had used two mornings prior were still where they had left them, piled in the centre of the training yard ready to collect once more. Devi was eager to train. He could count the number of times he had held a sword on one hand, and he was certain he was one of the least experienced trainees left when it came to combat. If he was ever going to seek the Aether Stones, he would have to become adept with a sword, no matter how long it took. If he had to train for the rest of his life, he would do so, but he would be grateful if his progress came a little more quickly.

"Gather around!"

Farruk's booming voice filled the yard as he strode out of the Keep. Devi still hadn't quite managed to come to terms with the way his body shook when Farruk spoke. Whispers amongst the trainees were that Farruk had been to The Sands, and if he had, he had clearly made it back to tell the tale. Devi wondered whether Farruk had ever needed to unsheathe his sword, or whether his voice alone had been enough to send the Sand Dwellers crawling back into their caves or disappearing into the dunes.

"Make it quick," Farruk yelled. "The sun won't wait for us."

The trainees frantically began to form a circle around Farruk, and he stood at the centre of it like the great eye of a storm. Devi quickly found a place at the edge of the circle, and he saw a handful of other trainees hurrying behind him to fill in the gaps elsewhere.

"Today," Farruk said. "We spar. The Sands will eat you alive if they wish, but the Sand Dwellers are at least mortal. If you train hard, you'll be as much a threat to them as they are to you."

Farruk picked up a wooden sword from the pile at his feet.

"Remember," he said, dropping into his ready position. "Your shield arm is out in front but only as a counterbalance. Your sword arm is back ready to strike should the opportunity arise. Your primary goal is evasion. Retaliation is secondary."

Silence lingered over the yard for a moment.

"Well come on then," Farruk yelled. "Pair up. Let's see you."

Almost instantly, each of the trainees descended on the pile of swords like ants on the discarded stone of a peach. As they had the previous morning, the trainees quickly formed into pairs and dispersed amongst the training yard, whilst Devi stood, content to allow the crush of bodies to subside before collecting a blade of his own.

He looked across the yard and saw Orlain already in the throes of battle with a boy he did not recognise, but striding towards him was another of his bunkmates. The boy held a sword in each hand, which hung loosely at his sides.

"Looks like it's you and me," the boy said.

Devi groaned. He was in no doubt the boy had been sent by Orlain, just as his partner had the last time they had trained combat. He had little choice but to accept his challenge, however, and it wasn't clear any of the other remaining trainees would present any easier opposition.

"Let me just grab a –"

Devi stepped towards Farruk and the pile of swords.

"Here, take this one," his bunkmate said, grinning and nodding towards the sword he now held outstretched towards him.

Devi briefly looked over the blade.

"Thank you," he said. "But I'll take one for myself."

Devi wasn't sure what the boy had to gain by offering him the sword, but he had no reason to believe the extension of kindness was genuine, and he was certain that any gain would occur at his expense. As Devi stepped forward to collect a sword of his own, however, Farruk sent him spinning back in the opposite direction.

"Where are you going, boy?" he said. "You have a partner. Turn around and fight him. There's no room for malingerers amongst the Seekers."

Devi gazed up into Farruk's enormous, brown eyes.

"I just need a…"

"He has a sword for you," Farruk boomed. "Accept his challenge or leave my yard."

Seeing no other option, Devi turned and took the outstretched sword by the blade. As he followed his bunkmate to an empty space across the yard, he inspected the weapon. Its handle felt solid, it seemed just as long as the one he had held previously, and he thought its weight felt similar too. He swung the sword forwards and then backwards, and it made a satisfying whip as it sliced through the air. Surprisingly, to Devi, the blade seemed fine.

"What are you waiting for?" Devi's bunkmate asked.

Devi swung his sword through the air a final time, and then he dropped into the ready position and examined his opponent. Like most of the other trainees, the boy was taller than Devi, but he looked heavy and slow. Devi hoped he could at least evade the attacks of his bunkmate for a while and tire him out. Then, when it came time for him to attack, he might be able to land a blow or two of his own.

"Nothing," Devi said finally. "I'm ready."

Devi circled away from his opponent, his legs wide and his body poised to spin to its left or to its right as necessary. His bunkmate circled too, closing the distance between himself and Devi with several short shuffles of his feet. He swung his sword, and Devi spun away easily.

The boy was roughly the same height as Devi's previous opponent, but he was even wider, and his body appeared far less muscular and defined than many of the other trainees. He swung again, but his attacks were slow, and Devi was able to twist away once more so that his empty hand stretched out behind him, and his sword was pointed in the boy's direction.

When the boy took another hacking swing with his own sword, Devi raised his blade to block the blow. A splitting crack punctuated the air, and Devi's sword fell apart in his hand, the top half of his blade falling to the dirt, the bottom half still attached to the handle in his hand.

Devi glared at the boy, his brow furrowed and his cheeks burning with anger. It was clear his sword had been tampered with, but despite Devi being all but defenceless, the boy did not relent in his attack.

He raised his sword above his head, poised to bring it violently down upon Devi. With little left to protect himself, and unprepared as he was to evade the attack, Devi simply closed his eyes, covered his head with his arms, and braced for impact. The impact did not come, however. Instead, the sound of wood against wood exploded around the yard again.

When Devi opened his eyes, he saw Vikas standing next to him, his own sword just inches from his face, trembling as it struggled against the blade of Devi's attacker.

Vikas whipped his sword arm around and thrust his left shoulder into the right shoulder of Devi's bunkmate, sending him stumbling back. Several pairs of trainees in the immediate vicinity stopped their sparring and watched on.

"You're going to strike a defenceless opponent?" Vikas barked at the boy, scowling.

The boy regained his balance and took a single step back in Vikas's direction.

"He had clearly yielded," Vikas said.

By now, it wasn't just a small circle of trainees that had turned to watch, but the entire yard looked on.

"There's no yielding in The Sands," Devi's bunkmate replied.

"We're sparring," Vikas shouted. "We're not in The Sands!"

"We will be soon," the boy said. "At least, some of us will be."

Vikas stared back at Devi's bunkmate, but the boy squarely held his gaze. Then, like a crack of thunder after a long, humid summer, Farruk's voice broke the silence.

"Why have your swords fallen still?" he boomed. "Why do you stand idle?"

The small circle that had formed quickly dissipated, and the trainees across the yard whose attention had been drawn turned their heads away once more.

"A Seeker should never be idle!"

Vikas turned to Devi as the trainees around them frantically resumed their sparring, disappointed they had neither seen the altercation escalate, nor had they seen

Farruk forced to throw someone out of the Keep, dwindling their numbers even further.

"You have to stay ready," Vikas said. "They've clearly got it out for you. Don't give them any opportunity."

Devi wanted to scream at Vikas. He had been there to ward off Orlain's advances when he had first arrived at the Keep, and Devi had been grateful for his interjection. He had thwarted Orlain's plan in the marketplace too, ensuring that Devi made it back to the Keep with something that would abate Farruk. Devi wasn't sure what he would do if he felt Farruk's mammoth hands pulling him from his bed and tossing him from the Keep, but he did know it was up to him, and him alone, to ensure that he never found out.

Devi didn't scream at Vikas, however. Instead, he simply nodded his assent, reaching to the ground to inspect the shattered remnants of his wooden blade.

"Come on," Vikas said. "Let's get you another sword. I'll spar with you."

Devi tossed his broken sword aside and made his way back over to the pile at the centre of the yard. He grabbed another sword, bending the blade across his leg to test its rigidity more vigorously. Then, when he began to make his way back towards Vikas, Devi looked up in the direction of the windows at the back of the Keep. Just as he had two days prior, he saw the red-haired girl staring back down at him once more. The yard was a hive of activity, pairs of trainees sparring with each other whilst Farruk yelled instructions. Yet, the girl's gaze was fixed squarely on Devi.

"Who's that?" Devi asked, nodding towards the window as he rejoined Vikas.

Vikas looked up towards the window.

"You don't know?"

Devi shook his head.

"That's Reya," Vikas said. "King Vagan's daughter."

Devi felt foolish. The pale skin, the crimson hair, the brilliant blue eyes. Of course she was Vagan's daughter. Like Vagan, all of Katai knew of Princess Reya, but Devi had never seen her for himself. Unlike Vagan, however, she looked just as Devi had imagined she would, only infinitely more captivating.

"Apparently she never leaves the Keep," Vikas continued. "Vagan keeps her locked up all day."

"Why?" Devi asked.

"Who knows? She's Vagan's only child, so maybe he is getting paranoid after all."

Devi continued to gaze up at the girl in the window. Then, he watched as she dropped from her seat on the ledge and disappeared from sight.

"Come on," Vikas said, adopting the ready position. "Let's spar."

With Vikas as a partner, Devi could feel his sword growing lighter and easier to control with each swing.

Vikas was a talented swordsman, and he put Devi through his paces. More than that, he was an effective teacher, pushing Devi far enough to test his limits, but not too far to overwhelm him.

"Have you fought before?" Vikas asked, wiping the sweat from his brow as he leaned back to dodge one of Devi's attacks.

The night of the Darmeenian raid immediately flashed across Devi's mind. He saw his father's body laying headless in the dirt, and he saw Jerod with his stomach sliced open, his vacant eyes still staring skyward.

"No," Devi said, swinging his sword fiercely towards Vikas's head, but its blade slicing only through air. "There's not much need for fighters on the farms."

"I've heard about the raids. The Darmeenians haven't come for you?"

"No," Devi said, his next attack lacking the same ferocity as the previous. "Not yet anyway."

"Who have you left back home?"

Once more, Devi found himself stumbling over his answer.

"Just my father. He doesn't know I'm here."

"Why not?"

Devi's attacks had slowed so significantly that Vikas took it upon himself to become the attacker, and Devi dropped into his ready position to defend.

"He wouldn't approve," Devi said.

"Wouldn't approve of his son becoming a Stone Seeker?" Vikas asked, incredulous. "That's every father's dream."

"Not mine."

"What *did* he want for you?"

"He wanted me to spend my life in the fields. Like he did. And his father before him, and his father before him."

"They were from the Hinterlands?"

Darmeen had its own farming tradition before Katai broke away, but Devi's dark skin and his father's passion for the fields gave him away. He nodded his head.

"You?"

"My father was in the Vanguard," Vikas said. "If I don't make it as a Seeker, that's probably where I'll end up."

Devi parried the blade of Vikas's sword with his own, and he attempted to spin away to his left. Before he was able to do so, Vikas turned his blade instantly back on Devi, raising it over his head and swinging it with force towards Devi's throat. Devi closed his eyes and winced, preparing himself for a felling blow for the second time that morning, but the blade came to a halt an inch from his neck, perfectly still and steady in Vikas's sure hands.

"If you don't make it as a Seeker," Devi said, opening his eyes. "There's no hope for any of us."

~

Devi ate quickly that evening. His stomach had been treated to a rich and nourishing meal the previous night, but his day out in the yard had been long and tiring. Though Vikas had worked him hard, Devi finally felt as if he was beginning to become accustomed to the sword. It didn't feel nearly as safe and sure in his hands as his scythe, but at the very least, it no longer felt insurmountably cumbersome. He knew, however, that if he was ever going to come close to matching Vikas, or Orlain and the other trainees for that matter, he still had a long way to go. So, he slurped down his gruel, gnawed his meat to the bone, dispatched with his chunk of stale bread, and headed to the back of the Keep.

Outside, Devi passed the broken sword he had tossed aside earlier that morning. It still laid in two pieces in the dirt where he had left it. He made his way to the centre of the yard, took up another blade, and stood alone in the darkness. He paused for a moment, closing his eyes and picturing Farruk in his ready position. He recalled the advice Vikas had given him that morning too, the slight adjustments to his posture and the subtle weight shifts that would allow him to maintain his balance. But as he opened his eyes and brought himself into his own ready position, his gaze was drawn by a figure lurking at the edge of the cliffs.

Even in the half-light of the moon, and in spite of her unusual attire, Devi immediately recognised Reya. He had seen her at the window earlier that day, and he had seen her a number of times since he had arrived at the Keep. Her red hair no longer hung in loose curls at her shoulders but was instead tied into a tight bun, and she no longer wore the ornate, flowing dress she had been wearing on his arrival. Instead, black leather trousers clung tightly to her legs, and a tight-fitting tunic and waistcoat revealed the cut of her body. She no longer looked like a princess. Instead, she looked more like a pirate.

Reya turned her head one way and then the other, as if to ensure she had not been followed. When she finally turned in Devi's direction, her gaze immediately met his own. She did not waver, however. Instead, she stared back at him, her blue eyes catching the light of the moon like pearls. As she had earlier that morning, Reya flashed Devi an enticing smile. Then, she turned back to face the sea and, suddenly and without warning, she leapt from the edge of the cliff.

XI

Down in Black Soul's Bay, the Tharakun somehow looked darker than it had from up high on the Salt Cliffs. Devi wasn't sure whether it was just an illusion, the shallow water glistening with a different hue now that he was level with the low sun, or whether his eyes were simply so heavy with sleep that they distorted the world around him.

Until Farruk had wrenched him from his hammock, Devi had laid wide awake, his body still but his mind impossible to quiet. Every time he closed his eyes, he had seen Reya standing on the edge of the cliff, her red hair stirring a little in the gentle breeze. He had watched again and again as she leapt from the cliff, unable to make sense of her actions. There was nothing below but jagged rocks and an unforgiving sea. The water had been as still as ever, but there was still no way she could have survived the fall. Now, standing at the edge of the water, where the waves swept up onto the flawless sand of the beach, Devi was still struggling to explain what he had seen.

Before him, were six small boats that had been moored by ropes attached to thick, wooden stakes driven into the sand. They slowly rose with the arrival of the waves, and they fell once more as the water retreated away again.

"This morning, you will take to the water," Farruk had said earlier, his voice resounding around the Great Hall where he had gathered the trainees. "A true Seeker must be a talented sailor as well as a fearless warrior. Tame the sea, and she will carry you to glory. Allow her to tame you, and she will take your soul along with your life."

An earthy aroma had drifted through the great, wooden doors that led to the mess as they opened, a couple of the King's Vanguard slipping between them. When he had first arrived in the Keep, the smell of the greasy, days-old meat and tasteless soup alone would have almost been enough to quell Devi's rising hunger. In that moment, his stomach had yearned for it.

"You are to fish for your breakfast," Farruk had said, reeling in the handful of trainees who had allowed their gazes to drift towards the mess. "The Tharakun is rich with sustenance. The Deep Sea and The Sands…"

Farruk paused.

"Less so."

The boats close to the shore were small, and as Devi waded out into the sea, the cold water reaching almost to his knees, he was grateful they were only large enough to hold five boys. He watched as Orlain and his four other bunkmates climbed over the side of one boat, and then as Vikas, Warwick, and Tsurzan were joined by two other boys he recognised from the yard in another.

He looked on as the sail that had been wrapped tightly around the short mast at the centre of Orlain's boat came loose, and then as it was pulled tight against the horizontal wooden poles that hung over each side of the tiny ship. The clanking of metal against wood echoed all around the empty bay, and Orlain's anchor glistened as it emerged from the water and was hauled up onto the deck. The ship's sail bulged in the gentle morning breeze, and it began to force its way through the water against the will of the waves.

Devi clambered out of the water into his own tiny ship, and immediately he felt his knees begin to grow weak. He had never stepped foot on a boat before, and the way it rose and fell with the movement of the tide was enough to send him clawing at its edges. His stomach rolled over itself, but as he looked back towards the shore, he saw the hulking silhouette of Farruk lurking just beyond the water's edge, and it was all he could do to stop himself from retching violently. Four other boys climbed into the ship behind Devi, and they each took a seat on the low bench that ran around each of its sides.

"We should get moving," Devi said, nodding his head in the direction of Farruk.

None of the boys in the boat moved.

"We should assign a captain. How many of you have sailed before?"

Once more, the boys remained silent and still.

Devi thought it likely he would be the only trainee to enlist without any past sailing experience. Now that the group had been whittled down significantly, he was almost certain of it. The four blank faces staring back at him told him he was wrong, however, and the other boats that were halfway out to sea told him he was already running out of time.

"Looks like I'm the captain," Devi said reluctantly.

Devi gripped the edge of the boat and made his way unsteadily towards the mast at its centre, his stomach churning as he moved. He looked up towards the top of the mast, exploring the mass of cloth that had been wrapped tightly around it. He pulled at the edges of the fabric, hoping it would come loose with nothing more than a simple tug, but it wouldn't budge.

"Someone pull the anchor up," Devi said, and he heard one of the other trainees behind him beginning to shuffle towards the back of the boat.

Devi thrust his hand up under the bottom of the sail, his fingers searching for some kind of mechanism that would drop the sail loose, but all he could feel was the smooth wood of the mast. Water splashed and rippled loudly behind him, but he could not yet hear the same clanking of metal he had heard when one of his bunkmates had hauled their anchor onto their ship moments ago.

"In Vagan's name," Devi cursed, swatting at the sails with his open palms.

He looked back in the direction of the shore once more and saw Farruk's shadow still lurking on the beach.

"Hurry up with that anchor," Devi shouted, grabbing a fistful of the sail and turning his attention on the trainee at the back of the ship.

From his seat on the low bench, the boy was looking up at Devi. If he was to stand, however, he would have been peering down his nose.

"Watch your mouth, farmer," the boy said calmly. "If you don't know how to sail, I'm sure you don't know how to swim."

Devi stared back at the boy for a moment, the threat lingering in the air like the thin mist that circled their tiny boat. Then, he turned back to the sail just as one of the other trainees reached towards the base of the mast and pulled a rope from the metal hook it was wrapped around. The sail came fluttering free, and the trainee pulled the rope tight until the cloth was stretched out across the horizontal wooden poles. Finally, Devi heard the clanking of metal against the wooden hull of the boat, and the trainee at the back of the ship dropped the heavy lump onto the deck with a thud. The gentle wind picked up just a little, and their tiny boat began to carry them away from Farruk and towards the horizon.

Though the ship sailed away from the shore directly towards the rising sun in the distance, Devi, still holding tightly to the mast, pulled at the sails until they began to veer away to the left. It was there that the Salt Cliffs jutted awkwardly out into the sea, where the King's Keep loomed overhead, and where Devi had seen Reya leap into the water the night before.

"What are you doing?" one of the trainees complained. "Everyone else is out that way."

"There's probably only tiddlers out here," another said. "Why do you think they've all gone straight into the deeper waters?"

"Let them fight over the large fish," Devi said. "We'll have our pick of the rest."

As their boat pushed its way gently through the water, rising and falling with the tide, riding the waves that continued to lap at the rocks to their left, Devi leaned over the edge and scanned the water. It was clear and blue, and he could see all the way to the bottom of the seabed beneath.

Every now and then, a school of fish would dart beneath the boat, their bodies so small but their numbers so plentiful that Devi could have reached down into the water and plucked out a handful. But it wasn't fish that Devi was searching for. It was Reya.

His stomach churned, not only with the rise and fall of the ship, but also with the thought of her lifeless body laying in the sand, the weight of the water long since having crushed the air from her lungs, her pale skin shrivelled and already beginning to grey.

Devi glanced up towards the rocks as they drifted past too, hoping he wouldn't see streaks of thick, red blood running down their sides, Reya's body perched on top, twisted and broken from the fall. The rocks were covered with nothing but green moss, however, and nothing perched on their tops but enormous, pot-bellied gulls, their stomachs likely full of the fish that darted to and fro around the hull of Devi's ship.

"Are we planning on catching any fish or not?"

Each of the other trainees leaned over the edge of the boat, their own eyes fixed to the water.

Devi lifted one side of their net from the deck, and one of the other trainees took the other side. They made their way to the back of the ship and looped the net over the metal hooks they found there, allowing the bulk of the mesh rope to fall over the ship's stern and into the water. Then, Devi pulled the horizontal bars beneath the sail towards him, and the ship lurched to the right, back in the direction of the horizon where the other trainees cut and weaved in their ships against the backdrop of the slowly rising circle of the sun.

To his left, however, Devi saw another ship some way off, which seemed to be sailing back towards Narkasee. It was slightly larger than his own, and its sails were jet black, only just visible now that the sun had risen high enough to lighten the previously pitch-black sky.

Devi stepped towards the port-side of his ship, and he raised his hand to his brow, blocking out the sun that glared at him from his right. He narrowed his eyes in the direction of the ship, and he was sure he could see a figure staring back at him.

The figure's red hair glowed like burning embers in the twilight of the early morning, and even from such a distance, the girl's blue eyes twinkled at him like the slowly dying stars above. Staring at him from the deck of the ship was Reya. Devi was certain of it. He watched as she moved behind the sail, disappearing from sight, then as the ship in the distance lurched to the left and began to sail away from him.

Devi's eyes stayed fixed to the ship. He couldn't have torn them away if he tried. The night before, only hours ago, he had seen Reya leap from the cliff to her certain death. Now, he saw her standing on the deck of a ship staring back at him.

Only a moment ago, Devi couldn't have been convinced it wasn't Reya on the ship in the distance, but suddenly his mind was flooded with uncertainty. King Vagan kept her locked up in the Keep at all hours. And she was the princess. How could she alone sail a ship larger than the one Devi and four other trainee Seekers had barely managed to force out to sea?

By the time Devi's tiny ship was making its way back into Black Soul's Bay, his mind was as full of doubt as his net was of fish. Some were so small that they swam straight through the holes in the mesh, but others were large enough to become caught there. Devi and his shipmates certainly didn't have the biggest fish, but it was possible they had the most. Some of the other ships had already made it back to shore, however, and it looked from a distance as if their own nets were just as bulging, if not more so.

As they had fished, the sun had separated itself from the horizon, and Devi saw Farruk wading out into the water, pulling the ships, trainees and all, closer to the shore to moor them in the sand again.

"We should haul this in," Devi said, looking out towards the other two ships that were still at sea. "If we hurry, we might not be the last ones back."

Two trainees took hold of the horizontal bars of the mast and turned them against the wind. Devi felt the ship lurch forward just a little as the sail filled. The two other trainees leaned over the back of the ship with Devi, each taking hold of the net.

"On three," Devi said. "One, two…"

On three, each of the boys pulled with all their strength, but the net barely moved. They each adjusted their positions, Devi propping his foot up onto the side of the ship for leverage.

"Again," he said. "One, two…"

Once more, the boys pulled, but their combined strength was not enough to haul the net aboard.

"Hold on," Devi said, and he leaned over the side of the ship.

There, beneath the water, the net had become tangled in the splintered rudder below the stern.

"It's caught," Devi said. "We'll need to pull it free."

He looked to the trainee to his left. Then, to the one on his right. Neither boy made any move towards the water.

"You *are* the captain," one of the boys smirked.

Devi had no idea how he had ended up being the one to take the lead. Either he truly was, having never stepped foot on a ship before, the most experienced sailor on board, or the other trainees were simply content to allow him to flounder as he struggled to captain their tiny vessel, certain Farruk would be watching on.

"Fine," he huffed.

Devi thrust his knees up against the lip that ran around the side of the ship. He leaned over the edge, burying his arms in the water up to his shoulders, the salty sea licking at his face. He tugged and yanked at the net, but the pull of the water held it tight against the rudder.

Devi stood up and approached the net from a different angle, leaning over the side of the ship once more. The water was cold and biting, and already his arms almost felt numb. Though he thought his fingers might snap from his hand at any moment, Devi finally found where the net met the rudder. He put one foot up onto the side of the ship, and he leaned over so far that he was forced to turn his face away from the water to prevent it from being submerged. He gave the net one final tug, and it burst free, expanding out at the back of the ship, the fish inside tossing and thrashing in the water. At the same moment, Devi found himself thrashing his own body back and forth in the net, his foot slipping from the slick side of the ship as he plunged into the deep, cold water of the Tharakun.

~

Devi stared longingly at the greasy lump of meat on Vikas's tray, and his body shivered violently. Though he had dried off quickly under the warm sun, the cold water of the Tharakun still seemed to be running through his bones. He watched as Vikas lifted the leg up to his mouth by the fractured bone and tore at it hungrily, and his stomach rumbled as he looked down at his own empty tray.

He had offered little resistance when two of the trainees that had shared his boat that morning came and whisked away his bread and his bowl, and he had offered even less when a third had returned for his meat. It was his fault they had gone without breakfast, and he was content to pay his debts, even if his stomach wasn't.

He had clambered out of the water and back up onto his ship in seconds, but the net had been pulled free from the boat entirely when he had fallen into it, and it was all he could do to untangle himself and haul himself out of the water without drowning. He had given no thought to attempting to ensure the fish did not escape. Even if he had, he would have stood little chance.

Devi was not content to see Orlain's gormless face bounding across the mess towards him, however, his four other bunkmates following close behind.

"Someone's hungry," Orlain scoffed, pawing at Devi's empty tray. "Looks like you worked up quite an appetite this morning."

Devi simply stared down at his empty tray. He was cold, and he was tired, and he was in no mood to indulge Orlain. He wondered whether Vikas might speak up on his behalf, but he merely sat in silence gnawing on his meatless bone, as did Warwick and Tsurzan.

"I'm talking to you, peasant boy," Orlain spat, slamming his own tray down on Devi's table.

Orlain cast a sideways glance at Vikas, but Vikas's silence buoyed him.

"Did you father do nothing to prepare you for this?"

Devi immediately flushed with anger, unprepared as he was to hear Orlain mention his father. Though his bones continued to clack with the cold, he felt a burning in his cheeks.

"You can't fight," Orlain said. "You can't sail, you can barely even keep hold of your own food. What *did* your father teach you?"

"Don't mention my father," Devi said, his voice low, his eyes still fixed on his empty tray.

"All you're good for is the fields. I'm sure your father told you that though, didn't he?"

"Don't mention my father!"

Devi's voice boomed around the mess almost as loudly as Farruk's. He was suddenly standing nose to nose with Orlain, the tips of his toes pressing him up towards Orlain's face. But Orlain didn't flinch. Instead, he held Devi's gaze squarely.

"There it is," Orlain sneered. "Everyone has a nerve to pinch, and it seems I've just found yours."

Devi could feel his chest heaving. He struggled even to breathe.

"What is it?" Orlain pressed. "Your father sent you here? You don't even belong in the fields, and he needed a way to get rid of you?"

The tiny muscles in Devi's eye began to twitch, and Orlain continued to peer down his nose at him.

"No, that's not it," he said. "He doesn't know you're here?"

Devi stared back at Orlain, and he curled his hands up into two tight, little fists.

"No," Orlain said again. "That's not it either."

Orlain fell silent for a moment, scouring Devi with his eyes. Then, he leaned in a little closer.

"He's dead, isn't he?" Orlain said, a smug grin settling over his face. "That's it, isn't it? I'm right. Your father is dead, and you've come here on some half-bit quest to honour his memory."

Devi felt a fire of rage burning within him. He wanted nothing more than to thrust his palms into Orlain's shoulders, send him sprawling across the stone floor, and pounce on him, pounding his fists into his smug, gormless face. But he did not. He simply stood there staring, whilst Orlain glared back at him, his expression all contentment and satisfaction.

Then, Orlain turned away from Devi, finally breaking his gaze after what felt like an eternity but glancing back over his shoulder in his direction.

"Don't worry," Orlain sneered. "I'm sure you're making him proud."

Devi's other bunkmates cackled like hyenas as they filed out of the mess behind Orlain. Devi stood for a moment longer, his arms trembling at his sides, the tips of his fingers dug so deep into his palms that he thought they might draw blood. Then, silently, he took his seat at the table opposite Vikas once more.

"I can't stand up for you every time, Devi," Vikas said.

His voice was soft, but he spoke with firmness and finality. Devi wished he hadn't spoken at all. He knew he couldn't rely on Vikas to stand up for him, and he had resented his intervention in the yard the previous day. As he watched Orlain retreat from the mess, however, he felt as if he resented Vikas even more for refusing to intervene. He had done nothing to deserve Orlain's scorn, and no citizen of Katai should turn a blind eye to injustice.

Devi knew it was not truly Vikas he resented, however. Someone needed to stand up to Orlain, but it wasn't Vikas. He needed to stand up to Orlain himself.

~

Out in the training yard, Devi could hear the Tharakun Sea lashing at the rocks, but the night was otherwise silent. He looked towards the edge of the Salt Cliffs, where he had seen Reya standing the night before, but he saw no figure silhouetted against the light of moon. What he did see was the large, wooden board and his name scrawled in thick, white letters at the very bottom of the pile once more.

Devi made his way over to the pile of swords at the yard. He picked one up and held it in his hand for a moment, trying to come to terms with its additional weight as he held his arm aloft. He swung the sword forwards and then backwards, turning to his left and to his right as he lashed out with the blade, and although he had grown used to the weapon somewhat, it still felt foreign and unfamiliar.

He thought back to his sparring sessions and the ease with which the other trainees swung their weapons, and he wondered how young they must have been when they had first gripped the handle of a sword. It had been a scythe that Devi had gripped in his small, innocent hands, and it was a scythe that he longed to grip once more.

Devi looked across the yard towards the empty stable that ran along one side. He carried his sword over and into the stable, and he scanned the dirt at his feet, which was littered with soiled straw. Laying, half propped up against the fence on the far side of the stable, was a long, wooden broom, and Devi crossed the stable towards it, hopping from left to right to avoid soiling his boots. He carried the broom back out to the yard in one hand, his wooden sword still gripped tightly in his other.

Back out in the yard, Devi dropped his sword. Then, he held the broom out so its handle crossed his body and its head laid on the floor by his opposite foot. He placed one foot on the handle of the broom, just above the head, and he jumped into the air, bringing both feet down against the base of the wooden handle and snapping the head of the broom clean off.

Devi dropped the broken handle beside his sword and ventured back towards the shacks beside the stable, returning with a short length of rope that was fraying and tangled, which he had found inside. It took him only a few moments to untangle the mess, and he wrapped the rope around the handle of the broom several times before reaching for his wooden sword.

Devi wrapped the rope around the sword too, and then he brought the two handles together, fastening them securely together with the rope so his sword was fixed perpendicular to the end of the broom, where its head had once been. It was a rudimentary scythe at best, but it was a scythe nonetheless.

Clutching the weapon in both hands, Devi made his way to the centre of the yard. Then, he dropped into the ready position that Farruk had demonstrated earlier that morning. He bent slightly at the knees, held one arm aloft at his shoulder, and stretched his other arm out in front of him to balance the weight. Now, however, at the end of his outstretched arm was the blade of his scythe.

Devi imagined Sand Dwellers coming at him, one at a time, from all angles. He spun away from the shadows, twisting his hips one way and then the other under the moon's silver light, and he didn't stop until the yard was too dark for him to continue any longer.

XII

Devi was already standing in the pitch black of his room when Farruk's giant fist pounded against his door. He heard the groans of his bunkmates in the darkness, dragging themselves from the comfort of sleep, but he had been up and dressed for some time already. By the time Farruk was pounding on the door next to his own, Devi was already halfway down the corridor heading for the mess.

There, he devoured his meat, picking the bone clean, he slurped down his thin soup, and he crammed his chunk of bread into his mouth as if it was not so hard that it cut up his gums. As the other remaining trainees were just beginning to file in through the great, wooden doors, Devi was already passing them on his way out to the training yard.

Devi stood at the centre of the yard, and he stared into the face of each of the trainees as they finally began to file out of the Keep to join him, some still wiping the sleep from their eyes and the soup from their lips. Even when Farruk emerged from the corridor out into the yard, Devi held his gaze for what almost felt like a moment too long. Although Farruk initially glared back at Devi, his enormous face all lightning and thunder, his expression twisted into a smile when he saw Devi already held a wooden sword at his side.

"At least one of you is keen," Farruk said.

When Devi finally saw Orlain's face beneath the stone archway, he caught his attention only for a moment.

"What are the rest of you waiting for?" Farruk yelled. "Grab your swords!"

Orlain hustled out of the Keep towards the pile of swords at the centre of the yard, and Devi followed him unblinkingly with his eyes. He watched as Orlain frantically looked towards Farruk, seemingly hoping he had not noticed that he had been one of the last to emerge, and then as he bent to collect a wooden sword from the pile at Devi's feet. When Orlain rose to standing once more, he found himself face to face with Devi, just as he had in the mess the night before.

"What are you staring at, farmer?" Orlain spat.

Devi simply glared back at Orlain, his face still and his expression dead.

"Watch yourself before I even that out."

The strike that Devi had taken across his cheek and his brow a few days earlier was still evident by the steadily darkening bruise it had left behind. With his sword in his hand, Orlain turned and walked away in the direction of his bunkmates across the yard. The second he heard Devi's voice, however, he stopped in his tracks.

"Where are you going?" Devi called.

For a moment, Orlain simply stood, either confused or incredulous that Devi had found the nerve to respond to him. Finally, he looked over his shoulder at Devi.

"Need a partner?" Devi asked, his voice as flat as his expression.

Orlain didn't even attempt to suppress his laughter.

"I do," he said. "But I'm not wasting my time with you."

Orlain turned to walk away once more, but he stopped again almost immediately.

"What's wrong?" Devi called. "Worried I might beat you?"

Orlain whirled around on Devi, his face already flushed with anger. Some of the other trainees that had scattered themselves around the yard stood looking on, their swords hanging limply at their sides. Even Farruk, who on any other morning would be bellowing at the trainees to hurry up and begin sparring, seemed to be watching on with interest.

"Trust me," Orlain said. "You don't want me to embarrass you in front of everyone."

"Or is it," Devi countered, pausing for just a second to allow the yard to fall completely silent. "That you don't want *me* to embarrass *you*?"

At that moment, Devi released his grip on the sword that he held in his right hand. The blade did not hit the ground, however. Instead, the wooden broom handle, which had been concealed by Devi's arm and back, slid down into his palm, revealing the makeshift scythe he had pieced together the previous evening. Devi gripped the handle tight, the wooden blade of the sword at its end hovering just above the dirt at his feet.

"What's this?" Orlain asked.

He no longer laughed, but his face twisted into an amused smirk once more. He raised his arms and spoke not only to Devi but to the entire yard.

"The farmer thinks he's back in the fields."

Devi heard a few snickers scatter around the yard, and he searched the faces of the trainees to see his four bunkmates grinning back at him.

Then, Devi whipped his scythe around his body, and the entire yard heard it cut through the air. He spun in a half circle, initially leaving his scythe behind but then immediately swinging it back in front of his body. He raised the weapon into the air and brought it down ferociously as he spun in another half circle, his gaze falling upon Orlain once more. The grin that had adorned Orlain's face had fallen to the dirt, and he stared back at Devi blankly.

"You can't fight with that," Orlain said.

When Devi remained silent, he turned to Farruk instead.

"He can't fight with that," he repeated. "That's not a sword. Stone Seekers fight with swords."

Devi also turned to face Farruk, and he watched as the giant of a man cast his gaze around the entire yard. All around, the trainees gazed back at him, awaiting his reply.

"You plan to seek the Stones?" Farruk asked simply.

Orlain failed to respond for a moment. Instead, he stared back at Farruk, confused.

"Answer me, boy," Farruk bellowed. "You have plans to seek the Aether Stones?"

"Yes… Of course," Orlain stammered.

"And yet, you are scared of a peasant boy with a wooden stick?"

Murmurs and sniggers rumbled around the yard once more, but this time Devi's bunkmates were silent.

"I'm not scared," Orlain insisted.

"Then fight him."

Devi watched as Orlain took his turn to gaze around the yard, the trainees all staring back at him, now eagerly awaiting his response.

"You'll regret this, farmer."

Orlain stepped towards Devi and laid his boot into the pile of wooden swords between them, sending them scattering across the yard. He kicked out at the blades in his immediate vicinity and bent to pick one or two up, tossing them aside.

Meanwhile, the trainees that had scattered themselves around the yard eagerly closed in on Devi and Orlain, forming a tight circle around them as they had previously when it had been Farruk at the centre. Farruk himself stepped aside, taking his own place in the circle to watch on.

"Assume your ready positions," he thundered.

Devi narrowed his eyes and stiffened his jaw. Then, he bent at the knees and turned his side to face Orlain, holding the blade of his scythe out in front of him.

"I suppose that's one way to keep your distance."

Orlain tossed his sword out towards the tip of Devi's scythe, knocking it aside with ease. Then, he turned to face Farruk.

"I can't believe you're going to allow this."

Devi glanced over in Farruk's direction too. The great man's face did not move.

"The boy wishes to fight you with a broom," Farruk said. "You may accept the challenge, or you may yield to him."

Orlain scoffed.

"Yield," he repeated derisively. "Very well. If the farmer wants me to hurt him, then hurt him I shall."

The crowd began to murmur in earnest as Orlain adopted his own ready position, and then Farruk's voice boomed around the yard once more.

"Fight!"

Orlain moved immediately. He lunged forward at Devi, sending a violent hack right towards his face. Devi ducked and spun out to his left, narrowly avoiding the second blow Orlain had thrown shortly after the first. Devi flicked the blade of his scythe lazily towards Orlain, but it lacked the conviction necessary to present any real threat. Orlain dodged the blow easily, and he was quickly upon Devi again.

Orlain swung towards Devi's face once more, but he did not conceal the attack, and Devi was again able to avoid the oncoming blow. Devi twisted away from the attack this time, allowing Orlain to lunge across his body and pass him.

Devi tightened his grip on the handle of his scythe. Somehow, even with the additional weight of the broom handle, the weapon felt lighter and more manoeuvrable than the sword alone. He had grown up clutching a scythe in his hands. It felt natural. It felt right.

Orlain launched his third attack, and Devi once more easily stepped aside, knocking Orlain's blade away with the handle of his scythe. Before Devi was able to retreat, however, Orlain swung his trailing elbow, and it landed flush against Devi's nose. Cheers erupted around the circle. Devi stumbled back, blood already leaking from his nostrils, but he quickly found his feet and assumed his ready position once more.

"What in Katai possessed you to step in with me?" Orlain asked, turning to face Devi, the blade of his sword extended out towards Devi's empty hand.

By now, Devi's heart was beating like a drum, and he suddenly felt as if he had made a terrible mistake. Somehow, he had managed to survive his first few days of training, and out of the crowd of hundreds that had arrived at the Keep to enlist, he was one of only a handful that remained. Orlain was quick, and strong, and relentless, however, and even with his scythe, Devi was no longer sure he could beat him.

But as he spoke, Orlain's voice seemed distant. Though he was only an arm's length away, Devi could barely hear him. Instead, he heard flames beginning to crackle into life around the yard, and he heard the pounding of horses' hooves against the dirt.

He suddenly felt as if he was no longer in the training yard but was instead in the field outside his home, watching the Darmeenians plough through his fields. He felt the fire burning around him, and he felt the blades of the killers closing in. He heard his father's voice too, calling out to him from the darkness.

In darkness lie all terrors true,
be they many, few, or one.
Yet, through the darkness, he pursues,
to lie in wait, the rising Son.

Devi circled away from Orlain, keeping his scythe poised and raised high, ready to deliver a counter-strike should the opportunity arise. Orlain circled towards Devi, and he struck at Devi's outstretched arm with his sword, knocking it aside and leaving Devi's body open and exposed. Orlain lunged forward and struck Devi solidly in the stomach with his fist, knocking the air from his lungs. Devi stumbled backwards, gasping to catch his breath before it left his body, but again he found his balance and prepared a new defence.

Devi breathed heavily. He felt a rock in his stomach, and it felt as if his nose had been split in two. Orlain was not about to relent, however. He held his sword above his head, gripping it with both hands, and he swung it down towards Devi like a lumberjack. Devi lifted his scythe and held it across his face, softening the blow enough with its handle to allow him to step to his left once more. Orlain turned in pursuit of Devi, swinging and hacking at his body like a man possessed, but Devi maintained his poise. He twisted and shifted away from Orlain's blade, his strong and slender body able to change direction far more quickly than Orlain was able to launch his lumbering attacks.

As Devi spun away from another of Orlain's heavy strikes, their eyes met, and Devi was suddenly present in the centre of the circle once more. He could hear the ravenous cheers of the trainees that encircled him, baying for blood, and he could see the frustration pulsing through Orlain's body as they began to move around the circle again. Devi knew he would never be able to defeat Orlain blow for blow, but suddenly he could sense his advantage. He knew, if he was able to lower Orlain's guard and catch him in just the right place at just the right moment, he would fall.

Devi spat a mouthful of blood onto the ground at his feet.

"My father *is* dead," he said simply.

"What?" Orlain huffed.

He was breathing more deeply than Devi had realised.

"You said my father is dead," Devi said. "You were right."

Orlain lunged forward and swung his sword towards Devi, but the effort was lazy and lethargic, and Devi was easily able to knock the blade aside before he was struck.

"But my father would be proud."

Orlain threw another lazy strike towards Devi, but Devi was again able to avoid it with ease.

"He taught me focus, and he taught me discipline."

Orlain mirrored Devi's movements now, circling away from him in an effort to catch his breath.

"Your father will be ashamed," Devi said. "When you tell him you lost to a farmer."

Orlain lifted his sword above his head with one hand, and he reached out recklessly towards Devi with the other. It was Devi who lunged forward, however, ducking low and passing beneath Orlain's outstretched arm so he was at his exposed back. Then, Devi thrust the handle of his scythe between Orlain's legs and pulled it back towards him, sweeping Orlain's feet out from under him.

Orlain crumpled to the dirt in an instant, his legs folding beneath him, his upper body bent awkwardly back over his lower half. His mouth hung open, and his vacant eyes glared directly up at Devi. Silence fell around the yard as Devi raised his scythe high into the air. Devi's mind was not silent, however. Instead, it echoed with the words of Psalm Eight.

Deep within the truest heart, there lies a darkness all but rare.

"I yield! I yield!"

Orlain's voice crawled frantically out of his throat. He placed his hands in the dirt in an effort to scramble away from Devi, but his legs failed him. As Orlain laid helpless in the dirt, Devi brought his scythe furiously down towards his face, but its blade barely grazed the tip of his nose before Devi brought it to a halt.

Every soul must do its part to bring the good Son's light to bear.

They were the same lines Devi had been sure his father was repeating silently to himself when he had challenged the Stone Seekers in the marketplace. He could have pulled his own scythe from the cart that day and gone hand to hand with the men. As fearsome as the Stone Seekers were rumoured to be, Devi had seen the way his father handled his scythe. His victory hadn't been in imposing his will, however. It had been in allowing the Stone Seekers to think they had imposed theirs.

Devi's scythe hung over Orlain's face, the point of its blade almost poking at his flesh.

"I yield," Orlain repeated.

Devi lifted his scythe and placed the base of its handle in the dirt beside him. He stood over Orlain, looking down on him as he had looked down on his father's broken and lifeless body.

Then, he gazed around the circle of trainees, most of whom looked back at him with blank shock and adulation, whilst others, like his bunkmates, scowled at him. He saw Vikas, Warwick and Tsurzan at his sides, and he saw his father in his face for a moment, smiling back at him proudly. Finally, Devi's gaze lighted on

Farruk, who stood to his left, towering over the trainees on either side of him in the circle. Before Farruk could step forward to raise Devi's hand, however, Devi felt Orlain's foot crack against his shin.

Almost instantly, Devi lost all control of his body. His legs buckled as Orlain's had only moments earlier, and he crumpled to the ground, his scythe clattering to the dirt at his side. Then, he saw Orlain glaring down at him, a vicious, cynical smirk plastered across his face. He watched as Orlain lifted his sword above his head, and then the yard fell away around him, and the entire world turned black.

XIII

Devi gripped his father's knife tightly in his hand, his arms hanging loosely at his sides. He cast his gaze out across the field towards the smouldering horizon, where the flames danced and swayed before the setting sun. The night was silent – no screams from the women and children who hurried past him, no thunder of horses' hooves against the dirt of the field, no battle cries. Even the fire did not hiss or crackle.

Devi stepped down onto the sand and began in the direction of the field. Cool steel glimmered in the dying light before him. Wherever his eyes roamed, there was a sword, or a dagger, or a spear beckoning him forward. They called out to him, desperate to make his body their home. Devi moved slowly at first but, as he began to approach the field's edge, he picked up his pace. By the time he reached the dirt, he was running. Devi carved a path through the flames, but they licked at his ankles as he ran, and smoke whirled all around.

Devi ran towards the centre of the field, where the horses were careening and the blades were swinging. Directly before him, Devi's eye fell upon a Darmeenian raider. His horse laid dead at his back, but his sword was drawn, and he circled slowly away from Devi, his body poised and ready to attack at any moment.

Across from the Darmeenian stood Devi's father. He held his scythe in both hands, its blade held out in the direction of the raider, and he shifted his feet so that he circled in the opposite direction. Then, he lunged, his arms bringing the blade of his scythe down upon the raider like a bolt of lightning.

The blade of the scythe found its place in the Darmeenian's neck, and he immediately fell to the ground, his sword falling to the dirt at his knees. Devi's father lifted his scythe high above his head once more, its blade dripping with Darmeenian blood. Within an instant, however, another raider had appeared, standing over the body of his fallen comrade. Then, another appeared at his side, and another appeared beyond him so that Devi's father was outnumbered.

Devi took off towards his father but not before the first Darmeenian had swung a lunging blow in his direction. His father parried the blow with the handle of his scythe and turned its blade towards the raiders. Once more, the Darmeenian lunged in his direction, and once more he was able to avoid his blade.

When the two other Darmeenians launched their own offensives, it was Devi who attempted to repel them. He arrived at his father's side just in time, ducking beneath the sword of one attacker and thrusting his father's knife towards his ribs. Devi's blade did not find flesh, however. It found nothing.

Devi turned to see his father parrying the blow that he had attempted to defend himself, and he dispatched the Darmeenian with a swift slice across the stomach. Devi's father spun in a half-circle, knocking the incoming sword off its path and bringing the butt of his scythe against the jaw of the second attacker. Then, he turned to face the two remaining Darmeenians.

Devi was behind the raiders now, and it seemed that, with their attention drawn by his father, he would be able to dispose of one or more of them easily with his knife. As the Darmeenians continued to circle, Devi leapt forward with his knife held aloft, ready to sink its blade into the neck of one of the attackers. Once more, however, the blade was left wanting, and Devi swiped at thin air. It was as if the Darmeenian had seen him coming and had shifted his body to avoid harm, leaving Devi to crumple into a heap on the floor.

Suddenly, Devi was overwhelmed. Darmeenian boots stampeded the ground around him, and occasionally a face flashed before him as it fell lifeless to the dirt. And the fire was closing in on him too.

Between the bodies and the flames, Devi searched for his father. When he finally found his face amongst the crowd, it was covered in blood, and his eyes were wide with terror. He was surrounded by Darmeenians, and he no longer held his scythe. Devi tried to scream out, but the night was still and silent.

Devi laid motionless in the dirt, the heat from the flames crashing down on him like a tidal wave, his lungs filling with thick, acrid smoke. The smoke seemed to search for him in the darkness. It sought him out from all corners of the field, and it drifted towards him incessantly from the burning orchards. It attacked his nostrils and infected his throat until he felt as if he couldn't breathe, and it squeezed every ounce of air from his lungs until his chest was so heavy that he thought his ribcage would cave in. He fought desperately to lift the boulder from his chest. Then, his eyes burst open, and he managed to swallow a tiny, gasping breath.

For a moment, Devi struggled to find a face in the darkness. He could barely breathe under the force that pressed his ribs against his lungs, and he struggled to shift the weight aside. In the chaos of half-sleep, he searched in the darkness for Farruk, grinning as he dragged him from his bed to toss him out of the Keep and out of training for good. But instead, he saw the glint of a steel blade at his throat, shimmering in the dim, orange light that drifted in from the corridor, and when his eyes finally met those of the person who sat on top of him, they shone back at him a brilliant, clear blue.

"What are you doing?" Devi whispered, a piercing pain splitting his head in two.

He spoke quietly – partly because he did not want to wake his bunkmates, and partly because it was all he could manage.

"Not so tough now, are you?" Reya asked.

As his eyes acclimatised themselves to the half-light, Devi glanced around the room. He was not in his hammock but was instead alone in a small, anonymous stone room containing only a single bed.

"What are you talking about?" Devi said, trying and failing to shift his body under Reya's weight.

Reya was not large, but she held Devi tight in place with her legs, pinning his arms at his side.

"You want to be a Stone Seeker," Reya said. "To defend my father and bring glory to Katai? How are you going to defend Katai when you can't even defend yourself against a girl?"

Devi struggled hard, and Reya giggled quietly as she held him in place.

"I saw you earlier," Reya said. "How could you let yourself lose to that smug boulderhead Orlain? I'm not very impressed."

"I wasn't trying to impress you."

Devi struggled again to pull his arms free, or at least to find some leverage with his legs, but again he failed.

"I don't think your father would be proud either," Reya said.

Devi did not speak. He simply stared back at Reya and continued to struggle.

"What was it you said to Orlain? His father would be ashamed that he lost to a farmer? Well, what if I slit your throat right now?"

Reya leaned her face in close to Devi's own. They were so close that their noses almost touched. Devi felt Reya's cool breath on his lips, and he felt the blade of her knife press against the flesh of his neck, just beneath his jawline. For a moment, Devi stopped struggling.

"Your father would be ashamed if he knew you lost to Orlain," Reya whispered. "Imagine how ashamed he'd be if he knew you were killed by a princess."

Devi almost screamed as Reya's teeth sank into his bottom lip. Then, suddenly, Reya leapt from Devi's bed, her bare feet landing silently on the stone floor, and she darted out of the room.

Devi scrambled to his feet and out of the room in pursuit, catching a glimpse of Reya's red hair as it disappeared around the corner to his left towards the Great Hall. Devi ran down the corridor as quietly as he could manage, and he saw Reya disappear on the opposite side of the hall. He crossed the great, open space after her and took off down the next corridor towards the back of the Keep.

The Keep was silent and empty, and Devi thought he had lost Reya for a moment. At the end of the corridor, however, he saw her standing over the threshold of the door that led out to the training yard. She glanced back in Devi's direction, her smile infuriating and enticing in equal parts. Then, she ducked out of the door and disappeared into the yard.

As Devi approached the door himself, he peered tentatively out into the darkness. The yard was half-lit by the moon, and he could hear the waves of the Tharakun Sea crashing against the Salt Cliffs. He stepped outside, the night air cool against his skin, but there was no sign of Reya.

Devi walked slowly out to the centre of the yard, where he had toppled Orlain earlier that morning. He turned in place, his eyes struggling in the darkness to find Reya. Then, silhouetted against the silver light of the moon, he saw her.

Reya stood near the edge of the cliff, just as she had two nights earlier, and once more, she wore the tight-fitting britches and waistcoat of a pirate. The loose curls of her red hair hung at her shoulders now, as they had when Devi had first seen her in the Keep beside Vagan, and they shifted a little in the gentle breeze that whispered through the yard, her eyes glistening with the stars at her back.

Devi began in Reya's direction. He walked slowly at first, but he soon found himself beginning to jog. Reya turned beneath the moonlight so that she faced the sea rather than Devi, and she took off running. Devi immediately found that his pace quickened until it matched Reya's own, and soon they were both running towards the edge of the cliff and towards the Tharakun Sea. By the time Reya reached the edge, Devi was only a step behind. He watched as Reya leapt from the edge of the cliff, her legs wide and her arms outstretched. Then, he did the same.

PART THREE

XIV

Devi's body hung in the air, silhouetted against the fullness of the moon. Though it felt as if he was still and motionless, he was falling – falling towards the all-consuming waves of the Tharakun Sea. The night felt eerily peaceful, and it seemed to Devi as if the world, for a moment, had stopped spinning, as if the clouds in the air hung there with him and the stars beyond had ceased to blink. Devi felt weightless. He felt free. Then, it was as if the world had been ripped from under him.

Devi's arms and legs began to flail as he plunged towards the water that was waiting for him below, and a sense of regret deeper than any he could imagine exploded within him. He closed his eyes and tried to bring his limbs under control. If he was going to slam into the water, he at least wanted to give himself the best chance of survival. He straightened his legs and pinned his arms to his sides. When he finally felt the impact of the water, however, it was not hard and unyielding as he had expected. Instead, it was soft. It caressed him like a cloud, enveloping his entire body, vanishing the sky and blinding his senses.

Devi felt himself continue to fall, but he did not hear the rush of water at his ears, nor did he feel the pressure slowly building as he plunged deeper and deeper into the sea. Instead, he still felt light, as if he had not yet hit the water at all.

Devi opened his eyes, ready for the saltwater to sting them. He was still enveloped in darkness, yet he felt no pain. Blind as he was, it was difficult for Devi to pair the inertia he felt in his body with the outside world, but he felt as if his fall was beginning to slow. Then, Devi finally landed, his body crumpling into a heap on solid ground, and the world around him was visible once more.

It felt to Devi as if he had been falling for an age. As he laid flat on his back, however, the top of the Salt Cliffs looking down on him, he realised it could only have taken him a few seconds to make the drop. What Devi also saw as he laid gazing up at the moonlit sky was a large, black sail, only half-loosed and flapping fitfully against its narrow mast. Devi laid at the base of the mast, and he realised the cloud that he had been momentarily enveloped within was the sail above him, and it had caressed his fall, dropping him softly onto the deck of the ship to which it belonged.

Devi forced his body slowly upright. He found himself on a small ship, similar to those he had seen sailing the Tharakun Sea for as long as he could remember, and identical to the one he was sure he had seen Reya sailing the previous day. He searched the deck of the ship for Reya and quickly found her in the bow. She was bent over a stiff, wooden winch, which clacked loudly as she forced its handle anticlockwise. A thick, metal chain slowly snaked around the base of the winch as it turned until a loud thud brought it to a halt.

Devi rose to his feet, and he immediately felt his stomach beginning to churn. He watched as Reya relinquished her grip of the wooden handle and strode towards him. Reya did not speak as she approached Devi, however. She did not even offer him a glance. Instead, she took up a loose hanging rope from the base of the mast and began to pull at it, heaving backwards with the entire weight of her body.

Above Devi, the sail that had softened his fall from the edge of the cliff began to stretch and tighten. The top of the sail was already flush with the top of the mast, but its low corner now inched towards the end of a wooden bar that ran perpendicular to the mast. Unfurling before Devi was a sheet of sheer black, dotted with hundreds of tiny, white specks. As he gazed up at the sail, it was as if he was looking through the clouds into the starry sky beyond.

Reya pulled the rope tight, stretching it beneath a metal hook at the base of the mast and wrapping it quickly around the hook's curves in a figure of eight until the sail was secure. Devi could feel the ship softly lurching beneath his feet, the waves of the Tharakun intermittently advancing and receding with the tide, and he struggled through deep breaths and a clenched jaw to stop his stomach from lurching along with it.

Without a word, Reya continued on past Devi towards the stern of the boat, which already felt as if it was beginning to drift away from the base of the cliff. There, she took her place behind a large, wooden wheel lined with thick, wooden spokes, which extended out beyond the wheel itself to form several short handles. Reya gripped two of the handles at the base of the wheel and heaved them towards the top. The ship lurched violently to Devi's right, and he almost failed to keep his feet. Reya gave the wheel a second one hundred and eighty degree turn and held it in place there.

Moments earlier, the ship had run parallel to the shore, but now its bow dragged itself towards the horizon, and it slowly began to move away from the cliff. A gust of wind picked up, and the rope that was tied tight to the base of the mast creaked a little, the sail it held in place pulling even tighter. The ship lurched again, and suddenly Devi's back was to the cliffs and the Keep, and the open sea stretched out before him.

Devi considered jumping from the ship for a moment. It had turned towards the horizon, but it was still close enough to the cliffs that he could reach the shore. The cliff face directly behind him was sheer, but it shallowed as it began to meet Black Soul's Bay further down. Devi had barely stepped foot on a ship before, however, and he didn't even know how to swim. The water might be shallow enough for him to wade – he had seen the bottom of the Tharakun from his ship the day before – but he didn't like his chances if it was deeper than it seemed.

"You won't make it," Devi heard Reya call over his shoulder.

She hadn't even needed to see his face to know his intentions. Devi turned to face her. He tried to bring himself to speak, but he quickly found that he was unable to do so.

"The crocs will get you," Reya said simply.

She turned the wheel in her hands back to her left slightly and held it there, straightening the ship's course. Wind filled the sails, and the ship split the water in two, sending soft, rippling waves away from its bow on either side. They echoed out across the water, gradually growing more and more faint until they settled into the stillness of the sea once more.

Devi looked up at the Keep that loomed over them from atop the Salt Cliffs. Reya was right. The small ship moved quickly, and in Devi's brief moment of hesitation, Reya had already put some distance between themselves and the cliffs. Even if they had been closer, Devi's body flailing in the water, trying its best to stay afloat, would have been an invitation too enticing for the crocodiles on the shore to resist.

Devi turned away from Reya and walked the length of the boat. It was small and manoeuvrable, and it seemed to cut through the water with ease, but unlike the tiny ship he had sailed, it appeared to be large enough to have its own hold below deck. When he had seen the ship sailing off the coast of Narkasee the previous day, Devi had been unsure whether it was Reya he had seen staring back at him from its deck. Now, there was no question that it had been.

"What's going on?" Devi asked, turning back towards Reya.

"We're sailing. Have you never seen a ship before?"

"Yes, I've seen a ship before," Devi said.

"Of course you have. I watched you fall out of one."

Reya giggled as she spoke, and the sound ignited sparks of anger inside Devi.

"I mean why are you sailing, and why have you brought me with you?"

Hanging from the middle of the ship's wheel was a short length of rope. Reya bent to one knee, pulling the rope tight there as she had at the mast. She fed the rope through a metal loop on the deck beneath the steering wheel, her fingers dancing as she tied it into a strong knot. She tugged at the wheel as she rose to standing, but it barely moved an inch.

"You want to find the Fire Stone, don't you?" Reya asked.

She made her way back towards the front of the ship, where a second mast, much smaller than the one at its centre, rose from the decking. A small, black sail hung loosely there, and it too was covered with tiny, white dots like stars.

"Of course," Devi replied.

Reya took hold of the rope that hung from the mast and pulled it tight. The small, black sail instantly stood to attention, stretched tight at the bow of the ship. Reya curled the rope around another curved, metal hook, tying it and pulling at it lightly to test its security.

"So, let's go and find it," she said.

"Let's go and find it?" Devi repeated, his voice flat and cynical. "Us? Now?"

"Why not?"

"Because we don't know the first thing about surviving in The Sands," Devi said, incredulous. "I've barely begun my training, and you're a princess, not a Seeker."

"Who says a princess can't be a Seeker? Isn't it the right of everyone in Katai to seek the Stones?"

Reya smirked at Devi, just as she had when she had pinned him to the bed moments earlier. Already, he hated that look. It made him feel stupid and weak. It made him want to wither away and hide. It made him doubt whether he even knew his own name.

"Every boy," Devi said finally.

"I'm sorry?"

"It's the right of every boy and every man in Katai to seek the Stones."

"Well did you ever think that the women and girls might enjoy a chance to win glory for their nation too?"

Devi fell silent. He felt like he was a boy again, being chastised by the village mothers for taking apples from the orchards.

"But why now?" he asked.

"I could ask you the same question."

Devi thought back to the night his father's head had been sliced from his body. As they had countless times since, visions of Rakhas's fields burning to a cinder flashed across his mind as if he was back there under the moonlit, ash-filled sky.

"Besides, my father keeps me locked up in the Keep all day," Reya said. "I have to do something to pass the time."

Devi remembered seeing Reya in the window of the Keep the first morning he had trained, and he remembered Vikas's words.

"So that's what this is for you?" Devi asked. "A way to pass the time? You're going to get us both killed because you're bored of having someone to keep you safe and protected?"

Reya bore down on Devi, her smirk falling from her lips as she strode across the deck. She didn't stop until her face was just inches from Devi's own, his lip still throbbing a little from where she had bitten it earlier.

"You're not the only one that wants to find the Fire Stone, you know? And besides, I'm not safe in the Keep, and neither is my father. He thinks its walls can protect us, but the longer we stay hidden behind them, the closer Katai comes to extinction."

Reya stepped back from Devi but continued to hold his gaze.

"You've heard the rumours, Devi. The Darmeenians are closing in. If we don't find the Fire Stone soon, they will, and that will be the end of Katai. I love my father, and I love Katai. I want to save them both."

Devi wanted to speak, but for a moment, he couldn't find the words. Until now, Devi had only seen Reya from a distance. Each time he had seen her in Vagan's Keep, he had barely been able to tear his eyes away from her. Since then, he had seen her leap from the edge of the Salt Cliffs, watched her sail a ship single-handedly, and had awoken with her teeth sinking into his bottom lip. Reya was captivating. She was wild. She was reckless.

But now, all of a sudden, she seemed immeasurably vulnerable.

"Why me?" Devi asked, his fledgling anger beginning to dissipate but his confusion remaining.

The smirk that had fallen from Reya's face returned with a vengeance. She made her way back over to the steering wheel at the stern of the ship and gripped the end of the rope that she had tied around the metal loop. She gave it one short, sharp tug, and the knot instantly fell apart. Then, she unhooked the rope, and took hold of the steering wheel once more, heaving it anti-clockwise for a full rotation. The ship lurched to one side, the sails tightening against the wind as it banked around to its left.

"This is my ship," Reya said, a mischievous glint in her eye. "I'm the captain, and I give the orders. Most of those other boneheads wouldn't be able to handle that."

"Boneheads?"

"The other trainees," Reya clarified. "They might be dense, but they certainly aren't spineless."

Devi felt his anger beginning to rise once more. He had never met anyone able to shift his emotions so dramatically.

"How do you even know how to sail when you just said yourself you spend all day in the Keep?"

"I spend all *day* in the Keep," Reya repeated. "But my father doesn't need to know where I am at night."

Devi looked to his left towards the Salt Cliffs. He and Reya were far out to sea now, and the Keep looked tiny, barely visible but for the dim orange light that glowed in the windows at its back. To Devi's right, the Tharakun stretched for as far as the eye could see, and the moon shone bright above the horizon.

"Well, Captain," Devi said. "I hate to tell you this, but The Sands are that way."

Devi pointed over Reya's shoulder, in the opposite direction to the ship's current course. Reya paused for a moment, content to allow Devi to continue to speak.

"And what kind of supplies can this thing hold?" he asked, raising his arms and looking from one end of the boat to the other. "I might not know much about sailing, but I know we need to eat. It will take weeks to sail to The Sands."

"We're not heading for The Sands," Reya said, once it was clear that Devi had fallen silent. "We're heading for Darmeen."

Devi was dumbstruck.

"Darmeen?" he asked.

"That's right," Reya said simply.

"Why in Vagan's name would we want to go to Darmeen?"

Reya crinkled her nose.

"Please don't say that," she said.

"Don't say what?"

"In Vagan's name," Reya sneered. "He's my father. It just sounds strange."

"Fine," Devi sighed, his patience long since having worn thin. "But why Darmeen? It's a death-wish."

"But The Sands aren't?"

Devi chewed his bottom lip.

"The Fire Stone is in The Sands," he said. "The Darmeenians killed my father and grandfather, and they enslaved my great-grandfather. Why would I want to go anywhere near that place?"

"So you can reach the Fire Stone," Reya replied. "And so we can save Katai from the same fate."

"But the Stone is in The Sands!" Devi said, exasperated.

"I know where the Stone is," Reya replied. "Everyone in Katai and beyond knows where the Fire Stone is. But we'll never reach The Sands in this thing."

Devi looked up and down the ship that continued to drift away from the Salt Cliffs. It was a meagre vessel, barely large enough to support a small crew of five or six and small enough to be sailed by as few as one.

"We've only got space for a few days' worth of supplies. You said so yourself."

"So what?" Devi asked. "We're using supplies to get to Darmeen, and then we'll just be picking up more supplies to sail back. It's not worth the trip."

Once more, Reya said nothing. Instead, she allowed Devi's mind to continue to work.

"Unless," Devi said, a light of understanding falling across his face. "We're going to switch to a bigger ship in Darmeen."

"Not just a bigger ship," Reya replied, her eyes catching fire. "The *biggest* ship."

It was Devi's turn to fall silent.

"The Darmeenians have been building the largest ship the seas have ever seen," Reya continued. "They've been working on it for years, and it's finally ready to set sail."

"How do you know this?" Devi asked.

"You hear whispers on the waves," Reya said. "But it's true, Devi, and that's our way out to The Sands. A ship that large will be able to sail for weeks on end without ever having to stop to resupply. It's set to sail further than any ship has ever sailed before, and we're going to be aboard it when it leaves."

Devi stared back at Reya. Though his training had been limited, he had at least begun to prepare his mind and his body for The Sands. After losing to Orlain, however, there was no way that he would be allowed to continue his training. Reya's plan was bold, it was brave, and there was a chance that it would now be his best hope of finding the Fire Stone. But Devi knew there was a much greater chance it would lead to his death.

Devi opened his mouth to speak, but the ship lurched suddenly, and he quickly clamped it shut once more. Then, he ran to the side of the ship, bent over its taffrail, and hurled the contents of his stomach into the Tharakun.

XV

By the time the sun rose, Narkasee was nowhere to be seen. Devi had spent the dwindling hours of the previous night watching from the stern of the ship as the tiny glowing orbs atop the cliffs had grown fainter and fainter until eventually they had dissipated in the darkness. He hadn't been sure whether the flame torches in the windows of the Keep had been snuffed out, or whether he and Reya had sailed so far that they were no longer visible, but it didn't much matter. For the first time in Devi's life, Katai was behind him, and before him was the open sea and eventually Darmeen.

The sun was warm, and it shimmered on the water of the Tharakun like the smouldering embers of a fire. The water itself was still and gentle, whispering only faintly as it rippled away from the bow of the ship. Until now, Devi had only imagined what it would be like to drift across the sea. He was used to the land, where he would stand gazing out towards tiny Katai sails from the edge of the fields. There, the coasts and the borders divided one country from another, one people from another, but the water belonged to no one.

Devi was laying flat on his back, still staring up at the rapidly brightening sky when Reya emerged from below deck.

"Good morning," she chirped, stretching her arms above her head and forcing her hips out in front of her shoulders in an effort to shake the stiffness of sleep from her body.

"Morning," Devi grumbled in response.

Reya laughed.

"Not a morning person then?"

"Usually, I am," Devi said, groaning as he forced himself upright. "But I couldn't sleep."

"I'm not surprised. The deck wasn't exactly made for sleeping."

Devi rubbed the back of his head.

"It's the only way I could stop myself from throwing up."

From her pocket, Reya took out a small, metal compass. She made her way to the front of the ship and looked out across the open water. Then, she held the compass aloft. Its little, red arrow bounced from left to right before it settled, quivering only lightly as Reya's hand shook with the motion of the ship. Then, Reya tucked the compass back into her pocket and made her way to the back of the ship. She loosened the knot at the base of the ship's steering wheel, allowing the rope to fall at her feet, and she gripped its wooden handles tightly.

Reya pulled the wheel of the ship around to the left just a little. She held it there for a moment, and then she stooped to pick up the rope from the deck of the ship, tying the wheel down and fixing the rope to the metal loop once more.

"Based on your performance the other morning, I'm guessing you don't know a lot about sailing," Reya said as she made her way back to the centre of the ship.

"Nothing," Devi said.

"And fishing?"

Devi shook his head.

"What *do* you know?"

"I know how to farm," Devi said immediately.

Reya laughed.

"That won't be much use out here."

Reya made her way over to the port side of the ship, where a mess of thick netting laid in a heap.

"Get on your feet," she said. "We're going to be needing breakfast, and our stomachs aren't going to fill themselves."

Devi stood, and the world around him immediately began to spin. He didn't feel as if he was caught in a whirlwind. Rather, it seemed as if he could sense the motion of the planet shifting around him. He stumbled a little, and for a second, he felt as if he was seven years old again, spinning in circles in the fields of Rakhas with the other farming children until they each collapsed into the wheat, their heads dizzy and their stomachs churning.

"You'll get used to that soon enough," Reya said, beginning to unfurl the mass of netting and holding a section out towards Devi. "Come on. You take this side."

Devi took hold of the length of net that Reya had already begun to untangle. Then, Reya took up the pile that still laid on the deck and began to work away at it. The net felt heavy in Devi's hands. It was constructed of thick lengths of rope that had been wound tightly together so that the holes between them were only big enough for him to slide a single finger through.

"Throw it over," Reya said, nodding towards the water below.

Following Reya's lead, Devi heaved the pile of rope in his arms over the side of the ship. The boat was not small, and it took only a fraction of a second for the net to hit the water. Devi felt a splash of cool, salty water hit his face, and he licked the moisture away from his lips.

On the taffrail beside Devi was a second large, wooden crank that he had never seen on another ship, and which had previously been hidden by the mass of netting. Reya took hold of the crank's handle and began to turn it. From the side of the ship, two straight, wooden poles began to emerge, around which the netting seemed to be attached. As the poles diverged further and further from the ship, the net spread wider and wider out in the water. Reya released her grip of the handle and stepped back.

"Think you can manage?"

Devi gripped the handle just as Reya had, and he began to crank it. The net, however, did not budge.

"You're going to have to try harder than that," Reya said.

Devi stepped one foot back and lowered his shoulders. He put his entire bodyweight behind the handle of the crank and began to force it laboriously around. The two poles slowly began to stretch out towards the sea once more, and Devi continued to turn the crank until the net was pulled tight.

"That's as far as it goes," Reya said.

When Devi rose again and looked over the side of the ship, the mass of netting they had hauled overboard stretched out and back, forming a pocket for fish to swim into. The top portion of the net was attached to the wooden poles, and the bottom of the net appeared to be weighted so that it was pulled down into the water, rather than simply being dragged along its surface.

"How long will it take to fill?" Devi asked.

Reya smirked a little. Devi had only fished once, and that had been just off the coast of Narkasee, where the water was teeming with life. Out in the vast depths of the Tharakun, food would be a little harder to come by.

"It won't fill," Reya said. "But give it a couple of hours and we should have something."

Devi's empty stomach rumbled. He had barely eaten the previous day, and it hadn't taken long for him to spill what little he had eaten over the side of the ship.

"There's yellowfin out here but not much else. We'd have more luck if we stuck to the coast, but the fishing boats will already be out. Besides, my father has probably realised I'm gone, and who knows where he'll be looking?"

Devi pictured King Vagan storming through the halls and corridors of the Keep, his cheeks flushed with anger and his voice bouncing off the thick, stone walls.

Looking up at the sky, Devi guessed the other trainees would have just finished their morning meal and would likely be heading out into the training yard about now. Reya's absence certainly would have been noticed, and it would undoubtedly be cause for great concern, but Devi wondered whether anyone would have even given him a second thought.

"There is one other thing out here," Reya said, making her way back over to the hatch in the floor that she had emerged from a short time ago.

A moment later, Reya returned from below deck once more clutching a large, metal spear. It had a vicious-looking barbed spike on one end and a long length of rope attached to the other. The rope had been neatly looped several times then tied to itself at the base of the spear.

"What are you planning to do with that?" Devi asked.

"I'm going to catch our breakfast. It won't be worth hauling the net in for a few hours, and I'm hungry now."

Reya carried the spear to the starboard side of the ship, and she tossed it to the floor. She leaned forward, placing her hands on the ship's taffrail and gazing out across the open sea. Then, she scanned the water in the near distance, slowly reeling her eyes in like a line.

Devi made his way over to Reya and stood beside her. He leaned forward against the taffrail too, his own hands alongside Reya's.

"How often do you come out here?" he asked.

Reya was silent for a moment.

"Most nights," she said. "Sometimes I'll sail, and sometimes I'll just drift. You've really never sailed before?"

"Never."

"I can believe that," Reya said, one corner of her mouth rising a little as she smirked.

She leaned to her left, her shoulder and elbow meeting Devi's own and knocking him ever so slightly off balance.

"I'm a farmer," Devi said. "Boats don't sail through the dirt. And besides, you'd look out of place with a scythe in your hand or behind an ox cart."

"True," Reya said. "Tell me about the farms."

Devi thought for a moment, but he found it difficult to begin. Every memory he had of his home began with his father.

"They stretch for miles," he said finally. "Like the sea. In the winter, the fields are bare, but in the summer, they're chest-high with crops."

"What do you grow?"

"Everything," Devi said proudly. "Wheat, corn, grain."

Devi thought back to the night he had watched the orchards burn on the horizon.

"Even fruit," he said.

"I'd like to see the farms someday," Reya said. "Before the Sands have wiped them away."

Devi and Reya each fell silent. The Sands had only just begun to nibble away at the farmland. They would take what was left of Rakhas soon, and eventually they would come for Narkasee too. It was a future neither of them wanted to imagine.

"Will you show me?"

Devi thought for a moment.

"I suppose I'll have to," he said. "After all, you've shown me the sea, so I guess in a way I owe you."

Devi felt Reya's hand slide over his own. It sent a bolt of lightning through his body, and it felt as if the entire world was melting away around him.

"It's beautiful, isn't it?" Reya asked. "The water."

Devi gazed out across the still and silent Tharakun Sea. Then, he turned his gaze on Reya, her blue eyes just as still and just as silent.

"It's stunning," he said.

Before he was even aware of the need to resist, Devi found Reya's hand wrapped around his wrist, his hand in the air and his palm facing out to sea. In the blink of an eye, Reya reached to her hip with her opposite hand, pulled her dagger from its sheath, and ran it across Devi's palm. She squeezed Devi's wrist tight, and a stream of thick, red blood ran down his hand and dripped into the ocean.

"What are you doing?" Devi yelped, yanking his wrist from Reya's grasp and examining the gash on his palm.

Streaks of blood rushed across his hand, finding its way between his fingers and beginning to explore his arm.

"Are you mad?"

Reya sheathed her dagger once more.

"It's only a little scratch," she said. "To a Seeker, at least."

Devi pressed at the edges of the wound. Reya was right – she had only nicked him – but the blood flowed freely, regardless.

"Why did you do that?"

Reya picked the tethered spear up from the deck.

"Wait," she said, resting the spear against her shoulder and tying the loose end of its rope around her waist.

Devi looked over the edge of the ship, just as Reya did. Then, he saw the tiny, black tip of a fin in the near distance. It snaked its way gracefully through the water, bearing down on their boat seemingly without effort.

"Blacktip shark," Reya said.

Devi's face was blank and expressionless as he glared back at Reya. He hadn't managed to keep himself inside his tiny ship days earlier, and by the coast of Narkasee, he would have been back on deck before the crocs on the shore had even managed to force themselves into the water. If he fell overboard now, he would be eaten alive in seconds.

"Don't worry," Reya laughed. "They're barely bigger than the yellowfin."

A second black tip appeared in the water, which was soon joined by a third, and it wasn't long before all three sharks were circling just below the edge of the ship, eagerly searching for the source of the blood in the water.

"Why couldn't you cut your own hand?" Devi asked, retreating a little from the side of the boat to ensure his hand bled only on the deck.

"Well, I'm going to catch the shark," Reya began.

She cocked her elbow and lifted the spear above her shoulder.

"And I'm going to gut the shark."

She pulled her arm back so the tip of the spear was level with her eye.

"But we're both going to eat the shark."

Reya held the spear steady, her body poised and strong like the string of a bow.

"There's no plunder without sacrifice," she said. "And it seems like I'm the one making all the sacrifices."

All of a sudden, Reya unleashed herself, hurling her spear into the sea, which instantly erupted as the shark flailed and thrashed beneath it. The water immediately began to turn red, and the rope that laid on the deck of the ship quickly began to unfurl. Reya braced herself, bending at the knees and placing one foot on the taffrail. She allowed the rope to pass through her hands for a moment longer, and then she clamped them shut.

Reya flew forward, her chest meeting her knee. She winced as the rope continued to pass through her hands, and Devi could hear its fibres cutting into her palms.

"This one's big," Reya said, forcing the words out through her laboured breaths as she struggled to bring the rope still. "I need your help."

Devi wiped his hand across his tunic, smearing it with blood. He took up a length of rope from the floor, and it tore into his own palms before it stopped unfurling. He took his place behind Reya, planting his feet to the deck of the ship, and he leaned back.

"On my word," Reya said.

Devi squeezed the rope tight.

"Heave!"

Both Devi and Reya leaned back, hauling the rope along with them with the full force of their bodies.

"Heave!" Reya yelled again, and again they did the same.

Each time Reya gave the signal, Devi pulled with all his might, doing his best to ignore the fact that his palms – one more than the other – were on fire. Between the two of them, it wasn't long before the rope was piled up at their feet once more, and only a short length remained overboard.

"Walk it back now," Reya said.

Devi wasn't initially sure exactly what the instruction had meant, but he was quickly able to follow Reya's lead.

He walked backwards as she did, not hauling the rope behind him any longer, but instead dragging it with him as he moved. Soon, Devi heard the shark thrashing at the water once more, and then the dull thuds of its body against the hull of the boat began to beat like a drum. Both Devi and Reya continued forcing their bodies backwards, and then suddenly the shark was aboard, throwing its body one way and then the other.

As Devi watched on helplessly, Reya drew her dagger and stood poised, waiting to strike. When the shark flipped itself over onto its front, Reya leapt onto its back and drove her blade into the side of the shark's head, just behind the gills. The shark's tail fin continued to flick intermittently from left to right, but otherwise the creature was still.

Reya stood next to the shark. It was roughly as long as she was tall, and it laid splayed out at her feet, the spear in its back and its blood painting the deck red.

"Is that the first shark you've ever caught?" Reya asked, turning to face Devi.

"It's the first anything I've ever caught," he said, panting.

"You did well."

Reya yanked the spear from side to side until it loosened. Then, she pulled it from the shark's back.

"Hope you're hungry."

~

Devi wasn't sure whether the water was more beautiful when the sun was at its fullest or when it had disappeared below the horizon. He and Reya had drifted across the Tharakun all day, and now he looked up at the night sky, the moon a little less than full, the stars around it flickering like a million tiny heartbeats. When Devi looked out across the sea, he saw exactly the same thing – a mirror image, a perfect reflection.

"You're not such a bad sailor," Reya said. "Considering you've never been on the water before."

She and Devi each sat with their backs against the taffrail of the ship, picking yellowfin from their teeth and gazing out at the sea on the opposite side.

"Thanks," Devi said.

"How do you like the water?"

Devi thought for a moment.

"It's nice," he said. "It reminds me of home in a strange sort of way."

"But you're a farmer," Reya laughed.

"I know. I just mean… It's peaceful out here. You have the sea; I have the fields. You have the water; I have the dirt. They're not so different really."

Devi felt Reya's gaze fall upon him, but he continued to look out across the Tharakun. He missed Rakhas, but as long as he was in Katai, he knew he was home.

"I'm heading down for the night," Reya said, groaning a little as she rose from her seat on the stiff boards of the deck. "We need to sail hard again tomorrow. You should try to get some sleep tonight too."

Reya walked over to the hatch that led below deck, and Devi laid down flat as he had the night before.

"Goodnight," he called.

Reya began to make her way down the steps, but she paused halfway.

"Devi," she called back.

Devi craned his neck, lifting his head from the deck of the ship.

"There's room for us both down here you know?"

An awkward silence lingered in the air. The water was still, and the sails hung quietly at their masts. Devi's muscles stiffened as they prepared to force him upright. Then, Reya spoke again.

"It's just… I heard you last night. You'll feel less seasick below."

"Oh," Devi said, releasing the tension in his muscles and allowing his head to fall flat against the deck once more. "It's ok. I feel much better now. But thank you."

Reya paused on the steps for a moment longer.

"No problem," she said.

Then, she disappeared below deck.

XVI

Devi hung over the edge of the ship, one hand on the taffrail, the other clutching his stomach. Though the water below was perfectly still, his stomach still turned uneasily, though less so than it had the previous day. He had managed to keep down the blacktip shark and yellowfin he had eaten the previous day, and though it still felt as if he might return them to the sea at any moment, it was finally beginning to seem as if his body could grow accustomed to being on the water.

Devi had risen with the sun. It had woken him the moment it had begun to peek over the horizon a short time ago, and already its relentless ascent to its perch high above him was well under way. The sun was warm, and it sent shards of light cascading across the flawless canvas of the water. Even the air itself seemed perfectly still.

To his left, Devi glanced up at the towering peaks of the Marakaya Mountains, and he felt his stomach drop when he realised how far south he and Reya had drifted overnight. The Marakaya Mountains were all that stood between the farmlands of Katai and the sprawling Kingdom of Darmeen. Once they were at his back, he would truly be far from home.

But Devi looked at the sails of the ship, which hung loosely at their masts. They were motionless, as if set in stone, and he wondered whether the ship would even be able to carry him and Reya any closer to Darmeen if the wind didn't pick up.

Just as Devi turned back to face the water, he heard footsteps ascending from below deck, and he turned to see a figure emerge from the hatch. He had assumed he and Reya were the only two aboard the ship, but the figure that emerged wore short, black hair cropped close to the ears and was dressed in a loosely fitting, black tunic. It wasn't until the figure turned to face Devi that he realised it was Reya that was staring back at him.

"Well," Reya said, stepping out onto the deck. "Don't just stand there. Say something."

Despite the instruction, Devi simply stared back at her.

"How do I look?" Reya pressed.

She held her arms out at her sides, her palms facing the sky, and Devi looked over her. She still wore the same black trousers and boots she had worn previously, and they still clung tightly to her figure. The loose, flowing tunic she now wore disguised her upper body, however, and did not follow the contours of her hips and shoulders as her waistcoat had done. Reya's eyes still shone a luminous blue, but her face seemed more rigid and angular now that it wasn't framed on each side by waterfalls of crimson. Even the brows above her eyes had been blackened, and they matched perfectly the hair that sat short and cropped atop her head, and which had been shaved tightly to the sides above her ears.

"You look…"

Devi struggled to find the words.

"Different," he said finally.

"Oh, wonderful," Reya said. "That's just what I was hoping to hear."

She turned slowly in a circle, allowing Devi's eyes to explore her from every angle.

"You look…"

Devi tried once more to find the right words, but again he failed. He found it strangely disconcerting to see Reya's delicate face, her pale skin and her soft button nose, framed by the crude lines she had shaved into her thick, black hair. The contours of her body too were hidden so that Devi's mind was forced to struggle with the illusion that she appeared much larger and broader than he knew her to be.

"Do I look like a boy at least?" Reya asked.

Devi thought for a moment.

"I suppose," he said. "In a way. But you're too…"

Devi's face twisted as his mind continued to attempt to solve the puzzle before him.

"Pretty," he blurted out finally.

Devi bit his tongue, and Reya froze mid-turn. She looked over her shoulder in Devi's direction, but Devi's eyes were already glued to the deck at his feet.

"Well," Reya said. "I suppose there are worse problems a girl could have."

She began to stride towards the back of the ship, her hips loose and her smile wide.

"And you don't walk like a boy," Devi said, peeling his gaze from the deck of the ship and meeting Reya's own. "Why do you want to be a boy anyway?"

"I thought I'd finally give my father his wish."

"His wish?"

"I am my father's only child. Everyone knows a king needs an heir, but my father has none."

"You think Vagan wishes you were a boy?"

"Of course," Reya said simply. "It's only natural. He's a paranoid old man but that's not the only reason he keeps me locked up all day. He is ashamed his only child is a weak little girl. He is ashamed Katai has no heir, and he has no one to continue to his legacy."

The words cut through Devi like a knife, but Reya spoke them as if they were meaningless. Her face did not shift, her lip did not quiver, and her eyes did not waver. It was as if the words had lived in her mind for so long that, when she spoke them aloud, they were empty and hollow, merely husks that had dropped their kernels only to be whisked away on the wind.

Silence lingered for a moment. Then, Reya's face twisted into a smirk, and she spoke again.

"Besides, I don't want to *be* a boy," she said. "I just need to look like one. By now, my father will know I'm gone, and word spreads fast. By the time we reach Darmeen, it's possible the whispers will have already arrived. It's unlikely people in Princi will be looking for me, but we can't be too careful."

Devi nodded in agreement. He didn't want to be found alone with Reya in Katai, and he certainly didn't want to be found alone with her in Darmeen. It had been Reya that had whisked him away in the dead of night, but he wasn't sure he could convince King Vagan that their roles hadn't been reversed. He wasn't even sure he would be afforded enough time to try.

"Besides," Reya continued. "Once we're aboard the ship, it'll be easier to stow away as a boy. I doubt they're taking many girls with them."

"Right," Devi said.

"So, what's wrong with the way I walk?" Reya asked, lowering her brow and glaring mischievously at Devi.

"There's nothing wrong with it exactly," Devi said. "You just don't walk like a boy. You walk like a girl."

"Show me," Reya said, stepping aside to allow Devi the length of the deck.

Devi walked the length of the ship as naturally as he could manage, but even walking suddenly seemed difficult and uncomfortable with an audience.

Reya laughed at Devi as he walked, and then she stepped forward to walk behind him.

"This is you," she said.

Reya pushed her chest forward and held her shoulders stiffly back. She plodded clumsily down towards the front of the ship, loudly grunting with each heavy step. Devi scoffed. He knew he was lighter on his feet than Reya was giving him credit for.

"Well, this is you," he said.

Devi turned at the front of the ship and began to make his way towards the back once more. As he walked, he placed one foot directly in front of the other and swung his hips theatrically from side to side.

"No, it's not," Reya yelled in protest.

She chased after Devi and was immediately upon him. She leapt onto his back and thrust her arms loosely around his neck. Devi reached his arms back and gripped Reya by the shoulders. He leaned forward and tossed her over his own shoulder, but he did not allow her to hit the deck. Instead, he used all his strength to hold her in mid-air, allowing her legs to straighten out and her feet to find solid ground. Then, he lowered her gently down until she was seated.

"And you fight like a girl too."

Devi paused for a moment, still bent over Reya with his arms hooked around her body, the words he had whispered still hanging in the air. His nose was pressed against the soft skin of her cheek, and his lips barely brushed against her ear. Reya's body felt perfectly still, and even her chest did not rise and fall with her breath. One moment bled into the next until Devi wasn't sure how long he had lingered there, and then Reya spoke again.

"You can change below deck."

Devi slid his arms slowly out from beneath Reya's own, and he stood upright. The air between them felt thick.

"Change?"

Devi stepped back from Reya, allowing her to rise to her feet, and then she turned to face him.

"You can't walk into Princi dressed like that."

Reya quickly looked Devi up and down. He was still dressed in the beige britches and tunic of a trainee Seeker.

"You'll have to change too."

Reya nodded towards the hatch that she had disappeared through each night, and Devi slinked away in its direction. When he emerged from below deck moments later, clad in the same loose-fitting tunic and tight trousers that Reya wore, he saw Reya at the bow of the ship, a small telescope held to her eye. In the distance, several tiny figures hovered on the horizon, their green sails barely visible.

"Sails," Reya said. "And they're Katai."

"Heading for Darmeen?"

"Heading home. Darmeen has several trade routes from Princi into The Hinterlands. At least to them they're trade routes. To our pirates, it's a hunting ground."

Reya slammed her telescope shut and turned towards the opposite side of the ship, where the heavy carcass of the blacktip shark still laid on the deck. Its stomach had been sliced open, and several chunks of flesh had already been carved from its side.

"We should eat," Reya said. "We must be getting close, and there's no point letting perfectly good blacktip go to waste."

Reya returned to the body of the shark, pulled her knife from her boot, and began carving away once more. She handed a strip of meat to Devi, and Devi sank his teeth into the flesh, tearing it away from the slick, dark skin of the animal with his teeth, blood and fat dripping down his chin as he chewed.

Far off in the distance, way out to sea, Devi caught a glimpse of another ship. It sat on the horizon as the Katai ships did, but it looked to be several times the size of those vessels.

"Look," Devi said, pointing out in its direction.

Reya took a single fleeting glance at the ship.

"Darmeenians."

"Is that the ship you've heard about?" Devi asked. "Have we missed it?"

Reya smiled and shook her head.

"No. That's just a regular trader."

"But it looks huge."

"Compared to a Katai ship, it is. But just wait until you see what they've been working on. It's going to be bigger than either of us can even imagine."

Way out in front of the ship, the Marakaya Mountains grew smaller and smaller until eventually they faded away completely.

"We'll reach land by midday," Reya said.

"You can see Princi from here?" Devi asked, raising his hand to his forehead and squinting his eyes as he gazed out towards the horizon.

"We can't just sail into Princi in a Katai pirate ship," Reya said. "We'll find somewhere to moor close to the mountains, and then we'll have to continue on foot."

"How long do you think that will take?"

"It's probably a full day's walk, but if we can catch a ride, we should get there by nightfall. We'll be close to the farmland, and we'll be just north of Darmaya. If we can find the main road, there should be plenty of carts we can make use of."

Reya made her way to the front of the ship, and she pulled the small sail there even tighter. Devi heard the mast creak, and he felt the ship lurch forwards a little.

"Come on," Reya said. "The wind is picking up. The sooner we get to shore, the sooner we get to Princi."

~

By the time Devi and Reya weighed anchor, the wind was blowing fiercely. The golden slopes of the Marakaya Mountains stretched away to their left, but they were low now and almost flat. In the distance up ahead, the Port of Princi Bay was just about visible. The coastline rose and fell with the roofs of the buildings there, and Devi could see the sails of several ships, some making their way into the port having successfully evaded the prowling eyes of the pirates, others making their way out to sea to try their own luck.

Reya leaned on the edge of the ship and gazed down into the water. She had loosened the sails and allowed the ship to drift as close to the land as she felt comfortable, but the water wasn't as clear as it was off the coast of Narkasee. Instead, it was murky and full of silt, and rocks beneath the surface were difficult to spot.

"We should be safe," she said. "Sharks won't swim this close to shore, and the crocs prefer our waters."

Reya climbed up onto the taffrail and waited for Devi to do the same. When he remained motionless on the deck, she looked back down at him.

"What's wrong?"

Devi glared back up at Reya, and the blank look on his face was answer enough. He was a farmer and had worked the fields of Rakhas until the day he had fled. He had never needed to swim.

"Just swing your arms and kick your legs," Reya said. "You'll get the hang of it."

Before Devi could speak a word in protest, Reya put her hands above her head and dove into the sea. A great plume of water burst up towards Devi where she had entered, and she emerged some way off, already driving her body through the waves.

Devi watched Reya for a moment from the deck of the ship. He wasn't particularly scared of the water, but he was anxious of the waves. They rose behind Reya, and he thought for a moment that they would come crashing down on top of her, consuming her body. Instead, Reya rose with the waves, and each time, they carried her a little closer to the shore.

Devi climbed up onto the taffrail, and he looked down at the water, the ship rising and falling beneath his trembling feet. For a moment, he thought he wouldn't be able to bring himself to jump. But then, he heard his father's voice in his head.

In darkness lie all terrors true,
Be they many, few, or one.
Yet, through the darkness, he pursues,
To lie in wait, the rising Son.

Just as Reya had done, Devi raised his hands above his head and dove forwards into the water. The sea exploded around him, and the salt stung his eyes as he plunged beneath its surface. For a moment, he struggled to find his bearings, but the sun was bright in the sky, and he forced his body back up towards its light.

When he reached the surface, Devi gasped for air, but he immediately found his mouth full of filthy saltwater. He turned towards the shore and began to kick his legs once more, forcing his face towards the sky each time he turned his head. The water was heavy, however, and his arms and legs seemed to flail helplessly, failing to impart their will on the sea. The pressure of the waves on his body was far greater than he could ever have imagined too, and it felt as if the air was being squeezed from his lungs as quickly as he could force it down.

Devi stole fleeting glances at the shoreline, and it didn't seem to be moving an inch. As he had watched on from the ship, the waves had seemed to carry Reya closer to the shore, lifting her along with them from beneath her body. Now that Devi was in the water, the waves seemed to crash down on him, forcing him towards the bottom of the sea rather than towards the shore. He continued to drive his arms forward and kick his legs behind, however, and the next time he looked towards the land, he saw Reya standing on the shore looking back out at him, and he knew he would make it.

"See," Reya said, taking Devi by the forearm and allowing him to share his weight with her. "I told you you'd get the hang of it."

Reya had been waiting on the shore for some time, but she was still struggling to regain her breath. The sun was high in the sky and, whilst the water would keep them cool for a short while, they would soon dry and begin to feel its heat.

Devi looked up towards the sun. Then, he bent at the waist and put his hands on his knees, taking several deep, slow, grateful breaths before he was able to speak.

"We can't stop," he said. "If the roads here are anything like back home, they'll be at their busiest around midday. If we're going to catch a cart, we'll need to keep moving."

"Then let's keep moving," Reya said.

~

The sun beat down relentlessly on Devi's skin, and it wasn't long before he wished he had taken one last bite of yellowfin before he leapt from the ship. His forehead poured with sweat, which ran down his cheeks and into his eyes until it almost felt as if he had not made it out of the sea at all. He and Reya walked steadily towards the road up ahead, and though it appeared empty, Devi could see the unmistakable mist of dust and sand that lingered around it, and he knew it wouldn't be long until another farmer's cart appeared in the near distance.

As he walked, Devi looked out across the vast expanse of fields on the other side of the road. Golden acres of wheat gave way to rich, green pastures, and each field was lined with rows of trees and hedges, some of which were decorated with plants and fruits in reds, purples, and oranges. The fields that ran directly alongside the roads were empty, but Devi could see farmers in the fields in the distance, toiling away at their harvest. Their heads popped up from amongst the crops momentarily before disappearing below once more.

Devi couldn't help but think of the fields of Rakhas, though they looked nothing like this anymore. All that was left of them was vacant dirt and smouldering ash, but he still remembered when they had been alive with colour. He saw wooden shacks at the edges of some of the fields, just like those that lined the streets of his own village back home, and he felt as if he would see his father emerge from one of the doors at any moment, beckoning him across the field to take up his scythe and put himself to work.

Devi had never been so far from home, and though Darmeen had always felt a world away from what he knew, it felt almost as if he was still in Katai.

When Devi and Reya finally reached the road, it was all but silent. Soon, however, Devi began to hear the low rumble of thunder in the distance, and he turned to see a single cart trundling down the road towards them and towards Princi. Devi looked around, but he saw nothing but sand. There was no way they could find somewhere to hide and steal onto the back of the cart unnoticed as it passed. If they were going to hitch a ride into Princi, they would have to force it to stop.

As Devi scanned the ground around the road up ahead, he saw several rocks, some large and some small. If a cart was to run over one of the larger rocks, it would likely be enough to damage a wheel. Devi had spent his childhood fixing broken ox carts with his father, and repairing the damage by the side of the road might be enough to secure them a passage into Princi by way of gratitude alone. But these carts likely travelled this road every day. Their drivers would be too experienced to overlook such a danger and, when they simply steered around the rock, Devi and Reya would be left behind.

Devi looked over one particularly large rock, but it wasn't the rock itself that had caught his attention. There, on top of the rock, basking in the heat of the early afternoon sun and barely noticeable thanks to the light brown colouring across its back, was a sand snake. Devi saw the cloud of dust beginning to pick up on the horizon, and he knew just what to do.

"Quick," he said to Reya. "Get on the ground."

Devi grabbed Reya by the arm and dragged her the short distance that remained between them and the large rock at the side of the road.

"Lay down there," he said.

"Why?"

"Don't ask questions. Just trust me."

Reya scanned the ground beneath her feet. She reluctantly lowered herself first to her knees and then to her back.

"Roll around a little."

Reya glared back up at Devi.

"Hurry up," he insisted. "Just do it."

Reya began to roll her body from side to side unenthusiastically. Devi bent down and pulled one leg of her trousers out of her boot.

"And now moan," he said.

Reya stopped rolling and sat bolt upright.

"What do you mean moan?" she said, her voice sharp and her eyes accusatory.

Devi put his foot on Reya's shoulder and pushed her back towards the ground.

"Just moan," he said. "Like you're in pain."

Devi turned back in the direction of the oncoming cart. It was making slow and steady progress towards him, and he could hear its wheels thundering against the ground now.

"Just hurry up. Before it gets here."

Reya held Devi's gaze for a moment. Then, she huffed a short breath and laid back down in the sand at the side of the road. She rolled from side to side once more and began to moan convincingly.

Devi turned to face the cart that was inching ever closer. He threw his hands above his head and waved them frantically from side to side. He jumped up and down too so that he was a frenzy of action. As the cart drew near, he began to yell above Reya's agonising moans, begging the cart driver to stop.

At first, the cart did not slow, and Devi thought the driver was going to continue right on past him. Devi began to point in the direction of Reya, however, rolling and writhing on the ground at his feet, and the cart pulled up to a stop beside him.

"Thank you so much," Devi said, breathless.

"What's his problem?" the cart driver asked, nodding towards Reya.

"Sand snake," Devi said. "He doesn't have much time."

Devi dropped to his knees beside Reya and stroked the back of his hand against her forehead. Reya suddenly let out a piercing wail and clutched desperately at her ankle.

"Please, sir," Devi begged. "Take us with you to Princi."

The cart driver looked Devi dead in the eyes. Then, he looked Reya up and down. He didn't seem convinced, and Devi was sure he was going to snap his reigns and drive his horses on. Just then, however, Reya leapt to her feet, abandoning all pretence of injury.

"Stop!" Reya called out, just as the driver was preparing to pull away. "I have money!"

Devi turned to face Reya as she pulled two gold coins out of her pocket.

"Two now, two more when we arrive."

The driver looked down at the coins, one of which bore King Vagan's face on its upturned side. He looked over Reya sceptically, turning his nose up a little. Then, he reached out and snatched the two coins from her palm.

"Alright," he said. "You boys better jump on the back."

"Thank you, sir," Devi said, already moving towards the back of the cart. "You won't even know we're there."

"Make sure I don't," the driver huffed.

Devi followed Reya to the back of the cart and waited as she hoisted herself up onto the burlap sacks that were stored there. Then, he climbed into the back of the cart himself, the driver snapped his reigns, and the cart began to move again.

XVII

"Reya."

Devi nudged Reya's sleeping body with his elbow.

"Reya, wake up. I think we're almost there."

The sun was low in the sky as the farmer's cart began the final leg of its journey into Princi. Devi and Reya had sat atop the burlap sacks in the back of the cart, riding the bumps and dips of the road as comfortably as they could, whilst the horses' hooves up ahead relentlessly pounded the dirt and sand beneath them. The horses were less sturdy than the oxen that Devi was used to, but they were much faster and were able to cover an impressive distance in little time.

Devi turned to face the front of the cart, and he peered over the top of the burlap sack that he was leaning against. On each side of the road, the fields had given way to several clusters of buildings constructed primarily of timber and packed sand, each appearing to have been shoddily thrown together by unskilled hands. Their walls were sloped, their roofs uneven, and some were crumbling at the corners. Most of the buildings appeared dark and empty, but off in the near distance, Princi glowed a gentle orange, the light of the setting sun coalescing with the flames of the torches that had already been lit for the evening ahead.

"We're getting close," Devi said, nudging Reya again, more firmly this time so that her half-closed eyes shot open.

Reya groaned a little as she forced herself upright and looked ahead of the cart. Then, she turned back to Devi and shot him a grave look.

"You should have woken me sooner," she said.

"Why?"

"Because we need to get off this cart."

"But we're not even in Princi yet."

"Exactly," Reya said, ensuring that her voice remained low enough to be masked by the wheels that rumbled beneath her. "I handed that man two copper coins with my father's face on. And you saw the look he gave us when I was rolling around on the ground. He didn't buy it. Not for a second."

Suddenly, Devi understood why Reya looked so panicked. She was right – the driver of the cart hadn't taken their bait, but he had been content to allow them to ride in his cart as long as there was something in it for him. There was no way for him to know who they were, but it hadn't taken him long to figure out they were up to no good, and the coins would have all but confirmed they were from Katai. As soon as they were in Princi, and Reya had handed over the remaining coins she had promised, the man would turn them over to the Darmeenian authorities.

"We need to get off this cart," Reya said again as she shifted her body forward to its edge.

Devi did the same, and their legs dangled over the back of the cart as it continued to rumble over the uneven ground below. Devi looked back over his shoulder at the driver, whose eyes were fixed on the road ahead. Devi had kept his word. He and Reya had been silent, and it was possible that the driver had forgotten about their presence entirely, but Devi wasn't eager to wait around to find out.

"On my signal," he said.

Reya nodded her assent.

Devi scanned the road ahead. There were a handful of shacks on one side and a single long, low building made of packed sand on the other. Devi kept his eyes forward as the cart approached the buildings. Then, when they were shrouded in the shadows of the walls on either side of the road, he gave Reya a gentle nudge with his elbow.

"Let's go," he said.

Devi forced his body into the air with his hands and propelled himself from the edge of the moving cart. As soon as he landed, he rolled forward over his right shoulder, harnessing the momentum of his body and breaking his fall. Then, he rose and darted to the side of the road, forcing his back against the wall of the closest wooden shack. He looked across the road, and he saw Reya in a similar position, pressed tightly against the wall of the building there.

The rolling thunder of horses' hooves continued to fill the air, and the wooden wheels of the cart continued to thunder against the sandy road at Devi's back. He had hit the floor with a thud, but he was almost certain that the sound had been masked and that the driver would be unaware of his and Reya's absence until he arrived at his final destination.

Devi held his position until the rumble of the farmer's cart had grown so faint that it had all but disappeared. Then, he peered around the corner of the wall that his back was pressed against, and he made his way out into the middle of the empty road. On the opposite side, Reya emerged from behind another of the wooden shacks, and she joined Devi at his side, each casting their gaze down the short stretch that remained between themselves and the port city of Princi, the smaller of Darmeen's two capital cities.

Even from afar, Devi could hear the bustle of the marketplace and the port. It hung in the air like the buzzing of a distant swarm of locusts, and it grew slowly louder and louder as he and Reya began down the road in its direction.

When Devi had looked out across the endless fields thick with wheat from the back of the cart, he had felt as if he was back in Katai. Even as he walked past the wooden shacks and packed-sand buildings that the fields had given way to, he was reminded of home. The closer that he drew to Princi, however, the less familiar Darmeen felt. Already, the clusters of buildings on each side of the road had begun to form neat and regimented lines that criss-crossed at right angles, and up ahead it looked as if they were no longer made from wood and sand but instead by sturdy blocks of stone. Even the dusty ground beneath their feet eventually gave way to stone blocks that had been sunk deep into the dirt to form roads and paths that snaked away from the central passageway. Soon, the buildings became so densely packed that Devi and Reya were surrounded on all sides, and as they continued to walk, the streets became busier too.

The bulk of the crowd, which seemed to grow with each passing step, was heading in the same direction as Devi and Reya – towards the centre of Princi. There were some amongst it that swam against the tide, however, likely heading back out towards the wooden shacks between the city and the fields. Some in the crowd were dressed in rags similar to those that Devi had grown used to wearing himself, but others wore thick, ornate robes that enveloped their bodies and brushed the blocks of stone at their feet, and their necks and wrists seemed to be adorned by heavy, gold jewellery, which glimmered under the soft light of the torches that lined the streets.

As Devi moved amongst the crowd, he couldn't help but feel conspicuous. The clothes that Reya had given him were nondescript enough not to draw attention, but still it felt as if those that passed him were aware that he was not one of them.

Alleyways cut between the buildings, and shadows lingered there, hidden from the searching glow of the flame torches in the main streets. As Devi turned a corner between two rows of buildings, he heard the whispers of the sea for the first time, and he knew that they must be drawing near to the port. At the end of the street, however, a throng of people were gathered beneath a great stone archway. Some lingered in small groups, withered sandals on their feet and woven baskets tucked under their arms. Others pushed through and made their way back up the street towards Devi and Reya.

"Follow my lead," Devi said, stepping in front of Reya and lowering his head to make himself as inconspicuous as possible.

Devi approached the crowd, and Reya followed. They pushed their way through the small gaps that they could find, fighting against the tide that now flowed more heavily against them. When Devi passed under the stone archway and raised his head on the other side, the sight was enough to stop him in his tracks.

A vast, open area stretched out before him. The ground was covered with large stone bricks that had been perfectly cut and arranged alongside each other with tremendous precision. Spilled across the stone floor was a sea of people larger than any Devi had ever seen, and they cascaded throughout the space like gentle waves. All across the area, stone structures rose from the ground, and they were covered at their tops by lengths of fabric stretched thin. They looked just like the wooden structures in the market in Narkasee, only sturdier and topped by roofs of white, rather than the green of Katai. The Narkasee market would be all but empty by now, and many of the stalls here had also been abandoned. Small crowds of people continued to gather around a handful of the structures that were still occupied, however.

"It's enormous," Devi said, as he and Reya made their way slowly through the marketplace.

"This is Darmeen," Reya said. "Everything is bigger here."

Devi thought back to the ships that he had seen lining the horizon as he and Reya had begun to approach land. The single Darmeenian trader had dwarfed the Katai vessels. In his mind, he tried to picture the ship they had come in search of too, but he struggled to imagine anything much larger than the Darmeenian trader that he had seen could remain afloat.

Then, Devi's head snapped to his right as the sound of a cracking whip suddenly split the air.

"Get moving," he heard a gruff voice bark from the same direction.

A short distance away was a large stone platform, raised above the ground so that it would have been level with Devi's shoulders. On top of the platform, a man stood with a whip in one hand, which dangled loosely at his side. The other hand pointed at the ground, where a dark-skinned man laid face down, his palms flat against the stone, struggling to force his body up. The first man lifted his whip once more and snapped it against the second man's back. Devi felt the tail of the whip sear into his own flesh as he watched on. But the man on the ground did not falter in his efforts, nor did he collapse in pain. Instead, his arms trembling violently, he forced his upper body from the ground and locked his elbows.

"See," the first man yelled, as if he had somehow triumphed. "He is strong! He is fit! Most importantly, he is resilient!"

The crowd that had formed around the man murmured as he spoke. Those amongst it were dressed in long, white trousers that had been tucked into their high boots so that they swelled at the thighs. They wore patterned tunics that clung tightly to their bulging midriffs, and they wore wide brimmed hats that hid their eyes and their necks.

"I'll offer twenty pieces," one man in the crowd shouted.

The lower portion of his face was covered almost entirely by a thick, grey moustache, which seemed almost to have spoken on his behalf.

"Twenty pieces?" the man on the platform scoffed. "He's worth fifty, at least."

"Twenty pieces and no more," the man in the crowd grumbled.

The dark-skinned man continued to hold his position, his chest pointed at the ground, his arms still locked in place.

"Twenty five pieces," another man in the crowd yelled.

"Still too little," the man atop the platform shouted back. "Will anyone offer forty?"

Devi looked towards the back of the platform. Rows of cages were lined there, and though each of them was empty, Devi knew that, if he and Reya had made it to the market earlier, they would each have been filled with another half-naked body. Though all that was left of him was his father's stories, Devi couldn't help but think of his great-grandfather, stolen from The Hinterlands like the man on the platform and sold as a slave by the Darmeenians. The cages at the back of the raised platform appeared old and rusted, and it was possible that it may have been one of them that had held his great-grandfather all those years ago.

In that moment, Devi felt ready to clamber up onto the platform, tear the whip from the slaver's hand, and rip a hole in his ornate tunic as he brought it against his own back. He could almost hear the screams of the slaver as the whip tore his flesh apart. Devi knew he would be thrown from the platform the second he stepped foot upon it, however. He also knew that the men in the dwindling crowd would be just as willing to place a price on his head the moment that they discovered that he was from Katai. There was nothing that Devi could do for the man on the platform except make it back out of Princi alive and head for The Sands.

Devi turned to face Reya. Her jaw was stiff, and a steely mist had settled in her eyes.

"Let's go," Devi said.

"Let's go," Reya repeated.

As Devi and Reya continued to follow the gentle calling of the sea, they heard the slaver's whip crack a final time. Either the man at his feet had finally collapsed and the whip was his punishment, or a price had finally been settled, and the slaver couldn't resist lashing out one final, parting blow. Devi and Reya would never know.

By the time they reached the opposite side of the marketplace, the area had thinned out significantly. The market was lined by a low wall on its far side, and just above the wall, Devi could see the rippling waters of the sea. He knew that the port itself must be below, though it was not yet in sight.

On the water, the large, wooden ships that he had seen from a distance earlier made their way into shore, lumbering across the waves entirely without the grace and elegance of the ship that he and Reya had sailed. They looked slow and cumbersome, but their sides were lined with cannons, and Devi could only imagine the size of their holds.

As Devi began to approach the low wall at the edge of the marketplace, the tip of a mast began to rise above the smooth, flawless edges of the stone. It grew taller and taller as he neared, great, white sails also beginning to come into view. When he finally reached the wall and gazed down the sandy slope on the other side, his breath left his body entirely.

There, sitting low in the water between two great, stone walkways that jutted out into the sea, was the largest ship he had ever seen – the largest ship anyone had ever seen. It faced the horizon, and its stern was as wide as the King's Keep. Several ornate sculptures had been carved into the wood at the back of the ship, and they each weaved around the sculpted letters that formed its name – The Kraken. The front of the ship looked to be adorned by a great figure in the shape of a child, which had been carved into the wood of the bow, though Devi could not quite make it out from his position far off. Countless masts rose from The Kraken's deck, and they were lined with enough white fabric to form a thousand sails. It looked as if the whole of Katai could board the ship, and there would still be room on the deck.

Directly below Devi and Reya, the low wall gave way to a steep, sandy slope that led down to the dock. The dock itself was another great, stone walkway, which spanned the entire length of the coast, and hundreds of men scurried to and fro across it. At regular intervals along the dock, shorter, narrower stone walkways cut out into the water, and boats had been moored at a number of them. Compared to Reya's ship, Devi thought they had looked enormous. Compared to the behemoth that sat in the centre of the dock, they looked tiny.

Devi and Reya watched from afar as scores of men made their way up a long, wooden ramp towards the deck of The Kraken, bending at the waist to roll large, sturdy barrels ahead of them. A line of men ran in the opposite direction too, back down the ramp empty-handed and out onto the dock. There, waiting for them at the base of the wooden ramp, was another collection of barrels, and each man tipped one onto its side and began rolling it up towards the ship once more.

Away at the back of the dock stood several great, stone structures that were covered by white fabric, and wooden boxes were stacked high beneath them. Devi and Reya each watched as one man dug his hands into one of the boxes and pulled out an armful of fresh, silver fish. He tossed them into an empty barrel before turning his attention to the stack of boxes alongside the fish.

There, he found a small, silver tool like a tiny shovel, and he dug it into the contents of the box. When the man lifted the shovel out of the container, it was heaped with glittering, white salt. Devi watched on as the man tossed the salt into the barrel over the fish, and then as he repeated the process a number of times, first heaving an armful of fish into the barrel, then layering them with a heavy scoop of salt.

"We're just in time," Reya said. "They must be leaving tonight."

"How can you tell?" Devi asked.

"They're packing fresh fish. They won't want all those barrels sat on the ship for days rotting. If they know anything, salting and packing should be the last thing they do before setting sail."

Devi and Reya each continued to watch the men as they worked. When the barrel appeared to be full, the man that had packed it took up a lid from a pile on the ground and laid it in place atop the barrel. Then, with the butt of the tool that he still held in his hand, he pounded the lid securely into place and tipped the barrel onto its side. A second worker took control of the barrel, rolling it towards the base of the wooden plank that led up to the ship, and a third worker appeared from further down the dock, rolling an empty barrel into place beside the first man and standing it upright.

"Any bright ideas?" Reya asked.

Devi's eyes scanned the docks, and his mind searched for a way to get himself and Reya onto the ship. The dock was busy – far too busy to simply sneak onto the ship directly. But Devi's eyes drifted towards the rows of empty barrels that were being wheeled over to the boxes at the back of the dock, watching as the men filled them with fish and salt before securing the lid.

Then, they followed the trail of barrels to the base of the wooden plank that led up to the ship.

"I think I might have something," Devi said. "Think you can climb inside one of those barrels without being seen?"

"I think *I* can. But I don't think you can."

Devi turned to Reya. Her face bore the same sneering, teasing expression that had already begun to leave a sour taste in his mouth.

"You just worry about yourself," Devi said, and he emerged from behind the rock.

Devi scurried down the side of the hill, ducking behind rock formations and making use of the long grass as he went. Reya followed close behind. When they reached the low wall that gave way to the docks below, Devi sat on the ground and peered over its edge. The drop was significant, but he was confident that he could make it safely if he hung off the wall first. The white fabric that stretched across the wooden rafters of the structure would conceal him from above, and the boxes of fish that were stacked high would hide him from the workers on the docks.

"I'll go first," Devi said. "You follow after."

"Yes, Captain," Reya replied, smirking.

Devi waited until another batch of empty barrels had been deposited, and until the men out in front had begun to fill them with salt and fish. Then, he made his move.

Devi climbed over the edge of the wall and gripped the rough stone as tightly as he could. He allowed his feet to fall towards the ground, and he winced as the stone dug into the tips of his fingers. Then, he allowed himself to fall, landing on his heels and toppling over backwards. Before he was even able to push himself up from the ground, Reya made a flawless landing next to him.

"Take your time," she said, already shuffling towards the stacked boxes of fish.

Devi and Reya each crept between the boxes until they were within earshot of the men working out in front. The men continued to scoop salt and armfuls of fish into the barrels, pounding the lids into place once they were full, before turning their attention to the empty barrels that had been rolled over to replace them.

"What now?" Reya asked.

Devi had planned to find his way into one of the barrels, but the men were working too quickly, and the empty barrels did not stay empty long enough for him to find his opportunity. Just then, however, Devi heard water splashing from across the dock, and a commotion suddenly picked up.

"You fool!" Devi heard one of the men close to him shout, and as he peered around the stack of boxes that he leaned against, he saw the man vacate his post and start running towards the ship.

At the base of the wooden plank that led up to the ship, Devi saw a man gripping a barrel that was hanging perilously over the water. He was leaning back, trying with all his might to drag the barrel back to safety. All the while, fish fell from the barrel and into the sea below.

"Quick," Devi said. "Now."

He shunted Reya in the direction of the empty barrels, his eyes scanning the dock for any workers that had not been distracted by the commotion. Reya leapt to her feet and clambered into an empty barrel just as the man on the plank lost his grip, his own barrel tumbling into the water. The first splash was followed soon after by a second, the worker himself being tossed into the sea to retrieve it.

Devi rose to climb into his own barrel, lifting two lids from the ground to secure both himself and Reya inside. Just as he did so, however, he looked up to see the men returning to their posts. Devi stood, with one leg inside his barrel, and he stared back at the men that were bearing down on him.

"Do you want to join him?" one of the men yelled.

"I'm sorry?" Devi said, his heart beating through his chest.

"I said do you want to join him?" the man repeated, pointing one arm back in the direction of the water that he had just tossed another worker into.

"No," Devi said.

It was the only response that seemed anything close to acceptable.

"Then stop fooling around and get back to work."

Devi removed his leg from the barrel and looked around. Each of the men made their way back to their posts and continued to scoop salt and fish into their barrels.

"What did I say?" Reya teased, her voice echoing around the wooden container at Devi's hip. "I knew you wouldn't make it."

"Shut up," Devi barked, and he kicked at the base of the barrel.

The man glared at Devi as he arrived back at his post. He took an empty barrel from the row, and Devi could see Reya out of the periphery of his eye looking up at him. The man carried his barrel a short distance further down the line and began to fill it with fish, his eyes still locked to Devi's own. Devi held the man's gaze as he reached into a box himself and took out an armful of fish.

"Don't you dare," Reya whispered viciously from inside her barrel.

Devi held the fish over the barrel's opening and looked down at Reya.

"I haven't got much choice," he said, and he dropped the fish onto Reya's head.

Devi turned back to the stack of boxes and took up one of the small, silver shovels. He scooped out a shovelful of salt, the man to his right still staring intently at him, and he dropped the salt into the barrel too.

Finally, the man looked away, scooping up another armful of fish, picking up his pace so that it matched the rate at which he had been working before the disturbance. Devi took up one of the two lids that he had dropped and placed it on top of the barrel.

"Sit tight," he said, peering down at Reya. "I'll come and find you tonight."

Devi thrust the butt of his shovel onto the lid until it was held securely in place. Then, he tipped the barrel onto its side, and he watched as Reya was rolled away across the dock and up the plank onto the ship. Then, he took another empty barrel from the row, scooped up another armful of fish, and tossed it inside.

XVIII

Devi waited until the sky was pitch black and The Kraken had settled on the open water before he went in search of Reya. The great ship had lumbered away from the dock shortly after the sun had set, and Princi, like Narkasee, had quickly faded into the darkening mist of the horizon.

Initially, the ship had been busy and alive, its deck awash with sailors and workers of every rank and station. They had hurried to and fro hauling anchors, hoisting sails, and plotting courses, and Devi had done his best to remain out of sight. He had lingered near the great stern of the ship, where a stairway on either side led up to a raised platform that housed the steering mechanisms, and several doorways between them seemed to lead below deck. He moved this way and that as the other workers did, ensuring that he appeared busy with the examination of a rope or the hauling of a barrel, but ultimately he had done nothing to contribute to the successful launch of the ship, his efforts only serving to create the illusion of meaningful work.

Once the ship was surging slowly but relentlessly through the water, the commotion had quickly died away, and the ship had become as still as the sky above and the water below. Men still stood on the platforms at the very peaks of the masts, and occasionally a sailor would adjust some length of rope at the base of one of the countless sails that hovered above the deck like great clouds, but most were already somewhere below. They had likely spent all day loading the ship, and the true work of sailing such a gargantuan vessel would likely begin with the rise of the sun. Devi didn't blame them for taking the opportunity to sleep. If he could find somewhere to curl up until morning, he would. But he needed to find Reya.

Devi leaned over the ship's taffrail, partly because it seemed as if the sickness he had felt every time he had previously stepped foot on a ship might be returning, and partly so that he cut an inconspicuous figure, hidden somewhat by the darkness of the night, his body camouflaged in front of the thick, wooden pillars that held the taffrail aloft.

As Devi gazed down the side of the ship, he marvelled once more at the size of the vessel. On Reya's boat, he had been barely more than an arm's length from the sea. Now, he felt as if he was standing atop the Salt

Cliffs, peering over their edge at the still waters of the Tharakun below. Until he had seen it for the first time, Devi could never have imagined a ship so large. It was almost a wonder it was even able to remain afloat.

Still gazing down at the water, Devi slowly shifted his body along the taffrail to his left. The steering mechanisms atop the platform at the stern of the ship were manned, and a handful of sailors lingered in small groups way down at the bow end, but the area of the deck immediately behind Devi was empty, and the doors were silent and still. It seemed that those above deck would be there until morning, and the same could be said of those below.

Devi turned around and leaned his back against the taffrail, his elbows resting on top. There looked to be seven doors set at regular intervals between the two sets of stairs that led up to the stern platform. The glass windows of six of the doors were black, but the door at the centre glowed a dull orange. Devi wasn't sure where the door led, but he was confident there would be people behind it and that he would remain above deck should he choose to pass through it. He wanted to avoid close contact with people as much as possible, however, and he knew he needed to get below deck if he was to find Reya. With six black doors to choose from, and no indication where any of them might lead, Devi simply looked from left to right to ensure he had not drawn any unwanted attention, and he slipped through the one closest to him.

As Devi pressed the door quietly shut behind him, he was immediately shrouded in almost complete darkness. Only the light of the moon shone through the thin, glass windowpane at his back, struggling to illuminate a short, narrow passage ahead of him, as well as the first few steps of a staircase that seemed to lead below deck. Devi placed his hand on the wall of the passageway to guide him, and he began to tread slowly and carefully down the steps.

"In darkness lie all terrors true," Devi whispered to himself as the light slowly disappeared behind him.

As Devi groped his way forward, it felt as if the wall bent around to his left, the staircase doubling back on itself as it continued to fall away into the bowels of the ship. Devi followed his hand around the corner, his feet finding a second set of steps, and once more he began to descend. Eventually, the wooden boards beneath Devi's feet flattened out, and he knew he had reached the first of the lower levels of the ship.

Reya had been right when she had invited him below the deck of her own ship. Though the water was calm to begin with, the ship felt even more steady than it had above deck. It still rocked gently from side to side, however, slowly lumbering away to its left a little before slumping heavily back to its right. Devi crept forward in the darkness, but his hands could no longer find anything solid to guide them. Instead, he could only hear the creaking of wood on both sides and the gentle breaths of the waves as they lapped at the ship's hull.

Then, Devi heard a sudden hiss away to his right, and he stopped in his tracks. The sound burst forth into the stillness of the air, but it quickly faded away. It sounded almost like the hiss of a rattlesnake or the angry protestations of a stray cat. When Devi turned to face the noise, however, he saw a tiny orange flame glowing in the pitch black.

The flame floated slowly upwards, and then, for just a moment, it lit the face of a man. The flame flickered a little, and it appeared to increase in size, but suddenly the tiny flame died away completely, and a second larger flame replaced it. The larger flame lit the man's face, and Devi could see that its source was a small candle that the man held out in front of him.

The man's face was dark and bearded. His eyes were set back beneath his brow, and his hair hung in thick strands across his forehead. Behind the man's head, Devi could see the thick fabric of a hammock knotted around metal hooks, and the creaking of wood all around him suddenly made sense. He was surrounded by men who were sleeping silently, their bodies swinging from left to right with the motion of the waves, their weight tugging at the wooden beams that their metal hooks and hammocks were attached to.

Devi stood motionless in the centre of the room. He glared over at the man who laid back in his hammock, his candle held in one hand at his chest. The man's other hand appeared at his mouth, and it left a small, brown cigar between his lips, which the flame of the candle lit.

As the man laid back and smoked, Devi was able to get a good look at him. His face was marked by a long scar that ran from the brow above one eye down his cheek almost to his mouth. He appeared to be wearing a white tunic, which matched the colour of his hammock, but between the two appeared to be a beige cape, which extended over the man's head in the form of a loose-fitting hood. Devi was in no doubt that the man was a Darmeenian Stone Seeker. He and Reya had not seen a single Seeker thus far, but it was clear now that they must have been aboard before they had even reached the dock.

Devi began to shuffle backwards as slowly and as silently as he could, doing his best to retrace his steps exactly. He had not encountered any obstacles in the darkness as he had made his way down and into the room, but he could see nothing beyond the glow of the candle away to his right. He had no idea how many other Seekers were around him, and he had no idea how close he was to them. Devi continued to back away until his heel hit the last of the steps that he had descended moments earlier. There, he turned, clambered up the steps as silently as he could manage, and emerged back out onto the deck.

The night air was cooler than below deck, and Devi gulped it down. He hadn't even realised he had been holding his breath, but his chest heaved in an effort to refill his lungs. He made his way past the other two doors on the port side of the ship, figuring that they, like the door that led down into the Seeker's quarters, would likely lead him towards people he had no intention of meeting. There was only one person Devi was searching for, and she was currently trapped inside a barrel filled with fish. Devi made his way to the starboard side of the ship and, still without any indication of which direction he should take, ducked through the first door that he found there.

Once more, Devi was shrouded in darkness, but the moon lit the first few steps of a staircase that led down beneath the deck of the ship as it had before, and Devi thought he could see the faint orange glow of a flame from below. He descended the steps, his hand again following the wall as it doubled back on itself. Making his way slowly down the second set of steps, and crouching slightly to allow himself to peer ahead, Devi approached the end of the staircase. There, he saw a single flame torch at the end of a long corridor, which was lined on either side by wooden, windowless doors. He had gambled with two doors already, and he was not eager to try his luck again, but the corridor seemed to give way at its end to another set of steps that led even deeper below deck.

As Devi approached the bottom of the third staircase, he finally breathed a sigh of relief. In the faint, orange light from the torch above, Devi could barely make out a long, narrow room that was lined on each side by hundreds upon hundreds of barrels. He paused for a moment and listened, but the space was completely silent. He could just about feel the rhythm of the ship as it moved against the waves, but he couldn't hear a sound.

"Reya," Devi whispered as he moved. "Reya, are you in here?"

He tapped on each barrel as he passed, but none offered him a response.

"Reya," he whispered again.

For a moment, Devi thought he heard his name from somewhere up ahead. He stopped, but the room was still silent.

"Reya," Devi said once more. "Is that you?"

This time, he was sure he heard a response.

Devi continued to make his way down the narrow space, tapping at the barrels on his left and his right as he went. Then, he heard a voice up ahead, clear and distinct yet muffled by the confinement of a barrel.

"Devi, if you don't hurry up, I swear I'll…"

Devi smiled.

"What's that?" he called out, a little louder than his previous whispers had been. "I didn't hear you."

"Devi," Reya growled, her voice low but terrifying nonetheless.

Devi tapped against the next barrel, and Reya tapped back. He took hold of the lid and pulled, but it was stuck tight.

"I think I may have been a bit heavy-handed earlier. Can you push from inside?"

Devi dug his fingers beneath the ridge of the lid and pulled as hard as he could manage. He heard Reya's hand thumping at the bottom of the lid from inside the barrel, and finally they managed to pull it free.

Reya stood upright, her upper body emerging from the barrel but her lower half remaining inside. She glared at Devi in the half-light, and Devi stepped back a little, the smell of the salted fish almost enough to overwhelm him. He could just make out Reya's face, and it glistened a little in the darkness. He couldn't tell whether she was covered with sweat or salty fish juice, but he wasn't sure that it much mattered.

"You took your time," Reya grunted, lifting herself out of the barrel.

Before Devi was able to reply, the light at the end of the passage suddenly grew brighter, and footsteps sounded against the wooden boards of the stairs he had descended a short time before.

"Get down," Devi said, and he and Reya each ducked behind a barrel.

As the light at the bottom of the stairs continued to flood into the narrow passage, Devi peered around the edge of the barrel that he hid behind. Walking towards him, Devi saw a small boy, with a flame torch in his hand. The boy looked to be slightly younger and slightly smaller than Devi himself, and he stopped at one of the first barrels, tugging at its lid. Just as Devi had on his first attempt, the boy failed to pull the lid free. He bent at the knees and explored the barrel with the light of his torch. It didn't seem to be what he was looking for, however, and he began to make his way down the narrow passage towards Devi once more.

The boy swung the torch from left to right as he continued to look over the barrels, and soon he was almost upon Devi. Devi hugged tight to his barrel as the boy wandered close, the light of the torch filling the narrow passage around him. Just then, a second set of footsteps began to echo at the far end of the passage.

"Boy!"

The footsteps were accompanied this time by the low, grumbling voice of a man.

“Show yourself, boy,” he called into the darkness.

The boy paused for a moment, and Devi thought he saw him turn back in the direction of the man who called out to him.

“The captain needs his rum,” the man shouted. “Keep him waiting any longer and it’ll be a beating for you.”

Devi turned to face Reya, who was hidden behind a barrel slightly further along the passage. He opened his mouth to whisper, but the boy was too close. Instead, he moved his lips silently.

“The captain,” he mouthed.

Reya had heard the words too, and her eyes flickered in the light of the torch. Devi nodded towards the boy just on the other side of the barrels, and Reya nodded back at him. It seemed to Devi that she knew his intentions.

The second the boy had passed Devi’s barrel and he had sight of his back, Devi grabbed hold of one of the boy’s ankles, and he came crashing to the floor. Reya was immediately upon the boy, and Devi watched as she pulled her knife seemingly out of thin air, held it to the boy’s throat, and clamped his mouth shut with her other hand. The torch the boy had carried now laid on the floor, but Devi quickly picked it up and held it over the face of the boy, whose eyes were wide with terror, his entire body trembling violently. The boy looked back up at Devi, and then his eyes shot over to Reya, who continued to hold her knife close to his throat.

"Don't say a word," Reya whispered.

She grabbed the boy by the collarbone with her free hand and forced him up against the side of the ship behind the barrels. At the same moment, the man emerged from the steps and into the half-light of the narrow passage. Devi scrambled to his feet, and he turned to face the man with the flame torch in his hand.

"There you are, boy," the man said, striding down the passage in Devi's direction. "What are you doing down here?"

When the man was only a few paces away, Reya popped up from behind the barrel, her knife sheathed and hidden once more, the trembling boy concealed away at her back. The man stopped dead in his tracks.

"Oh," he said. "There are two of you down here."

The man narrowed his eyes, and a knowing grin fell over his face.

"Never mind," he said. "I know exactly what you're doing down here."

"We're getting the captain's rum," Devi said.

"Well that's funny," the man replied, still smirking. "Because the rum stores are upstairs."

He grabbed Devi by the shoulder and shoved him back towards the wooden steps at the other end of the passage.

"And you, boy," he said, shoving Reya away in the same direction.

Devi and Reya marched back towards the stairs as the footsteps of the man followed close behind. They climbed the stairwell and emerged back out into the corridor that was lined with doors. Devi opened the first door on his right and, just as the man had suggested, it was lined with metal shelves on both sides, which were stacked with row upon row of bottles of rum. Devi grabbed a bottle by the neck and shut the door behind him.

"Hurry up," the man grunted as he joined Devi and Reya in the corridor once more. "Or it won't just be the captain that gives you a beating."

Devi and Reya clambered back up the second set of steps more quickly than they had the first. The man was close behind, and he stepped back out onto the deck of the ship just moments after they had emerged themselves. Though Devi had led Reya and the man out of the narrow passage and up onto the deck, he assumed the man would take the lead once he was able. The three stood awkwardly on the deck of the ship, however, each looking to the other to be the first to move.

"Get a move on!"

The man screamed suddenly in Devi's face, and he struck him across the cheek with his open palm. Then, he pointed in the direction of the door at the centre of the ship, the windows of which continued to glow a faint and distant orange.

"Get the captain his rum," the man yelled, his eyes level with Devi's own.

Devi stepped away from the man in the direction of the captain's cabin, and Reya began to do the same. The man placed a hand on Reya's shoulder, however, stopping her in her tracks.

"Not you, boy" he said, his voice low now. "I think you two have seen just about enough of each other. Off to the kitchen with you."

Devi opened the door and looked back towards Reya. Her eyes met his own across the deck as she was led away by the man, his hand still locked tightly to her shoulder. Then, Devi turned away, closed the door behind him, and began down the long corridor towards the captain's cabin.

XIX

"What took you so long, boy?"

The captain was a small man with the stomach of a man twice his size. He wore a pistol at his hip, but his stomach bulged over its handle so much that it would have been exceedingly difficult to draw. His face was long and narrow, however, his nose thin and bony and turned down towards his mouth at its tip. He sat behind a large and ornate oak desk at the back of his cabin, and he was dressed in a long, blue overcoat, the collar of which stood tall and stiff at the back of his neck.

Two men stood behind the captain, one on either side, and a line of men stood opposite, but they craned their necks around to glare at Devi as he entered.

"I'm sorry, Captain," Devi said, loitering awkwardly by the door he had just passed through. "I lost my way."

"Well don't just stand there," the captain barked. "Rum! Now!"

As Devi stepped forward, he felt the captain's eyes, as well as those of the other men, scouring him from head to toe. He thought back to the boy he and Reya had left below deck. He was unassuming, indistinctive, and forgettable, and he had seemed to be roughly Devi's age and height. There would be thousands of boys like him in Darmeen, and there were likely one hundred others like him on the ship. For once, Devi was grateful that he was equally unassuming and equally indistinctive, but he still couldn't help but feel conspicuous as he approached the captain's desk.

Devi held the bottle out towards the captain, and the moment he did so, he caught a flash of the branded scar that ran across his wrist – the two interwoven heads of wheat that marked him as a child of Katai. If there was one thing about him that *was* distinctive, that was it. Should the captain ever discover he was from Katai, Devi would be tossed overboard without a second thought. Reya, too. Devi did his best to hold the captain's gaze as he reached for the rum bottle, and he snatched his hand away the moment he was able, pulling the sleeve of his tunic down over his palm and holding it there with the tips of his fingers.

The captain continued to glare at Devi as he took the bottle and pulled the cork from its neck, and for a moment, Devi thought his efforts to hide his scar had been in vain.

"Well?" the captain said.

It seemed to Devi that he expected something more, but he had handed over the rum. If the boy below deck had been expected to collect something else, Devi had no idea what it was.

"Glasses," the captain roared, his voice all ash and gravel.

Devi's eyes frantically darted around the cabin. It was a large room, wider than it was long, and it was decorated ornately by rugs and cushions and fabrics that hung from the ceiling and walls. It did not appear as if they had been arranged with any particular thought or discretion, but rather had been placed wherever they might happen to fit. Two great pillars stood on each side of the cabin, and various piles of wooden boxes and barrels were scattered across the space.

One side of the cabin was lined with wooden shelves, some holding colourfully bound books and sculpted ornaments, a number of which laid fallen on their sides or were dangling perilously over the edge of the shelf. Directly behind the captain, several windows allowed the light from the moon to seep in, but a number of flaming lanterns hung from the ceiling regardless, and on the other side of the cabin, Devi's eye's lighted on a wooden cabinet that held the tiny glasses it seemed were his responsibility to collect.

Devi hurried over to the cabinet, took up as many glasses as he could carry, and returned them to the captain's desk. The captain handed the bottle of rum to the man at his left shoulder, and the man began to pour.

"Two more," he grunted, and Devi hurried back to the cabinet to retrieve two additional glasses.

The man with the bottle poured the rum into the tiny glasses until it reached the very top, occasionally spilling some of the contents onto the captain's desk. Each other man that stood around the desk took up a glass and threw the rum back.

"Finally," the captain said once he had slammed his own glass down onto his desk. "A voyage has never truly begun before the first shot of rum."

He then turned to face Devi once more, and his eyes narrowed.

"Where is your glass, boy?"

"I didn't fetch one for myself," Devi said meekly.

"Well why not?" the captain asked. "Every Darmeenian, man or boy, needs his rum. Fetch a glass."

Devi felt as he had when the Darmeenian cart driver had looked him over at the side of the road. The driver had known in an instant that he and Reya were not from Darmeen, but Reya's promise of two additional coins had incentivised him to maintain the illusion for the duration of their journey towards Princi.

The captain did not share the driver's motivations, however, and Devi did his best to convince himself that, if the captain had realised he wasn't the boy he had sent below deck, if he had seen Devi's scar, or if he felt any suspicion at all for that matter, he would likely already be at the bottom of the sea. Regardless, Devi tugged at his sleeve once more, ensuring it covered his wrist completely, and he held it there in his palm as he hurried back towards the captain's desk with a tiny glass of his own.

"Another," the captain announced, raising his glass from his desk and holding it towards the man at his side.

The man poured out a second shot for the captain, and then he filled the glasses of the other men around the table. They each raised their glasses to drink, but the captain raised his hand before they threw the shots back for a second time.

"One for the boy this time," the captain said. "He may have taken his time about it, but the bottle was delivered by his hand, after all."

Each of the men around the desk turned to face Devi, and it took every ounce of strength he possessed to stop himself from squirming under their glaring eyes.

"Thank you, Captain," Devi managed to force out, his mouth dry. "But I'd prefer you all enjoyed it."

The captain's face was dead and expressionless. He glared at Devi intently, his jaw still and his eyes unblinking.

"And I would prefer," he said, speaking slowly and assuredly. "That you followed your captain's orders.

Devi watched as one of the captain's men filled his glass with rum.

"To Darmeen," the captain said, raising his glass.

Devi picked up his own glass from the desk.

"To Darmeen," the other men repeated.

Devi held his glass aloft, and a small amount of rum spilled over its lip onto his fingers. Already, he could smell it. Devi had pilfered from his father's ale barrel before, but he had never drunk rum. It smelled like fire and poison.

Devi glanced at the captain, who was still staring him down expectantly.

"To Darmeen," Devi said, and he threw his shot back.

A fire rose in Devi's chest and set his throat alight. His eyes watered as he fought tooth and nail to keep his mouth clamped shut, knowing that, if he opened it, he would bring forth a bout of coughing and spluttering that would never end.

The captain continued to glare at Devi for a moment longer. Then, he sank back into his chair, and a smile fell across his face.

"I like this boy," the captain declared. "He is small, but he can hold his rum. He is a true Darmeenian."

Devi breathed out deeply and suddenly. He had been holding in a lungful of air since he had first swallowed down his shot, and as it left his body, Devi felt as if his throat and nostrils had been opened up like great caves. His head spun a little as the rum hit his stomach, and he already felt a little hazy. It usually took three or four trips to the barrel before the ale began to take its effect.

"Pour him another," the captain said. "We drank without him, now he must drink without us."

Devi considered resisting, but one look at the captain changed his mind. He had only just stepped foot on The Kraken, and he had no idea how long he would be aboard the great ship. The last thing he wanted to do on his very first night was disobey the captain's orders, especially since he had been fortunate enough to find his way directly into his cabin.

Devi set his tiny glass down on the desk once more, and it was filled to the top with rum. He took a deep breath, bracing himself for the flames he was about to pour down his throat. Then, he picked up the shot glass, held it to his mouth, and tossed his head back.

This time, Devi was unable to suppress his body's urges. His chest exploded, and he fell towards the desk coughing uncontrollably, his fingers clutching its edge as he tried to stop the cabin from spinning wildly around him.

"There it is," the captain roared, a hearty laugh erupting from his belly.

The other men around the table laughed too, and one even smacked Devi on his back as he spluttered violently, gasping for the clean air that would quell the fire in his throat.

"He could barely handle one," the captain laughed. "I knew he wouldn't manage two."

The captain took the bottle of rum and plugged the cork back into its neck.

"That's enough fun," he said. "Away with you, boy."

He raised his hand and flicked his wrist, shooing Devi away from the desk. He did not gesture towards the door, however. Instead, he seemed to usher Devi away towards the side of the room.

Devi retreated unsteadily back towards the cabinet from which he had retrieved the glasses moments earlier, and he stood there against the wall, cupping his hands together at his waist. The cabin lurched vigorously from side to side, but Devi was unable to determine whether this was down to the waves or the rum.

Across the room, Devi watched through hazy eyes as the captain reached into a small pocket at the breast of his waistcoat and pulled out a tiny, golden key. Then, the captain leaned down to his right and pulled open a drawer. From inside, he took out a huge mess of papers with both hands, some of which had been tied together by a thin rope in a loose knot, others of which were splayed out at all angles. The captain dumped the pile on the desk before himself and the other men, and he began to sift through them, pushing some aside and placing others back in the drawer to his right.

When the captain had located the papers he was searching for and had spread them across his desk, several of the men leaned in close, and they each gazed down at the mess intently. Their bodies crowded the desk, and the cabin continued to teeter so that Devi was unable to make out exactly what it was they all pored over.

"Firstly, men," the captain said. "Congratulations on a successful departure. We've waited a long time for this, and we're finally underway. We're also aboard the largest vessel the seas have ever known, so to depart without a hitch should be commended."

The captain's men each murmured their assent.

"Secondly," the captain continued. "I must apologise for the secrecy surrounding our voyage. I trust it's no mystery where we are heading, but any information beyond that which a peasant could surmise has the potential to jeopardise the venture. Word has already begun to spread that we are close to the Fire Stone, and it seems it has spread even further than we realised. I trust you understand the need for secrecy."

Once more, the men around the desk nodded and murmured in agreement.

"Now that we are finally underway, I can be a little more forthcoming with the details."

Devi stood as still as he could manage, and he focused his ears on the conversation taking place across the room. He already knew they were heading to The Sands, and he already knew why – everyone in Darmeen knew, and there were plenty in Katai who knew too. No one seemed to know the captain's precise plans, however. Not even those who stood around his desk.

"It's no secret we sail for The Sands," the captain said. "But we're sailing deeper than anyone has ever sailed before."

The captain's men each shot glances at one another around the desk.

"The path we will sail will be different from past voyages too," the captain said. "First, we sail due north, well clear of the coast. We are under strict orders from King Baelor not to engage – not with pirates, not with traders, and certainly not with Katai. There's enough firepower on this ship to level half of Narkasee but our primary objective remains the same – to reach The Sands. The rest can wait."

Devi's ears burned. He had only seen barrels of salted fish being loaded onto the ship, but he knew the workers must have spent days filling it with all manner of other goods before he and Reya had arrived in Princi. He never imagined he would be sailing on a ship filled with explosives, however. At least, not enough to level a city.

And had the captain's words simply been a turn of phrase, or were there truly plans to attack Narkasee? He had referred to The Sands as the *primary* objective. *The rest can wait*, he had said. Did this mean Narkasee would be a secondary objective somewhere down the line? Devi listened intently as the captain continued to speak, though he forced his body to remain still, and he forced his wandering eyes to gaze anywhere but in the direction of the captain's desk.

"Once we are clear of Katai," the captain continued. "We sail due east for twelve days. Ten if the wind is behind us."

As he spoke, Devi couldn't help but watch as the captain trailed his finger across one of the large sheets of parchment he had sprawled across the desk. Though it was difficult to control his focus, Devi surmised that the large sheet must be a map, and the map seemed to plot The Kraken's journey.

"We remain clear of the coast even after Katai is at our backs. We have the largest ship the seas have ever seen. I'm not taking any risks of running aground. And we might have enough supplies to survive months at sea, but time is still of the essence. We take advantage of the deep waters until we near the landing spot. Only then do we sail in close."

Devi stole another fleeting glance in the direction of the captain. He watched as he searched the mess of papers on his desk once more, locating a second sheet of parchment that appeared to be much like the first, only smaller. As he had done with the first, the captain unfolded the sheet and laid it flat on the desk for the men around him to see, pinning its curled edges down with the tips of his fingers.

"When we arrive in The Sands," the captain said. "We have one day to set up camp. No more. We will land here."

The captain pointed to a spot on the map, and the men around the desk leaned in closer to see. It seemed the captain had a map of The Sands as well as of the sea.

"We will weigh anchor as close to the coast as we can, and the dunes along this ridge should protect the camp from any storms that might pass through. Didrik, you will leave immediately, and you will head out to the west."

The captain glanced up from the map at one of the men that stood on the opposite side of the desk. He wore beige britches that were tucked into dark brown boots just above his ankles, as well as a white tunic, and a scabbard hung from his shoulder to his left hip, where a sword was sheathed. The man had long, brown hair that appeared to have been slicked back with some kind of grease, and Devi instantly recognised the long scar that ran from his brow down one side of his face.

"Einar, you will also leave immediately, but you will head south."

Einar was dressed in much the same fashion as Didrik, but his hair was blonde and cropped much shorter. He nodded as the captain spoke.

Even if Devi had not seen Didrik below deck, his attire, coupled with the fact that he and Einar were the only men in the room other than the captain that wore swords at their hips, made it clear they were each Stone Seekers. Not only that, but they seemed to be the leaders of their battalions.

Devi thought back to the first time Farruk had woken him from his sleep, his enormous fist pounding at his door and his thundering voice booming down the hallways of the King's Keep. He remembered seeing Farruk for the first time too, striding out of the Keep with fury in his voice but passion in his eyes. If these men were even half as formidable as Farruk, Devi knew it would be in his best interest to avoid them wherever possible.

"These," the captained continued, dragging his finger slowly across the map. "Are the routes you will take.

Each has been designed to cover as much ground as possible, whilst ensuring your paths will overlap and you do not waste time covering territory that is thought to be vacant."

The captain looked up at the two men, turning from one to the other.

"You will not deviate from your routes. Any deviation from your route puts the entire venture at risk and will be severely punished. Is that clear?"

"Yes, Captain Heller," each of the men said.

Devi finally had a name that he could pair with the captain's face.

"Good," Captain Heller muttered, reigning in the large sheet of parchment and folding it into a much smaller square.

"Captain?" one of the men began.

"Speak on."

"What follows? When we have the Fire Stone, what are our orders?"

A menacing grin fell across Captain Heller's face. His hand disappeared into his drawer once more, and this time, it pulled out a book, which he dropped onto his desk with a thud.

"When we have the Fire Stone," the captain said. "We finish what Katai has started, and we take back what is ours."

He opened the book before him, placed the smaller, folded sheet between two pages, and slammed it shut once more. He dropped the book back into the drawer, and he swept his arm across his desk, cramming the mess of papers in after it. Then, he forced the drawer shut, slamming it several times in the process.

"Right," Captain Heller said, his voice suddenly bright and airy. "Now that's taken care of…"

He slipped his key into the lock on the drawer, turned it, and Devi heard the lock click shut. Then, he dropped the key back into the tiny pocket on the breast of his waistcoat.

"We can get down to the real business of sailing."

Captain Heller took up the bottle of rum from his desk and looked across the room at Devi.

"Boy," he called out. "Fetch another bottle."

Devi nodded to the captain and made his way over to the cabin door. His feet were unsteady beneath him, and he stumbled wildly, almost toppling over into a heap on the cabin floor. He heard the captain and his men laughing again as they watched on. Then, as he reached the door and turned the handle, Devi heard the captain's voice call out to him over his shoulder.

"And don't dawdle this time."

It was the smell of cooked meat that first dragged Devi back towards consciousness. He couldn't remember the last time he had eaten a hot meal – the legs of meat in the mess back at King Vagan's Keep were cold and slimy, and though the soupy gruel was supposed to be hot, it was never more than lukewarm. Devi's eyes remained closed, however. His head was sore, and his mind felt groggy and slow. It wasn't until he heard a gentle voice calling out that he truly felt compelled to force himself from his slumber.

The voice seemed to call out for the captain, and it was accompanied by the quiet creaking and clicking of a door being pushed open and closed. When Devi finally managed to pry his eyelids apart, the cabin was hazy and blurred, both by sleep and by the pain that throbbed in his head.

Devi looked towards the door, and he saw a figure standing with its back to him, one hand still lingering on the handle. When the figure turned to face him, Devi found himself staring up at Reya. Instinctively, he flashed her a smile, but she simply glared back unimpressed, turning away and walking towards the desk that Captain Heller was still slumped over.

"Captain," Reya said again, her voice a little louder now.

She placed a metal plate down on the captain's desk, and Devi knew immediately it was the source of the smell that had reached him even in his sleep. He saw only a single plate, and his stomach roared as it realised what his mind already knew – the food in the Keep was rough, but it would be a long while before he ate that well again.

Devi watched as Reya reached out and nudged the captain, prodding lightly at his shoulder with two fingers.

"Captain?" she said again.

When Captain Heller still did not stir, Reya gripped his shoulder tightly and wrenched at it violently, her voice so loud that Devi wondered whether it might prompt the captain's men to come bursting through the door.

"What is the meaning of this?" Captain Heller roared, suddenly alive, fire and fury in his eyes. "Who dares to wake me?"

Reya stepped back from the captain's flailing arms, but she did not flinch. Even when his eyes lighted on her, she stood unmoved.

"Explain yourself, boy," Captain Heller said. "Before I have you strung up on the mast."

"I'm sorry to have woken you, Captain," Reya replied calmly. "I brought your breakfast."

It was only now that the captain's nose was drawn towards the warm, rich aroma of blackened sausages wafting up from the plate beneath it. He glanced down at the plate, and the ire in his face dissipated, leaving behind only a mask of contentment.

"Oh. Very good," Captain Heller said. "You are dismissed."

He took up the two-pronged metal fork from the plate and thrust it into one of the sausages. Devi could hear the sausage almost wheeze as the air and fat inside leaked out. Then, the captain lifted the sausage from the plate, and half of it fell away, a light mist of steam snaking out from its centre.

"You heard me, boy," Heller said. "Away with you."

He waved his hand at Reya as he had at Devi the previous night, dismissing her from his cabin. Reya gave a low bow and turned for the door. As she strode across the cabin, however, her eyes locked to Devi's own. Her face was twisted and angry, and she nodded her head towards the door that she was about to leave through.

When she gripped the handle once more, Reya glared at Devi, widening her eyes and scrunching her lips together. Then, she turned the handle and disappeared out into the passage.

Devi forced himself from the floor, and he saw that Captain Heller's eyes fell upon him instantly. The blank look on his face told Devi that he had forgotten about his presence entirely.

"Oh, it's you, boy."

"I'm sorry, Captain. I was sleeping."

Captain Heller speared the second half of his first sausage and thrust it into his mouth.

"Make yourself useful, boy," he said, fat and grease spilling over his lips and chin.

Devi brushed the dust from his britches.

"Yes, Captain. I will fetch a bottle of rum for you, Captain."

Devi made his way across the cabin and out of the door, but there was no sign of Reya in the passage that led back out onto the deck of the ship.

When he stepped out through the second door, unlike the previous evening, the deck was alive with activity. Men called from the deck up to the rigging, from the rigging to the nests, and from the nests back down to the deck. Hundreds of bodies hurried to and fro like scorpions across hot sand, each on his way to, or already engaged with, some task vital to the upkeep or navigation of the ship.

Devi had all but forgotten how enormous the ship was. The captain's cabin was larger than anything Reya's ship could have accommodated, but when compared to the ship as a whole, it was a dusty cupboard. It had been difficult enough to find the ship's massive stores of rum the previous evening. Devi had no idea how he would find Reya and the kitchen.

"Watch yourself, boy."

Devi turned to his left to see two great, hulking men bearing down on him. They held a large, wooden box between them, which would have flattened Devi if he had not managed to scurry out of their path at the last moment. As Devi stepped forward, however, he felt a rush of wind at his ear, and a pile of thick, heavy rope in loops suddenly landed at his feet. Startled, Devi leapt aside, and a bare-chested man landed where he had stood only a moment before with a thud as loud and explosive as that of the rope. The man didn't even acknowledge Devi's presence. He simply hauled the rope over his shoulder and took off towards the bow of the ship.

Devi scanned The Kraken's deck. Everywhere he looked, men were at work. When finally he did lay eyes on a solitary, stationary sailor, he hurried over and tapped him tentatively on the shoulder.

"Can you please tell me where the kitchen is?" Devi asked, his instinct being to offer too much by way of politeness rather than not enough.

The sailor wheeled around on Devi, his broad shoulders bare and browned.

"What?"

The man's grunting voice reminded Devi of one of his oxen.

"The kitchen," Devi repeated.

"How should I know where the kitchen is?" the man grumbled.

Devi turned to walk away, but the sailor's muscular arm suddenly appeared in front of his face.

"Down there somewhere."

The man pointed back in the direction of the doors towards the stern of the ship, one of which Devi had just passed through, and two of which he had explored the night before. On one side of the captain's cabin, the door had led down to the rum stores, and the food holds were likely down there too. On the other, the door had led down to the sleeping quarters of the Stone Seekers. Devi made his way over to the doors on the lefthand side of the cabin and passed through the one in the centre.

Below deck, the ship was as alive as it had been in the open air. Down in the dark and narrow corridors and stairwells, however, Devi was surrounded by boys as well as men. They scurried through the passages like rats, some carrying boxes and bottles, others empty-handed. The passages were longer and more winding than Devi had imagined they would be, weaving and joining and plunging further and further below deck like a great labyrinth. When Devi turned one of the countless corners, he spotted Reya's jet-black hair up ahead. He called out her name, but she did not stop and turn.

"Reya," he called again.

She must not have heard him the first time.

Devi pushed through the mess of bodies in the narrow corridor, but already the crowd was beginning to thin. As Devi followed Reya around another bend, which split off in three different directions, he found himself following her down a near-empty corridor, only a single boy walking back in the opposite direction.

"Reya," Devi called a third time, quieter now that he did not have to shout over the din.

Initially, Reya did not turn, but the instant the other boy had passed Devi and disappeared around the corner, Reya spun on her heels, utter fury in her eyes. She grabbed a handful of Devi's tunic and thrust her forearm up into his throat, driving him against the wall of the narrow passageway.

"What's wrong with you?" Reya spat, bringing her face so close to Devi's that he could feel her hot breath against his skin. "Do *not* call me Reya here. Are you trying to get me killed?"

The thought hadn't occurred to Devi, but now that it did, he felt foolish. Beyond foolish. He felt dangerous. The Darmeenians would never have set eyes on Reya before, but they would certainly know the princess of Katai by name, and though word would already be spreading about her disappearance, they had likely set sail before the rumours could travel as far as Princi.

"I'm sorry," Devi said. "I didn't –"

"You didn't… You didn't what?"

Devi didn't speak. He simply allowed Reya's anger to free itself. She pushed herself away from Devi and sent a series of lashing, open-handed blows at his chest and shoulders. Devi raised his hands to defend himself against the assault, but he quickly relented. Though Reya continued to strike him, her attacks were weak and careless. Devi knew that, if Reya wanted to hurt him, she would be quite capable. Yet, her assault was feeble and easy to withstand. Devi watched her anger slowly fade, and he saw the vulnerable eyes of a frightened animal staring back at him.

"Why did you let him take me?" Reya said, finally allowing her hands to fall to her sides, the passage at her back still empty and quiet.

Though she had been the picture of anger only a moment ago, now she merely looked wounded.

"I didn't let him," Devi protested.

"Then how did I end up down here? Alone."

The lids of Reya's eyes quivered, and her pale cheeks seemed to flush a little. Devi had sensed the vulnerability in her voice when she had spoken of the importance of reaching the Fire Stone, and it was all too obvious again now.

"I'm sorry," Devi said. "But what could I do?"

"You could have argued," Reya said, but her voice lacked conviction.

"And have them throw me overboard? Then where would we be?"

Reya fell silent. She knew Devi was right.

"I just didn't expect us to get separated so quickly."

"Neither did I."

Devi hadn't felt altogether safe in the captain's cabin, but he felt it best not to share his own anxieties with Reya. Ultimately, whilst he had been getting drunk with Captain Heller and his men, Reya had spent the night in the darkness below deck, scared and alone.

"I'm on kitchen duty from now until we arrive," Reya said glumly. "There are hundreds of boys on this ship, and they managed to find the only girl and put her in the kitchen."

Devi did his best to stifle the laughter that rose suddenly in his stomach. He didn't make a sound, but he couldn't prevent his mouth from rising a little at the corners. When Reya saw this, her face exploded with rage, but she was immediately forced to relent to the laughter that bubbled and swelled in her own stomach.

"Don't you dare laugh, Devi," she said, barely managing to suppress a smile.

She and Devi stood in the empty passage smiling at one another, and the tension and apprehension of the previous days seemed to dissolve just a little.

"Come on," Reya said, two boys joining them in the narrow corridor again. "We shouldn't talk here."

Reya led Devi through a maze of passages until they reached the kitchen. They had not been alone in the corridors for long, and they were soon joined again by boys who scurried in all directions.

Despite the size of the ship, the kitchen was a tiny room deep beneath the deck. There was a single porthole in one corner, and the heat inside was almost insufferable. In the centre of the space, a large, shallow pan hung from three metal poles that joined above its centre. Below the pan, a low wall had been constructed of bricks, and the area inside the wall had been filled with sand. At the centre of the sand was a sizeable fire, which heated the contents of the pan directly above until they hissed and spat at the boys passing to and fro about the room.

Devi and Reya made their way to the back of the room behind the pan. Reya handed Devi a spatula, and they each began to prod at the sausages, rolling and turning them over so they cooked evenly on all sides.

"I don't suppose those are for us?" Devi asked.

"Not until they start to rot."

Devi's stomach roared. He was even more glad it had been Reya that had been pulled away below deck. If he had to spend all day cooking hot sausages but never getting the chance to taste one, he wasn't sure he would make it to The Sands with either his mind or his body in one piece.

"So, what's the captain like?"

Reya leaned in close to Devi and spoke quietly enough that the fat hissing in the pan, coupled with the general commotion of the kitchen, masked her voice.

"His name is Captain Heller," Devi replied. "And he likes his rum."

"A Darmeenian captain who likes his rum?" Reya asked, her tone all mock surprise. "Who would have thought?"

Devi leaned in even closer to Reya.

"He has maps," he said.

Reya turned to face Devi for a moment, her eyes alight. She quickly turned back to the pan, however, fixing her gaze on the sausages that she rolled back and forth with her spatula.

"He has a map of the sea," Devi continued. "And one of The Sands. We're sailing for ten days, maybe twelve. Then, they have two battalions of Seekers, and they have their routes mapped out already."

"They must be pretty certain they know where to find the Stone. Either that or they're getting desperate."

"I think we're more desperate than they are."

Reya turned to face Devi once more, her eyes burning into his own.

"We need to get hold of that map, Devi."

For a moment, Devi considered telling Reya what else he had overheard – the firepower on the ship and the talk of Narkasee and Katai. He wasn't certain of anything, however, and King Vagan was back in Narkasee. He didn't want her spending the duration of their voyage worrying about what was to come next, and he certainly didn't want her risking the venture, and their lives, trying to prevent it. If the Darmeenians were planning to attack Katai, obtaining the Fire Stone would be the best way to stop them.

"He keeps the maps locked in his drawer, but he keeps a key in his breast pocket," Devi said. "We'd need to get hold of that key first."

"He was out pretty cold this morning," Reya said. "I had to give him a hard shake to wake him. We can just wait until he passes out and take it from him."

Devi thought for a moment. It was true the captain seemed to be a heavy sleeper, especially when his belly was full of rum, but there would be no way of knowing how far gone he was.

"It's too risky," Devi said. "We'd need a way to make sure he was completely dead to the world."

Reya's face twisted into a smirk.

"No," Devi said, his eyes frantically darting around the kitchen to ensure his raised voice hadn't drawn any attention. "Not *dead* dead. Just unresponsive."

Just then, a man stumbled through the door into the kitchen. His torso was bare, and his skin was deathly pale. His cheeks were somewhat sunken, and his eyes were black and bloodshot. It seemed as if he could barely stand.

"Fenocci," the man forced out.

The kitchen continued to bustle with activity, no one acknowledging the man that had just entered.

"Fenocci," the man said again. "Please tell me we brought fenocci."

He wavered as he stood by the kitchen's entrance, his legs weak and his body hunched over. Devi thought back to the moment he had first stepped foot on the tiny Katai fishing boat, his stomach turning over itself violently. He thought back to the first night he had spent aboard Reya's ship too, hurling the contents of his stomach into the water below.

"I've barely slept a wink," the man said. "And I can't keep anything down."

Devi and Reya each watched as one of the boys on the other side of the room made his way over to the cabinets that lined the kitchen. The boy reached into the very top of one of the cupboards, where a handful of small, glass bottles rattled around on a shelf, and he took one down. He made his way over to a barrel of freshwater, took a wooden beaker from a basket beside it, and plunged it into the bucket, pouring water back out of the beaker until it was only half-full. Then, the boy handed the beaker to the man, who already appeared beyond relieved.

The boy removed the cork from the top of the glass bottle and tilted its neck ever so slightly towards the man's beaker. He allowed only a drop of the liquid inside to fall into the water, and the man eagerly drank it down.

"Thank you," he said, the gratitude in his voice sincere and more than palpable.

Without a word, the boy took the wooden beaker back from the man and tossed it back into the basket. He plugged the cork back in the glass bottle and returned it to the cabinet. Then, he returned to his duties, the man disappearing into the darkness of the corridor once more.

When Devi turned to face Reya, he expected her to look as confused as he felt. Instead, an irrepressible grin fell across her face.

"That's it," she said.

"What's it?"

"The fenocci. The Darmeenians use it to treat sea sickness. It only takes a drop to numb the body enough that it no longer feels the rise and fall of the sea."

"But Captain Heller doesn't get seasick," Devi said. "And he drinks enough rum to numb his body anyway."

"So, we lace his rum with fenocci. More than just a drop. And we'll make certain he'll be dead to the world."

Devi nodded slowly as he considered the plan. If the fenocci was as strong as Reya had suggested, it could easily work.

"Tonight?"

"You think you can keep the key and the maps hidden for the next ten days?" Reya asked.

She was right. They would have to bide their time – keep a low profile until they were close to The Sands.

"When then?"

"I'll let you know when."

Devi nodded.

"I should get back to the cabin. The captain will be wondering where I am. I told him I'd bring him another bottle of rum."

"Right," Reya said.

Devi saw the same vulnerability in her eyes that he had seen in the corridor moments ago.

"We'll meet in the rum stores each night," he said. "Just keep your head down during the day."

Reya nodded.

"I should get back," Devi said, but he didn't move.

He could feel himself being drawn to Reya. He wanted to wrap his arms around her and embrace her – not simply to reassure her, but also to reassure himself. They were aboard the largest ship to ever set sail, and they were surrounded by Darmeenians with no possible chance of escape if they were discovered. They had each left behind everything they had ever known, and they each had no one else in the world to turn to but the other. Devi's presence was already beginning to draw sideward glances from the Darmeenian boys, however, not least because he seemed to be offering very little in terms of a contribution to the workings of the kitchen.

"I'll see you tonight," Devi said, and he ducked out of the kitchen, trying his best to keep his eyes forward and resist the urge to cast one final look in Reya's direction.

XXI

The bottles of rum on the shelves rattled as The Kraken bounced over yet another wave. The shelves were more than half-empty, Captain Heller and his men having drained their stores far more quickly than Devi could ever have anticipated. A single empty bottle rolled back and forth on the floor along with the rhythm of the water, but this, along with the gentle creaking of the ship's hull, were the only subtle indicators that Devi had not been plunged into the depths of unconsciousness, shrouded as he was in complete darkness.

Though Devi had never sailed before he had landed on the deck of Reya's tiny ship, he found that days at sea passed in much the same way as those on land. He was hungry most of the time, thirsty even more often, and tired almost always. He devoured the rations of salted fish and pulses that were handed out twice daily, and he was never absent when the freshwater barrels were drained. The barrels had not lasted long, however, the last having been emptied shortly after the ship had sailed clear of the coast of Katai.

Devi had hoped he might catch a glimpse of Narkasee or the Salt Cliffs as they passed, but The Kraken had sailed so far north that there was nothing to see but still water on all sides.

The most striking similarity between life on the ship and life in Katai was that Devi was not idle for long enough to dwell on his fatigue, his hunger, or his thirst. Captain Heller kept him scurrying about the ship at all hours, fetching food and rum, and delivering messages on scraps of torn parchment to the first mate, the quartermaster, or the boatswain.

Devi even ventured down into the Seekers' quarters on occasion. There seemed to be about fifteen men in each battalion, and he noticed that their bunks were always impeccably kept. Their routines were so strict and orderly that Devi thought it likely he could have tracked the passing of the days not by the changing sky overhead but instead by the movements and machinations of the Seekers.

At night, Captain Heller and his men would drink rum in his cabin until the early hours of the morning, occasionally blessing Devi with a glass or two when they were at their most merry. Devi hoped he might develop a tolerance for the stuff, or at least warm to its taste, but every time he threw back a shot, his throat burned and his head swam. Once the water barrels were empty, however, he had little choice but to be grateful. It was certainly preferable to drinking seawater, after all.

In the darkness of the rum store, he tilted his head back and downed another mouthful from his near-empty bottle.

"Save some for me."

Reya's fingers prodded against Devi's cheek as they searched in the darkness for the bottle.

"And for Captain Heller," she said.

Reya's hand slid over Devi's own and found the bottle still held close to his face. She gripped it by the neck and took it from him, and Devi could hear the liquid sloshing in the bottle as she tilted her own head back to drink. Then, a burst of shattering glass sounded away to Devi's left, and he felt the bottom of his britches immediately begin to grow damp.

"Watch it," Devi said, pulling his leg up to his chest away from the stream of rum that was quickly spreading across the floor.

"It's disgusting," Reya replied, smacking her lips. "It must be tainted. You can't taste that?"

To Devi, all rum seemed to taste the same - bitter and acrid. If the bottle was tainted, he would never have known.

"Grab another," Reya said.

Though the rum store was cloaked in thick, impenetrable darkness, it still seemed to Devi as if the room was spinning. Even Reya, who could usually hold her rum far more easily than Devi, couldn't prevent herself from slurring a little as she spoke.

"I think we've probably had enough," Devi said. "And besides, I know you were joking, but we really should save some for Captain Heller."

"Screw Captain Heller," Reya yelled, barely managing to force the words out through her laughter. "Screw him and his burnt sausages."

Devi reached out for Reya in the darkness, and he shook her by the shoulder.

"Keep your voice down," he said. "Someone will hear us."

Devi tried his best to speak scoldingly, but Reya's laughter was infectious, and though she fell quiet, he knew it was not a result of his attempted reprimand.

"It's hot tonight," Reya said, her fingers finding Devi's own and sliding between them.

With her other hand, she seemed to pull her moist, sticky tunic away from the skin of her chest.

"We must be getting close."

The Kraken had been on the water for days, and it had steadily grown warmer and warmer as it had ventured deeper and deeper into The Sands. With the exception of their first, Devi and Reya had spent every night at sea together in the darkness of the rum store, but each night that passed had grown more and more humid, and they had each found themselves getting less and less sleep.

"I don't think I'll be able to sleep down here tonight," Reya said. "Not in this heat."

Devi thought back to the years he had spent sleeping half-naked on the wooden stoop outside his father's shack, with nothing to cover him but the blanket of stars in the sky. He was used to the heat. The farmlands in the south of Katai soaked up the sun, but it was nothing compared to The Sands.

"It should cool down now the sun has set," Devi said.

"Not nearly enough."

"Perhaps we should go up and sleep on the deck."

"No," Reya said. "We'll just be put to work. It might be the middle of the night, but no doubt there'll be someone who could use us."

The rum store fell quiet for a moment. Then, Reya's fingers slipped from between Devi's own, and he felt her lift herself from the floor.

"Where are you going?"

Devi could see nothing, but he heard two thuds and then the shuffling of Reya's bare feet against the deck.

"Nowhere," she said.

"Then what are you doing?"

Reya seemed to stand more still now, but Devi could still hear the rustling of her clothes.

"I'm undressing."

Devi was silent for a moment, and he was grateful that Reya couldn't see his face in the darkness.

"Are you sure you want to…"

Devi struggled to find his words.

"Do you want me to leave you?" he asked finally. "I can give you some privacy."

"It's pitch black," Reya said. "You can't see me, can you?"

Devi was shaking his head before he realised his reaction was the perfect illustration of the point Reya was attempting to make.

"No."

"Well then I should be fine."

Reya's voice was muffled for a moment.

"But you've left me alone below deck once already," she said. "If you want to do it again, there's nothing stopping you."

Devi could hear Reya's clothes rustling in the darkness as she stripped them away from her body. A thick bead of sweat ran from his temple down the line of his jaw, and his own tunic clung uncomfortably to his sweaty chest.

"I don't want to," he said. "But do you mind if I…"

Once more, Devi found himself unable to complete his thought.

"There's nothing stopping you," Reya said again.

Devi pushed himself to his feet, finding one of the shelves at his back for balance. Tentatively, he began to unbutton his britches, but he felt sheepish and shy. Though he could still hear Reya undressing herself beside him, he couldn't help but feel as if she was luring him into a ruse, ready to pull open the door and flood the rum stores with light from the flame torches beyond, revealing his naked body. He pulled his britches down over his legs, stepped out of them, and pushed them aside with one foot. Then, he pulled his tunic over his head and dropped it on top, forming a small pile.

Devi bent at the knees and placed his hands on the floor by his hips. He allowed himself to fall backwards slowly, first onto his elbows, and then until his back was laid flat. The wooden boards of the ship felt rough against his skin, but the air felt much cooler now that he wasn't covered by moist, cloistering clothes. Reya, however, continued to undress.

"What's taking so long?" Devi asked.

"I'm going as quick as I can," Reya insisted. "It's not my fault boys can get away with wearing next to nothing."

"But you're dressed as a boy," Devi laughed.

"On the outside. But you can't see what's going on underneath."

Suddenly, Devi found himself imagining what Reya could have been wearing beneath her tunic. He pictured her body wrapped tightly by fabric to hide its shape, and he began to see inch after inch of her pale skin as, layer by layer, the fabric was unwound. Then, he heard a gentle thud as Reya dropped her own clothes to the ground.

Devi sensed Reya lowering herself to the floor beside him, and he could feel the heat from her body.

"You know," Reya said. "I used to be scared of the dark."

"Really?"

Devi struggled to believe someone so bold could be afraid of mere darkness.

"When my father would lock me in my room inside the Keep, I would scream and cry endlessly. I was convinced there were monsters lurking in the shadows, and I would beg for him to let me out. It wasn't until I started sailing that I grew to tolerate it."

"In darkness lie all terrors true," Devi said instinctively.

"What does that mean?"

"It's a line from one of the Psalms."

"The Psalms?"

Devi was taken aback for a moment. Everyone he had ever known had constructed their entire lives around the Psalms. It felt strange to introduce them to someone who had never come across them, and he struggled as he considered the best way to describe them.

"We lived by them on the farms," he said finally.

"Teach it to me," Reya said.

"I don't know if –"

"Please."

Devi felt Reya lean a little closer to him, and for the first time, he felt her naked skin brush against his own.

"Ok," he said. "Say it after me – In darkness lie all terrors true."

"In darkness lie all terrors true," Reya repeated.

"Be they many, few, or one."

"Be they many, few, or one."

"Yet, through the darkness, he pursues."

Reya repeated Devi's words after him once more, and again as he completed the Psalm's final line.

"To lie in wait, the rising Son."

The words sounded strange on Reya's lips. They had been the last words Devi had ever heard his father speak, and they brought him a strange sense of comfort.

"Everyone has fears they must face," Devi said, elaborating on his explanation of the meaning of the lines now that Reya had heard them in full. "But if you face your fears, the Son will be there to meet you when the darkness subsides."

"Who is the Son?" Reya asked.

"He's the saviour," Devi explained. "He will come to redeem us and to lead us."

"Do you really believe that?"

Devi used the silence and the darkness to think.

"I don't know," he said. "Some people say the Son will be our salvation in this life. Others say you meet the Son when you pass on, and he judges the man you've been."

"And what do you think?"

Devi considered repeating the same words to Reya that he had spoken to his father. He thought about telling her that the Son was merely a fiction - a story to provide hope and a reason to rise with the sun - that the lines of the Psalms had been spoken for generations and little had changed. But he didn't.

"My father said the Son is in us all," he said instead. "The strength to banish the darkness is the light you find when it subsides. To meet the rising Son is to merely make it through the night."

"He said?"

A silence hung in the air for a moment.

"Your father doesn't say this anymore?" Reya asked.

Devi remained silent. Only the gentle breaths of the waves and Reya's rising and falling chest whispered in the darkness. Devi couldn't imagine speaking about his father to anyone. Reya had repeated the words that he had spoken to Orlain in the training yard, so she must have also heard him tell Orlain that his father was dead. Even if he could find the words to confirm what she already knew, however, Devi would never be able to bring himself to explain how, whilst his father and the rest of the village had perished, he had managed to survive the night. Fortunately, Reya did not force him to speak again.

"Teach me another," she said instead.

Devi thought for a moment. He had known all ten of the Psalms by heart for as long as he could remember. Each had its own lesson to teach, and each meant a little something different to him. All ultimately culminated in Psalm Ten, however, the promise of the arrival of the Son and the redemption of a nation.

"For when it seems that all is lost."

Reya did not repeat the lines after Devi this time. Instead, they simply lingered in the darkness as he spoke them aloud.

"And the holy kingdom is set to fall. The Son will rise to levy the cost and give his life to save them all."

"So the Son is the saviour."

Reya echoed Devi's words.

"But he will lose his own life saving his people."

Devi thought back to the night of his father's death. He had seen the Son in his father, as well as in every man and boy that had stood and fought in the fields. They had been willing to give their lives to save each other, and in this way, they had each embodied Psalm Ten itself. Devi's heart twisted in his chest. He knew he had been given the opportunity to do the same, and he was the only one that had not taken it.

"Something like that," he said simply.

Devi felt Reya's fingers slip between his own once more, and he turned his head to face her. Though the room was still shrouded in impenetrable darkness, he could feel that she was staring back at him. Her gentle breaths lingered on his lips, and their faces were so close that their noses almost touched. All it took was a whisper to break the silence.

"I'm glad you're here with me, Devi," Reya said.

For a moment, Devi was certain that he could just about make out Reya's brilliant, blue eyes gazing at him in the darkness, but they quickly faded, and her gentle breaths began to slow.

Devi pulled Reya's body close to his own, and he turned his face away from her. He allowed his eyes too to fall closed, but he knew that, even more than usual, his chances of drifting off to sleep were vanishingly thin.

XXII

When one of the lookouts way up in The Kraken's mess of masts and sails had called *land ho*, Devi knew they were drawing near. At first, only a sliver of sand was visible on the horizon, as if there was a crust on the sea. But soon, the rolling dunes of The Sands rose and fell like waves off the starboard side, and Devi had watched as the great ship edged closer and closer to the coast. He had noticed that Captain Heller and his men had been staying decidedly more sober too, and when he overheard them discussing the practicalities of making their landing, he knew the time had come.

He stood in the darkness of the rum store once more, trying his best to navigate a path between eagerness and anxiety. When the door finally creaked open, a flood of orange light poured over the threshold, lighting Reya's face from below.

"Sorry," Reya said. "I couldn't get away."

"We need to hurry," Devi said. "Do you have it?"

"I have it."

Reya set the lantern that she carried down on one of the shelves, and Devi gently pushed the rum bottles there aside. The last thing they needed was for The Kraken to go up in flames. From her waistband, Reya pulled a small, glass bottle, and Devi recognised it as one of the fenocci bottles he and Reya had seen used to treat sea sickness during their first morning on the ship.

"Let's make this quick," Devi said. "The captain is already asking for his food. The sooner we get you back up to the kitchen, the sooner you can fetch his dinner."

He began lifting bottles from the shelves, inspecting them in the low light of Reya's lantern until he had found one that hadn't already been emptied. He pulled the cork from the bottle and held it out in Reya's direction.

"How much do you think we'll need?"

"I'm not sure," Reya said. "They only use one drop for sea sickness, so how about we try…"

Reya thought for a moment.

"All of it," she concluded, smirking.

"All of it?"

"Why not? We want to be sure they go down."

"But do we want to be sure they don't get back up?"

Reya shrugged.

"Doesn't matter to me."

Devi's face twisted with discomfort. He held the rum bottle aloft and examined its contents. The bottle was almost full to the brim, touching the bottom of the cork that had been thrust into its top.

"There's no space," he said.

"Then we better *make* space."

Devi's discomfort grew. He placed the small, glass bottle on an empty shelf and pulled the cork from the top of the rum bottle.

"Bottoms up," Reya said.

Devi lifted the bottle towards his mouth, and the smell almost overwhelmed him. A shot glass full of the stuff was unpleasant, and he had tolerated the occasional mouthful since the freshwater barrels had emptied. But a bottleful was overpowering.

Devi took a deep breath in, then exhaled sharply. He brought the bottle to his lips and took a large, full swig. The liquid attacked his throat, and he immediately began to splutter. He managed to force some of the rum down his throat, and it burned like fire, but some he spat over the empty shelves and across the floor at Reya's feet as he doubled over. His eyes were streaming, and his lungs were squeezing his chest tight as he struggled to breathe through the urge to cough.

Reya couldn't stop herself from giggling.

"I thought you'd started to get used to the stuff."

She grabbed the neck of the bottle and snatched it from Devi's grip. She stared at him, holding his gaze as she lifted the bottle to her lips and tilted her head back. Devi watched as the rum filled the neck of the bottle, bubbling as it struggled to find its way past Reya's lips.

With her eyes fixed on Devi's own, Reya swallowed one mouthful of rum, allowing her cheeks to fill again before swallowing a second. Then, she brought her head forward and smirked mischievously at Devi as she wiped her lips dry.

She took the small, glass bottle from the empty shelf, pulled out its cork with her teeth, and poured its entire contents into the rum bottle. She tossed the glass bottle aside, and it shattered on the floor. Then, she grabbed the cork, placed it back in the bottle of rum and shook it vigorously, blending the fenocci with the alcohol.

"Here," Reya said, thrusting the bottle of rum into Devi's chest. "Tell the captain I hope he chokes on it."

Devi hurried back to Captain Heller's cabin, but when he arrived, he found it empty. He wasn't sure whether the captain had stepped out for some air or to get his own look at the dunes that rolled away off the starboard side of the ship. Or perhaps, more worryingly, without Devi there to do so on his behalf, he had gone in search of the food that Devi had promised was only moments away. Devi was supposed to return with the rum, and Reya was supposed to join them with his food shortly after, but it was possible the captain's empty stomach had already led him from the cabin.

Devi made his way across the cabin and placed the bottle of rum on Captain Heller's desk. There was a mess of papers spread across it, and just as Devi was about to turn away in search of the captain, he saw that his desk drawer was wide open.

Devi cast a fleeting glance back towards the cabin door. The corridor beyond seemed dark, lit only by a glimmer of the silver light of the moon. Then, without hesitation, Devi grabbed a handful of the papers on Captain Heller's desk. His eyes devoured them hungrily, and he found himself tossing them back on the desk in an instant, eager to devour something more. He spread the papers around with hands, trying to take in as much as he could, but they were disorganised and chaotic. He saw maps of the sea, details of star positions, and countless records of the supplies the ship was still carrying, as well as those they had already run through. Then, Devi turned his attention to the open drawer.

He made his way around the desk and stood just by Captain Heller's chair. He reached into the desk and pulled out the journal he had seen Captain Heller lock away during his first night on the ship. Though he knew Captain Heller could return at any moment, he pulled the book out slowly and carefully, as if the gravity of its contents necessitated a measured approach. He laid the book flat on the desk and opened it.

Devi flicked through page after page of logs, and they seemed to each detail only the mundane operations of the ship. Some contained the fleeting thoughts of the captain himself, most seeming to have been scrawled hastily down at the height of his intoxication, but Devi was in search of something specific.

Protruding from between two of the pages of the journal was the stained corner of a sheet of parchment. Devi flicked quickly forward through the pages until he found the sheet, and he saw it was the map of The Sands that the Darmeenian Seekers were to use. He saw their routes plotted across the rise and fall of the dunes, he saw the location where Captain Heller seemed certain they would find the Fire Stone, and he saw the plans for the camp that would be waiting for them once they had obtained it.

As Devi returned to the pages of the journal itself, his entire body turned cold. There, before him, was a hastily drawn map of Katai. It was crude, and it lacked detail, but Devi could see the farmlands, he could track the coastline, and he could see Narkasee perched on the edge of the Salt Cliffs.

In the water just off the coast, surrounded by Darmeenian sails, The Kraken loomed. It seemed as large as Narkasee itself, and its guns were turned on the city. Outside Narkasee's walls, rank upon rank of what Devi could only assume were Darmeenian soldiers lined up to lay siege to the city, and in the south, amidst the farmlands of Rakhas and beyond, were countless more men. Any doubt that Devi had harboured about the Darmeenians' plans, any hope that he had misunderstood Captain Heller's words and they sailed only for the Fire Stone, immediately dissipated. The Darmeenians knew the location of the Stone, and when they had secured it, they would turn their attention to Katai.

Devi closed the book, and he placed it back in the drawer, trying to remember the exact position in which he had found it. Just then, he heard the door to the cabin creak open. Devi looked up, expecting to see Reya staring back at him, a metal plate filled with sausages in her hand, but instead, he saw Captain Heller.

"What are you doing, boy?" Captain Heller asked, his voice unusually low and measured.

For a moment, Devi panicked. Then, he dropped to his knees and scooped up an empty rum glass from the floor.

"I've brought you a fresh bottle of rum, Captain," Devi said, holding the glass up for Captain Heller to see and making his way around to the other side of the desk.

Captain Heller crossed the cabin and slumped into his chair. He eyed Devi closely as he took up the bottle of rum, poured it into the glass, and slid it across the desk in the captain's direction. Devi watched as Captain Heller's eyes slid to his right, and then as his right hand quietly pushed his open drawer closed. The captain leaned forward, his hand reaching towards the glass that Devi had filled, but instead he snatched up another glass from the desk, placing it down in front of Devi.

"Join me in a drink," he said.

Devi looked at Captain Heller, and his gaze was returned blankly.

"Thank you, Captain," Devi said. "But the rum stores are almost empty. I'd prefer you were able to enjoy what's left."

"Nonsense," Captain Heller said, lifting Devi's glass from the desk and slamming it down once more. "Our arrival draws near. We weigh anchor in the morning. We must celebrate."

Devi paused for a moment.

"Really, Captain, I –"

"Pour," Captain Heller insisted.

Devi's fingers trembled as he pawed at the cork in the bottle. They felt distant, the rum he had consumed below deck already seeming to take its toll, slowing his mind and unsteadying his limbs just a little. He watched as his glass filled with the rum and fenocci concoction, and he lowered the bottle to the desk, placing the cork back in its top once more.

It was now that Captain Heller finally lifted his glass from the desk. He held it aloft and looked expectantly towards Devi.

"To Darmeen," he said.

Devi stared down at his own glass. His mind was already a little hazy from the rum alone, but he could see no way to avoid downing the fenocci too. There was a chance that he could handle a single shot, however, and perhaps he would be able to avoid drinking for the rest of the evening whilst the captain slowly sent himself into a stupor.

Devi reached down and lifted the glass from the desk. His motions mirrored Captain Heller's as they each lifted their glasses to their mouths, but the captain held his there, his eyes boring into Devi's own. The rum alone had smelt fiery, but along with the fenocci, it smelt almost toxic. Devi opened his mouth, threw the shot glass back, and swallowed. Captain Heller, however, returned his glass to the desk still full.

"On second thoughts," he said. "I think I'd prefer to wait until I have something in my stomach. Where is your little friend with my dinner anyway?"

Devi's throat roared and his head swam. It felt like the entire world had flipped upside down in an instant, but his body had been left behind. He had no idea how he was going to remain conscious for the rest of the evening, much less remain standing. He heard the door to the cabin creak open once more, however, and he looked gratefully back in search of Reya. But, once more, it was not Reya that entered. Instead, Captain Heller's men filed in one after the other, some making their way across to the captain's desk, whilst others lingered closer to the door.

"Ah," Captain Heller said, his voice light and triumphant. "Didrik, Einar. Tell me, is there anything worse than an empty stomach?"

The men looked at the captain confused.

"Few things I can think of," Didrik said, whilst Einar simply shook his head.

"And what do you think the boy will bring today? Sausages? Merely bread and salted fish, perhaps?"

"I'm not sure, Captain," Didrik said, Einar once more remaining silent.

"And tell me," the captain continued. "How long do you think we will lay siege to Narkasee before it falls? I give it… perhaps half a day."

Didrik, Einar, and every other man in the room turned to face Captain Heller, and Devi watched as Didrik nodded in his direction.

"Captain, perhaps we should discuss these matters later."

Captain Heller brushed Didrik's concerns aside almost immediately.

"We need not worry about him," he said, turning to face Devi. "You've already availed yourself of the information, haven't you, boy?"

Devi's heart ceased beating. The cabin rocked from side to side, and the room already seemed to be spinning.

"I don't know what you're talking about, Captain," he said.

"Of course you do," Captain Heller insisted, his voice still bright and airy. "So why don't you tell me what you think? How long before Narkasee falls, and we finally get our hands on that traitorous wretch you call a king?"

Devi's eyes darted around the cabin. They flashed over the windows at Captain Heller's back, open to the world beyond but too small for him to dart through with any real urgency. He turned back to scour the door, but the captain's men lingered close, their suspicion evidently heightened by the captain's words. There was no escape. If Devi was going to make it out of the cabin alive, he would have to fight his way out, and the chances of that seemed as likely as reaching into his pocket and finding the Fire Stone there waiting for him.

Before Devi could open his mouth to respond, he heard the door creak open for a third time. He watched as Reya walked into the cabin, a plate of sizzling sausages in her hand, but before he could call out for her to run, the captain's men had slammed the door shut behind her.

"Why don't we see what your little friend thinks?" Captain Heller snarled.

The mock delight in his voice had been replaced by sinister malice. Reya's eyes met Devi's own, and as she made her way across the cabin towards Captain Heller, he could see fear and confusion rising within them.

"We've just been discussing," Captain Heller said, turning his attention to Reya. "How long it will be before Narkasee burns."

Reya glared back at Captain Heller as she placed the plate of sausages on his desk.

"The farmlands are already burning," the captain continued. "The city must already be starving. She won't be able to hold out for long."

Reya turned and made for the door, but Captain Heller's voice boomed around the cabin.

"Seize them," he roared.

Captain Heller's men set upon Devi and Reya almost instantly, and though Devi struggled, he wasn't close to strong enough to resist the strength of three grown men. Reya, however, yelled as she kicked and thrashed.

"Get your hands off me!"

She sank her teeth into the arm of one of the men, but he took a handful of her hair and brought his open palm across her face. Captain Heller rose from his desk, and he lowered his face to Devi's own.

"Are these the Seekers they're sending to The Sands now?" he spat. "Katai grows weaker with each passing day."

Captain Heller stormed past Reya and out onto the deck of the ship. The captain's men each followed, dragging Devi and Reya along with them. Though Devi struggled initially, he quickly succumbed to the overwhelming strength of the men. Reya, however, continued to lash out, and it was only when one of the men struck her across the face for a second time that she relented.

The Kraken moved slowly through the water, and its deck was quiet and still.

"Katai wishes us well," Captain Heller roared.

The men that lingered at all corners of the ship turned their attention to the captain.

"So well," he continued. "That they have sent two messengers to tell us directly."

The captain's men pushed Devi and Reya towards the centre of the deck, and Devi felt the eyes of the Darmeenians upon him. The stars above and all around swirled and darted through the sky, and although the water was still and the ship moved slowly, the fenocci made it seem as if the deck was lurching violently from left to right. Captain Heller stepped towards the very edge of the ship, and he turned back to face Devi, beckoning him over with a finger. The captain's men forced Devi towards the taffrail, and Captain Heller grabbed a handful of his tunic in one hand, taking hold of his wrist in the other.

"This boy is from Katai," Captain Heller said, holding Devi's wrist aloft so that the sleeve of his tunic fell away from his branded scar. "He is a long way from home, and he must grow very sick and weary. How cruel it would be of us to keep him from her any longer."

Captain Heller hauled Devi's body up onto the taffrail of the ship, and Devi swayed uncontrollably as he looked down at the water below. It felt like he was peering off the edge of the Salt Cliffs into the still water of the Tharakun once more.

"Please," Devi said.

Captain Heller dragged Devi's face down to the level of his own.

"Please," Devi said again. "I just wanted to see The Sands, and I dragged him along with me."

Devi looked back towards Reya, who returned his gaze without hope.

"Do what you want with me, but don't hurt him."

"Oh, don't you worry about that, boy," Captain Heller whispered. "We won't be hurting *her*. *She's* far too precious."

Captain Heller thrust his hands into Devi's shoulders, and the world gave way beneath him. The stars flashed across the sky, and the last thing Devi saw as he fell away towards the water below, was the captain's men dragging Reya away.

PART FOUR

XXIII

Devi's mind was silent, and his body was distant. The entire world around him was shrouded in darkness. It seemed as if a lifetime had passed since he had felt Captain Heller's palms against his shoulders, looking back helplessly as Reya was pulled away by his men, but somehow he still felt his body drifting slowly through the water towards the bottom of the Deep Sea. He wondered how deep the water was and how long it would be until he felt himself come to rest on the seabed. The Sands themselves were vast. It was only natural that the water that surrounded them would be just as immense.

Though Devi's limbs felt far off, almost unreachable, he sensed a fire in his chest, searing across his collarbone and down through his ribs. His mind was hazy, but he did his best to focus on the pain. If he could reach out and grab it, feel it, he would know that he was conscious. And if he was conscious, he was alive. Whether he would remain alive long enough to force himself back towards the surface of the water was another matter.

Devi made an effort to slow his breathing, but with each laboured breath, the pain in his chest intensified. It felt as if it was spreading down his arms and out into the very tips of his fingers. It wasn't until he could finally feel his hands and his wrists that Devi realised he shouldn't be breathing at all. He was plunging through the depths of the sea, and he was filling his lungs with water in the meantime. Devi began to cough and splutter, trying his best to dispel the water from his body, but his throat and mouth were dry. They burned almost as intensely as the muscles in his arms, and he could hear his rasping voice echoing around him.

As Devi's body fell still once more, he finally felt present enough to tear his eyes open, and he expected to feel them burn in the saltwater. But they didn't. His vision was merely blurred and clouded. He closed his eyes and forced them open again, and he tried his best to lift his chin from his chest.

Slowly and painfully, the world around Devi began to come into focus. He was not, as he had thought, plunging through the water any longer. He could vaguely remember being consumed by the sea, but he could not recall the moment the world had gone black. And though he did seem to be surrounded by darkness, faint light glimmered all around him, illuminating the space in which he found himself.

As Devi continued to blink the haziness from his eyes, he saw stone walls all around. But these were not the smooth, refined, beige stone walls of the Keep. Instead, they were cold and grey, uneven and moist with cold and dankness. Bolted to the walls, Devi found one or two flame torches – the source of the low, orange light that washed over his body. He looked up, and he groaned a little as the muscles in his neck screamed out. Then, he heard movement to his left.

Forcing his head painfully around, Devi saw that he was in a small cave. The burning across his chest grew sharper second by second, and he could now feel that his hands were bound behind his back, his arms pulled tight against his body, the muscles between them tense and stretched.

As he looked to his left, Devi saw two hooded figures. Their bodies were draped in loose, sand-coloured cloaks, and the space beneath their hoods where their faces should be were vacant and anonymous. For a moment, Devi thought he might be hallucinating, his body laying at the bottom of the sea filled with water, his mind throwing images at his unconscious like nightmares. He watched as one of the hooded figures nodded in his direction, and the other began to move towards him.

Devi's head jerked back as a thin, bony hand took hold of him. He could feel that his scalp was thick with sweat, and the knuckles of the figure's fingers dug painfully into his skull. Devi stared up towards the roof of the cave, and a large droplet of condensation dripped onto his cheek, splashing his face. Then, the head of the figure appeared above him, and Devi was able to examine it closely for the first time.

Unlike the rest of its cloak, the figure's hood did not hang loosely. Instead, it protruded out from its skull, standing stiff and rigid and curving around what should have been the figure's face. Where Devi should have seen a pair of eyes glaring down at him, however, he saw nothing.

Though the vague shape of a face remained, the figure's features appeared to have been eaten away by The Sands. There were merely two shallow holes in place of its eyes, as well as a narrow slit for its mouth, and there was a subtle ridge that suggested the shape of a nose, but each was covered by a smooth, beige skin the colour of sand. Though it seemed to have no eyes, Devi could feel the figure glaring down at him, and though it seemed to have no lips and no tongue, no cheeks and no jaw, from somewhere beneath the hood, the figure spoke to him in a gruff, gravelly voice.

"It's about time," it said.

The only response Devi could manage was a groan. His hair tugged painfully at his scalp, and the muscles in his chest were on fire.

"We were starting to think you might never wake up."

The hooded figure released its grip of Devi's head, and his chin slumped against his chest once more. His head felt heavy, and he barely had the strength, or the control over his body, to hold himself upright.

"Where am I?" Devi managed to force out.

"You know exactly where you are," the figure said.

"The Sands," Devi muttered. "But where?"

"Indeed," was the figure's only reply. "The Sands."

Devi groaned again. With all the strength he could muster, he forced his head from his chest and held it upright.

"Where are the others?" the hooded figure asked.

"What others?"

Suddenly, Devi felt his cheek explode as the figure lashed out a limb from beneath its cloak and struck him in the face.

"There is no use being deceitful," the figure spat, its voice seeming to emanate from its entire body. "Not if you value your life."

Devi breathed heavily. A thick streak of saliva ran from one side of his mouth down his chin, and he was sure he could taste blood on his lips.

"I'll ask you again. Where are the others?"

"I don't know," Devi said. "I'm alone."

Devi felt his cheek erupt once more, and he watched as blood and saliva splattered on the floor at his feet. He knew the answer the figure was looking for, but if he gave it up, there would no longer be any reason to keep him alive.

"We've seen your ship," the figure said. "Do you take me for a fool? There must be hundreds of you."

This time, Devi kept his mouth shut. He knew he risked another bolt across the face, but as long as he had information the figure needed, he hoped he would receive little more than that.

"How many of you were aboard?" the figure pressed.

Still Devi remained silent. This time, he felt a closed fist crush his nose against his face, and blood immediately began to leak out across his lips.

"Don't think I won't kill you, boy."

Devi licked away the blood.

"You won't kill me," he said.

"I have killed many Darmeenians. You think I would hesitate to kill another?"

"I'm no Darmeenian," Devi said, his voice low and laboured.

"Who else possesses a ship of that size?"

The figure's voice was full of fury, and it echoed around the tiny cave.

"I will not warn you again. Do not attempt to deceive me."

"I came on the Darmeenians' ship, but I'm no Darmeenian."

"Then who are you?"

"I'm from Katai," Devi said.

Devi did his best to turn his palm face p behind his back. He wasn't sure whether his branded wrist would be enough to convince the figure he was from Katai, but it was worth a try.

"Darmeen. Katai. It matters little," the hooded figure said, glancing over Devi's shoulder to where his wrists were tied. "You seek the Fire Stone."

"I do," Devi said.

"And you are not the only Seeker. Where are the others?"

Devi knew he was playing a risky game. There was every chance the figure would slit his throat and go out looking for the Darmeenians without his help. For the first time, however, buried deep below the anger and the fury, Devi caught a hint of desperation in the voice that scolded him.

"Free me, and I will tell you," he said.

The anonymous face of the figure seemed to laugh. "Tell me, and I will free you."

Devi sensed his advantage.

"You know there are Seekers out there," he said. "You know they are searching for you, and for the Fire Stone, but you do not know where they are or when they will arrive. Release me, and the information is yours."

The figure swooped in closer to Devi's face. Devi held what should have been its gaze for a moment, but its vacant features were eerie and uncanny, and he couldn't prevent himself from turning his cheek. As it moved, the figure's robe swept and fluttered loosely, as if there was some ethereal body beneath, material yet somehow transient. Then, Devi felt a thin, bony hand crawl up his chest and settle on his throat. Its fingers pinched his windpipe, and suddenly it was painful to breathe.

"The information will be mine," the figure hissed. "You may give it to me, or I may take it from you, but I will have it one way or another."

Devi struggled to swallow down a few gasping breaths, but he knew there was only one way he would make it out of the cave with his life.

"You may torture me," he said. "But I'll die before I speak. Then, the Darmeenians will arrive, and you'll die too. And the longer you spend torturing me, the closer the Darmeenians get."

The figure's grip on Devi's throat tightened, but Devi managed to force out a few final words.

"You have no choice. Either you release me, or we all die."

The figure's hand lingered on Devi's throat. For a moment, it squeezed so tightly that Devi couldn't breathe at all, and then the figure finally released its grip.

"Go and fetch Sadikah."

The figure turned back to its companion across the cave, who immediately slipped through the wooden door opposite Devi. As the door opened, Devi struggled to catch a glimpse of what laid beyond, but all he could see was a dark and gloomy stone corridor. The figure that had stood over Devi made his way behind the chair that he was tied to and, for a moment, Devi hoped he might feel its fingers once more, this time untying the ropes that continued to bind him. The figure simply settled behind him, however, its robes falling so still and so silent that Devi couldn't help wondering whether it was capable of vanishing into the stone as well as into the sand.

As Devi sat, slumped over to one side, the throbbing in his face dragging his mind even more steadily back towards lucidity, he gazed around the cave. It was merely a small, low hollow in the stone, and Devi assumed he must be deep below one of the mountains or rock faces he had seen lining the shore from the deck of The Kraken. The stone was grey and somewhat moist where it met the floor and the roof, but as he looked across the walls to his right, Devi noticed they were covered by faint, brown markings, so subtle that they were difficult to make out in the dim light afforded by the pair of flaming torches close to the door.

The markings seemed to be paintings of some kind, their lines too precise and uniform merely to be part of the stone's natural colouring. As he inspected the markings closer, Devi saw that the lines resembled The Sands themselves, some rising and falling like the dunes by the coast, others sharp and jagged like the mountains he felt sure he was buried beneath. Across the desert, there seemed to be countless figures spanning the entire breadth of the cave's wall, flooding out around and between the dunes and the mountains. The figures seemed to be robed like those inside the cave itself, and they were countless in their number.

What Devi also noticed was that the robed figures all seemed to coalesce, their lines all leading to one spot at the very centre of the wall, where they all met to form a small circle. At the centre of the circle stood a single figure, but this figure was not robed. Instead, he stood in stark contrast to the countless figures around him, small enough that Devi quickly became convinced that the figure was merely a boy, and different enough that it was clear he was not of The Sands.

As Devi narrowed his eyes and tried to get a closer look at the boy, the wooden door at the other end of the cave creaked open, and another hooded figure walked in. The figure paused by the door for a moment, and then it glided over the threshold, seeming almost to float beneath its cloak, which spilled out across the floor like liquid. The vacant space where the figure's face should be glared at Devi, its invisible eyes seeming to take in every inch of him.

Then, Devi watched as two coarse, withered hands emerged from beneath the cloak. They reached towards the hood of the figure and pulled it back, the hood itself coming to rest on the figure's shoulders, revealing a layer of perfectly smooth, beige skin beneath.

Devi saw now that the suggestion of a face sat at the front of a hairless head, with a ridge on each side that gave the impression of ears, even if it was impossible for Devi to confirm that this is what they were. Just like the stories he had heard since he was a boy, the figure looked like a man whose features had been worn away by The Sands, wiped from his face like the ancient civilisation that had been wiped from the land, leaving behind nothing but vague semblances of what had once been.

In its right hand, the figure held a golden staff, and Devi followed it from its base, which rested against the stone floor of the cave, all the way to the circular embellishment he found at the top. There, embedded in a setting of gold was the Fire Stone. Though no man in

Katai had ever laid eyes on the Stone, Devi was certain that he was the first. It shone with an irrepressible incandescence that seemed all but otherworldly. It held his eyes as captives, and it seemed to burn with the fire of a thousand generations.

Devi could hardly tear his eyes from the Stone, but he watched as the figure's coarse hands reached towards the top of its skull, and it seemed to take its skin in its bony fingers, pulling it down and peeling it away from the bone. What laid beneath the skin was not bone, however. Instead, Devi found himself gazing into the face of a man. His skin was wrinkled and greying, and his cheeks were sunken, but it was the face of a man like any other. Of this, Devi was in no doubt. The man gazed across the cave towards Devi through two blackened eyes, and he stepped towards him.

The man stood over Devi, and Devi glanced up towards him. He moved with a grace and elegance almost beyond mortality, but somehow he appeared fragile. Devi felt as if he had seen the man's face before in every beggar that sat at the edge of the streets in Narkasee, and in the helpless eyes of the men and women that laid motionless in the fields of Rakhas.

"You are from Katai?" the man asked.

"I am," Devi said.

"And you think because you are not from Darmeen that you are not our enemy?"

The man spoke gently, but his voice was fortified by a distinct air of forthright authority.

"Katai is no one's enemy," Devi said defiantly.

"Katai seeks the Fire Stone just as Darmeen does. The Fire Stone belongs to my people. Whoever wishes to take it from us is our enemy."

"Katai seeks the Fire Stone," Devi confirmed. "But merely to keep it from Darmeen. Every kingdom has its right to defend its people. It is Darmeen that wishes to change this, not Katai."

The man held Devi's gaze, his face stoic and unmoving.

"Then, if you do not wish to take the Fire Stone from us," he said. "Why have you risked your life coming here?"

"It is as I said. If Darmeen obtains the Fire Stone, Katai will be lost forever. If we are able to keep the Fire Stone from Darmeen, Katai may live to see another day."

The man continued to stare back at Devi, and for a moment, Devi was certain his intention was to kill him.

"Kill me if you wish," he said, failing to prevent a hint of desperation from creeping into his voice. "But to kill me is to wash away all knowledge of the Darmeenians and their plans. I know their numbers. I know the location of their camp. I know the routes that their Seekers plan to follow. Kill me, and the Seekers will find you. Perhaps you will be able to fend them off as you have before. But they will send more. And more. And more. They will send their Seekers until the Fire Stone is theirs."

Devi looked around the cave, a mere sunken hollow beneath the rock of the mountains. Then, he looked back at the man, his tired eyes sunken beneath a withered, wrinkled brow. He looked as if he held the weight of the world on his shoulders, and he looked almost as desperate as Devi felt.

Devi thought back to the stories he had heard of the Sand Dwellers, passed from mouth to mouth all over Katai, and likely all over Darmeen too. According to the stories, the Sand Dwellers lived amongst the sand, basking in its glory rather than cowering from it. They were faceless warriors. Their eyes and noses had been worn away by the wind and the storms, but their blades were sharp, and they could vanish into the dunes at a moment's notice as if they were made of vapour.

Though there seemed to be a kernel of truth in each of the tales, it was clear to Devi now that they had been protected by husks of deception. It was true that the Sand Dwellers lived amongst the sand, but their caves seemed a meek and meagre shelter, and they certainly did not seem to bask in its glory. It was also true that they were faceless, but their features were merely hidden beneath a skin of protective fabric, shielding them from the harshness of the desert. And it was true that they could vanish into the dunes, their long, flowing robes the colour of sand, but beneath them, they were all flesh and blood like every other man.

The Sand Dwellers seemed to have forged a life for themselves amongst the dunes, but if the Darmeenians were ever to reach them, Devi was in no doubt that, just like Katai, they would be overwhelmed.

"Katai must keep the Fire Stone from Darmeen," Devi said. "But you must do the same. It seems your time is running out just like ours. Alone, neither of us can stand against the Darmeenians. Together, perhaps we have a chance."

The man continued to look at Devi for a moment longer. Then, he slipped a dagger from a sheath at his waist and stepped around him. Devi could feel the man lingering at his back, and when his hand fell upon Devi's shoulder close to his neck, he thought for a moment that he had made a terrible misjudgement. Devi held his breath and waited, expecting to feel the man's knife running across his throat at any moment. Instead, the man's cold, withered fingers slid down to his wrist, and the cool metal of his blade began to cut the rope away.

Devi's arms fell to his sides, and pain shot through his muscles like water down a riverbed. His arms hung loosely for a moment before he made an effort to lift them, massaging his forearms with his fingers and kneading the pain away like a baker with his dough. Then, Devi looked up at the man as he stepped before him once more and reached out his hand.

"I am Sadikah," the man said.

XXIV

Devi followed closely behind Sadikah, the invisible eyes of the anonymous, robed figures that he passed following him as he made his way down another narrow passage. Behind him, Devi could still feel the presence of the Sand Dwellers that had been there to greet him when he awoke, but he no longer felt the touch of their cold, bony fingers against his skin.

Inside the small cave in which he had awoken moments earlier, the stone walls had been wet and grey, and it was clear to Devi that they had been hollowed out of the rock of the mountains that lined the coast of The Sands. Outside the cave, the passages cut and weaved through the rock in all directions, and Devi was in no doubt that he was beneath the jagged peaks he had seen from the deck of The Kraken. Though it was clear he was underground, there still seemed to be a thin layer of sand covering the ground beneath his feet.

Sadikah walked in silence, and Devi did the same, but the Sand Dwellers that they passed invariably lowered their heads in a subtle bow, each muttering a few muted words to which Sadikah responded merely with a subtle nod of his own. Each of the Sand Dwellers wore the same long, flowing, beige robes that concealed their entire bodies, and it unsettled Devi somewhat to know there could be almost anything lurking beneath them.

Up ahead, the narrow passages seemed to give way to a wider, more open clearing, where several of the Sand Dwellers seemed to have congregated. As Devi followed Sadikah down the last of the narrow passages and out into the clearing, a gentle gust of wind seemed to swirl around the space, lifting Sadikah's robes from the floor just a little as he walked ahead. The clearing seemed to give way to another shorter, wider passage to Devi's left too, which rose on a shallow incline away from his position. As Devi craned his neck, he saw a thin slit of brilliant, white light - the relentless sun beating down on the endless desert of The Sands.

Then, Sadikah turned to face him.

"If you'll excuse me for a moment," he said. "They are waiting on me to depart."

Sadikah turned away in the direction of a group of Sand Dwellers that lingered by the wide opening of the passageway to Devi's left. As he did so, the two Dwellers behind Devi stepped forward, each taking hold of his arm in one hand and his shoulder in the other. But Sadikah turned back to face them, and he waved them off.

"Unhand the boy," he said. "And allow him his space."

Immediately, the Sand Dwellers released their grip of Devi's arms and stepped back from him.

Devi watched as Sadikah approached the group of Dwellers that awaited him. They each bowed their heads low, just as the others had, and they gathered around Sadikah as he approached. For a moment, Devi was reminded of the trainee Seekers and the way they would all congregate around Farruk, ready to hear his wisdom and heed his instructions.

Devi could see that a handful of the figures had pulled their robes aside, revealing sheaths at their hips, which seemed to hold short swords with blades that curved so far back that they almost touched their handles. Devi watched one of the Dwellers as he adjusted his sheath, tightened the laces of the lightweight boots that reached his knees, and tucked a smaller blade inside one of them. Then, the figure pulled his robes around his body again, and he almost seemed to vanish beneath them.

As Sadikah spoke what appeared to be his parting words, the Sand Dwellers each pulled their stiff, rigid hoods over the flawless, beige skin that covered their faces. Then, they each turned away from the clearing, making their slow and steady way up the wide, sloping passage towards the desert until they disappeared from sight.

"My apologies," Sadikah said, returning to Devi's side. "You must be hungry. Allow us to see to that."

Sadikah turned to the two Sand Dwellers still close at Devi's back, whose faces Devi still had not seen. Devi considered declining the offer, but his stomach rumbled in protest, and the Dwellers moved too quickly to allow him to do so, regardless. Without a word, each of the men retreated, vanishing up another narrow passage close by, and Sadikah began to lead Devi once more.

As he followed Sadikah across the clearing and down another narrow passage, the stone walls around him seemed to change. They were no longer the same dull grey as the rock of the mountains, but instead they seemed to be a withered and pale brown. They no longer seemed to be formed of a single, sheer face of rock either, into which the caves and passages had been carved. Instead, there appeared to be seams where several chunks of rock met, almost like bricks, the corners and edges of which were ragged and crumbling.

On his left and his right, Devi passed several archways in the rock, some of which gave way to other long, narrow passages that seemed to snake away even deeper into the mountains. Others, however, gave way to small, cave-like rooms similar to the one he had awoken in a short time earlier, only they too were lined with pale, brown stones like bricks. Though he only caught fleeting glances as he passed, some of the walls appeared to have been decorated with scenes similar to those he had seen in the cave earlier too, depictions of hordes of Sand Dwellers all congregating in the sand.

As he passed the small, hollowed-out caves, Devi was taken aback to see several figures staring back at him, their hoods pulled down around their shoulders and their faces exposed. The Sand Dwellers were varying in their number, but they were far from varying in their condition.

Some rooms contained only a single Dweller, seemingly surrounded by his meagre possessions - a ragged blanket on the floor for his bed, a wooden shelf that was all but empty, and a pile of loose robes and boots. Other rooms contained what appeared to be small families, huddled together at the centre of their cave, cloistered by the broken remains of the furniture around them.

Invariably, the faces of the figures that stared back at Devi as he passed, like Sadikah's, were pale and sunken. Their skin was withered and thin, and their eyes were yellow and bloodshot. They sat upon the floor in their tiny caves, each within arm's reach of the others, not only because the meagre space would barely allow them to be any further apart, but also because there seemed to be few other sources of comfort close at hand.

As they reached the end of the long passageway, Sadikah and Devi arrived at another wooden door, and Sadikah pushed it open, holding it there for Devi and ushering him inside. Like the tiny rooms they had just passed, the space was a small, cave-like area, filled by little other than ragged blankets and rotting, wooden furniture scattered haphazardly wherever it might fit. The space was slightly larger than those they had passed, however, and at its centre was a wooden table, which was lined with two low, wooden benches.

Devi hadn't been sure what to expect when he passed through the doorway into Sadikah's room. Each of the Sand Dwellers he had seen so far had appeared meek and fragile, withering away beneath The Sands in the tiny hollows they seemed to call their homes. Each of them seemed to revere Sadikah, however, almost immediately sending for him when Devi had awoken, gathering around him before departing into The Sands, and even bowing their heads at him as he passed. It was clear that Sadikah was their leader, but his face was just as withered, and his room was just as meagre.

"Please," Sadikah said, gesturing towards one of the benches. "Take a seat."

Devi did as he was asked, and he took a seat at one of the benches. Glancing around the room, he saw that

Sadikah's walls matched those of the rooms that they had passed earlier - lined with withering, beige bricks the colour of sand, which were covered with faded, painted lines. Devi searched the walls for the same figure he had seen in the cave earlier, and which he had struggled to find in the caves along the passageway - the image of the boy around whom the hordes of Sand Dwellers congregated - but the lines were so faded that he could barely make them out.

Sadikah made his way over to a decrepit, wooden cabinet at the back of the cave, and he found a wooden beaker there. He held the beaker into a small hollow that was formed in the wall, and Devi heard the rippling of water as the beaker filled. Just then, a knock sounded at Sadikah's door.

"Enter," Sadikah called.

The withered face of another Sand Dweller pushed the door open, and he came crawling into the room, a wooden plate trembling in his hand.

"Ah, thank you," Sadikah said, gesturing for the man to place the plate in front of Devi. "It's not much, but I hope it will suffice."

Devi looked down at the plate, which was covered by thin slices of some green fruit or vegetable. Its skin was pale, and its flesh was almost translucent. Beside the slices was a handful of what appeared to be some kind of nut, and two dry, dusty balls that Devi thought could have been formed of maize or some other grain.

"Thank you," Devi said, the rumbling of his stomach more muted now, as if it was unsure what to make of the offering.

The Sand Dweller retreated from Sadikah's room, bowing his head subtly as he backed away and pulled the door closed behind him.

Delicately, Devi lifted a slice of the green fruit from his plate, and it flopped around between his fingers. He rolled it between his thumb and two fingers and slipped it into his mouth. Though the plant was far less moist than any fruit Devi had tasted before, it was surprisingly sweet, and he immediately took up a second slice and slipped it into his mouth whilst he continued to chew away at the first.

"I apologise for the heavy-handedness of my men earlier," Sadikah said.

Devi's nose still throbbed, and he could feel the blood that had trickled across his lips already beginning to dry.

"We have grown increasingly wary of -"

Sadikah paused for a moment.

"Visitors."

Devi swallowed the slices of fruit, and he took up one of the maize balls, which crunched loudly as it fell apart between his teeth. He looked up at the fragile, withered face of Sadikah, and he saw a wounded animal, ready to lash out at anything he might perceive as a threat but desperate to find some path out of the forest, where he could rest and recover.

"It's understandable," Devi said.

He wished his village, along with the rest of Katai, had been a little more wary of visitors, stocking their farms with swords as well as sickles and scythes, and maintaining the signal towers that had petered out on the night of the raid rather than neglecting them and allowing them to fall dormant.

"I know you have grown to fear Katai," Devi continued. "But Katai is no one's enemy. It is true we seek the Fire Stone, but we seek it merely to defend ourselves against Darmeen. Katai wishes simply to live freely. If Darmeen possesses the Aether Stones, no one will live freely."

Sadikah looked back at Devi, his face grave and anxious.

"The Darmeenians are coming," Devi said simply. "But I know where they have made their camp. I know where their Seekers plan to search for the Fire Stone, and I know what they plan to do once they obtain it," Devi said. "All of this information will be yours."

"And what do you expect in return?" Sadikah asked.

"I expect nothing."

Sadikah eyed Devi even more closely.

"If you wish, you may cast me out into The Sands," Devi said. "Katai does not seek to *possess* the Fire Stone. Katai merely seeks to keep the Fire Stone from Darmeen. The information will be yours, and you may do with it what you wish. You know the desert better than anyone, and if you know the Darmeenians' plans, I have no doubt you will defeat them."

Devi paused.

"But they will return. And if you defeat them next time, they will return again."

Sadikah breathed deeply. It was clear he knew the truth of Devi's words. Devi could tell he had spoken the same words over and over again to himself countless times. If Devi already knew the Sand Dwellers were running out of time, then Sadikah knew it far more keenly.

"We have a common enemy in Darmeen," Devi said. "And we have a common enemy in The Sands. The desert has already wiped your kingdom from existence, and it will do the same to Katai. At least, it will if Darmeen doesn't do so first. You may cast me out into The Sands if you wish. Or, you may join me and strike back against Darmeen."

The Fire Stone glowed a menacing amber at the tip of Sadikah's sceptre, and Sadikah glanced in its direction before returning his gaze to Devi.

"Lead us to them," he said.

Devi held his hand to his eyes as he peered over the top of the sand dune. From a distance, The Kraken looked as large and imposing as it had up close, lurking just off the coast, barely moving with the ceaseless flow of the tide. Between the ship and Devi's position atop the ridge, countless tents had been scattered, and they were surrounded by the boxes and barrels that Devi had watched being packed and loaded back in the Port of Princi. Regardless, the ship still sat heavy in the water.

The camp was filled with people too, scurrying from tent to tent like ants in a nest. Devi wasn't sure how long the Seekers planned to stay, but it was clear they weren't as confident about finding the Fire Stone as it had first seemed, the camp appearing to be equipped to provide for them for weeks. At the very least, it looked as if it could provide for them long enough for The Kraken to sail back to Katai and rain hell on Narkasee before returning to collect them, if necessary.

As he ducked his head below the line of the ridge once more, Devi gazed from left to right along the face of the dune that rose up from the sand behind him. The Sand Dwellers had moved across the desert with enviable ease. Their feet had barely sunk into the steep waves of sand that rose and fell across the vast stretches of golden emptiness, and it had seemed as if they were walking on water. Devi, on the other hand, had struggled to wade through. Now, the Sand Dwellers sat waiting, their sand-coloured cloaks making them almost invisible. Though they numbered in their hundreds, Devi could hardly tell where the Dwellers ended and the dunes began. If he hadn't known where to look, he may never have seen them at all.

Devi watched as Sadikah broke rank and came gliding across the face of the dune towards him.

"What do you see?" Sadikah asked.

"Just as I expected," Devi said. "There's no sign of the Seekers. They must be out there somewhere."

Devi nodded back towards the vast wasteland he and the Sand Dwellers had crossed, grateful he had not been forced to traverse it alone.

"They have numbers," Devi continued. "But it's all sailors and cooks. Half will be boys, most won't even have weapons."

Sadikah slid up to the edge of the dune and looked out towards the camp for himself. The Fire Stone glowed a menacing orange in his sceptre, which he held close at his side.

"Captain Heller may be down there," Devi said. "Or he may be on the ship. Some of his men will be experienced seamen, but the rest are just here to maintain the camp. They won't put up much of a fight."

Sadikah already seemed convinced, and Devi suddenly felt as if he was speaking to reassure himself as much as anyone else. He clutched the handle of his sword tightly, and his stomach twisted in a knot. He had not held a sword since training, and its blade had been wooden. Though the curved blade he held now was smooth and ornate, Devi knew its beauty belied its capabilities – a single swing could leave a man torn in two.

"If I may?" Sadikah said, and Devi nodded his assent. "The dune gives way to the sand to our left, where a clear approach to the camp may be made."

Sadikah held an arm aloft, gesturing in the direction.

"A single force will likely overwhelm them, but the element of surprise may be even easier to obtain with two forces. I suggest that I lead a force to the base of the dune, which will attack from the exposed rear once you have made an initial assault from this position."

Devi pursed his lips and nodded. Sadikah knew The Sands much better than he did, and he was happy to acquiesce.

"Agreed," he said.

"Then I will wait on your lead."

Sadikah turned to his right, signalling along the line of Sand Dwellers with his hands. Then, the entire dune seemed to shift as several of the Dwellers began to creep away from Devi's position, making their way slowly down the ridge. Sadikah turned to his left and gave a similar signal. This time, only a handful of Sand Dwellers began to move away from Devi, and the others simply rose from their crouched positions, each inching closer to the edge of the ridge.

Though their weapons until now had been concealed, the Sand Dwellers alongside Devi slid bows out from beneath their robes. Each pulled an arrow from the quivers strapped at their waists, and they nocked the arrows in the strings of their bows. The dune continued to shift to Devi's left as Sadikah led his band of Dwellers around towards the far edge of the camp. Then, Devi watched as Sadikah turned back to face him, and he flashed a final signal in his direction. The Sand Dwellers at the edge of the ridge rose to standing, pulled back the strings of their bows, and waited.

Devi stared up at the men as their string arms quivered, holding the tension in their bows tight with every muscle and fibre in their body. But other than their quivering arms, they stood perfectly still.

Devi rose to standing too, and he stepped forward to the edge of the dune. He looked to his left, and he saw the dune fall still and silent once more as Sadikah and his men settled into their position. When Devi raised his arm, he heard the creak of the bows to his left and his right as the Sand Dwellers pulled their strings even tighter. Then, he threw his arm towards the ground, and suddenly a cloud of arrows hung high in the air. In an instant, the Sand Dwellers had each pulled another arrow from their quiver, nocked it once more, and sent a second cloud of arrows into the sky.

Devi watched as the first shower of arrows rained down on the camp at the base of the ridge. Some pierced the fabric of the tents, some drove their way into the wooden boxes and barrels that were scattered all over, and some fell harmlessly into the sand. A handful of the arrows, however, found the flesh of the Darmeenians that scurried about the camp, piercing their hearts and faces as they looked towards the sky.

Then, before he knew it, Devi was running. The second volley of arrows came crashing down on the camp below, and a third flew high into the air above him, but Devi didn't slow his pace. If anything, he ran even faster. His body felt wild and out of control as he barrelled down the face of the sand dune, and before he knew it, he had reached the bottom.

There, staring back at him, his eyes wide and his body stiff and immobile, was a single Darmeenian man. He clutched a wooden crate in both hands, and he stared up at the great dune behind Devi, which stormed in an avalanche down towards him. Without a thought, Devi raised the curved blade of his sword high into the air, where it glimmered in the light of the blinding desert sun for a moment, and he brought it sweeping across the Darmeenian man's stomach. The crate in the man's hands fell to the ground, and half a dozen rotting apples spilled across the sand. Then, the contents of the man's stomach spilled out alongside them, and his body crumpled into a heap.

Devi stared down at the man, and for a moment, he couldn't convince himself that what he saw was real – that the thick, red blood that dampened the sand was the same blood that dripped from the blade of his sword. He looked deep into the man's eyes, and it felt as if he was back in Katai looking into the eyes of Jerod, whose own stomach had been sliced open at the hands of a Darmeenian.

In that moment, it felt as if justice had been served. But it wasn't the Darmeenian at Devi's feet that had cut Jerod open. There likely wasn't a single man in the camp that had been in Rakhas the night it had burned. Devi stared at the blood on his sword before returning his gaze to the man who laid lifeless on the ground. Then, a storm whirled around him as the horde of Sand Dwellers came crashing down onto the sand like a wave, flooding across the camp and sweeping Devi forward like the tide.

Brilliant metal flashed to Devi's left as the blades of the Sand Dwellers cut through the air. To his right, Devi watched as the cloaked figures cascaded across the sand, their own arrows snapping beneath their feet as they stormed past him. Darmeenian men stepped out of their tents, their faces all horror and confusion for the brief moment before they were greeted by a sword. Then, they slumped to the ground like beached whales, their bodies making their homes in the sand, where they would rot and wither and perish under the sun until all that was left was their brittle bones.

The Sand Dwellers moved with a grace and elegance that Devi had never known. They drifted across the sand liked birds through the sky, twisting and gliding effortlessly, hardly deigning to beat their wings. They used their swords as Devi used his hands. It was as if they had been born with curved blades in their tiny fingers, or as if they had never been born at all but had merely emerged from the sand clutching the weapons. Their cloaks waved and swayed in the gentle wind as their bodies spun, and together they looked like a great sandstorm sweeping across the desert, laying waste to everything in its path.

As Devi cast his gaze around the camp, he saw a handful of Darmeenians beginning to mount some semblance of a counter-offensive, but they were disorganised and haphazard. The few men with sheaths at their hips drew their swords and engaged the Sand Dwellers, but they were quickly surrounded and dispatched. Even those that managed to challenge one of the Dwellers man to man were unable to do little more than briefly prolong their inevitable fate.

When Devi saw Sadikah sweeping across the sand with his own band of cloaked warriors in tow, he knew the camp was already theirs for the taking. Sadikah raised his sceptre into the air and swung it ferociously towards the Darmeenian that charged in his direction. The man's skull instantly split in two, and he ploughed into the ground, his body half-covered in sand by the time it came to rest. Sadikah leapt into the air, twisted his body in a half-circle, and brought his sceptre down on the shoulder of another man, whose back was turned. The man's neck contorted awkwardly, and he too slumped to the floor.

It was then that Devi finally caught a glimpse of the power of the Fire Stone. He watched as Sadikah held his staff high above his head, and the Fire Stone seemed to glow with an unworldly luminescence. When Sadikah swept the Stone across the dry, dusty ground, waves of flames snaked away from it, each seeming not to race away from the Stone itself in the direction that it had begun, but instead seeming to act of its own accord, seeking out the Darmeenians that continued to scurry desperately to and fro around the camp.

It was clear there was vast, unbridled power within the Fire Stone. If the Darmeenians had not yet laid siege to Narkasee, the Earth Stone would still be buried deep within the Keep, its power just as fertile, yet dormant for the time being, and Devi shuddered as he contemplated the power that would be unleashed if the Stones were combined.

As death and chaos hung in the air, Devi found himself running once more. The Sand Dwellers had flooded past him into the camp, and he followed after them now. Confused Darmeenians wandered past him, their faces bloodied and their bodies sliced and torn, and Devi cut them down as he ran. He swung the curved blade of his sword so violently that it seemed to scream as it sliced through the air. Then, in the corner of his eye, Devi caught the glint of a blade.

Before he knew it, he had raised his own sword to block the oncoming blow, twisting away from his attacker in the way that Farruk had shown him, and thrusting his sword into the man's stomach. Devi watched the light fade from the man's eyes for a second.

Then, he pulled the sword out, and the man slumped to the ground.

A second Darmeenian stood alongside the man that laid in a bloody heap before him. He stared back at Devi, his wide eyes full of terror and confusion. Devi raised his sword again, ready to cut the man's head from his body, but the man simply cowered. He raised his hands above his head, closed his eyes, and awaited his felling blow. But Devi paused.

Deep within the truest heart, he thought to himself. *There lies a darkness all but rare.*

The man that cowered before him was Darmeenian, but he appeared merely to be a cook. Devi felt certain that Darmeen was the enemy of Katai, but he felt less certain the same could be said of every man and woman in Darmeen. After all, King Vagan himself had once considered himself Darmeenian, and without him, there would be no Katai.

Every soul must do its part, Devi decided. *To bring the good Son's light to bear.*

His sword lingered in the air, blood dripping down his arm and the sleeve of his tunic, its blade glimmering in the light of the sun. The Darmeenian man lowered his trembling arms and opened his eyes. He looked back at Devi for a brief moment, and then he took off running.

Behind the man, several other Darmeenians followed. Devi watched as they fled past him, scrambling up the dune that he and the Sand Dwellers had just descended. What awaited them in The Sands, they could not know. Their chances of survival would be remote, but their chances of living to watch the sun set again would all but vanish if they were to remain in the camp. The camp itself fell still for a moment, and then a single Darmeenian man scurried out of a tent and up the dune after his compatriots, never breaking Devi's gaze as he scampered past him.

The sand was thick with blood, and a deathly silence lingered in the air like a heavy mist that had drifted in off the water. Everywhere Devi looked, he saw bodies, either already lifeless or steadily inching ever closer to death. Devi looked down at his feet, and his worn, hide boots were splattered red. The sand beneath him was dry and cracked, and it eagerly drank down the blood that he and the Sand Dwellers had spilled.

Then, Devi's eyes drifted to the motionless man just in front of him. It seemed unthinkable that it had been his blade that had stolen the life from his body. Devi felt that, if he were to drop to his knees and shake the man by the shoulders, he would wake up, as if he had merely been caught in a bloody nightmare. But deep down, he knew the truth. The moment his blade had pierced the man's skin, he was gone.

Devi remembered dropping to his knees beside his father's lifeless body, and in that moment, it had seemed as if life was so fragile and so fleeting, and Devi had never felt closer to death. He felt scared now, but what scared him most was the vitality that coursed through his veins. As the Sand Dwellers began to swarm around him, wiping their own bloodied blades on their sand-coloured cloaks, Devi felt powerful, almost invincible. He would likely never lay eyes on the man that had taken his father from him, but all around him laid the lifeless bodies of the Darmeenians that would accept vengeance on his behalf. He also knew that, in just a few short moments, he would come face to face with the man that had taken Reya from him.

"Are you ok?"

Sadikah arrived at Devi's side, the Fire Stone in his sceptre still glowing a fiery orange.

"Devi? Are you hurt?"

Devi stood in silence for a moment. Then, he turned to face Sadikah.

"They're still on the ship," Devi said, choosing to answer a question that Sadikah had not asked rather than the one that he had. "Let's go."

The far edge of the camp gave way to the beach, and the water continued to roll up and down the shore. Where the water met the sand, several small boats had been moored, their lines tied to wooden stakes that had been driven into the beach like those back in Black Soul's Bay. Devi strode towards the boats, and Sadikah followed closely. The two bands of Sand Dwellers merged into one great, faceless horde behind them once more, and they began to fill the boats that had carried the Darmeenians from The Kraken to the coast.

Devi and Sadikah each climbed into the same boat, and Devi found two great, wooden oars inside. Two Sand Dwellers took the oars from Devi, each taking their seats at the centre of the boat and preparing to row. Devi made his way to the bow, and he turned back to see the Sand Dwellers tearing the wooden stakes from the sand and tossing them into the water, dampening their robes as they clambered through the shallows and up into the boats themselves. Then, they were on their way, dozens of tiny, wooden vessels each ploughing through the tide towards the great shadow of The Kraken that loomed in the water ahead of them.

Devi stared up towards the deck of the great ship as they slowly drew closer and closer. The camp at their back had been crawling with Darmeenians, but now all that remained was their lifeless bodies, and the deck of The Kraken appeared to be entirely empty. There was no sign of the sailors that had steered the gargantuan vessel from the Port of Princi Bay deeper into The Sands than ever before, no sign of the Seekers that would be in search of the Fire Stone in Sadikah's sceptre, and no sign of Captain Heller.

Devi's tiny ship knocked into the hull of The Kraken. Looking up, the ship seemed to loom over him like the great face of the Salt Cliffs, and in a second, the Sand Dwellers were clinging to its side, hanging from the ropes, nets, and pulleys there like beetles scurrying up the bark of a tree. They hoisted their bodies out of their boats and climbed towards the deck of the ship, some reaching the taffrail almost before Devi was even able to reach up and grab hold of the ship's netting for himself.

By the time Devi reached the top, the deck was already swarming with Sand Dwellers, their sandy robes standing stark against the blue sky now that they were no longer concealed by the dunes. Devi clambered over the taffrail and onto the deck, and Sadikah followed close behind.

Though the deck was packed with bodies, an eerie silence hung in the air. The Sand Dwellers each stood in silence, and the camp at Devi's back was now lifeless and still. Then, away to his right, Devi heard the creaking of a door, and he turned to see Captain Heller stumbling out of his cabin, his tunic torn-half open, revealing a filthy chest, and a half-empty rum bottle in his hand.

"What is the meaning of this?" Captain Heller spat, his words slurred, his chin moist with saliva.

Devi could see the confusion in the captain's face from the other side of the ship. His eyes scanned the deck of The Kraken, undoubtedly expecting to see his shipmates but instead being confronted by a horde of faceless figures. Devi watched as Captain Heller's body swayed from side to side, his eyes twisting and squinting as they struggled to determine whether what they saw was real, or whether it was merely part of some drunken stupor. Then, the captain's eyes fell upon Devi, and they narrowed even further as they struggled to place him.

"The Katai boy," Captain Heller said finally, his lethargic mind slowly beginning to piece together the fragments of understanding it had been able to glean.

With a speed and dexterity belying his state of intoxication, Captain Heller reached for the pistol at his hip and turned it on Devi. Devi stood perfectly still as a cloud of smoke masked the captain's face and a single shot sounded across the deck. Ahead of Devi, at the centre of the ship, the shot ripped into the great mast that held the main sail, sending splinters of wood flying across the deck, whilst Captain Heller's pistol also clattered to the floor, his body consumed beneath the robes of several Sand Dwellers.

"Unhand me," Captain Heller roared, his voice muffled, his words even more slurred than they had been previously. "Don't think I won't –"

The captain fell silent as one of the Sand Dweller's drove a clenched fist into his ribs. Then, the Dwellers lifted him from the deck, carrying him towards Devi and Sadikah as his feet searched frantically for the wooden boards that lingered just beneath them. Captain Heller continued to struggle, but his efforts were futile. The Sand Dwellers held him firmly in place, and one of the men grabbed a handful of his hair, holding his head still so that Devi could look directly into his eyes.

"Where is she?" Devi said.

His voice was calm and stoic, but he felt a fury burning inside him.

"Katai scum," Captain Heller said. "You're a kingdom of thieves with a traitor for a king."

Devi glared back at Captain Heller, but his face remained unmoved.

"Where is she?" he asked again.

Captain Heller sucked the saliva that ran down his chin back into his mouth, and he spat it in Devi's face. Devi stared back at Captain Heller as the odorous string of thick saliva ran down his cheek. He pulled the sleeve of his tunic over his hand and wiped his face dry. Then, he gripped the handle of his sword tight and held it up to the captain's throat.

"Look around," Devi said calmly.

He watched as a thin slit of red blood burst through Captain Heller's skin beneath his blade and ran down his neck.

"Your ship is empty. Your camp is empty. Your men are dead, and your Seekers are wandering the desert in search of a Stone they'll never find."

Devi could almost see the blood and rum slowly draining from Captain Heller's face. His eyes darted across the deck of the ship, where the countless anonymous figures of the Sand Dwellers continued to lurk. He tried to look back towards the shore too, but the Sand Dweller behind him held his head firmly in place.

"Katai men are not so merciless as those of Darmeen," Devi continued. "I could kill you where you stand and find Reya myself. Instead, I'm giving you the opportunity to redeem yourself. Tell me where she is, and your life will be spared."

Captain Heller stared back at Devi. In his eyes, Devi saw the same melange of terror and confusion he had seen in the eyes of the man that he had struck down back at the camp. It was the same look he had seen in the eyes of his neighbours as they fled across their fields, away from the Darmeenian raiders that laid waste to their farms and their homes. Devi knew little of death, but already he had discovered that it looked the same in everyone.

"She's in the Seeker's quarters," Captain Heller said, his voice weak and defeated.

Devi turned to Sadikah and pointed towards the door that he had passed through during his first night on the ship, when he had found himself amongst the Seekers' hammocks as he searched for Reya. Without a word, Sadikah turned to the handful of Sand Dwellers to his left, and they hurried away towards the back of the ship, disappearing through the door that Devi had pointed to.

Devi turned back to face Captain Heller, and he pressed his blade even more firmly against his neck. Captain Heller squirmed, clenching his jaw and gritting his teeth as the tiny wound that Devi had started opened up a little further.

"Now now," Captain Heller said, allowing a little more desperation to creep into his voice than he had likely intended. "I told you where she is. Stick to your word."

The deck fell silent and still, and Devi's mind was calm. For a moment, he heard only the waves lapping gently at the hull of The Kraken, but then, he heard dull thudding and muffled screams away to his right.

"Please," Reya screamed as she emerged out onto the deck. "Let me go."

Devi couldn't see Reya's face, but he could hear the fear in her voice, and he caught flashes of her pale skin as she struggled against the grip of the Sand Dwellers.

Then, one of the men stepped aside, and Reya's eyes immediately found Devi's own. Just as Captain Heller had, Reya stared back at Devi blankly for a moment. Then, she broke free from the Dwellers that crowded around her, each of them releasing his grip and standing aside, and she sprinted across the deck towards Devi. Devi felt Reya's arm slide around his waist as she barrelled into him, and he watched as Captain's Heller's eyes moved from his own face to Reya's.

"Don't even look at her," Devi snarled.

The captain's frantic eyes met Devi's once more.

"I told you where she was," he said. "Now let me go."

Devi stood fixed in place. He pulled his sword back gently so that it scraped across the captain's skin, not firmly enough to draw more blood, but just firmly enough to let him know that his life was still in Devi's hands. With the point of his sword still resting on Captain Heller's throat, Devi paused. He could see the captain's lip trembling, his eyes still now but somehow just as frantic.

"You said you would release me," Captain Heller said, his voice lacking all authority. "Now release me."

Still, Devi did not move. Instead, he kept the point of his sword fixed squarely on Captain Heller's throat.

"Release me," Captain Heller yelled. "I demand that you –"

Devi forced the point of his sword through the flesh of the captain's neck, and his words withered away to nothing. Blood spilled from the captain's throat and mouth, covering his tunic and his bare torso beneath. For a moment, his body stood still and vacant on the silent deck of the ship, the sound of blood gurgling in his throat masking the gentle whispers of the tide. Then, Devi yanked his blade free, and Captain Heller's lifeless body slumped into a bloody heap at his feet.

XXVI

When Devi had watched the last of the dunes fade away and drop over the horizon from the stern of The Kraken, he had known he was back in Katai waters. The dunes had steadily grown smaller and smaller away to his left, but now that they had given way completely to the dry, cracked desert that continued to creep its way towards the farmlands in the south, Devi knew he had ventured into The Sands and made it out with his life. In all of Katai, only a handful of people could claim such an accomplishment, but Devi felt no sense of pride, no sense of joy, and no sense of victory. Instead, he felt lost, and he felt hopeless.

Devi continued to rest his elbows on the taffrail of the ship as it lurched and lumbered its way back towards Narkasee. In his hands, he held Captain Heller's journal tightly, unsure whether he should simply release his grip and allow it to plunge into the Tharakun Sea below. He scoured the pages, scanning the coastline and plotting roughly where he thought The Kraken might be. He and Reya had been sailing for some time, and he anticipated it would be little more than a day until they reached Narkasee. When they arrived, however, though their ship also carried Sadikah, the Sand Dwellers, and the Fire Stone, Devi knew it wouldn't be to a hero's welcome.

On the pages before him, just off the coast of Narkasee, Devi could see several tiny ships drawn by the hand of Captain Heller himself, and he knew it wouldn't be long before the Darmeenian fleet sailed around the Salt Cliffs and cut through the waters of the Tharakun. Amongst the ships, he saw the great, hulking silhouette of The Kraken, and though he knew its guns would no longer be turned on Narkasee itself, Devi knew it would take far more to turn the tide in Katai's favour.

As he followed Captain Heller's map inland, Devi's eyes ran over hundreds of tiny dots scattered outside Narkasee's walls. Darmeen would soon begin their siege on land as well as on the water, and he knew they had more than enough manpower to overwhelm Narkasee's scant defences. Even if the initial siege force was somehow repelled, Devi saw countless more tiny dots on the pages before him making their way up through the farmlands to supplement the attack. Narkasee would defend itself. Of that, Devi was in no doubt. But he could see no way that it wouldn't eventually fall.

"Would you like me to fetch you some fenocci?"

Reya sidled up alongside Devi, her body close and her voice even closer. After spending so much time at sea, Devi had finally managed to become accustomed to the rise and fall of the waves beneath him, but his stomach turned over itself at the mere mention of fenocci. But he said nothing. He merely continued to stare down at the pages.

"You're the captain of the largest ship the seas have ever known," Reya teased. "You can't be seasick."

It was clear to Devi that Reya was trying her best to lighten his mood. Though he appreciated her intent, he couldn't force himself to smile.

"I'm not sick," he said simply.

"What's wrong then?" Reya asked, the tone in her voice immediately more sincere. "Have you seen something new?"

She nodded her head in the direction of Captain Heller's journal.

Devi closed the journal and stood upright. He looked Reya in the eyes for a moment, and then he returned his gaze to the water.

"No," he said gloomily. "I see the end of Katai, just like before."

The statement hung in the air like the light mist that seemed always to have settled around The Kraken. When they had sat together in Captain Heller's cabin and pored over his maps and the pages of his journal, both Devi and Reya had seen the future laid bare before them. It had seemed perilous then. Now, as they drifted ever closer towards Narkasee, it seemed inevitable.

"We have the Fire Stone, Devi," Reya said. "And my father still has the Earth Stone buried within the Keep. Darmeen possesses only the Water Stone."

On another day, Devi may have found Reya's optimism endearing. In that moment, however, all he heard was naivety.

"We may have more Stones," Devi replied. "But Darmeen is vast. They have the numbers to overrun Narkasee. You've seen Captain Heller's plans for yourself. There's a force at Narkasee's walls as we speak, and they alone may be enough to take the city. With the additional forces making their way up through the farmlands, there's no way we can hold them all back, with or without the Stones."

Reya's face turned grave. Devi knew she wasn't so foolish as to believe that Katai had gained the edge. She knew Devi was right. She had just been trying her hardest to convince herself otherwise.

"Besides," Devi continued. "We may have the Stones now, but we won't have them for much longer. Once they take Narkasee, Darmeen will take the Fire Stone and the Earth Stone along with it. Then it's only a matter of time before they find the Wind Stone, and there'll be no going back."

Both Devi and Reya fell silent. Devi laid out in his mind the plan they had discussed over and over again in Captain Heller's cabin, and though he knew it would buy Narkasee some time, he knew it would only delay the inevitable.

"There must be something we can do," Reya insisted, either less willing or less able to relinquish her fragile grip on the little hope she still managed to cling to.

Devi stared out towards the horizon, where the dry and dusty desert had begun to give way to the jagged cliffs that lined the entire coast of Katai, and where Rakhas would soon appear.

"There's nothing we can do," Devi said. "It may be possible to hold off the initial force, especially now that we have The Kraken, but there's no way to stop their reinforcements from joining them. We'd have to siphon our own forces away from Narkasee, but that would only make the city easier to take. And it's not as if the fields were made for fighting. There's no cover. There's nowhere to build defences, even if we had the time to do it. We need to cut the head from the beast, but we have no blade sharp enough."

Devi's head pounded. He had ventured into The Sands and retrieved the Fire Stone. It was what he and every other boy in Katai had dreamed of, but he couldn't help but feel as if he had failed Katai, regardless. Even with the Fire Stone, it was all but inevitable that Narkasee would fall, and Katai would fall along with it. He and Reya would make it back to the city in time to help mount its defence, but Devi could see no way that their efforts would be anything more than symbolic. They would not allow themselves to succumb to Darmeen without a fight, but succumb they would.

As Devi continued to gaze out towards the cliffs, he watched as they slowly began to fall away into the water. They grew smaller and smaller, and the fields atop them rolled closer and closer to the edge, until eventually Devi could make out the point where the very edge of the fields met the very edge of the cliffs. It was the point where, as a young boy, he would stand and gaze out across the vast expanse of the Tharakun and watch the Katai ships slicing their way effortlessly through the water, their green and black sails dancing against the flawless cobalt sky.

As The Kraken drew steadily closer, Devi began to see the burnt and broken remains of Rakhas itself, the charred corpses of the few wooden huts that remained barely managing to hold themselves upright. It seemed an age since Devi had last laid eyes on Rakhas, and though it looked nothing like it once had, it still felt like home, and he was intent on seeing it one last time.

"Pull her in close to shore," Devi said to Reya.

Reya looked back at Devi, a blank, quizzical expression falling across her face.

"I promised I would show you Rakhas one day."

~

The water was warm and amiable as it washed over Devi's feet and around his ankles. The surf dampened his hide boots, but after the days he had spent aboard The Kraken and amidst The Sands, the sensation was a refreshing one. He pulled their rowboat up onto the shore, where a narrow stretch of sand quickly gave way to the shallow hill that led up to the village of Rakhas. As Devi looked back out towards The Kraken, which loomed in the water some distance off, it felt strange to see a Darmeenian ship in Katai waters, but he knew that, before the day was out, the coast around Narkasee would be swimming with white sails.

Devi immediately began across the sand, and though Reya and Sadikah followed in his path, they allowed him to venture ahead a little, and he arrived at the base of the hill before they had even crossed the narrow beach. As Devi began the slow and steady climb up the hill, he could feel Reya and Sadikah's presence fading, and by the time he had reached the top, he knew they were holding back.

At the top of the hill, a vast expanse of fields spread out before Devi. As a child, when he would turn away from the water and back towards his village, he would be greeted by an endless sea of golden wheat plants, each glimmering under the light of the sun, gently swaying back and forth as if beckoning him back towards his home. Now, all he saw was death and ruin. The fields themselves were black and charred. The soil was still thick with dust and ash, and the only remnants of the crops that had once stood proudly side by side were the fragile, blackened flakes that crumbled to dust the moment Devi stepped foot on them.

"What happened here?"

Devi heard Reya's voice, soft and gentle, at his ear. He sensed her body lingering beside his, and though he could not feel her touch, he could feel her warmth.

"The Darmeenians," Devi said. "They burnt it to the ground."

His voice sounded hollow and vacant, as if the words had risen out of him rather than having been spoken aloud.

"They came just before nightfall. They came on horses and set fire to the orchards. Then, they came for the fields and for us."

Devi felt Reya's touch now. Her arm slid around his waist and pulled him close. Then, he felt her cheek come to rest against his shoulder.

"They killed everyone," Devi said simply. "Just cut them down. My friends, my neighbours… My father."

Reya's fingers pulled at Devi's hip, and he felt her head shift against his shoulder so that she was gazing up at him. But he couldn't bring himself to meet her gaze.

"I'm sorry," Reya said. "It means little, I know. But…"

Devi remembered weeping the same words into the smouldering soil the morning after. He remembered burying his face in his father's chest and telling him he was sorry. But the words hadn't been enough to bring him back. Nothing ever would be.

Without a word, Devi broke away. He stepped forward into the fields, and he was sure he could still feel the fire burning against the soles of his feet. He left Reya at the edge of the field, with Sadikah a little further behind, and he walked back towards his village.

As he walked, Devi kept his eyes fixed to the dirt, and it wasn't long before he came across the first body. Its bones were tainted by the black soil that continued to amble across the field like a tiny sandstorm, but huge chunks of half-rotten flesh still clung to the carcass, the sunken eyes of the skull and the broken ridges of the rib cage almost visible beneath. An acrid smell seemed to linger over the entire field, but up close it was utterly unimaginable. The closer that Devi drew to the village, the more bodies he stumbled across. They laid scattered across the earth like grotesque seeds, eventually to be consumed by the soil.

It still seemed impossible to Devi that these men and women were his countrymen, his neighbours. Though he could recognise the rotting and withered faces of some, as well as the muddied and charred rags that remained of the clothes of others, he couldn't bring himself to believe that these were the people he had worked alongside day after day, year after year in the fields. It didn't seem possible that the faces that had once held such life and such vitality could be the same faces that had all but melted into the dirt.

Devi saw their weapons at their sides too – the axes and sickles and knives they had used, not to defend their lives but merely to prolong them. The fields had been aflame, and the Darmeenians had whipped around them on horseback, their silver swords glistening under the light of the rapidly rising moon. They must have known there was no hope for survival, but they had stood and fought for Rakhas regardless, willing to die protecting it rather than to live without it.

As he neared the edge of the field that he had crossed, Devi caught a glimpse of another blade glistening in the dirt. The blade itself had been charred and blackened by the flames, and its wooden handle was crumbling away in places. Regardless, it was still in one piece, and Devi lifted it from the ground.

Grasping his scythe in both hands, Devi immediately found himself back in the fields on the night of the raid. As he had cowered away in his home, forcing his body into the corner beneath the window, clutching his father's knife, he had wished he had been holding his scythe. He had wished he was out in the fields, standing alongside his father and his neighbours, turning his blade against those who threatened both himself and Katai.

As he looked around the fields now, a blanket of darkness fell over them once more. Suddenly, the fields were alive with flames again, and a metal blade flashed across Devi's face as a Darmeenian on horseback swung his sword in his direction. He wished he could take back the night. He wished he could be standing side by side with his father, their voices bellowing the lines of the Psalms into the darkness as they gave their lives for Katai and for each other.

In darkness lie all terrors true.

And it was then that Devi knew what he must do. The Darmeenians had made their way into Rakhas once, and Devi had cowered away. The next time they dared to venture into Katai's farmlands, Devi would be there to meet them, and this time, he would be ready to fight and willing to die.

Still clutching his scythe, Devi made his way back across the burnt and ravaged field towards Reya and

Sadikah. He looked up towards Reya as he stumbled through the dirt, and for a moment, he wished things could be different.

He had barely begun to know Reya, and there was still so much about her that he wanted to discover. He wished this wouldn't be the last time he would gaze into her brilliant, blue eyes, which seemed to lure him towards her; he wished it wouldn't be the last time he would hear her voice; and he wished that, if Katai could live to see another day, he and Reya could each be there to celebrate it together. But he knew things couldn't be different. There was still a chance that Narkasee would stand, but the chances that he would be there to see it were vanishing quick.

"Narkasee is waiting," Devi said, arriving at the edge of the field and standing across from Reya.

Reya gazed back at him, her eyes all warmth and comfort, and for a brief moment, Devi felt his entire body go weak.

"Let's go," Reya said.

"I'm not leaving."

Reya's face twisted with confusion.

"What do you mean you're not leaving?"

"You must go," Devi said. "But I'm not coming with you."

"But... Why?"

"You must go," Devi repeated. "Deliver the Fire Stone and defend Narkasee. Return to your father and stand alongside him."

"I'm not leaving you behind," Reya said. "You have to come with us. Narkasee needs you."

Reya gazed deeply into Devi's eyes, and Devi forced himself to tear his own gaze away.

"You belong to the sea," he said finally. "My place is here. There's enough firepower on The Kraken to level half of Narkasee. Captain Heller said so himself. Take the ship and turn it on the Darmeenians. Blow their fleet out of the water and drive their soldiers into the ground."

Devi spoke with venom and conviction, as if his words alone could ignite The Kraken's guns.

"And what will you do?" Reya asked.

"I will cut the head from the beast."

"Alone?"

"We have no time. There's no other way."

"But you'll die," Reya begged. "You'll be outnumbered a thousand to one. How can you possibly hold them off alone?"

Devi was silent for a moment before he finally spoke.

"For when it seems that all is lost," he said. "And the holy kingdom is set to fall."

Reya continued to gaze at Devi, and she mouthed the final lines of the Psalm silently along with him.

"The Son will rise to levy the cost and give his life to save them all."

Reya pulled her body close to Devi's own. Devi gazed down into Reya's eyes, and the fields seemed to fade around him. For a moment, it felt as if he and Reya were the only people in the world – as if they were the beginning and the end.

Devi brought his palm gently against the pale skin of Reya's cheek, and he felt her lips against his thumb as she smiled. Reya pushed herself up onto her toes, tugging lightly at Devi's neck as she leaned in towards him, and when their lips finally met, Devi knew nothing short of death would be enough to tear them apart.

Devi released his grip of Reya's waist and allowed her body to fall away from him. His hand lingered on the small of her back for a moment before it fell to his side. Then, he dropped his scythe to the dirt, turned away from Reya and Sadikah, and began to walk. He walked through the charred fields, past the burnt and broken remnants of his village, and he didn't stop walking until Rakhas was at his back and The Kraken was lumbering across the waves towards Narkasee once more.

XXVII

The heavy wooden wheels of Devi's cart rattled against their axles as he dragged them through the soil. The earth was dry, but the dirt was loose, and the wheels seemed to sink deeper and deeper with every step that he took. On the back of the cart were stacked several barrels, each identical to those that Devi would drag home from the market with his father at the end of each harvest season. They were heavy with oil, forcing the wheels of the cart even further into the dirt as they thudded against the wooden boards.

As Devi turned the corner at the very edge of the field, he wondered how his oxen had not keeled over in the dirt before sunset each day. They were great, hulking beasts, and he was merely a boy, but dragging the cart up and down the fields had left his body aching and tired.

The dirt at the edges of the fields was difficult enough to navigate, but the fields themselves were thick with wheat crops that had not yet been harvested, and there was barely room for the cart to squeeze by without having to roll over the golden plants. Devi had hoped he might stumble across at least one of the farm's oxen milling around in the grasslands that surrounded the farm, but they were all long gone, as were the farmers.

Behind the cart, Devi left a damp trail in his wake. He had turned one of the barrels of oil on its side and tied it down at the very back of the cart, pulling the stopper from its top and allowing the oil to stream out onto the dirt. He had followed his father around the edges of the fields in Rakhas countless times, dampening the soil beneath their feet, and as he began to drag the cart along the final stretch of earth towards the dusty road, he wished he had him by his side again.

The final edge of the field was where the dirt was at its thickest, and Devi was forced to pull with all his might as the wooden wheels of the cart churned through it. When he finally made it to the dusty road, he was just about ready to collapse, but he knew his work had only just begun.

Devi dragged the cart up onto the road, looking out across the field on the opposite side, which, like the fields beyond, he had already lined with oil earlier that morning. As he always did during harvest season, he made sure he was out before the sun had even begun to rise.

Devi dragged the cart to the side of the road, and he allowed the great wooden beams he had used to pull it to fall to the floor. He made his way around to the back of the cart, where the open barrel continued to spill oil across the ground. There, he tore a strip of his sleeve away from his tunic and held the rag beneath the stream of oil. He moved the rag around, allowing the oil to dampen it completely, and then he tossed it over his shoulder, and the oil dripped down his chest and his back.

Devi clambered up into the bed of the cart, put his foot on the back of the barrel, and kicked it out onto the ground. The barrel shattered on impact, its remaining contents flooding out across the road, instantly darkening the sand around the cart.

Then, Devi turned his attention to the other barrels, which were still full. He shifted each of them to the edge of the cart and jumped back down to the ground. He hoisted the barrels up onto his shoulder one by one and carried them to the edge of the road, where sand met soil. He set two barrels down at one edge of the road, turning them on their sides just beside the great pillar of the signal tower at the corner of the field. Then, he set the other two down on the other side of the road, also rolling them onto their sides.

When the back of the cart was empty, Devi took a moment to look over it. Then, he placed his shoulder beneath the bed of the cart, equidistant between its front and back wheels, and he forced the side of the cart from the ground. The cart tilted away from Devi, but it quickly came crashing back down. The moment it did, however, Devi thrust his shoulder into its underbelly once more, forcing it from the ground again. The truck tilted away from him, its wheels rising a little higher into the air, but again it came crashing back down.

This time, Devi forced his shoulder against the side of the truck with such force, thrusting his body upwards through his heels, that the truck lurched away from him, hung for a moment on two wheels, and then tipped all the way over, thumping against the ground that was already thick with oil. Its boards shattered and splintered on impact, and if anyone but Devi was to stumble across the cart, they would be forgiven for assuming it had toppled over on a broken wheel, sending its cargo of barrels sprawling across the road.

Devi turned his back on the cart and began up the road in the direction of the wooden shacks at the other end. They stood in narrow rows just like those in the village in Rakhas. As he walked, Devi explored the fields with his eyes. They were as golden as his own would be at the height of the harvest, and he almost imagined he could see the blades of countless scythes glimmering in the sun as they carved their way through the vast sea of wheat plants. These crops had been abandoned along with the village itself, however, news of the Darmeenian invasion clearly having spread as quickly as the fires that had consumed Rakhas.

Devi wondered where the farmers and their families had ended up. Undoubtedly, some would have made their way north to Narkasee. The capital city was ultimately where the Darmeenians were heading, but its walls were taller and thicker than those of their wooden shacks, and they would stand more resolutely against the Darmeenian invasion. Some would have made their way west towards Kartan too, and some may even have stopped to take refuge in Doku along the way. Those with the resources and the know-how may have taken to the hills, seeking out some desolate spot to call their own for a short time, but whatever the outcome of the invasion, they would need to move on again eventually.

As he drew close to the other end of the field, the wooden beams of another cart came into view. Devi had stashed the cart close to the wheat crops before he had lined the edges of the fields with oil, and he made his way over to it now, dragging it just a little further from the signal tower at the corner of the field and just a little closer to the road. He didn't want the cart to be visible from a distance, but he wanted to be able to reach it in a hurry, and he wanted to reduce the distance he would have to drag it later as much as possible, heavy as it was with the oil barrels he had stashed in the back.

When he was satisfied with the cart's position, Devi continued on towards the wooden shacks that lined the edge of the field. Many of the doors to the shacks stood open, but there were no men or women sitting on their porches. Nor were there any children running between the houses or through the shadows cast across the sand.

Devi made his way towards one of the shacks that stood with its door wide open. They were all empty, but somehow it felt less invasive to step through a door that had been left open than to force his way into a home that had been shut up tight.

Despite moving lightly, the wooden floorboards creaked under Devi's feet. He stood in a house almost identical to his own, perched on the periphery of a large field. Outside, the crops beyond the window at the front of the house rose majestically towards the sky, and they glistened like gold under the light of the sun.

Across the room, a wooden table was dressed in a cloth, and various wooden plates and items of cutlery laid scattered across it. Four chairs stood around the table, each skewed awkwardly and positioned without conformity, as if they had been hastily abandoned. Devi had only stepped foot in one building, but he knew the others that lined the field would be the same. Nobody had been here in days, maybe even weeks. The families that made these houses their homes would have fled the second they received word that the Darmeenians were on their way.

Devi collected the scythe he had stashed by the door the previous night when he had arrived in the village. He had spent the night on the floor of the house, his eyes closed but his mind alive, and he had been out in the morning before the sun, having barely managed to find a wink of sleep. Devi held the scythe in his hand for a moment, exploring its long wooden handle with his fingers. Then, he ran his palm along its blade, which was dull and muddied from harvests gone by. He took up a large stone from the table at the centre of the room and sat on the wooden floorboards in front of a fire he had prepared but had not yet lit.

Devi ran the stone along the length of the scythe's blade with a single smooth motion. Bright, orange sparks rained down around his feet, but they petered out and died almost instantly. As he ran the stone along the blade once more, Devi was sure he could hear a dull, booming thud somewhere far off. The sky outside the window was bright and blue, and there were no storm clouds in sight. He knew he was a long way from Narkasee, but he imagined that perhaps it was the great guns of The Kraken finally opening fire that he could hear.

Devi wiped the dry, solid dirt away from the edge of his scythe with his finger, and he ran the stone along its length once more. Already, the very tip of the blade was beginning to shine as if it had been made new again.

The fields outside the window were silent, but as Devi continued to sharpen his blade, the dull thudding in the distance returned, louder this time. It echoed around the rolling hills that surrounded the farmland, barely managing to drift through the open door and reach him before it died away. But it reached him loudly enough that he could no longer dismiss it as a mere trick of his tired mind. The thudding grew steadily louder and steadily more frequent until there was only one explanation Devi could provide. It wasn't thunder rolling in over the hills, nor was it the sound of The Kraken's guns booming away off the coast of Narkasee. It was the sound of Darmeenian feet marching in unison towards him.

Devi forced himself from the floor, his body already heavy from a lack of sleep and from hauling the heavy carts around the fields. He stepped towards the fire he had prepared in the pit at the edge of the shack's front room, and he lowered the blade of his scythe towards it. He brought his stone against the blade once more and ran it along the length of its edge. Though the sparks had previously petered away at Devi's feet, they now fell upon the sticks and kindle he had arranged, clinging to the torn rags sodden with oil that he had placed beneath them and erupting in tiny, orange flames. The fire immediately began to crackle as it came to life, and Devi could already feel its warmth.

From his shoulder, Devi took the sodden rag he had stashed there at the other end of the field. It had dampened his tunic, and it no longer dripped with oil, but it was still soaked through. Devi brought the rag against the muddied blade of the scythe, and he began to wipe it across the dirt. The clods of dried soil began to fall away, and soon the blade shone as if it had never been muddied at all, its edge once more sharp enough to cut through wheat plants with ease, and to cut through flesh besides. Regardless, Devi continued to move the rag smoothly across the blade until its metal not only shone, but until it was covered by a thin layer of oil.

On the still and silent air, the steady pounding of Darmeenian footsteps continued to drift in through the open door. Whilst the fire continued to crackle away, Devi stepped through the door and out onto the wooden steps. The dull thudding he had heard from a distance now sounded immeasurably closer, and the thuds were now so frequent that they blended together into a single relentless drone. Way off in the distance, far beyond the golden wheat fields and out towards the green hills that rolled across the horizon, Devi thought he could just make out the tiny figures of countless men cutting the valley in two and making their way steadily towards him.

Devi stepped back inside and made his way over to the fire. Though it was corralled by the pit of sand and stones that held it, the flames had quickly grown, and they rose almost as high as Devi's knees. Devi turned the blade of his scythe towards the ground, and he held it out towards the flames. The flames hissed and spat as the oiled blade briefly found its home within them, and Devi watched as the blade itself caught alight. He lifted the scythe from the fire, and it continued to burn like a smouldering crescent moon.

Outside, Devi's scythe whispered in his ear as the flames that licked its blade danced and swayed. They continued to burn as Devi climbed down the wooden steps onto the sand of the road, and as he made his way across the road towards the fields. Devi approached the cart he had dragged beside the signal tower earlier until he was level with it – at the centre of the road where he would be in full view of the oncoming Darmeenians, rather than concealed by the wheat plants like the cart itself. And there, he stood. Waiting.

Devi felt the warmth from the steadily rising sun as well as from his flaming scythe. The morning was all but over, and the sun was drawing close to its peak in the sky above, the sky itself clear and blue, entirely unsullied like a blank canvas. A gentle breeze washed across

Devi's face and sent the flames of his scythe this way and then that, whilst the dull rumbling of footsteps in the distance continued to roll towards him. They seemed to beat with the same rhythm as his heart – slow, steady, and relentless - and he almost found himself getting lost amongst it. Then, on the crest of the horizon far off beyond the fields, Devi saw the figures of the Darmeenians looming once more.

At first, Devi felt as if he was looking upon a single figure, the long, winding body of some snake or eel slowly growing as it made its way steadily towards him. As the Darmeenians grew closer and closer to the fields, however, Devi was finally able to discern individual men amongst the ranks. They marched side by side, but Devi couldn't tell whether they stood ten across or one hundred. He could see that the men began to narrow as they made their way up the road that ran between the fields, however, those at the edges folding into the ranks behind until they were narrow enough to span only the width of the road itself.

He watched as the Darmeenian men steadily made their way up the road towards his position, cutting the fields perfectly in two. Eventually, Devi was able to see the pale skin beneath their helmets, and when he was finally able to make out the shapes of their faces, one man at the very front of the ranks raised his arm, and the entire body of men behind him came to a halt.

The man that seemed to lead the Darmeenian advance stepped forward, his menacing eyes fixed on Devi. He was still some distance away, but Devi could see the confusion in his face. The man kept his arm raised as he took several steps in Devi's direction, only lowering it when he had put some distance between himself and the army that waited at his back. As the man drew steadily closer, Devi held his own position, standing perfectly still and gripping the handle of his scythe a little tighter.

XXVIII

Reya sat behind Captain Heller's desk, the high back of his chair looming above her head, a mess of papers from his drawer spread out before her. Her red roots had begun to show days ago, and a thick strip of crimson now ran down the middle of her head, splitting the jet black hair on either side in two. Her face was rigid and stoic as she pawed at the papers, her eyes dancing over the map of Katai and its surrounding waters that sat on top of the disorganised pile.

Captain Heller's journal laid close by too, still open and revealing the plans that she and Devi had pored over for so long. If she had made it back in time, the Darmeenians would be engaging Katai's defensive fleet, biding their time until the beastly shadow of the Kraken came lumbering over the horizon to pull their enemy to the bottom of the ocean. Then, the great ship would turn its guns on Katai itself, reigning a storm of metal and fire down upon Narkasee. No longer.

The door to the captain's cabin creaked open, and Sadikah stepped regally through.

"We draw near," he said simply.

"How far?"

"We can see the coast."

"Any sails yet?"

"Not yet. But we see smoke. A lot of it."

"Thank you, Sadikah," Reya said. "I'll be right out."

Sadikah nodded, and he withdrew from the cabin.

Reya took a deep breath, and she rose from Captain Heller's chair. She tucked the seat under the great oak desk, sceptical that the captain had ever done so for himself. Then, she crossed the cabin to the low cabinet that stored books, empty frames, and other items that Captain Heller had deemed necessary for the voyage. They had grown dusty during their time at sea, and Reya felt certain Captain Heller had never laid his hands on a single one of the items. Reya took up the small telescope she saw there and made her own way out of the cabin.

The air was fresh and piercing as Reya emerged onto the deck of the ship. She had sailed since she was old enough to find her way out of her father's Keep and down the side of the Salt Cliffs to the tiny ships waiting below, but stepping out onto the deck of The Kraken felt like something entirely new. The great ship lumbered across the waves, careening from left to right with the rhythm of the water, relentless and inevitable as it bounded towards Narkasee. All across the deck, the Sand Dwellers made diligent work of the tasks that Reya had set for them. Each man had only taken on a single role, but together, they were responsible for keeping the ship ploughing forwards.

Reya made her way towards the bow of the ship, where she found Sadikah casting his gaze out towards the horizon. Just as he had informed her, Reya could already see black smoke rising in the distance, darkening the sky and standing in stark contrast to the brilliant white of Katai's clouds. Reya lifted Captain Heller's telescope to her eye and pointed it in the direction of the smoke. She could not yet see Narkasee, but she knew it wouldn't be long until the Salt Cliffs began to rise into view.

"Are the gunners ready?" Reya asked, lowering the telescope and turning to face Sadikah.

"They are," Sadikah confirmed.

"Have them open the hatches."

Sadikah gave a low, solemn nod.

"As you wish," he said, and he left Reya's side, making his way to the back of the ship and disappearing below deck.

Reya looked out towards the horizon once more, lifting the telescope to her eye. There, far off in the distance, she could just about make out the very top of the King's Keep, its crenelated walls punctuating the smooth plane of the horizon. As The Kraken rose on the wave that forced its way beneath its hull, the entire Keep flashed into view for a single moment, perched as it had been for so long on the very edge of the Salt Cliffs, before it disappeared from view once more.

A great rattling of wood challenged the roar of the waves below as Sadikah and the Sand Dwellers hoisted the gun hatches open, and Reya felt the entire ship rumble as they rolled The Kraken's great guns into position. In that moment, Reya felt as grateful as ever that the guns would no longer be trained on her father's Keep, nor on Narkasee itself.

"Tighten the main sail," Reya called.

A number of Sand Dwellers hurried about the great mast at the centre of the deck, and the ship lurched forward as the main sail drew even tighter. Reya slid the telescope shut and thrust it into her waistband. Then, she turned away from the bow of the ship and followed in Sadikah's footsteps towards the doors that led below deck.

"Alter our course two clicks north-west," she called up towards the ship's great steering wheel.

The Kraken slowly banked to the starboard side so that the ship moved towards the King's Keep, and the coast ran along its port side.

"And prepare to make haste."

Below deck, the walkways and passages were pitch black, the torches that previously lit them having been torn from the walls for the purposes of igniting the cannons. When Reya entered the first of the gun rooms, however, light poured in through the open hatches. Though the ship itself felt steadier below deck, the world outside seemed to thrash and writhe violently until it felt to Reya as if the ship was rolling over on itself. It felt unnerving to be so much closer to the water, and it felt as if she might fall through one of the gunports and into the Tharakun at any moment.

Reya looked out through the hatches, and she could see Narkasee clearly now. The King's Keep sat at the top of the Salt Cliffs, and the city spread out behind it. Then, between Narkasee and The Kraken, the first sails appeared in the water.

"Are they ready?" Reya asked, locating Sadikah at the far end of the gun room.

"They are ready," Sadikah confirmed.

By the time Reya returned her attention to the water, another set of sails had pierced the horizon. Then, another. Then, another. Soon, the horizon was so littered with sails that they were impossible to count.

"Tell the gunners to ready themselves," Reya said. "Pile the cannonballs, load the cannons, and light the torches. But wait for my signal to open fire."

As Reya looked out across the familiar waters of the Tharakun Sea, the hulls of the ships on the horizon were now visible, as well as their sails. Some of the ships were dressed in the green of Katai, but there were countless sails in Darmeenian white too, each undoubtedly buoyed by the arrival of The Kraken. As for those on board the Katai ships, Reya struggled to imagine their terror. They were already outnumbered, and now they had a behemoth the likes of which the world had never known bearing down on them.

"When you feel the ship begin to turn," Reya said, finding Sadikah's eyes. "Let them have it."

Sadikah nodded, his expression steadfast and resolute.

Back on the deck of the ship, Reya saw that not all of the sails were filled by the wind, and not all of the ships continued to cut their way through the waves. Instead, some laid half-consumed by the water, their flaming bows reaching desperately for the clouds, masked only by the thick plumes of grey smoke that signalled their demise like gruesome beacons. It seemed each of the ships that laid wounded or half-sunk bore the green and black sails of Katai, whilst almost all the ships that continued to sail bore the white of Darmeen.

Reya made her way up the steps towards the stern of the ship, where two Sand Dwellers awaited her, its great wooden steering wheel in their hands.

"Sadikah could use you below deck," Reya said, stepping between the Sand Dwellers and taking the wheel from them. "He will guide you."

Each of the Sand Dwellers stepped aside, almost bowing as they allowed Reya to take over.

"Yes, Captain," they each said, and Reya watched as they hurried away down the wooden steps to her left.

Then, Reya turned her gaze to the sea. Standing at the stern of such a large ship, she felt invincible, but she knew this was far from the truth. Beneath her feet was enough firepower to level half of Narkasee. Devi had relayed the words to her from the mouth of Captain Heller himself. Such firepower would be more than enough to blow the Darmeenian ships from the water, but Darmeen's army did not begin and end with its fleet. She knew that, beyond the walls of Narkasee, a vast army marched on the capital, and she knew there were thousands more making their way up through the farmlands behind them. If Katai was to survive, it would take more than The Kraken's guns to make it happen.

"Loosen the mainsail," Reya yelled, her voice loud enough to reach the bow at the other end of the ship.

She took the wheel in both hands and thrust it clockwise around its pivot.

"Loosen the mizzens and prepare to come about!"

Reya watched as the deck below her erupted with activity. She held the wheel of the ship firmly in place as it lurched around to its left, the port side where the gunports hung open turning to face the ships that continued to cut through the water.

Then, a great, thunderous roar shook the immovable vessel, its guns bellowing in their ports and flying backwards towards the centre of the ship. Reya almost fell to the deck, unable to maintain her balance amidst the great burst of energy, and she struggled to hold the wheel in place. Then, she heard the low rumble of the guns' wheels as the Sand Dwellers rolled them back towards the open hatches, and a second volley followed only moments later.

The scene off the port side of The Kraken was one of chaos and confusion. Several Darmeenian ships had been struck during the first volley and were already on their way to the bottom of the Tharakun, whilst others had narrowly avoided being struck by the second. Darmeenian sailors leapt from their decks as they abandoned their ships, undoubtedly cursing The Kraken's gunmen for their recklessness and negligence, but the Darmeenian ships that still sailed continued in their pursuit of the Katai vessels, firing their own tiny guns as they followed.

As Reya hoisted the great, wooden wheel of the ship back around in the opposite direction, holding its position steady, the world again split in two. Reya braced herself more adequately during the third volley, and she managed to keep her feet.

This time, many of the guns missed their targets, sending their great, heavy cannonballs to the bottom of the sea rather than into the hulls of the Darmeenian ships. Regardless, a handful of masts were broken, sails were torn, and decks were splintered. By the time the fourth volley sounded, tearing one Darmeenian ship in two and blasting a hole in the bow of another, there was no longer any illusion that the damage was accidental. It was clear it was the Darmeenians that were under attack, rather than the ships of Katai.

Just then, the great, wooden column that held the ship's wheel erupted in a mess of wood and splinters, and Reya found herself sprawled out on the deck of The Kraken. She could feel the ship lurching back to its right, and she struggled to dispel the ringing in her ears as she clambered back to her feet, tying the wheel down to hold the ship steady once more. A second explosion erupted to Reya's left, and she felt the impact as the side of the ship was struck.

Sadikah must have given his command to fire at precisely the moment Reya had begun to make her way below deck. The entire ship shook with thunderous force as it was driven down into the water. The cannon's forced themselves into the boards beneath their wheels, storming to the back of the gun deck, and Reya almost found herself tumbling down the steps that led from the raised stern back onto the deck.

When she made it down to the first gunroom, and her head had stopped spinning, Reya looked out of the nearest gunport to see half of the Darmeenian fleet laying in pieces across the Tharakun Sea, the other half abandoning their pursuit of the ships in front. She thought for a moment that they might turn to face The Kraken, pointing their own guns back in an attempt to repel her counterattack, but only a handful had been foolish enough to risk the endeavour.

Instead, most of the ships broke ranks and sailed towards the edge of the coast, doubtlessly with the hope of rounding the easternmost point of Katai and finding refuge past the Salt Cliffs until they reached Darmeenian waters once more. Several of the Katai ships set off in pursuit, however, firing their own light guns at the white sails, hoping to tear them to shreds and slow them down enough that they could board and take prisoners. But unlike the others, one particular green-sailed ship seemed to be making its way directly towards The Kraken.

"Hold fire," Reya called.

She wiped the blood from her brow, running her fingers across a wound that was deep and fleshy. She searched the gunroom for Sadikah, and it wasn't until she saw the gaping hole in the side of The Kraken that she located him. Sadikah knelt beside the broken bodies of two lifeless Sand Dwellers, their limbs twisted and contorted beneath them. All around them laid the shattered boards of The Kraken's hull, broken and splintered like the bones of the men that had stood behind them.

Sadikah crouched over the bodies, embracing them within his own. The guns had fallen silent, the water beyond their ports even more so. He muttered low words beneath his breath, placing his thin, trembling fingers over their eyes, and Reya saw the Fire Stone glow in the setting of its sceptre. Reya held back for a moment, eager to allow Sadikah the space to grieve, but as she stepped forward to offer him what little comfort she could, he raised his head once more and rose to his feet.

"What now, Captain?"

When Reya emerged from below deck once more, with Sadikah following close behind, she found the horde of Sand Dwellers lined up along the taffrail, surveying the hollow corpses of the ships that sank slowly towards the bottom of the Tharakun. She joined them there, casting her own gaze over the graveyard of sails, and her eye was drawn across the water, where the green sails of the tiny Katai ship bounced across the waves in her direction.

"Find a ladder," Reya screamed, turning away from the taffrail and darting about the deck. "Someone find me a ladder."

When one of the Sand Dwellers returned with a rope ladder, Reya immediately rushed back to the edge of the ship. The ladder was enormous, and though it barely reached the water below, it was only with the assistance of the Sand Dweller that Reya was able to toss it over the side.

Reya heard the thudding of boots against the wooden hull of the ship, and a few moments later, she saw a figure dressed in the green and black attire of a navy sailor clambering over the taffrail.

"What in Vagan's name…"

The man began to speak, but he quickly lost his words. Perhaps it was the ordeal he had just been through that silenced his tongue. Perhaps it was the sheer size of the gargantuan vessel he stood upon. Or perhaps it was the sight of the horde of countless faceless men staring back at him.

"Take me to my father," Reya said.

The man cast a blank gaze all around the ship. Then, his eyes fell upon Sadikah, who stood at Reya's shoulder clutching his golden sceptre, the Fire Stone gleaming against the brilliant blue and white sky like the Katai sun.

"Do you not hear me?" Reya said, her patience already wearing thin. "Take me to my father."

The man's eyes finally fell upon Reya, and despite her ragged appearance – her hair a cropped mess of black and red, her brow torn open and spitting blood across her cheeks – he realised immediately who he was speaking to. Suddenly, the man was frantic.

"Yes, Princess," he said, ushering Reya towards the edge of the ship and the ladder he had just clambered up.

Reya lifted one leg over the ship's taffrail, and then the other. She began to lower herself down onto the ladder, but she paused, finding Sadikah's face in the crowd that lingered on the deck.

"Will you join me, Sadikah?" Reya said. "My father will be eager to meet you."

The ladder felt weak and unsteady as Reya clambered down. It swayed a little in the breeze, and its ropes creaked and moaned with every step so that she felt as if she might plunge into the Tharakun at any moment. Eventually, however, her feet found the deck of the ship below, and Sadikah followed her close behind.

After the days she had spent aboard The Kraken, the Katai ship felt like a toy. It seemed almost as if she could reach from the bow to the stern if she was to stand below the main mast and hold out her arms. When the anchor was hauled onto the deck, and the mainsail was loosed, however, the ship moved with a speed and dexterity that the great Darmeenian ship could never have managed. It was only a matter of moments before the ship was gliding across the waves, and she and Sadikah were bouncing back towards Black Soul's Bay.

XXIX

Devi's eyes remained fixed on those of the Darmeenian captain that stood at the centre of the road. Behind him, a vast army loomed, countless men standing side by side across the width of the only road that ran north through the village towards Narkasee. Devi had seen countless tiny dots scrawled on the maps in Captain Heller's journal. Their numbers had seemed vast as he had looked upon the page, but now that he saw the faces of the men in the distance, it felt as if half of Darmeen stood before him.

If everything Devi had seen in Captain Heller's journal had gone to plan, Darmeen's attack on Narkasee would already be well underway. He knew Reya and Sadikah would be able to buy the city some time, turning the guns of The Kraken against the Darmeenians themselves, but he also knew their efforts would be in vain if the supporting force was able to make it to Narkasee's gates to join the siege that was already underway. Standing alone in the fields, facing down an entire army, Devi knew the future of Katai rested on his shoulders, and on his shoulders alone.

"Step aside, boy," the Darmeenian captain called out.

He lingered a short distance down the road from Devi, and he seemed to be somewhat confused by his presence. Devi imagined how he must have appeared – ragged, filthy, and clutching a flaming scythe. He felt the power of the flames coursing through his body, and he knew he must have seemed an eerie apparition. Even with an army at his back, it was no wonder the man seemed tentative.

As Devi stared back in the captain's direction, however, he saw the same menacing glint in his eyes that he had seen in the eyes of the raiders as they had set fire to the fields of Rakhas. Soon, the fields here would be aflame, but this time they would not burn by Darmeenian hands, but rather by Devi's own.

"I said step aside, boy," the captain called again. "You have no business here. Step aside or you will be stepped upon."

Rather than step aside, however, Devi stepped forward. He lowered the flaming blade of his scythe towards the ground, and he touched it against the dampened soil at the edge of the field. Immediately, the oil he had poured there caught fire, and it snaked away from Devi towards the corner of the field, licking at the base of the wheat crops as it went.

The Darmeenian captain stared fixedly at Devi as he moved, and he took half a step forward from his position a short distance down the road.

As Devi shifted his scythe from one hand to the other, he glared back at the man, and he realised it wasn't only the menacing glint in his eye that seemed familiar. Standing slightly closer to the man than he had been previously, Devi could now make out his features more clearly, and he felt as if his eyes had fallen upon them before.

As he kept his gaze fixed to the captain, Devi reached down towards the dirt on the other side of the road, touching the blade to the dampened soil there as he had before. Again, the oil-soaked dirt immediately caught fire, and the flames snaked away from Devi, licking at the base of the golden crops that began to blacken in an instant.

The flames had not yet risen high enough to be visible above the wheat plants, but Devi had set fire to the fields in his own village countless times before. Each time, the fire seemed to spread more quickly than it had the last. He never ceased to be amazed by the speed and ease with which the flames would dance across the ground, leaping from one golden stalk to the next, seeming to gather momentum as the fire grew larger, rather than to lose it. He knew the flames on one side of the road would already be drawing near to the end of the first field, and it wouldn't be long before it began to make its way down the edge of the field beyond. And the field beyond that. And the field beyond that. The flames on the opposite side of the road wouldn't be far behind, and before too long, the entire landscape would be alive with flames.

The Darmeenian man took a second half-step forward and raised his arm into the air.

"Very well, boy," he called out, beckoning the men behind him forward. "You may perish if you wish."

In an instant, the ground began to shake with the dull rumble of Darmeenian boots. The low thunder that Devi had heard from a distance began to roll across the fields once more, and in that moment, Devi was certain he had seen the man before. He had been there on the night of the raid, riding his horse across the fields of Rakhas, bringing his flaming torch against their wheat and slashing his sword across the stomachs of Devi's neighbours. Devi had seen the man standing outside his house too, the moment before he had cut his father's head from his body.

All of a sudden, Devi felt as if his body was burning from the inside out. A fury like none he had ever known rose within him, and he wanted nothing more than to take off running, swinging his scythe from side to side until the man was nothing more than a mess of flesh and blood. He wanted to lash out in a fit of wrath and ire, and scream his vengeance into the sky. He wanted the man to run towards him too, to fight for the life that he was about to take, rather than to give it over willingly. But, though Devi remembered the face of the man, it was clear the man did not recognise him. He was a faceless figure, a mere boy amongst the dust and ash that had darkened the sky that night.

Devi knew that, one way or another, the Darmeenian captain would die. He could challenge the man and take his life with his scythe, but his death would be quick and painless. Instead, he was content to allow him to succumb to the flames.

Rather than take off running, Devi merely stepped forward again. He raised his flaming scythe into the air and began to hack away at the wheat plants in the field to his left. His blade sliced the crops in two, just as it would during harvest season, but the flames that ran across it leapt into the field beyond, and immediately, the fire began to spread.

Then, Devi turned to his right and swept the blade of his scythe across the wheat plants in the field opposite. Once more, golden heads of wheat fell to the ground at his feet, and flames spread out across the field before him, turning the crops from gold to black and already beginning to send thick, grey smoke up into the air. As Devi cast his gaze around the fields, the flames at their edges were now tall enough that he could see how far they had stretched. Already they had reached far beyond the ranks of men whose faces Devi could make out, and he watched as those men that were closer to him began to turn their heads towards the edges of the fields, where the rapidly rising flames steadily made their way towards them.

It seemed that a handful of men at the front of the ranks quickly recognised what was about to happen in the fields around them. Some turned and began to force their way through the sea of bodies at their back, but the army behind them continued to advance so that they were merely swimming against the tide, being carried slowly forward against their will. Those far off in the distance continued to push forward, seemingly unaware that there were flames snaking their way down the edges of the fields at their left and right and curling their way silently behind them.

The Darmeenian captain at the head of the army turned to face his men, and he took a few steps back in their direction as he saw them beginning to break rank. Devi heard the man's voice above the low crackle of the flames, but he could not hear his words. If his men had heard him speak, it seemed they chose to refuse his orders as even more began to turn away and scan the edges of the fields for a break in the flames.

Devi continued to step forward, swinging his scythe from left to right as he went, slowly drawing closer and closer to the Darmeenian captain and the army at his back. The captain turned back to face Devi, his eyes twisted with anger, and just as he opened his mouth to confront him once more, the entire world shook, and the air itself split in two.

Away at the far end of the field, the cart that Devi had upturned, along with the barrels of oil, exploded into a million tiny pieces. A great ball of orange flame burst into the air, and even from a great distance, Devi could feel its heat. The fireball spewed tiny comets of oil and flaming splinters of wood all across the field, and Devi watched as they fell upon the golden crops, immediately setting them ablaze.

Panic erupted around the fields with almost as much force as the burst of flames. The Darmeenian captain at the head of the army bellowed for his men to move forward, but they bolted away in all directions. Some followed their captain's orders and ran straight towards Devi. Others continued in their efforts to turn back and flee towards the rolling green hills behind them, and some even fled into the fields themselves, frantically trying to find a way behind the flames before they closed in on them completely. The fields were already roaring, however. The fire that Devi had set had already begun to work its way from the edge of the field in towards the road, and the great explosion of the cart and oil barrels had only served to hasten the process.

Devi gripped his scythe in both hands, and he turned away from the flames and the army of men that were beginning to gain on him. He looked towards the village beyond the fields, which was framed on either side of the road by a steadily rising wall of flames. The road between the fields was not yet alight, Devi declining to dampen the sand there with oil, but just beyond the wall of flames was where he had stashed the second cart that he had packed tight with barrels. It was towards the cart that he now walked, slow and measured, ready to drag it to the centre of the road and set it ablaze, closing what would soon be the only narrow space through which it would be possible to escape. Above the ever-increasing roar of the flames, however, the air was split once more.

It was not an explosion that erupted around the fields this time, but instead an awful, wrenching groan. Several great cracks filled the air, and as Devi turned to glance back over his shoulder, he saw the great signal tower at the far end of the fields lurching to one side. It roared as it teetered towards the fields for a moment, barely managing to keep itself upright, and then it came crashing to the ground, the flames that engulfed the field having eaten away at the fragile, rotten pillar that had held it upright.

For a moment, Devi was content. He had not planned for the signal tower to fall, but it would prove even more difficult for the Darmeenians to flee the flames at the other end of the field now, which would only mean that even more of them would perish. As he turned back towards the narrow break in the flames at the top of the road, however, Devi's heart sank. The signal tower up ahead, behind which the loaded cart was stashed, also began to creak and moan, and though its great height tended always to provide such an illusion, it too seemed to be lurching to one side.

Without a second thought, Devi took off running. He kept his eyes fixed on the top of the road and the village beyond. The fire at his back was already growing unbearably hot, and he knew the flames would have spread to the fields beyond, lining the ranks of Darmeenian soldiers on each side and trapping them on the road. The narrow passage up ahead was the only way out of the fields, and even that was beginning to steadily close, the edges of the fields that lined the road continuing to succumb to the fire set by Devi's flaming scythe.

Then, just as Devi was beginning to draw close, and just as he could almost feel the cool relief beyond the flames, the signal tower at the corner of the field up ahead came crashing to the ground, and the cart behind it erupted.

To Devi, it felt as if the earth had been pulled from beneath his feet. One moment, he was running, and the next, he was laying face down in the dry sand of the road, his skin hot with fire and his ears ringing loud.

Devi rolled around frantically in the sand. The barrels in the back of the cart had exploded as the signal tower had come crashing down beside it, and thick droplets of burning oil rained down all around, searing into his skin and setting his tunic ablaze. He swatted at his arms and legs with the palms of his hands, which were already covered in sand and beginning to blister. Then, just as he was satisfied he was no longer alight, he saw a flash of metal in the sky above.

Instinctively, Devi grabbed the handle of his scythe and held it across his face. The silver blade of the Darmeenian captain came crashing against the handle, and Devi was astonished it did not split in two. Devi rolled out to his left and scrambled to his feet just in time to deflect another of the Darmeenian man's attacks.

All around him, Devi could see nothing but bright, intense flames. The air was thick with dust and ash, clinging to his throat as he struggled for breath and masking the frantic rush of movement that surrounded him. He could feel the presence of the Darmeenians all around, clambering over one another in search of an escape, but it was only the face of the captain that found him amongst the smoke.

The captain swung his sword towards Devi once more, and Devi twisted away from the blow this time, hacking at the man's shins with the base of his scythe. Then, he spun full circle and swung his blade towards the man's stomach. The captain swatted away the blow with his own weapon, however, and lashed out with a furious back-handed attack. This time, it was Devi's turn to block the blow, and the blade of his scythe sparked as it met the metal of the captain's sword. The air was so thick with flames that Devi wasn't sure whether the blade of his scythe was still alight or whether the fire that surrounded him merely lent it the appearance.

The Darmeenian captain did not relent, however. He swung his sword violently at Devi, his face twisted with fury, seemingly unconcerned that the world around him had been consumed entirely by flames. Devi deflected the blows as they came, but the man was swift and efficient with his attacks, and Devi could barely move his scythe quickly enough to keep up.

Then, the captain feigned a prodding blow towards Devi's face, but instead he slashed at his thigh, his blade tearing through Devi's britches with ease and scoring the flesh of his leg. Devi cried out in pain, but his voice was immediately lost amongst the crackle and the roar of the fire around him.

The Darmeenian captain bore down on Devi, but Devi blocked his next attack and sent a lashing blow out towards him. When the captain turned away to evade it, Devi made a frantic dash through the smoke towards the top of the road, where he had been heading before the signal tower collapsed. The flames clawed at him as he moved, sinking their teeth into his tunic and his torso beneath it. Out of the smoke, a single Darmeenian soldier dashed across Devi's path, sending him sprawling across the ground once more, but the man merely darted off in the opposite direction, the thought of unsheathing his sword and plunging it into Devi's flesh barely even seeming to have crossed his mind.

Devi forced himself up and continued to stumble through the flames, but there was now no way to determine his position or direction. It was possible he was moving towards the edge of the field, but it was equally possible he was stumbling deeper and deeper into the heart of the fire. It was also possible, even likely, that even if he were to find his way to the end of the road, it would have been blocked by the fallen tower and consumed by flames like the rest of the field. Devi looked towards the sun for guidance, but the air was so thick with smoke that he could barely make out the sky beyond.

As he continued to stumble in the darkness, Devi glanced down at his leg. His britches were thick with blood, and the wound beneath them looked deep and vicious. Even if he made it out of the field, he would likely bleed out before he could reach the village.

Devi stopped. His lungs were heavy with smoke, his eyes were thick with dust, and it felt as if his skin itself was alive with flames. He bent over double, his chest heaving, barely able to breathe. He tried his best to keep himself upright, but he found himself teetering over like the signal towers at each end of the field, and before he knew it, he was laying flat on his back looking up towards the dust and the ash that darkened the sky above.

In that moment, Devi knew he would die. Though he had known his chances were remote, he had hoped he might somehow find a way to make it out of the fields and back to Narkasee before the day was over. He wanted to climb up the Salt Cliffs and over the wall of the Keep to find Reya safe inside. Even more, he wanted to walk through the gates of Narkasee, the Darmeenian soldiers having perished or fled, succumbing to the guns of The Kraken, the swords of the Vanguard, or merely their own fear and desperation.

As he laid in the burning field, Devi thought back to the days he had spent planting seeds, ploughing the earth, or harvesting crops. He thought back to the nights he would sit on the veranda of his father's house, watching the full moon rise high above the orchards far off in the distance. And he thought about the night the orchards had been consumed by flames, just like the field around him. He thought about the Darmeenians riding their horses across the fields of Rakhas, and he thought about his father, helpless and alone as their blades tore his body apart.

Devi thought of Reya too. He could almost hear the guns of the Kraken still firing in his mind, as well as the frantic thoughts of the Darmeenians beyond the walls of Narkasee, desperately wondering when the army of reinforcements would arrive. But they would never arrive. The Darmeenians would die in the field alongside Devi, Narkasee would stand, and Katai would survive. Reya would sail the Kraken into Black Soul's Bay, and soon she would discover that Devi had not returned.

For a moment, Devi hoped she would feel saddened, but his heart quickly shifted. He didn't want her to mourn him. He wanted her to be happy. For a brief moment, as Devi gazed skyward, the smoke cleared just a little, and he felt as if he was looking into Reya's brilliant, blue eyes one last time.

"For when it seems that all is lost, and the holy kingdom is set to fall."

Devi spoke the lines of Psalm Ten to himself almost silently as he waited for the flames to consume him.

"The Son will rise to levy the cost and give his life to save them all.

END OF BOOK ONE

LEAVE ME A REVIEW

Reviews are incredibly important for all authors, but especially so for those that are self-published. They help to build the trust and credibility that we don't get through working with a traditional publisher.

If you enjoyed **THE BOY OF DUST AND ASH**, please take a few moments to leave it a review:

FOLLOW ME ON SOCIAL MEDIA:

@JOSHUANEALYAF

THE AETHER STONES SAGA
BOOK TWO

BE THE FIRST TO FIND OUT
ABOUT PRE-ORDERS:

ABOUT THE AUTHOR

With a lifelong passion for science fiction, fantasy, and all things dystopian, Joshua Neal is a self-published Young Adult Fiction author looking to inspire a new generation of young readers.

Having taught English in Secondary schools and Further Education colleges for over seven years, Joshua has seen first-hand the formative influence a good book can have. He began writing in order to continue to bring the wonders of fiction to those who have already had the privilege of experiencing it, and to provide a thrilling introduction to those who have not.

Not content simply to provide an engaging read, Joshua attempts to make some life's difficult existential questions accessible to a young audience, encouraging them to question everything from the nature of the relationships we form to the nature of the universe itself.

WWW.JOSHUANEALFICTION.COM